The Housegirl Becoming Angela

Eileen K. Omosa

Janna,
Books take us
to new places
Welcome to
Angela.
Thanks
Eileen

Copyright

The Housegirl Becoming Angela ~ A Novel

First Published, 2018
Canada
We Grow Ideas/Eileen K. Omosa
The Housegirl Becoming Angela
ISBN: 978-1-9991828-3-0

www.EileenOmosa.com

Acknowledgements

I am grateful to every individual consulted while I went about creating *The Housegirl Becoming Angela.*

The following people made a professional contribution:

Content editor: Kyle V. Hiller

Copy editor: Robert `Babu' Wagner

Cover design: cathyscovers.wix.com/books

Wardrobe editor: Darleen Masakhwe

Book design template by BookDesignTemplates.com

DEDICATION

To all the girls and women making decisions and choices during unpredictable times. Through sheer effort, you prove to society that positive change is possible.

She can't run from her obligations, even when her mind warns her to.

Angela cannot afford to lose this job as a house girl for Ronny's children, no matter what his sister or mother-in-law say or do.

While busy with her duties as a housegirl, Angela gets entangled in a web of struggles at Ronny's house. Frightened, her first reaction is to run, abandon her job, but she cannot. She has a child to provide for and save money to realize her lifelong dream of a university education. And, if she leaves, who will take care of Ronny's children–their mother has been dead for only twelve months.

While Ronny fumbles through work and grief, Angela, his twenty-three-year-old housegirl "mothers" his children. He focuses on his CEO tasks until society insists, he should marry.

Ronny gets practical, analyzes his needs, and prepares a checklist of what he prefers in a wife. It matches Angela.

Friends and family unleash daggers, eager to get Angela out of the picture.

How will Ronny convince Angela to change her title from housegirl to wife, give him his second chance?

Buy this standalone book to experience a story of unexpected love, romance and family sagas.

CONTENTS

Chapter 1

Ronny sat on a black recliner, hunched forward while he cupped his cheeks in both hands. Worried.

Who would take care of his children while he worked as CEO of the family business, give his father enough time to recover from a stroke?

"Auntie," the shouts from Mia and Betty, Ronny's eight- and six-year-old daughters, startled him back to reality.

The girls ran towards the front door into the house ad Ronny glanced at his Rolex as he heard a key turn and the door swung open.

Rose walked in, elegantly dressed in a vintage black Alaia pencil skirt, a cream silk blouse and a cardigan providing jacket length warmth.

Mia and Betty held onto Rose, one on each arm.

Rose paused, stretched her six-inch heel of Lavender Oracle Mary Janes shoes backwards and kicked the door shut. "Where is the baby?" She asked, looking from Betty to Mia.

Ronny watched as his daughters pulled Rose towards the family room.

Nikko looked up from the blue and yellow Lego blocks he was assembling. He pressed his elbows to the carpet for support and stood up. "Auntie, auntie."

Rose's pencil skirt overstretched as she squatted, picked up the three-year-old and kissed him on the forehead. "Hello kiddo, auntie is here to play with you."

Nikko waved a half-built Lego car he had assembled. "Auntie, see my car."

Rose went back into the living room, her nieces in tow.

"Hi Ronny," she kissed her brother on the cheek. "Please gather your courage, you still have the children to love." She kissed him on the other cheek before she added, "Mum sent over some food." She touched his shoulder. "She wishes you could take the family back home."

Rose sat on the sofa adjacent to Ronny's chair.

Betty jumped on her toes. "Food, food from Grandma." She paused and asked, "Did she pack ice cream for our dessert?"

"We will find out when we open the food containers," Rose said.

Nikko struggled out of Rose's hold. "I want to build my car." He hurried away, to the family room where he lay down on the carpet, next to his sisters who had arrived ahead of him and were watching TV.

The left side of Rose's mouth twitched upwards into a smile as she watched Nikko. Her eyes darted back to Ronny who had reverted to his earlier posture.

Her eyes scanned the room and stopped at a black-framed photo of Bella, her sister-in-law. The photo lay on a side table next to Ronny's recliner.

Rose wiped a tear off her cheek as she walked closer to a wall adjacent to the fireplace, filled with framed photos of Ronny's family at different events, some showing the life-stages of each child.

"Did you say there was food?" Ronny interrupted Rose from perusing the photos.

"I have been waiting for you to come help me carry it," she said without turning to his direction.

"Really, that much food, just for the four, five of us?" Ronny asked while staring at the back of his younger sister.

She sniffed back tears before she turned and faced him. "Not that much food, but the huge containers." She spread out both arms to demonstrate size.

"Mmhhh."

Rose picked her car keys from a glass coffee table in the center of the room and walked to the door. She clasped the knob and looked at Ronny over her shoulder saying, "I will drive into the garage."

"Okay," Ronny agreed and took long strides towards the kitchen.

The children left the family room and followed their father.

"Auntie just walked out. Are you also leaving us?" Mia asked.

"Yes, to bring food from Auntie's car. Grandma does not want any of us to sleep hungry," Ronny said without

3

turning back. He walked past the kitchen, opened the pantry door and walked into a corridor to reach the entrance to the car garage. He pressed the garage door opener mounted to the wall.

As the door pulled upwards, then inwards into the roof, Rose drove a maroon Highlander inside.

Rose got out of the car, opened a side door and pulled out a hotpot before she said, "Please pick the larger one from the booth of the car," lifting her chin towards the back of the car before she walked away.

She placed the food on the kitchen island before she stared at Mia standing nearby and asked, "Where is your brother?"

Mia put the book she had been reading on the granite countertop and walked past the dining room to the family room. "Auntie, Nikko is here, playing."

Betty giggled. "Auntie is afraid that our brother will get lost inside the house."

The family assembled at the dining table. Ronny sat on the chair previously used by Bella, to the right of Nikko on his highchair.

Betty tapped a spoon on the mahogany table. She scowled at her father before she turned to Rose sitting on her right-hand side. Mia sat to Rose's left.

Rose was oblivious to the glare as she served lightly buttered mashed potatoes, a deep brown chicken stew and still crisp white cabbage, into Nikko's compartmentalized blue plate.

4

Next, she picked Betty's plate.

Betty took the plate from Rose. "I know, you want to serve me vegetables."

"Vegetables are good for your stomach," Ronny said as he served food into his plate. He started with ugali, a polenta-like food cooked out of maize flour and water.

Betty picked one roast potato from the serving bowl.

Rose looked at her. Betty smiled back. "I will use a spoon when I serve soup."

"You better," Rose reprimanded her.

There was silence at the table, except for the click, click sound made by the stainless-steel spoons hitting plates.

Betty lifted her plate and emptied the little soup she had served into her mouth. She replaced the plate on the table and looked at her father across the table, pointed at him with the spoon in her right hand. "You are on Mummy's chair. Here's Dad's chair," as she pointed to Rose.

Ronny glanced at his sister before he made eye-contact with Betty. "It is okay baby. I will sit here, next to Nikko, as Mummy did."

Betty thinned her lips. "Mummy is dead. Why are you sitting on her chair, and not yours?"

Mia's fork dropped onto her plate of half-eaten food, splashing some soup onto the sides of her glass of water. She said, "Grandma said we could only leave her house if we promised to be good, to each other." She picked the fork. "She also said we should let Mum rest in peace." Mia choked on her words as she looked around the table.

It had been just over twelve months since their mother died. Mia still remembered the day. Two days before schools closed for the Easter holiday. She had been happy to see Pauline, her grandmother at their school, though she questioned why they needed to leave before school was over for the day.

Pauline had hugged each girl tightly and asked them to gather their items and leave for home, their father wanted to see them.

As Joseph, the family driver drove them home, Mia had wondered why their usually chatty grandmother was so quiet.

Immediately Betty had mentioned the words, "Mummy died," Mia had recalled how on arrival home, their father had hugged all the three children into one-fold before he said, "Mummy died."

There was total silence.

After dinner Rose cleared dishes from the table and ran the dish washer.

She entered the family room where Ronny and the children sat together on a three-seater sofa watching TV. She pointed from one child to the next, "Mia, Betty, please go bathe. Call me if you need any help."

Rose turned to Nikko. "You will come with me when I stand up," as she sat down on a nearby two-seater sofa.

"Auntie, I want to bathe now," Nikko said as he ran towards the staircase located on the foyer between the family room and the corridor leading into the visitor bedrooms.

Rose followed Nikko. She held his hand, and they climbed the stairs as she said, "Promise me you will fall asleep after I splash lots of warm water on you."

"Yes. And we read a book, as Grandma does," Nikko said, grinning.

Rose did not respond, fearing the tears gathering in her eyes would stream down her cheeks. She worried that the boy had forgotten his mother in just a year. He was now referencing his grandmother. Why? She questioned, though she knew the answer. Nikko was barely two years old when his mother died.

Rose wished Ronny had stayed another year at their parent's house, for Pauline, their mother to take care of her grandchildren.

Thirty minutes later, Rose walked into the living room and joined Ronny. "I left my boys with their grandmother, my mother-in-law. I will be here for some days." She frowned while she asked, "Why did you insist on leaving our parents' house?"

Ronny picked the remote and turned off the TV. "I have been away from this house for an entire year. Time to gather back my family. I wish you had brought your kids over, that way you would stay longer."

"I'll stay until schools open," she said while serving wine she had picked from the drink's fridge in the dining room. She gave one glass to Ronny. "We need to find and train house workers. Why isn't Margaret coming back to work, her job?"

"Margaret said her husband needed her back home." Ronny focused his eyes on Bella's photo on the side table. "But I have a feeling she reacted, after Mum reminded her Bella would be here if she had not delayed her travel back to the city. She would have been in the house that fateful day, called for help when Bella needed it most. I wish the chef had not gone grocery shopping that day." He said in a shaky voice.

He switched on the TV. "I doubt Margaret will come back. I guess her plan was to take care of the children for one year, appease Bella's soul. The reason she asked to leave immediately after we returned from Bella's memorial."

He took a sip of wine and placed his glass back on a stool. "Margaret has taken care of the children for the past six years. It's time for me to find a different housegirl." He sighed, loud enough for Rose to hear.

Ronny spoke, avoiding Rose's eyes. Looking at her only made him tenser, made him more afraid. Where would they be now if their mother had died when they were young, less than ten years old? Would Henry, their father have managed as their only parent and CEO of his company?

"The worker for Gladys, my neighbour, recommended someone for the vacancy." Rose said as she clasped her cheeks between her hands. "Though I wonder if she can leave her job at a restaurant, and, I did not like her age."

The smile that had replaced the tightened muscles of Ronny's face faded. "Any person with a good reference will do. Make sure they are not one of those who run away with people's children." His mouth twisted into a smile, "Though this compound is secured."

"I will drive her here tomorrow evening for an interview, after he shift at the restaurant." Rose stopped talking and listened to the news on TV.

The newscaster reported about parents struggling to get transport back to the city after the Easter school holiday.

When the news shifted to floods from the extended April long rains, Rose massaged her wrist. "There is another one, a suitable one, an older woman. We can wait for her to travel from upcountry."

"Did you say the restaurant worker is already in the city? Bring her, we try and see if she can get along well with the kids, that's all I need. ASAP."

The skin on Rose's forehead loosened as her eyebrows pulled in and her long eyelashes batted up and down, opening and closing. "I fully understand that things are hard, but we should not bring in someone who is too young." She forced a smile. "It's not your job to babysit another young person."

Rose tilted her neck upwards, like she was listening to someone from upstairs. "I'd assumed you would continue to live with our parents, for Mum to mind the kids while you focus on the Company."

Ronny chuckled while he massaged the back of his neck. "Mum raised us well. I don't want to burden her in raising my children. That is my job as their remaining parent."

Ronny appreciated the welcome his parents had accorded him and his children in the last one year. Residing at his parents' house gave him what he needed to mourn his wife. He had also adjusted to managing the family business while his father recovered from a stroke.

He was now determined to lead his life without the daily support from his mother and her many house workers. Ronny wanted to be a parent to his children, give his mother a chance to assist their father through his recovery process. "How can someone already working at a restaurant in the city be too young for the job of a housegirl?" He questioned.

After the struggle he went through to convince his mother that he needed to move back to his house, Ronny felt he did not have much energy left to debate on who was old enough to be a housegirl. It was okay to have whoever was available if they were of legal age to work.

What Ronny needed was someone with a good reference and old enough to mind his children. Make sure they woke up on time each morning, ate breakfast and were on time for school. "Just bring the one available. I need to get back to work, establish some normality in my life." He shook his head. "I can have a max of two workers in the house, if the upcountry one shows up."

Rose watched as her brother heaved himself out of the chair, stood upright, all six-foot and two inches of him.

He stretched his arms upwards and yawned, before he made his way towards the dining room.

Rose followed him.

Halfway, he stopped. "As always, feel at home in any one of the guest bedrooms. No need to wake up early unless you have somewhere to go." He winked at her and walked on.

He paused in the dining room. "I will take the baby monitor with me," he picked it from where Rose had placed it.

Rose's lips parted to say something, but Ronny spoke ahead of her. "No need for you to walk up and down these stairs." He looked upwards, blinked many times, like his head hurt. He held to one side of the banister as he walked upstairs, something he could not do thirteen months ago. He always preferred to jog when going upstairs.

On his way up he heard a faint, "Good night," from Rose.

While taking an unusually long shower, Ronny juggled ideas in his head. He searched for the right words to use the next day. He needed to break the news to his children that their home address would change in the next few days.

After a year of grief, he knew he would never find peace in their current house, the place where Bella met her death. His growing dislike for the house was the other reason he had agreed to reside with his parents after Bella's funeral. Since then, he had rarely visited his house, except on few occasions to pick necessary items for his children.

11

The family had been back to their residence for fifty-two hours now. The two days had been days of great fear and anxiety. Fear that he or his children might miss a step, tumble downstairs to their death.

Chapter 2

Ronny entered the kitchen and walked past the chair he had vacated a few minutes earlier. He was content that his children would stay in the family room where he had served them their favourite banana crisps.

Arms crossed on his chest, he leaned against one of the hanging cupboards in the kitchen. The position gave him a better viewpoint of Rose and Angela.

Rose had positioned her chair opposite from Angela at a small round table at one corner of the kitchen. Anyone could tell that Rose was in search of evidence to dismiss Angela as a potential housegirl.

Although Cynthia, a long-term housegirl to Gladys, had provided a recommendation for Angela, Rose was determined to find fault so that Ronny could not hire her, evidenced by her increased agitation as the interview progressed.

Angela had maintained a facial expression that was hard to read, neither happiness nor sadness. Instead, she sat with her back straight on the chair, her left hand clasped on top of the right one, on the table. She must have practiced for that position, to steady her shaking fingers and hold her shoulders squared without much push of her chest forward.

Ronny listened without commenting. He did not want to antagonize Rose on the many intrusive questions she asked Angela. He distracted himself with occasional glances outside, through the panel of kitchen windows.

"Are you tidy enough to take care of The Henry's grandchildren?" Rose asked.

Angela's eyelashes lowered, more out of the implied shame than anger. "I have always made personal neatness a priority. I shower daily and I never repeat clothes. I put things in their rightful place, and I clean up wherever I see dirt." She glanced at Ronny, and back to Rose very quickly, like she had been slapped back.

Rose bit her lower lip before she said, "Anyway, they wouldn't let you work at the restaurant if you were not in order." She glanced at Ronny and back to Angela. "Do you harbour any wild dreams to invite your boyfriends into the compound of your employer?"

"I would never do that, even if I had one. I respect workplaces."

"Did you say you don't have a boyfriend? Remember there are none in this compound. Okay?" Rose warned.

Angela nodded.

Ronny was growing impatient. He glanced at the clock on the wall, concerned that his children would run into the kitchen and interrupt the interview. Worse, he would not like them to hear the intrusive questions Rose was asking Angela.

To distract himself from the long time the interview was taking, he set water to boil in his Fallow kettle and made himself a strong cup of tea. He placed a pot of hot water, two cups, tea bags, a sugar dish and spoons on the table, in between Rose and Angela before going back to his former position.

A moment later he turned to the window and stared outside, but he was attentive to the interrogation. "How do you plan to make friends with the children if you have not studied any child psychology?"

Ronny jerked back and stared at Rose. He sipped from his cup, to stop himself from asking if she was interviewing for a teaching position at her private school.

He tried to read Angela's reaction to the question but saw none. His mind wandered off. He questioned what could have forced such a beautiful young woman into the life of a restaurant worker, now struggling to convince Rose that she could make a good housegirl.

Ronny's brow pulled inwards as he thought of his two young daughters, Betty and Mia. He worried if something would ever go wrong in their lives, to force them into the world of work, to earn money at a tender age.

His forehead warmed up into a sweat as he thought of how life had suddenly changed for him and his children when his wife died suddenly, through an accident.

As he had done many times in the last twelve months, he said a silent prayer, asking God that nothing should happen to him. He would do his best to support his children until they were old enough to take care of themselves.

His hope was that Angela, as young and timid as she looked, would be a good housegirl for his children. And with that, he made a promise to himself, that in return he would be a good employer.

"Eleven thousand, five hundred." Angela's words pulled him back to the interview.

Ronny joined in the discussion on Angela's expected pay. "If she can prepare food for the children, make sure they do their homework and go to bed at the appropriate time, we cannot fail to agree on money."

On seeing Rose's lips part, Ronny held his hand in front of his face, an indication to Rose not to talk while he said, "She may leave now." He retrieved his phone from his trouser pocket. "Did you mention that your employer will require a one-week notice?"

Angela looked at Rose before she muttered, "Yes, Sir."

Ronny chuckled, fully aware of the murderous expression on his sister's face.

He addressed Angela, "Come back next week, Wednesday." He tapped on the screen of his phone and lifted it to his ear while still addressing her. "Bring enough clothes for a three-month probation period." He walked to the kitchen door leading outside.

Rose followed Ronny. When he turned and looked at her, she stood and stared at him until he finished speaking on phone then addressed her. "No need to worry, I've called someone to drive her back to town."

He watched as Rose's eyelashes flapped open and close before she said, "Sounds like you have decided to hire her, after all she will be in your house."

Rose opened the door. "Come on, you're good to go," she called to Angela without looking at her.

Ronny walked back into the house as Angela followed Rose outside.

Rose growled to Angela, "Have a good night." She kicked the door closed with her bare foot, turned and walked back into the kitchen.

She hastened her stride into the family room where Ronny had joined his children. She stood with hands held akimbo. "Kids, you have a housegirl. Your Dad asked her to start work next week."

"Why next week and not today?" Mia asked without turning from the TV screen.

Ronny's left side of the mouth drifted upwards into a smile as he asked Rose, "Did you not want to introduce Angela to the children before seeing her off?"

Her eyes widened. "You will introduce her when she reports for duty."

"How did you find her as a person?" he asked.

"Hahaaha! I was doing the interview well, the way we interview house girls, when you interrupted, and ended our discussion."

He glanced to his left and right, where his children sat then said, "We will have a housegirl from next week. She can prepare delicious food and check your

17

homework. Will you get out of bed in the morning when she asks you to?"

"Yeees," Betty, the second-born child responded while watching TV.

Ronny muted the TV and received an immediate series of glares from the children, the attention he needed. So, he spoke. "As I had told you, I found a house for us, not far from here." He lowered his hands and scooped Nikko, his three-year-old from the carpet. "Young man, are you excited? You will bring all your toys to the new house."

Nikko's face beamed as he ran towards his toy box at one end of the room. He went down on his knees and struggled to open the cover.

Rose touched the sofa beside her and sat down, saying, "I thought it was a joke when you said you had put your real-estate agent into a fast-paced assignment, to find you a house." She tilted her head upwards, like she was inspecting the high ceiling. "What about this one?" She waved a hand in the air into a half-circle.

Ronny did not answer Rose's question, instead he called, "Nikko, come."

He watched as his son left the side of the toy-box, carrying many toys in both hands. Ronny said, "Grandma said you all go stay with her for some days. She does not want the movers to drop heavy boxes on your feet."

Nikko ran towards Rose who threw both arms open and he fell onto her lap. She cuddled him and massaged his head. "You will go and be spoiled by Grandma."

Ronny leaned back on the chair and entwined both hands at the back of his head. "Grandma will come with you on Tuesday, then you will see your new bedrooms."

"No, Dad," Betty said while looking at Mia. "Can we go see the empty house before they fill it up with all the tables, chairs and beds?"

"We can go see the house tomorrow, after you pack your travel bags." He lowered his hands back to position while saying, "I will do some office work in the morning before we go to Grandma's house in the afternoon." He smoothed Betty's hair backwards. "We can stop by the empty house for you to see it."

Rose stared at Ronny while she spoke, "That is a good opportunity, to visit an empty house. You could even play ball, if the living room is as huge as your current one."

Ronny unmuted the TV before he said, "Not really. It is smaller, all the rooms are on one floor. No staircases for people to fall down." He stood up as Rose asked.

"Why move your family from this palatial home, into a smaller—? she stopped talking on noticing her brother's gritted teeth and pulled-in brows.

Rose walked to the kitchen and Ronny followed her saying. "I would have asked Angela we pay her employer for the one-week notice, but I think it will be better if she starts work at the new house."

Rose grumbled. "Does that mean you have made up your mind about her?"

"Was that not the reason you brought her over, to be interviewed for a job?"

19

"I brought her because Gladys had talked to Cynthia her houseworker, who asked Angela to come for the interview. Gladys mentioned the age after I had agreed to the interview."

"Is she not of legal age to be a housegirl?"

Rose did not respond. She opened the fridge and closed it.

Ronny followed her into the pantry. "What are you looking for? I ordered take-away." He watched as a smile relaxed Rose's face. She let her hands fall to her side, like she had accepted some defeat. She walked to the kitchen window and looked outside.

Since the family returned to their house, Ronny had relied on frequent food deliveries from his parents' house and take-away from restaurants, a practice he did not want to continue now that they had less than two weeks before schools opened. That was the other reason he asked Angela to report for duty when she said she could prepare a variety of food dishes, a skill that he and his sister lacked in equal measures.

"Excellent choice, we can eat take-away until your housegirl arrives next week. Any plans to employ a chef?" Rose said while still facing outside.

Ronny continued to hold some worry about why Rose did not want Angela hired as the housegirl he was so urgently in need of. He wished she could see that he did not have many options now that he had moved back to his house. He needed to make things work. If his children received good care, he would be freed to focus more on his CEO duties. His success in managing the Henry Technologies Inc. would please his father, lead to his quick recovery.

Henry had worked hard to build the company. He would be heartbroken to see it crumble due to his illness.

Ronny was determined to lead the company to further success. He wondered why his sister was focused on which woman could be or not be the housegirl for his children. "Let me know when the lady from upcountry arrives." He pulled a chair and sat. "We can interview her as well."

He stood and walked out of the kitchen, but paused before reaching the door, and said, "I am going to the gym." He flicked his fingers. "Do you want to join me, or stay with the kids and receive the dinner? I already paid." He hurried off.

Ronny held onto one side of the banister as he took one stair at a time. Something he would have never done thirteen months ago, when getting ready for the gym, located next to his car garage, meant running upstairs for a change of clothes.

He was relieved as he closed the bedroom door behind him. He was happy that one more night and his children would vacate the house which held bad memories for them. His hope was that no girl or woman would ever walk down those stairs, wearing high-heeled shoes.

Shoes that Bella loved, but they never loved her back.

Chapter 3

Angela did not stop her silent prayer of thanks on her drive from Muthaiga to the city center.

She stayed alert, reminded herself not to let the smile in her eyes escape through her mouth. Ronny's driver might think she was not of sound mind, which would jeopardize her job as a housegirl.

The car came to a stop outside KENCOM, the public transport vehicles' terminus.

Holding onto the partially open door of the Subaru Impreza, with one leg dangling outside, Angela turned to the driver and released her full smile. "Thank you very much for driving me all the way. You've saved me a lot of time," she said as her leg touched the pavement.

"Welcome. This ride was ordered by the boss."

"Thanks, and see you next week," she said as she pushed the door to close. She retained her smiled as she watched the car drive off.

She exhaled and lifted a hand to her chest as she walked to a strategic point from where she had an unobstructed view of approaching matatus–minibuses used for public transport. It did not take long before a matatu number eight came to a halt at the bus stop.

Unlike on most other days when she would be tired while boarding a matatu after work, she still had energy. The manamba manning the entrance into the matatu looked at her longer than necessary. Angela guessed that he was suspicious of her smile, an expression which most matatu travelers lacked in the evening.

She was suddenly aware of the stuffiness of the matatu but did not abandon her smile as she walked to the back row, the only place with three empty seats. She thought of how different air could be.

The scent in Ronny's house was like all the flowers from Naivasha flower farms, destined for Europe. She recalled the fragrance from Rose, fantasizing until it helped neutralize her harsh words during the interview. She wouldn't mind meeting with Rose again, just for a chance to inhale her perfume and maybe get the name right this time.

Angela neared her seat as the four people already comfortable at the back returned her smile, each assuming her smile was for them.

The vehicle was in motion before the two passengers on the passageway reached the vacant seats beside her. Angela acknowledged each person as they sat down.

She wished it was possible to share her happiness with someone in the matatu before she arrived home, to share her news with the three women she shared a house with. But she knew better not to.

A ride in a matatu going to Kibera, a low-income residential area of the city, meant that many of the passengers had toiled throughout the day, many for minimum pay.

There were also some who could have lost their jobs that day, while others could have traveled to the city or industrial area early in the morning, with hopes of getting a temporary job. Now they could be going home empty handed.

Like in many other big cities, there were also people scouting for easy prey, to snatch a handbag, a wallet or a phone.

The familiar buildings alerted Angela that her bus stop was not very far. Aware that matatus rarely waited long enough for passengers to alight, she went nearer to the exit.

Showing her sparkling white teeth, she asked the manamba to let her off at the next stage, *"Nashuka hapo kwa Mama samaki,"* a stop commonly referred to by the elderly lady who deep-fried and sold tilapia fish by the roadside.

As predicted, the matatu slowed down just long enough for her to jump out. When she frowned at the manamba, he stared back and shouted, "This vehicle is a moving object, not stationary like your house."

As her feet hit the muddy sidewalk, Angela reflected on his words, questioned if some houses in Kibera could qualify as mobile objects.

Many of the houses in the area lacked a solid foundation. With that thought, she said another silent prayer, thanking God that she and her housemates lived in a more stable house, rented by Cynthia.

Cynthia, popularly known as Aunty C, worked as a housegirl for Gladys, Rose's friend and neighbour.

Cynthia was an aunty to Brenda, Angela's best friend from high school.

The one-bedroom house where Angela resided with Jane, Phoebe and Concepta was rented by Cynthia. Cynthia, who resided at the compound of her employer, did not need her house in Kibera though she paid the landlord the monthly rent.

The house was for Cynthia's side business. She sourced girls with good references from rural homes, accommodated them at her rented house until they found jobs in the city. Others found jobs that demanded they moved out, as Angela would be doing soon.

Each of Cynthia's tenants paid her their share of rent. In most months, the total rent was more than what she paid the landlord.

The aromas of fried fish caught Angela's attention. She stopped by Mama samaki and enquired, "How's business today? I hope no fish has escaped from your bubbling oil," Angela called out to announce her arrival.

Mama *samaki* said her byes to another customer before she turned to Angela, "Welcome my child. I hope those tall buildings in the city have treated you well."

"More than well," Angela said, restraining herself from sharing that she would be starting a new job soon. She did not want to alert Mama samaki that she would soon lose a customer. Unlike her housemates who preferred meat, Angela bought fish on a weekly basis, her gift to the house, aware of its nutritional value.

Angela paid for a medium-sized tilapia fish, two onions and four tomatoes.

They exchanged pleasantries on each other's welfare and the latest happenings in the locality before they said their byes. Angela left for her house, a few minutes' walk away.

When Jane and Phoebe arrived, Angela had showered and cooked ugali, vegetables and fish stew for their supper.

"I hope that aroma is from our house," Jane announced as she unlocked the door and walked in, with Phoebe right behind her.

Angela rummaged for something she could not name. She silently rebuked herself for having not thought of how to break the news to her housemates.

Should she tell them of her interview and job offer, or wait until she reported for duty?

Reflecting on how tough Rose had been during the interview, Angela worried she might turn up at Ronny's house on Wednesday and be told the position had been filled. In confusion, she said, "I went for a job interview today, at a charming home. If I get the job..." she trailed off as she scanned the faces of Jane and Phoebe for reaction.

Phoebe clapped her hands into a loud sound as her face lit up with a smile. "A higher pay means you will continue to feed us well, the nice food," she said as her nose pulled in the fish aroma.

The delicious aroma of fish was rare in their house. Breakfast was mainly a cup of tea. An accompaniment of bread, mandazi or roasted groundnuts was a luxury afforded by one of them as a gift to the group. Supper was mainly ugali and vegetables on most days, while beans or beef was served as a specialty on Saturdays and Sundays.

The four women had a routine to help them co-exist peacefully in the shared accommodation. They held weekly meetings where they discussed cleaning chores, the menu, and costs, and a cooking roster. Each woman put her share of the combined costs into a common purse hidden in a kitchen cupboard.

While considering how much information to share, Angela noticed a sneer on Jane's face.

Jane had resigned her job as a room cleaner in a hotel in the city. She preferred her current job as a washerwoman. She walked around estates, knocked on house doors and asked if they had clothes for her to wash and iron. Her plan was that one day she would be asked to stay on as a resident cleaner in one of the houses of rich people. She had not been able to secure her dream job for more than seven months now.

Angela wriggled her fingers. "I don't know about the pay yet, but I will reside in the compound of my employer."

In the past, the four women had voiced their desire to find jobs where they would live at the compound of their employer, just like Cynthia. Such a job enabled one to save on travel time and money for transport, rent and food.

For Angela, the position of a housegirl would also mean physical security that worried Joshua, her older brother. He'd never stopped reminding her to be careful, alert on her security. There were days when Angela left the house at five o'clock for an early morning shift or arrived home past eleven at night on days when she worked an evening shift.

Residing at the compound of her employer meant she would have no worries on personal security. She needed to be safe for her son. "Aunty C referred me to the job, I will start next week," she said.

Jane held one hand akimbo, "Lucky you. Does that mean you are giving us a short notice for rent? You know how Cynthia wants the same total amount of rent, be it two, three or four of us living here?"

"Mmhhh," Phoebe nodded.

Angela decided very quickly that she would afford to pay rent for next month. Ronny had mentioned they would not fail to agree on her pay, and his home displayed niceties as only seen in movies and furniture magazines. She would still be making a saving from transport, rent and food. "I will pay my full rent for next month. Aunty C would have found another girl to join you by then."

Jane, the shortest of them all, at five-foot two inches, threw her arms wide open and hugged Angela. "You are a sister. Please find for me a similar job in your new neighbourhood."

"Muthaiga," Angela added.

"Muthaiga?" Phoebe glanced at the corrugated roof of their house, with no ceiling to block her view. "That means you will be working for one of the bigshots." She chuckled. "Sounds like time to enjoy the delicious food in our kitchen. Is there cake for breakfast tomorrow?"

Phoebe threw her handbag onto the only chair in the house, a three-sitter sofa in the room that served as a kitchen and living room. The threesome lined up and washed hands at a nearby sink before they served food and went back to the sofa. Each carried a plate filled with food.

As they ate, Jane who sat between the other two women on the sofa, asked, "Will you take your beddings with you?"

The question reminded Angela that Jane had never stopped commenting on the blanket and sheets she had bought during her second month in the city.

Angela resolved it would be better to leave Jane with a social debt. "I will leave my sheets, blanket and pillow for you, I hope you don't mind."

"Why would I mind receiving a gift from a sister like you?" Jane asked.

"Thanks. That means I can come back if I do not fit into the position, or when I come for a visit on my off days—"

"All you need is to ask Concepta, so you can use her bed. After all, she seems to like working as a night receptionist at that city hotel." Jane said before she stuffed her mouth with food, holding a fish bone back in her hand.

29

As Angela washed her plate, she told herself that she must make her job as a housegirl possible. She had sensed, at least from Jane, that she would not be welcomed back to the Kibera house. She bid Jane and Phoebe to a good night, explaining that she had an early morning shift at work.

From her top bed on one of the two double-decker beds in the bedroom, Angela made a phone call to Cynthia. "Auntie, is it an appropriate time to talk? I went for the interview today."

"How did it go?"

"I think okay. The lady who interviewed me was very detailed. But the man asked me to report for work next week, Wednesday. Thanks Auntie."

Cynthia released a soft laugh. "Nothing comes easy, as you already know from your restaurant job. Your task is to focus on the duties of a housegirl, keep the children comfortable and happy." She chuckled then added, "That's how we win the hearts and money of these rich people. Okay?"

"I will do my best Auntie," Angela said in a lowered voice. "Good night Auntie. It is okay if you find another person to take over my bed here." Angela said, no longer afraid that Rose might find someone else for the post. She would remain positive, report for duty as asked by Ronny, the person she would be working for.

"I have supported my four children from my job as a housegirl." Cynthia said as a matter of fact, "You can support your son and university education from the same." She paused and cleared her throat before she added, "Good behaviour and focus on your work tasks are the ways to survive any job. I know you'll make me proud. Good night," She said and ended the call.

Angela had wanted to thank Cynthia again. She still uttered the words to herself. "Thanks Auntie. I will not bring any shame to you or myself. Good night."

In her nightly prayer, Angela included a thank you for Cynthia, and to Brenda her friend through whom she'd come to know Cynthia. She also thanked her stars that Ronny came to her rescue from Rose.

A smile remained on her face as she checked one more time that her morning wake-up alarm was set.

She was content that she would soon start a job of taking care of young children, in place of the opportunity she had lost of being at home to take care of her son.

Chapter 4

The Subaru Impreza stopped at the bus stop where Angela had disembarked a week ago. She saw the driver turn her direction before he unlocked the passenger door.

She opened the door, placed her bag of clothes on the foot mat then climbed in. She sat and rested her feet on the bag while holding her handbag to her chest, tightly.

She turned to her right. "How are you? Thanks for picking me up, my name is Angela."

"You may throw it to the back seat," the driver said while pointing at her luggage.

"My name is Joseph. I was given your name from the house."

Assured that it was safe to join the main road, he drove off, towards Muthaiga.

Thirty minutes later, Joseph turned into a private road that was different from the one where Angela had interviewed for the job.

She panicked, worried what to do if the interview had been a scam, for kidnapping. She said a silent prayer, asking God to spare her life for the sake of her son.

Angela reached for her phone cautiously, wanting to be sure of the exact location, in case she needed to make one last call to her brother.

She unzipped her handbag and looked inside as the vehicle came to a stop and two side-by-side gates opened. A security guard stood to attention as they drove inside.

Should she ask where they were? Her dry lips refused to part as they drove on a long-paved driveway which ended at the front of a vast single storey house. The compound appeared as extensive as the one of last week.

Darting her eyes to the many glass panels on one wall of the house, she saw the three children she had seen at the other house.

A release of breath alerted Angela that she had not been breathing. She was relieved, no one in their right mind would kidnap her into a house with children.

Her prayer shifted, asking God that if Rose was still in the house, she would be less tough on her. That she would have some mercy and let her prove herself in her role as a housegirl.

Joseph directed Angela to the kitchen door into the house.

Angela took unsure steps into the kitchen where she came face to face with Rose. A cold feeling formed, spreading throughout her stomach.

~~~~~~

Five days later, Angela felt a little relief when on Monday morning, Rose loaded her suitcase and drove off in her jungle green Pajero.

The days Angela spent under the watchful eye of Rose were days she would not forget.

Though the house was dusted clean by commercial cleaners before and after the movers arranged individual items in specific rooms, Rose made Angela clean the new toilets and bathrooms.

Angela gathered strength, reminding herself that she needed to be strong for Edmond Babu, her son, named after her paternal grandfather.

She also did not want to put Cynthia in an awkward position by abandoning a job she had highly recommended her for.

There was also her plan to go to university to study foods service and hotel management, a program she had qualified for with above average grades from high school.

Her want for a career in food service was part of the reason she had relocated from the village to the city. Her strategy was to work at a restaurant, the best way to keep her career dream alive.

Angela's life-long ambition was to be a proprietor of a restaurant or hotel. That dream was shattered when three months into her holiday after completion of high school, she had started to vomit, mostly in the morning hours.

Priscah, her paternal grandmother had assumed it was malaria and rushed her to hospital. The lab results indicated negative for malaria.

Instead of getting better, Angela continued to vomit whenever she ate. Then her grandmother had asked her to lie down on the bed, on her back, so she could check for signs of any stomach related infections.

Immediately Angela pulled her dress up to her chest, the wrinkles on Priscah's face had turned into deep furrows as her small eyes disappeared into their sockets. Angered. "I see the line from your belly button downwards is dark enough. Have you opened your legs to men?"

Priscah had yanked the dress down from Angela's chest. "Your stomach is tender, like you are on your way to becoming a mother."

With those words, Priscah had struggled onto her feet and left the room.

There and then, it had dawned on Angela. The results of the night in December when she had joined her friends to celebrate their completion of high school. The contact with that boy had lasted no more than five minutes.

She was now alone with a baby on the way to take care of.

The sound of the car garage door alerted Angela to the arrival of Ronny. She busied herself with the food cooking on the gas cooker.

Ronny placed a paper bag from a renowned Italian bakery on the kitchen island. "How was your day, what about the children?"

"We are fine. They are in the family room."

He walked away towards the dining room.

"Daddy, daddy, daddy." The three children ran to him.

With his back turned, Angela scrutinized Ronny as he walked away. She inhaled the scent of the cologne he left behind and tried to guess the designer name without success.

She tilted her head upwards for a better view of his well-trimmed black hair. She levelled her head to his broad-squared shoulders hidden within a well-fitted black suit, courtesy of the tailors at Hugo Boss.

Angela was impressed with the way a tiny amount of the collar of his white button up shirt peeked out of the neckline of his coat with every step he took. "God gives too much material things to some people, then takes away their happiness," she mumbled to herself.

She watched as he let the leather bag, he was pulling beside him stand on its wheels. He threw open his muscular arms as he lowered his sturdy body towards the floor.

Nikko fell into his father's open arms, followed by Betty and Mia. He scooped up the boy and stood upright before he extended his right hand and touched the heads of his daughters, one after the other. "I missed all of you, my babies, did you enjoy your day?"

Angela turned away to mind the food, hide the smile on her face. She was openly impressed by the fact that a CEO of a renowned technology company in the country and beyond, lowered all his power to receive his children in his arms.

Betty looked up at her father. "Angela said we watch TV for only one hour. Why?" she shrugged her shoulders.

"Because you have school tomorrow," Ronny said as he placed a hand on Betty's shoulder.

She tilted her neck backwards, faced upwards and made eye contact with her father. "But Auntie and Grandma never stop us from watching TV?"

"We will have new TV rules, especially now that schools are opening."

He turned to Nikko, still leaning on his left shoulder. "I will stay with you while your sisters go bathe. Go shower, that way we'll have time to play after dinner, before you go to bed."

"Dad," Mia moved closer and leaned against his thigh.

Ronny placed Nikko on the floor and frowned at Mia. "No more arguments. I am tired from working all day. I had to leave work early to be home with you."

He regretted his words on seeing the expression on the faces of his children.

None of the children moved. All he saw were six pleading eyes turned upwards.

He felt sorry. He remembered for the thousandth time that he needed to withhold his angry outbursts. His children had no mother to cry to.

He sighed and forced a smile. In a softer voice, he said, "Go and bathe now. After dinner we can discuss when and how long you'll be watching TV."

Ronny watched as Mia and Betty walked away, with haggard shoulders. "When you are done, bring a paper and pencil so we can work on a program for all of us," he called out as Mia and Betty ran off through the family room, to the corridor leading to their bedrooms.

By the time Betty and Mia returned, dressed in matching pink pajamas, Angela had placed dinner on the dining table.

Angela retreated into the kitchen and busied herself, wiping the already clean counter tops. She was waiting for the family to eat. After, she was to clear the dishes from the table before serving herself from the leftovers.

Ronny and the children washed hands and sat at the twelve-seater table, one of the many items he bought for the new house. Except for their clothes, the children's toys, utensils and few items inherited from his parents, he had replaced all the other items from the previous house.

"Angela!" Ronny called.

"Sir," she answered and hurried out of the kitchen. Her hands hanging in front of her pink and white checked apron.

He took a glance at his children and back at Angela. "Come to the table with a plate. One of the new rules is that you will eat from here, with everyone else."

Her medium-sized lips parted but no words came out.

Ronny could tell that she was not breathing, too scared to utter a word. He had overheard Rose spell-out house rules to her. She was to eat from the kitchen after everyone else, never from the family dining table.

She seemed to count her steps to the kitchen. She came back carrying a plate, tightly held between both hands.

"Your seat," Ronny pointed to the empty chair on the right side of Nikko's chair. "That way, you can assist Nikko while you both eat."

He watched as she washed hands at the nearby sink and occupied the chair as instructed. He sensed that she would have liked to protest, remind him that her place was in the kitchen. He maintained a no-nonsense expression on his clean-shaven face. He did not leave any room for her to explain.

Angela followed the commands given. She did not want to defy her employer. Losing her job was not one of her options. She had resigned from her job at the restaurant where the manager had not been happy to see her go. He had been angry after begging her to withdraw her letter of resignation, without success.

Angela was one of the promising young employees at the restaurant. Within her fourteen months of employment, she had worked herself from her duties of floor cleaner and dishwasher loader, into a regular food server during peak hours.

She had to make her job as a housegirl work. It would be hard to approach the restaurant manager to return to her tasks. The chances were high that Cynthia would have already found someone to interview for the job at the restaurant and her now vacant bed at the house in Kibera.

The salary for her job as a housegirl was enticing enough. Eighteen thousand a month, and she did not have to pay for the two bed-room staff quarters she occupied. In no way would she want to lose the job.

She served herself less food than she would have wanted to eat. She paid more attention to Nikko than the food on her plate.

Whenever she looked up, she saw the stares from Betty and Mia. The two girls sat across the table from her, on either side of their father.

Angela understood why they were surprised to see her eat from the family table, something she had not done since her arrival. She now sat on the chair previously used by Rose.

Ronny was not oblivious to the frequent glances from his daughters. He focused on eating as the food was delicious.

Angela had prepared a bowl of roast potatoes, millet *ugali*, a beef stew and *Sagaa*, an indigenous vegetable also called spider plant. She had also prepared a small bowl of rice for Nikko.

Once or twice, Angela locked eyes with Ronny and quickly looked away by turning to Nikko. She assumed that Ronny was looking her direction because he wanted to be sure that his son was eating his food.

The thought of getting Nikko to eat his food reminded Angela of her own three-and-a-half-year-old son back in the village.

She picked a spoonful of food from Nikko's plate into his mouth. The more she could help Nikko to eat well and stay healthy, the more assured she would be that her own son, five hundred kilometers away in the village, would be well-fed by her grandmother, using the money Angela sent home every month.

Chapter 5

While Angela cleared the dining table and loaded the dish-washer, Ronny assisted Nikko with his evening bath. He played a nursery rhyme on a mini stereo, rocking him to sleep.

Ronny lowered the light on the bedside lamp and tiptoed out, carrying the baby monitor to the family room. He lowered the TV volume, getting Mia and Betty's attention.

"Remember you had an assignment, a timetable for your week-day evenings and weekends."

Betty pushed Mia to one side of the sofa, making room for their father. Ronny saw the gesture and occupied the space. Ronny was glad that his daughters were now happy, unlike at the dinner table.

Mia held a pencil and a paper on a leather clipboard, and the discussions began.

Ten minutes later, Angela took reluctant steps towards the family room. Ronny had asked her to attend the session. As she neared where the family sat, Ronny pointed her to a nearby chair.

Mia jerked out of the sofa and stood up, the clipboard in her hand. "Angela, Dad has helped us come up with a list of activities to do whenever we are home." She shrugged her shoulders. "He insists we watch only one hour of TV on school days."

She pointed at Angela with the pencil in her right hand. "You started all this, about one-hour TV," Mia sputtered.

Ronny held Mia's right hand, lowered it to her side as she continued to speak. "Do you want to hear the new weekend program?"

Angela nodded and said, "Yes," aware that Betty and Ronny were looking at her.

Mia read out the list. "Monday. Wake up with the first alarm, shower and get dressed in our school uniforms. Get to the dining table at seven sharp and eat breakfast promptly. Pick up our bag packs, after which Angela opens the house door and walks us to the car. She locks the house and accompanies us to school."

"Tuesday. Wake up with the first alarm, shower and get dressed in our school uniforms. Get to the dining table at seven sharp and eat breakfast promptly. Pick up our bag packs, after which Angela opens the house door and walks us to the car. She locks the house and accompanies us to school."

Ronny looked at the clock on the wall. "Good. Now read out your evening schedule without saying each day of the week. We need to observe your bedtime, which is fast approaching."

Betty looked at Ronny, then Mia. "Can Mia sit down now, as we do at school?"

"Sure. She has stood enough for the evening," Ronny said, grinning.

Mia made herself comfortable beside her father as she said, "Angela. We agreed that you will take a break from cooking on Saturday and some Sundays. Dad said if we behave well during the week, he will take us to the Club and buy food for us. He will also take us to Grandma's house or to Auntie Rose when you go away on your off day."

Betty who had been lying on her father's lap sat upright. "Angela, what do you do on your off days? Maggie used to visit her family on the other side of the city."

Ronny looked from Betty to Mia. "What if you read your after-school program first, before the weekend one?"

"Dad, Mia is trying to explain to Angela why we did not cry after you said we watch only one hour of TV," Betty explained.

They all laughed, including Angela who was sitting with her hands loosely crossed on her lap.

Mia's eyes went back to the paper in her hand. "Monday, arrive home from school, eat a snack, do homework or read a book, then watch cartoons on TV or go outside to the playground and jump around."

Betty raised her hand. "And Dad said we each have a designated day to choose a cartoon we can all watch." She stood and jumped up and down on her toes, giggling. A moment later, she stopped and sat down. "I know which cartoon I will choose, but it is my secret."

Mia stood up and looked at the paper in her hand. She turned to her sister. "I have not finished reading the activities for our evening. Where did I stop?" She asked as she ran her index finger across the paper. "Yes. Watch TV or play outside the house. At six-thirty, go bathe. Seven o'clock, sit at the dining table, pray and eat dinner. Brush teeth, story time with Dad, and be in bed by eight-thirty."

Ronny tickled Mia on the armpit. "Well done my baby."

"Dad, I am not a baby. I am a big girl."

He turned to Betty and tickled her. "And you, are you still my sweet little girl?"

Betty giggled. "If you let me watch more TV and eat lots of chips."

Ronny nodded as he looked at Angela.

She looked away, muttering, "That is a good list of activities. We can make a copy and pin it up and look at it if we forget something."

"I will not forget, maybe Betty," Mia said as she looked at Betty.

Betty made a funny face, waged her tongue out at Mia.

Angela looked at the clock. "I see your bedtime is approaching. I will come with you and show you where you will find your school uniform each morning." She stood up and looked at Mia.

"It'll be good if we follow the program from today onwards, since tomorrow is a school day." Mia said before she leaned over and kissed her father on the cheek. "Good night, Dad." She walked away.

Betty leaped onto her father's lap and circled her arms around his neck. She tried to align her small round face into Ronny's oval one. "Good night, Dad." She pointed a finger at his nose. "Go to your room, not your office. Okay?"

She slipped down to the carpeted floor, away from Ronny's hand tickling her armpit.

Angela tried to stay steady as Betty hung onto her arm while they walked to their bedrooms.

"Angela."

She paused from her stride on hearing Ronny call her.

"If you have a few minutes we will look at the weekend schedule."

She did not move, trying to decide if he wanted her to turn back or proceed with the girls and come back later.

He must have read her confusion. He added, "After you are finished with the girls."

Reassured, Angela walked on. She was determined to teach the children how to find their clothes and keep their rooms neat. In the days she had been with them, she had been the one to select their clothes for each day. Over time, she decided that Mia and Betty were old enough to select clothes for themselves each morning.

Angela knocked on Mia's door before entering.

Mia sat on her bed reading a story book.

Angela beckoned her. "Come to your wardrobe," she said as she opened the double wardrobe doors. "The left side has your school uniforms, including P.E and swimming clothes. Each morning, you pull out a skirt, blouse, vest and sweater."

She pulled a drawer open. "You will pick a pair of socks and underwear from the drawers."

Betty jumped onto Angela's back.

Angela held Betty's hands to the front of her shoulders, as she continued to explain to Mia. "As you can see, the right side of the wardrobe has your regular and church clothes."

Mia nodded with a smiley face. "Too organized, hard for me to miss anything," she said as she smoothed a hand across her many clothes on the right-hand side of the wardrobe.

"Mine now," Betty said as she slid down from Angela's back and skipped towards the door.

"Come with us, you need to see Betty's wardrobe as she has seen yours," Angela called Mia.

The trio walked out.

Angela knocked on Betty's door, sending both girls into loud laughter. Angela placed a finger on her mouth. "Shhhh. It's nighttime and the baby is sleeping," as she pointed to Nikko's room, right next to Betty's. They laughed again, though not as loud as the first time.

Mia asked, "Did you forget that we are with Betty? Why knock on a door when there is no one inside?"

"It is a nice practice to get used to," Angela explained as they walked inside. "That way, you will not enter a bedroom and find the person inside has dropped their towel and is pulling up their underwear. Would that be nice?" She turned from one girl to the other. "It would

47

not be good for your eyes or for the person getting dressed."

The girls laughed out again.

"So, can that be our first bedroom rule, to always knock on a door and wait for a response before opening?" Angela asked, looking from Mia to Betty.

They nodded.

At Betty's wardrobe, Angela repeated similar instruction from Mia's room before she asked the girls to follow her to Betty's bathroom."

"Mia, you will do the same in your bathroom. Place all your used clothes inside the basket," Angela said as she pointed towards the lime-green net basket at one corner of the bathroom.

Hang your used towel on the towel rack to dry. All garbage must be inside the wastepaper basket. Easy to do with that nice scoring ring."

Each child had a fancy waste-bin in their bathroom. The bins had a basketball net at the top to encourage children to aim for when tossing garbage into the container.

Angela walked out of the bathroom. "You will never lose your favourite items if you place things where they should be."

"Are you saying someone will come to the house and take our items from our rooms?" Mia asked.

Angela paused her step. "Not a person. Dad has set the Rumba to clean your carpets and bathroom floors every Tuesday and Wednesdays. However, Rumba does not know dirt from your items on the floor." Angela said, not bothering to add that she had spent time picking up clothing from floors of the children's bedrooms and bathrooms.

"Aaah," Mia said.

"Any other questions for me? I need to go and discuss my weekend schedule with your father."

"Dad said the weekend is your day off. Maybe he wants to discuss the time you will come back," Mia explained.

Betty followed them to the door, holding a toothbrush. "Angie. I have a question."

"Yes." Angela answered, amused at her new name, the version that her mother liked to call her.

Angela missed her mother more, each time she looked at Mia, Betty and Nikko, three young children without a mother. Angela made a promise to herself, she would try her best, give double love to these children - the mother's love she missed, and the mother's love she could not give her son.

"What will happen if we mess up our wardrobe or bathroom?"

A smile engulfed Angela's face. "Not much, except that you will spend your TV time arranging your room."

Angela threw her arms open and gave Betty a good night cuddle. "Brush your teeth and get between your sheets, they've been waiting for you all evening."

"But dad has not read me a story," Betty called out as Angela and Mia left her room.

Angela stepped back into the room. "I will be sure to remind him when I get to the family room. Go, finish your brushing from the bathroom sink." She walked out and pulled the door closed.

When they reached Mia's door, Angela knocked, opened the door and spread out her arms. She cuddled Mia. "Good night and sleep tight. No story books in bed, okay?"

Mia nodded, stepped inside and closed the door behind her.

Chapter 6

Ronny questioned what could have kept Angela for so long. He checked the time on the clock one more time before he walked away, into the living room.

His hope was that Angela did not forget about her job and busy chatting with the children, instead of letting them sleep as scheduled.

Angela walked into the family room. There was no Ronny. Fear gripped her, she worried that she had overstayed. As she entered the dining room on her way to the kitchen, Ronny coughed, attracting her attention.

She changed direction and went into the living room. "Sorry for the lateness."

"Did the girls take their time to get to bed?"

"I was showing them where to find their uniform each morning and how to leave their wardrobes and bedrooms organized. Betty asked if you will read her a story tonight."

He clasped his cheeks between his hands. "A storybook? Did she say which one?"

Angela shook her head no.

He stood up. "I will be back shortly; you may continue with your evening." He took long strides out of the room.

Upon arrival in the kitchen, Angela wiped the already clean counter tops and swept the kitchen floor.

She pulled out a food tray and loaded it with cereal bowls, teacups, two cereal-jars, spoons and sugar. She moved to one end of the kitchen and squatted to fetch a set of lunch boxes from one of the cupboards.

When she lifted her head up, she almost jumped, scared to see a tall figure standing by the kitchen island. She had not heard Ronny walk into the kitchen.

"Did I scare you?"

She did not respond as she recovered from being startled.

"The door alarm is already set, and the night security people are on duty. There are no bad people in the house to scare you," he said, trying his best to get her to relax.

Angela looked at Ronny from head to toe, then looked away on realizing that she was staring.

Ronny's eyes followed her as she picked three lunch carriers to the kitchen island.

He pulled a high stool out of its place and sat, resting both hands on the grey marble top island. He let the paper in his hand drop onto the countertop and motioned Angela to a stool.

"If you stay that scared every time I talk, you'll end up breaking all the glasses in this house, and that could mean no more water drinking for us," he said with a smile on his face. He was pleased to see a mild grin on Angela's face.

His eyes were on her slender body as she pulled a stool and sat at the edge. She still appeared ready to jump off at any moment.

He mused on what she could be thinking. That he had come to the kitchen to grab and drag her into his bedroom. There were many stories circulating in the city of some men who took advantage of their female house staff.

One side of his mouth twitched upwards into a smile. He pondered how to let Angela know that he had no such plans. She was in his house to mind his children while he focused on the family business. He was still grieving his wife, and strangely, he had lost the excitement he used to have on seeing young women.

Before he married Bella, there had been more than enough ladies ready to bare their hearts and bodies to him. There were many reasons for their interest. One, he held the title of Mr. Handsome from votes at one of the city members' clubs. Two, he came from a wealthy family. Many people in the city and beyond wished to be associated with the Henry family.

He coughed out a smile. In the past he had not had a reason to look at a housegirl twice. They were raised by their mother even though there was always a group of workers within the family compound. And Margaret, the woman who had minded his children for six years was a grandmother, in her sixties. He tried to recall who was the worker before Margaret, no name came to mind.

He did however, secretly acknowledged that Angela was young and a beauty. He liked her long heart-shaped face and oval eyes. For now, there was no need for her to be afraid of him. He had a reputation to keep.

His objective was to make sure his young children received loving care in order to lessen their grief from the loss of their mother. The reason he needed to interact with Angela, know who she was as a person, her aspirations, and any challenges that could impact on her tasks as a housegirl.

Once the children were happy at home and at school, he would focus all his energy on managing the family business. He needed to succeed, give his father time to recover from a stroke. Ronny knew that his success in managing the family computer soft-ware company would help his father recover faster.

The Henry Technologies Inc. had started off as a small software support company in the late 1970s. The company grew very fast in the 1990s as computer and cell phone technologies became more widespread, the world over.

By 2012, the company was the place to go to within Kenya and other countries in eastern, central and western Africa.

Ronny wanted to pick up the pieces and make some-thing good out of the death of his wife and his father's illness. "As you saw, the children have developed a sched-ule to provide some sort of guidance to their free time," he said, pushing Mia's handwritten schedule towards

Angela. "Do you have suggestions on additions or subtractions?"

Angela picked up the paper and glanced through. "Is it okay if I spend my Saturdays baking for the family? I'd love to have a place to try out new recipes."

Ronny smiled, having noted that she had changed the topic. "Will that include cake? I like chocolate cake," he said before he waved a hand away, to dismiss his words. "Forget about cake, your food is already delicious enough. When do you plan to take your weekly days off?"

She looked up at the hanging cupboards right in front of her view. "I do not have many places to go to, except visit friends at university. And go to church on Sundays."

He extended a hand and received the paper from her. "University?"

He watched as she bit her fingernails. "I am supposed to be at university. My classmates are now in third year. I visit some of them."

"Is that why Rose said you will leave this job after three to four years?" He asked, wanting to hear more on why she did not proceed to university like her friends.

She inhaled. "It is a long story," she said as her eyes focused on the granite top. "I plan to save money for my university fees, to study food service and hotel management. I qualified from high school."

Angela had developed interest in food from an early age. As a young girl, she liked to sit on a small stool in their family kitchen whenever her mother was cooking. She would watch, only interrupted whenever her mother asked her to go fetch something or chop onions or tomatoes from a small table by one corner of the kitchen.

Life for Angela changed at the age of twelve, when her mother died.

Their father remarried when she was 14 years and her stepmother slowly pushed her out of the family kitchen and house, into her paternal grandmother's house.

Angela perfected her cooking skills from the kitchen of her grandmother, where she relied on limited ingredients to prepare tasty food.

When she was in secondary school, the predictably bland taste of food made her resolve, that she would one-day work at a big hotel. She needed to prove that one can prepare tasty food for large groups of people.

Noticing her pulled in eyebrows, Ronny decided he would not ask further questions about university and her off days. She could be one of the many bright children from very poor families. A relative or good Samaritan could have paid for her through secondary school. Now she had to work, earn money to pay for herself through university.

"You are welcome to stay here every day, but you must have your legal off days, even if it means staying in your room." He chuckled, "I do not want to entertain future court cases, purporting I denied you your off days."

Her eyes widened. "No, I cannot lie."

He stepped down from the stool and handed the paper back to her. "Prepare a list of the ingredients you will need for your recipes. Be sure it is healthy food for the children. Weekends are our most convenient time to go shopping."

She nodded. "Can I use the children's computer to type this out?" She asked, waving the paper.

"What church do you attend? We are Catholic, if you find it convenient to come with us."

"Public transport seems not to exist in this part of the city. I can join the family to church if that is okay with you."

She did not tell him that she, too, was Catholic and liked to sing with the church choir.

He walked a few paces away then paused. "You may use the computer. Tomorrow evening remind me to give you the Wi-Fi password. Good night." He walked away.

Relieved, Angela found herself inhaling his cologne, she found that over the last few days she liked to do that each time he left a room. She watched as he walked towards the living room, the path to the side of the house where his bedroom, office and visitor bedroom were located.

Assured that she had ready all the items she would need for breakfast, she left for her sleeping quarters.

Angela was not very tired compared to the other days when Rose was around. Today she had energy left to check out the details of her living area.

She paced the living room, counting a total of twenty-five steps from one end to the other. On her second walk, she stopped and sat on the L-shaped sofa-seat, facing a thirty-inch TV on a grey matching stand.

The door leading outside was usually bolted from the inside, the preferred entrance being the one from the kitchen of the main house. Using the internal entrance meant that she walked along a corridor between the car garage and the outside wall of the house.

Next, she went to the kitchenette at one end of the living room, partially hidden by a half wall. Leaning over, she opened the tap by the sink and immediately closed it, after water splashed out.

Back in the living room, she made a mental note to one day add her photo or her family photo, to make the room really hers.

The larger of the two bedrooms had been her choice of sleeping area. It was twenty minutes to ten according to the clock on her bedside table. She confirmed that the alarm was on before she left for the bathroom.

The two bedrooms had a shared the bathroom, which was conveniently situated between them. Being the only one using the quarters, for now, Angela had no reason to bolt the door from the other bedroom.

Her wish was that she would be the only one working for the household, if only to enjoy being the sole occupant of the quarters. Although Rose had said a second worker was to be hired soon.

As she let water flow down her body in the shower, she repeated to herself that she would manage the work of preparing food for the family, getting the children ready for school, checking their homework, entertaining them and loading the dishwasher after meals. The work was nothing compared to the tasks she performed at the restaurant.

She hurried into bed, needing to relax in the soft bedsheets and mattress before her five-thirty alarm went off. She had set the clock thirty minutes earlier. The extra thirty minutes gave her enough time to pray and shower before she left for the kitchen at six.

This part of her workday felt glorious to say the least, having resolved that being a housegirl was as important a job as being a CEO in a corner office in the city.

Before she reported for the job, she and her friend Brenda had spent a day at Gikomba, a large open-air market in Nairobi, where, given time, one can find gently used designer items at a very affordable price.

Optimistic that she would save more money from being a resident housegirl, Angela had spent the entirety of her meagre savings at the market. This was a purchase that resulted in a bag of clothes. She had become the new owner of several neutral but stylish dresses, blouses, skirts and long trousers.

She had always dressed in a few black dresses of differing lengths, for her job at the restaurant. She liked to pair some of the dresses with the Zara blazers she had bought at a sale. Her Bata loafers gave her casual outfits an appearance of seriousness.

This tactic of having some sort of uniform was one that she planned on using in future, as a student at the national university, and later, as an employee at one of the large hotels in the city. Nothing was going to stop her from achieving her dream.

Chapter 7

A t six o'clock, Angela was in the kitchen.
It was the first day of the second term of the
school year and she was determined to show
Ronny that she could handle the job tasks of a
housegirl. Not only meeting the set expectations but going beyond them.

Rose had mentioned that Ronny preferred millet
porridge for breakfast, so she found herself whisking porridge first. She covered it to simmer while she prepared
tea.

She warmed milk and poured it into a glass jug,
fetched a glass jug filled with the fresh juice she had
blended and carried the items to the dining table.

Angela looked at the clock for the tenth time that
morning as she hurried back to the kitchen. She sieved tea
into a thermos, served porridge into an ochre brown ce-
ramic bowl and placed both items on a tray.

The sound of glass startled her.

As she approached the dining room, she saw Ronny
pouring juice into a glass. He was dressed in formal black
trousers and a well-ironed white shirt.

"Good morning, Sir," she called out as she placed the tray at one edge of the table.

He finished gulping the juice. "Good morning, Angela. It's okay to call me Ronny, all employees in my office do," he said as he pulled a chair and sat.

"Breakfast is served, Sir." Her left hand shifted to her mouth upon realizing that she had used Sir, again.

She turned to the clock on the wall, six-thirty-five meant the alarm clocks in the children's rooms would go off soon. She needed to go wake Nikko up.

Ronny lifted the bowl of porridge out of the tray. "Thanks for the porridge."

"I was wondering if you wanted to say a prayer," she mumbled.

"Thanks. We will do that with the children."

Angela saw one side of his mouth lift into a smile. She took one more glance at the food on the table. "Enjoy your breakfast, Sir. I will go get Nikko ready."

She sniffed his fresh cologne then walked away, aware of Ronny's eyes on her back.

He took the first sip of porridge as he wondered why he suddenly liked the person who took care of his children. He brushed the thought aside. It was okay, even normal to like someone who lived in the same compound and took care of his children. He focused on eating the delicious breakfast made just the way he liked it, porridge and sweet potatoes.

He took another sip of porridge as he scanned the well-arranged breakfast items on the table. A table mat resting below a bowl, matching side plate. A spoon, fork and bread knife rested on the left side and a cloth napkin on the right. Shared food items such as the jug of milk, fresh juice, bowl of fried eggs, beans, bread and drinking water lined across the center of the table.

Angela's first stop was at Mia's door. She knocked and entered as the alarm went off. She stood still, watched as Mia kicked off her bed coverings and lifted her legs off the bed.

Mia rubbed her sleepy eyes. "The night went by so quickly, back to school after being on a sad holiday."

Without further thought, Angela switched off the persisting alarm. She placed a hand on Mia's shoulder. "I am sorry to hear of the struggles you are going through. I am here to assist in any small way."

She watched helplessly as Mia wiped tears off her cheeks. "I don't want anyone at school to talk about their mothers."

"I hear you." She gently massaged Mia's shoulders as she sniffed back tears in her eyes. "After school I will tell you how I handled that feeling when my mother died."

Mia jerked her head upwards, to make eye contact with Angela. "You have no Mum, like us. Do you have a father?"

"Yes, my father is at our home in the countryside. Do you want us to pray now? We can pray when you go to eat breakfast. That way the prayer will be for Betty and Nikko and Dad, all of us," Angela said as she extended both hands out.

Mia grasped Angela's hands for support and stood up.

Angela gave her back a soft pat. "Go and take a quick shower, we don't want to be late for school." She released Mia's hands and watched her walk into the bathroom and the door closed behind her. Angela left the room as she dried tears from her cheeks. No time to weep.

A little happiness engulfed her when she opened Betty's door and heard water splashing in the bathroom. She left for Nikko's room, aware that she was running out of time if the children were to leave the house in time for school.

At seven o'clock, Angela walked out of Nikko's room holding his left hand. She knocked on Betty's room but received no response.

The voices from Mia's room worried her, afraid that the girls might be crying and comforting each other.

She knocked and opened the door. "Let's go eat breakfast." She was relieved to see that Mia and Betty were dressed in school uniform and having a normal sister talk.

The foursome walked to the dining room.

"Nikko, are you happy today is a school day?" Angela asked as she assisted him onto his dining chair.

Nikko smiled at his father seated across from him at the table. "Dad, I am going to play with my friends. Many, many friends." He lifted a hand and waved with open fingers, indicating how many friends he would play with at his kindergarten.

"Good morning my big boy. It's almost time to leave for school." Ronny greeted Nikko before he shifted eyes to Betty and Mia as they took their chairs on either side of his.

"There are my beauties, smart and ready for school. Did you have a good night sleep?"

Mia nodded.

"Good morning Dad. Did you sleep?" Betty asked.

Angela mumbled, "Just a minute, I forgot the bibs." She hurried off to the kitchen and came back with three bibs. She handed one to Mia and another to Betty.

Betty slipped hers on, but Mia placed her bib on the table and said, "We are waiting for you to pray."

Angela finished fitting on Nikko's bib and asked, "Who wants to give thanks for the food?"

Mia turned to Angela. "We start with the prayer you promised, for everyone, before I pray for the food."

Angela noticed that Ronny had paused his eating. She said, "Time for prayer," as she bowed her head. "Lord, we thank you for the peaceful night and for today's renewed gift of life. Take care of each one of us as we leave the safety of our home."

Ronny cleared his throat. Angela stopped then continued. "Protect us as we travel on busy roads back to school. Bless all the students and teachers and parents. Please God, make the children at school not to talk too much about their mothers. But if they do, please bless Mia, Betty, Nikko and Dad with the courage to tell them that their Mum is in heaven with the angels. Amen."

She was surprised to hear a loud "Amen" from the children and Ronny.

Ronny stood up and walked away. "Enjoy your breakfast, and do not forget about the time to leave for school."

Angela served portions of cereal for both Nikko and Betty, then added milk. While the cereal soaked, she served juice into the children's cups and lifted Nikko's cup. "Nikko let's count how many minutes it takes to drink all your juice."

She turned to Mia, then Betty handing over the bowls. "We need to see who eats enough breakfast to stay in their stomach until lunch time."

Twenty minutes later, Angela and the children had finished eating breakfast. They walked to the kitchen island, picked up their snack and school bags and followed Angela out of the house, into the waiting car.

Ronny was already in the car when Angela and the children boarded.

"Today I will drive with you to school before I go to my office," Ronny said from the front passenger seat.

John, the elderly family driver greeted everyone and asked if they were ready. Assured, he started the engine and drove off.

The first stop was at Mia and Betty's private school where Ronny introduced Angela to the class teachers and the school principal as the new housegirl for his children.

They then drove a short distance to Nikko's kindergarten where Ronny made similar introductions.

Nikko was all smiles, with a wave of "bye Dad, bye Angie, bye, John." He left his bag by a row of shelves and joined the other children who were busy playing with toys.

John drove to the city center. He was observant, easily maneuvering through the morning traffic; which had increased as parents and drivers took their children back to school.

The practice was that on the first day of school, even the children who usually used school or public transport were taken to school by their parents.

Angela was quiet in the seat behind John, aware that the seat behind the co-driver, back left, was mostly used by Ronny.

Afraid to stare to the front of the car, not sure if John or Ronny would see her through the driving mirror, she focused her eyes outside.

They joined Thika Road and she now saw more *matatus* on the road. As expected, she saw that the *matatus* slowed down just long enough for a passenger to hop inside.

Her attention drifted off, back to the early morning since she woke up. She worried if Ronny had liked his breakfast. She wondered if he minded that the children arrived at the table five minutes late, though they left the house at the scheduled time. She made a promise to herself, she would make the next morning better.

Angela's eyes opened wide, frightened by the sound of breaking that swayed her in her seat, with John coming to an abrupt stop.

Ronny said. "I wish we had more traffic police on the road at this time of day, that *matatu* driver needs to be booked for bad driving. They need a punishment program which finds and takes such drivers back to driving school."

John checked the mirrors. "The problem is that the *matatus* make these abrupt stops only in front of civilian cars. That driver needs to cut a GK, government vehicle." He chuckled. "I have seen a GK car block such a *matatu* and call the police to come arrest him."

Ronny added. "The police officers forget that we pay the tax that employs the government officers. They need to protect us civilians, as well."

John checked the vehicles behind and beside them, then changed lanes to exit to Museum Hill. "There is one police officer on this road that I like, problem is he is on duty after rush hour. If he had been nearby when that matatu cut into my lane, he would have directed the *matatu* off the road, asked for the ignition key and gone back to his traffic duties."

"And then?" Ronny asked as the traffic lights turned green and John exited into University Way. "The policeman keeps the ignition key and gives it back at the end of his shift. If the matatu driver approaches him, he radios for another officer to come arrest the driver." John laughed, "You know what that means, the driver will never behave badly on the road again, he would have lost money."

"Is he the one to lose money or the owner of the vehicle?" Ronny inquired.

"Whenever other *matatus* see one of their own parked by the roadside with a policeman nearby, they will behave, otherwise they will also lose their key, and be left out of rush hour, the most profitable time of day for the transport business. The driver and *manamba* sometimes keep the difference of money between what they collect, and the standard amount the owner expects to receive at the end of each day. That is the reason they are always in a hurry to ferry passengers."

"Mmhhh," Ronny nodded.

When John did not say more, Angela looked outside as the car drove into the basement of a tall glass building. Angela recalled, from her visits to the city center, that this was Henry Technologies Inc.

A man in a black suit and dark sunglasses appeared out of nowhere, giving a quick salute before he opened the car door for Ronny.

Angela became very attentive. She watched as the man closed the door and took Ronny's computer bag as they walked side-by-side to the elevators marked private.

The man swiped a card and the elevator doors parted. Ronny stepped in and the man followed.

The elevator doors closed.

Angela heard John say, "I will drive you home before I come back to work." He pressed a button to lock the doors, then drove off.

At the exit from the parking garage, while waiting for the gate to sense the car ID and open to let them out,

John asked, "Did Ronny give you my phone number?" The gate opened, and he drove out.

"Not yet," Angela said as she opened her lady bag and removed a pen and a small writing pad. "I will write it down."

"I will give it to you when we get back to the house," he said as he drove off and joined the morning traffic on Moi Avenue and exited to University Way.

Angela spent time looking at cars on the busy streets and back to John. She juggled words in her head, wanting to say something, ask a question on what she saw, how Ronny was received on arrival. She wondered what John would say if she started a conversation on the issue. Would he view her as nosy?

As they exited to Gigiri Road, Angela pondered if John was also part of Ronny's security. Why else would they drive all the way from home without one and find one on arrival. "I always assumed that only government officers had security people guarding them," she mumbled, loud enough for John to hear.

"Who else has security?"

Angela regretted starting the conversation. "Sorry, I thought the man who received our boss looked more like those security people."

"Hahaaha," John laughed as he maneuvered the car off the public road into the private road to Ronny's compound. "Am I allowed to say you qualify for your job without the training?"

"Eeeh?" Angela exclaimed.

"Not many people in your job position have been that observant. I am happy, it means you can walk around with his children without their bodyguards." He parked the car near the kitchen door into the house, fished his wallet from his inner coat pocket, removed a business card and extended it to Angela who had alighted from the car.

"That's my private phone number. Keep it well. Call me whenever you need transport or in an emergency."

He watched as Angela unlocked the door, walked inside and disarmed the ticking house alarm.

Angela looked out through the window and saw the car drive off. She questioned if John too was trained as a personal security man. Why did he mention she could call him in case of an emergency? Is that how the rich live, always protected?

~~~~~~

After dinner Angela cleared the table and loaded the dishwasher.

As she arranged breakfast bowls and cups on a tray, from the corner of her eye she saw Ronny walk to the kitchen.

Remembering that Angela still became scared whenever he spoke with her, Ronny pasted a smile on his face. "The children are asleep, and I read a storybook with them," he stated.

"Thank you, it means they will wake up on time tomorrow," she said.

"How did you find their first day of school?" He asked while looking at her for any nonverbal communication.

"Fine, though I was surprised at how fast time went by."

Not wanting to sound like she could not handle the duties of a housegirl, she added. "It is hard to say on day one, I will need more time to get used."

"Let me know if we should extend Nikko's school day to four in the afternoon. He can sleep at daycare and come home with his sisters."

She laughed then lifted a hand to her mouth before she said, "Today was a struggle getting him out of his school at mid-day. I had to wait for the parents of Conrad and Molly to arrive, only then did he agree to leave."

"Okay, remember to record any other occurrences of this nature, have reasons at the ready to change his schedule if he wants to stay at school longer."

"Okay," Angela said as she questioned herself silently. Did reporting the boy to his father imply that she had failed to convince him to come home, and in turn failed in her task?

Ronny said good night halfway through her internal questioning and walked away before he paused at the entrance to the kitchen. "That morning prayer was interesting. Do we expect a similar one tomorrow?"

"It will depend on what the children ask for."

He walked back. "Did they ask today?"

She looked at his face to gauge how much to reveal. "Mia cried in the morning, saying she was afraid to go to school, in case other students talked about their mothers."

"Ooh!" Ronny said as he leaned on the kitchen island with arms crossed at the elbow.

"I told her we would all say a family prayer, asking God to guide us in case of such a moment," Angela watched as the expression on Ronny's face changed, his eyebrows pulled inwards.

"Any other feedback since they came home from school?"

"They have been happy, we followed the schedule," she answered.

"Okay. Thanks, and good night." He walked away, not wanting Angela to see his own misty eyes.

After a year of talking with his children about their new reality. A year of comforting them, assuring them he would always be there for them, they would be his priority, Ronny had assumed he would now be the only one to struggle through the death of his wife.

It was disheartening for him to learn that Mia was back to her past struggles whenever her friends talked about their mothers.

Ronny was glad that Angela was confident enough to pray for all of them during breakfast. If the children had been happy after school, it meant that Angela's prayer worked. Or had she comforted Mia before breakfast. He would find out.

Chapter 8

Ronny was in his office preparing for a meeting with a major business client later in the day, when he felt a weight lift off his shoulders. He was, at the same time, also aware of the fact that his friend Bill would soon knock on his door.

Unlike a few months ago when a social or business meeting bothered him, sapped his energy, he was energetic that morning. He looked forward to the two meetings and other CEO tasks.

Bill had asked for a morning appointment and Ronny had agreed without asking what his friend would come for that early in the day.

Ronny and Bill had been friends since secondary school, their initial bond was furthered when they had attended the same university in England. Their friendship had continued over the years, despite their busy schedules that prevented them from having frequent social meetings.

Bill worked as Director of Communications at his father's firm, the Broaders Group of Companies.

Seven weeks had passed by since Angela started working as a housegirl. She had learned her tasks quickly and possessed the right type of efficiency.

Due to this, Ronny felt at ease with the thought of sparing time to meet with his close friends. He had become comfortable enough with Angela's performance that he could leave the house early, and on some days arrive home just in time for the family dinner.

He also had more time to discuss company matters with staff at Henry Technologies Inc., unlike before when he felt like staff were wasting his time whenever they walked into his office, he had become more welcoming to anyone who convinced Lorna, his personal assistant, to let them in.

He heard a knock on the door. "Come in."

His friend William Broaders strode in saying, "At last I've found you. Why have you been MIA?" he asked as he extended a hand to Ronny.

Ronny swiveled back in his chair, then he got up and walked to the front of his desk. "Welcome brother, work has made me a missing in action person, nothing else."

The two men shook hands as Ronny patted Bill on the shoulder. "Don't fret, you'll soon start to see more of me, I now have a worker at home, like no other." He motioned Bill to a visitor's chair and walked back to his.

"Great you found someone," Bill chuckled. "Which of the ladies made it?"

The loud laughter leaving Ronny's chest caught Bill's full attention. "Not that type of housegirl, not one for me, but for my children."

Bill placed both hands on the desk and leaned towards Ronny. "When will you be back to the clubs, to pick one for yourself?"

"Ronny laughed again. "I am becoming more of a believer of the saying that God never leaves one totally helpless. Whenever I arrive home, the smiles on my children's faces give me more hope."

Bill was one of the friends who had been keen on ensuring that Ronny's healing progress was a continued process. He had tried many different tactics to get Ronny to get back to his earlier social life – all without much success.

Whenever Bill and other friends asked Ronny out during the week, he had an excuse at the ready, that he needed to be home to eat dinner with the children.

On weekends he preferred to socialize during the day when he could be at the club with his children. Not in the evening when most of his age-mates regrouped to watch a sport, play a board game or chat about the latest car models and other technological innovations.

"Good man," Bill said while checking time on his Cartier. "You need to surprise the girls at the club. I will be there with my wife and her friends tonight."

Ronny played with the wedding band he had refused to remove. He looked at the door like there was someone eavesdropping, then leaned closer to Bill. "I might come if you ask all the ladies from my company to attend." He chuckled "You should see how they care for me." He sat back upright. "Though I don't blame them, could be their way of showing concern for my loss, my wellbeing."

"It is a pity that we lost our lovely friend, Bella. But I cannot wait to buy you a beer and hear more about the remaining contenders."

There was a knock on the door and Bill turned to see who was at the door.

Lorna stood at the slightly ajar door and looked inside.

"Hello Lorna. Come in, come in." Ronny urged.

Lorna stepped inside. "Sorry to interrupt you —"

"You are not disrupting," Ronny cut in. "You are welcome, anytime, come in."

"The client scheduled for five o'clock sent an urgent request that we reschedule the evening meeting into an earlier time. They suggested three o'clock."

"As always, check my calendar and fit them in."

"I did, just wanted to let you know of the new time since it's a new addition."

"Thanks Lorna, your usual computer reminder will get me out of my chair on time."

"All is set, and I am only two steps away from your office," Lorna said.

As his PA, Ronny had allowed Lorna access to his children's school calendar. That way she was able to reconcile the two and prioritize his attendance at office or school events.

Lorna turned to Bill. "I need to have a permanent chair set up for you in this office. Your friend here," she pointed to Ronny, "always has a huge smile whenever you're around."

Lorna, now in her late fifties, had worked at Henry Technologies Inc. as far back as Ronny could remember, as his father's personal assistant. When his father went on an extended medical leave, Lorna became Ronny's PA, making it easier for Ronny to transition into his father's position as CEO.

Lorna had supported Ronny through the misfortunes that befell his family, each occurring in the space of four months. She was close by when he fell into a depression after the death of his wife.

Lorna also visited Ronny's parents often and met with Ronny as his family had relocated upon the death of his wife. Sometimes Lorna arrived with her women's prayer group to console the family. On one occasion when Ronny broke down during a prayer session, Lorna started a song to distract those present and, once their attention had been diverted, she guided Ronny out of the room.

As months passed, whenever Lorna visited and determined that Ronny was too haggard for work, she would go to the office and either reschedule his appointments or assign them to relevant departmental heads.

Ronny had never stopped thanking Lorna. She once coordinated two departmental heads, and their managers, to secure a big contract for the company. Instead of seeking to reschedule, she had encouraged the concerned staff to finish all work for the bid and attend the interview process – which had involved a presentation.

Having worked with Henry for almost thirty years, Lorna was accustomed to contents of company meetings, so she assisted the staff to refine the presentation. She travelled to Europe with the group and had felt proud after learning that the proposal had moved onto the next stage during the bidding process.

Lorna was glad that in the recent past an easy smile had returned to Ronny's face.

Ronny sat up. "Lorna, do me a favour. Next time, please lock my friend out." He pointed to Bill. "He is here this early, pestering me about needing to find myself a lady." He gave Bill's shoulder a little push.

Lorna's laugh marks deepened with her smiling eyes. "I have been telling my son here the same thing," she pointed towards Ronny. "We have been praying for you, it is now time to look around and find out what else God has in store for you." She chuckled as she walked out and pulled the door behind her.

Ronny tapped his desk for Bill's full attention. "I do not know how to thank Lorna, she is more than an assistant to me." He picked a pen from a nearby pen holder and rolled it between his fingers. "She took over CEO work when I was on compassionate leave." He chuckled, "I gave my assistants and the departmental heads leeway to make some important company decisions. They still checked their final decisions with Lorna."

Bill stood up. "Let me go ask her to find you a wife."

Ronny motioned Bill back to the chair. "She will assume that I sent you. Please do not, I prefer to make my own choice, if ever."

79

Bill took one step away from the chair. "I need to get back to Truphena Towers, lest Henry Technologies think I have come for a job."

He extended a hand to Ronny. "What time will you be done with your meeting? Let us meet at Windsa, at four-thirty." He glanced at his watch. "That will give us enough time to catch up before you start talking about the children eating dinner and going to bed."

"You need to convince your wife Georgina to make you a dad soon, then you'll see the value in eating supper with your family." Bill and Ronny fist-bumped quickly while Ronny said. "Promise to drive me home, no need for me to keep John waiting while we socialize."

Ronny and Bill walked out together. At the elevator, they said their goodbyes.

On his way back, Ronny pondered on what Bill and Lorna had both said, that he needed a wife. Did he really? "No," he whispered to himself.

~~~~~~

Ronny ended the meeting held in boardroom A and hurried to the private elevator down to his office on the sixty-fourth floor. He paused by Lorna's desk, checking to see if they'd heard back from the clients in Bahrain.

Assured that all related work tasks could wait for the coming days, he checked the messages on his phone as he walked into his office. There was no message from home, which meant the children were fine.

He typed a message to Angela. "Hello Angela, get the children to eat dinner and go to bed, I might be late tonight." He pressed send, gathered documents on his desk and locked them in a drawer.

A new message appeared on his phone. "We are fine. I will do that. Let me know when you arrive, to reheat food for your dinner."

Ronny read Angela's response twice, the smile on his face broadened as he typed a response, "I will let myself in and find food if need be." He read the message he had written before he deleted it.

On second thought, he worried that if he mentioned he would be at the club with friends, Angela might think that he had shifted his parental responsibility to her, not being home to eat dinner with his children as was his practice. He preferred to let her formulate her own stories until he arrived back to the house.

Ronny arrived at the club and was surprised when Rose walked in with a group of her friends. He turned to Bill. "You better have an explanation at the ready. How did my sister know I would be here?"

Bill lightly squeezed Georgina's hand while he addressed Ronny, "If you are not pleased to see your sister, I can have her as the sister we never had."

Rose and her group arrived. She looked at Bill, then the table and said. "I had assumed you would get a larger table for all of us."

Bill stood up and called a waiter to put two tables together for the group of seven.

Ronny was grateful when Rose sat next to him, on his left side. He would not know what to do if one of the ladies sat next to him.

"Nice to see you out and about," she whispered into his ear.

Ronny was now convinced that Bill's visit that morning was to conspire with Rose.

Ronny's face heated with mild irritation, annoyed that his friend, in collaboration with his sister planned and chose women to bring to him. It was no coincidence that Rose just turned up with three of her single girlfriends.

There and then, Ronny decided that he would treat all the five women at the table the same way he treated his sister.

At around eight o'clock Ronny decided to say his goodbye's. On the drive home he was glad that he had remained joyful throughout the night, though he saw Roses' agitation rise as the evening went on. He attributed this to his decision not to show any special interest toward any of her friends.

Ronny let himself into a quiet house. The kitchen lights were on though Angela was not there. He walked towards the children's bedrooms where he heard laughter from Betty's room.

Knocking on the door softly, he turned the knob and looked in. All the children jumped up from their seated position on Betty's bed and rushed to their father, "Dad!"

Angela looked at Ronny and back to the story book in her hand. "I will go back to the kitchen now that your dad is here to get you to bed."

"Have we been having a tough time getting to sleep tonight?" Ronny asked.

Angela looked at Mia, then Betty. "Nikko and Mia can explain why they are not in their rooms," she said before walking out of the room.

Ronny removed his coat and hung it on the door handle, sat on Betty's dresser stool and finished reading the story book. Then he walked Mia and Nikko into their bedrooms. The children were very cooperative through the ten minutes or, so he was with them. He questioned why Angela sounded snappy before she left Betty's bedroom upon his arrival.

Ronny was anxious as he walked to the kitchen. On his way he noticed that Angela had set food on the dining table.

He became reflective, questioned if Angela was annoyed with him and not the children. He did not recall a time when the children had a complaint about her. Was she unhappy that he had gone out for dinner with some woman? "Sorry I stayed out so long with my friends. Bill insisted that we meet at the club after work."

She looked up from the breakfast dishes she was arranging on a tray in preparation for the next morning. "I am not annoyed with anyone, just surprised with myself."

Angela could not get herself to tell Ronny of the coincidence that day. Unlike other evenings when the children followed their schedule, that day was different.

At some point Angela thought the children collaborated to punish her. How else could Mia cry for a full hour because she forgot her textbook at school. Angela had tried in vain to console her by telling her that everyone makes a mistake occasionally, the teacher would understand.

Explaining only made Mia cry more. The incident worsened when Angela asked if she would call the home of one Mia's friends and ask their parent to take a photo of the homework page and email to her. Angela was surprised when Mia said she did not want her to call, she would not do the homework.

The difficult evening had continued during bedtime. All the children said they would not go to bed until their father had arrived and read them a bedtime story.

No sweet words from Angela could convince them otherwise.

Ronny watched Angela from the corner of his eye. She touched the bowls on the tray, like she was counting them. "I was given a chance today but failed." She laughed.

He pulled a high stool and sat by the island. "You have so far done an excellent job. One small challenge from the children should not make you feel like a failure." He kept smiling, partly to help Angela change her expressionless face. She did not.

He sprang from the stool, went to the dining room and returned carrying a plate of food. He ate while stealing glances at Angela as she arranged more breakfast dishes on one side of the island.

Though he had eaten dinner at the club, he decided he would eat dinner again, if that could help Angela put some readable expression on her face. He wished she could say more, even ask him to detail every step of his day. He wished he could guess what she was thinking, troubling her. She had so far done a good job as a housegirl for his children, he needed her to stay on.

As time passed, he saw a sparkle on her faced. It turned into a smile as he wished her a good night.

Chapter 9

The last Thursday of June became one of the longest days Angela experienced since she started her job as a housegirl.

That morning Ronny had said, "It is more than two months since you started on your job, we need to revisit your probation period."

He had walked away and out the front door, not giving her a chance to ask the question in her mind. She would have liked to know why Ronny wanted to revisit her probation period after only two months into her job.

Angela went through the day in a daze, worried why they needed to revisit her probation period. Questions filled her mind as the day went by. She worried if Ronny had found her work unsatisfactory. If he planned to relieve her of her duties. Had Rose found someone to replace her?

She was unusually quiet on her morning drive taking the children to school.

Back at the house, she worked without taking a break.

In the evening Ronny spent his drive home planning how to introduce the topic to Angela.

He was scheduled for work travel to Europe, and later in the month take his father to Thailand for further specialized medical treatment. A friend at the company had recommended a medical facility in Bangkok that could help Henry recover from the stroke faster.

Ronny had spent a lot of energy that week in internal debates. He questioned if Angela was confident enough to take care of his children while he was away. She had done well so far, but he had no idea how she would fare while he was away, for most of July.

He considered different options, including taking Angela and the children to stay at his parents' house. He shelved the idea, on recalling that relocating the children would disrupt their schedule. Yet one of his objectives was to give them a steady, predictable way of life as part of their healing process.

Knowing how scared Angela had been in her first month of work, a fear she had overcome over time, Ronny worried that she might be reluctant to guide the children while at the house of his parents.

He thought of getting a chef to release Angela from her kitchen duties, until he remembered that she might not like that idea, having told him she liked to prepare food, try out new recipes in preparation for her planned study program at the university.

So far, he enjoyed the delicious meals she prepared.

Ronny liked her determination in performing her tasks, which had helped strengthen his resolve, not to have many workers within his house, which he never liked.

Ronny was brought up in a home with more workers than their family of four.

His father's idea of doing well economically was to have his wife be a stay-home-Mom. On top of that, he had employed a chef, a house cleaner, a gardener, drivers and watchmen.

The family had three dedicated drivers; one to drive Henry to and from work. One to chauffeur him and his sister to school. The third driver waited on their mother, to drive her wherever she wished to go.

Ronny never liked the crowd around him. He felt like he had no privacy. For that reason, he wanted to do the opposite for his children, raise them in a house with minimal workers. He would find the latest innovations to lessen the time needed to perform household tasks.

The many workers in his childhood denied him and his sister a chance to learn some basic life skills. They should have had opportunities to learn to prepare simple food items and keep a tidy bedroom.

This was the reason he had mechanized many tasks within his house and relied on outside commercial labour whenever he needed work done. He liked it that Angela was managing the children and food preparation on her own. He was willing to pay her more money, if she could continue to manage as the only worker in the house.

Ronny was reflective. He considered giving Angela a three-year contract, renewable annually, with employee benefits including medical cover.

He had bought a smart phone to give her that evening.

His main challenge was how to discuss the end of her probation period without making her feel like he was enticing her to stay on.

Though he was aware that Angela needed her job, or rather, the salary, he did not want to appear so desperate to have her stay, though he needed her to, especially now that he was to travel out of the country.

This far, he had not received any communication from the teachers about late homework or incomplete assignments. All thanks to Angela.

He attributed part of the success with the children's schoolwork to the fact that Angela loved education, she appreciated the value of working hard as a student. The reason she was determined to acquire a university education.

If Angela worked for three or four years, he would give her a bonus, enough money to cover her university tuition.

He reflected on his immediate need for Angela to stay with the children while he traveled to Europe, Thailand and Mombasa.

After dinner, Ronny tucked Nikko into bed before he went and read a storybook with Betty and Mia.

Angela wiggled her fingers out of fear as Ronny walked into the kitchen.

She relaxed a bit on noticing the smile on his face.

"How's your evening? Have we overworked you with too much housework?" he asked.

"Thanks, I am okay, the work is fine. It is like any other job where people feel tired at the end of the day," she said, hurriedly. She was worried about what information Ronny had about her probation period. "Did you say you had an issue with my work or probation period?"

"I am satisfied with your work so far. Tomorrow, after you take the children to school, go to the company office and ask to see Stella in Human Resources. She has your new contract."

"Thank you." Those were the only words that left Angela's dry mouth.

"Read the full contract before signing. They must have taught you about that in school."

He regretted his words about being taught at school, on seeing her pulled-in eyebrows as she fumbled with her fingers.

Ronny wished her a good night and left.

In the staff quarters, Angela went down on her knees and prayed. She thanked God for the good news of a contract, in contrast to the fear that had stolen her happiness all day.

She uttered a lengthy prayer. She mentioned all the things she was grateful for, including the suffering she had gone through, and struggles to feed her son without an income. She thanked God for her brother Joshua and his family.

When times had become too tough for her to provide for her baby, the only person who had sent her money was Joshua. She knew Joshua would have given her more money, but he too must have been struggling to provide for his family on a teacher's salary. She would call Joshua the next day, after signing the contract.

She retrieved a notebook from her nightstand drawer. She read through the details of her earnings and expenditures. She had been able to save most of her salary except for her personal expenses and the six thousand shillings she sent home every month to her grandmother, an increase from the previous three thousand.

Now, that she had saved more money, she would increase the money she sent to her grandmother, ask her to employ a house girl to help her with housework.

Luka, her father, was already paying one person to tend the crops on the farm. Having a worker in the house would release her grandmother fully to take care of her son and play more with him.

Before she climbed into bed, she ironed one of her Sunday-best dresses. A floral, lime green Kitenge she had bought from one of the many tailors in Kibera. The Kitenge was comprised of a knee-high skirt with a matching long-sleeved blouse. The neckline was low, yet not too revealing. The puffy shoulders pulled eyes away from her chest to her shoulders. She selected a plain, black jacket and a scarf to guard against the end-of-June cold winds.

She inspected her black pair of shoes and made a mental note to buy another pair soon.

Angela chose her attire well. She wanted to be presentable when she entered Henry Technologies Inc., the building she had only seen from the outside. She needed to give a good impression of the person who took care of the children of the CEO, the grandchildren of the founder of Henry Technologies Inc.

~~~~~~

Angela had mixed feelings as she rode the elevator to the eighteenth floor, where the Human Resources Department was.

She was happy and afraid all at once. Happy that she would sign a contract, a sign of more assurance that she had secured the job.

On the other hand, she was afraid of what the contents of the contract would be. Maybe they would ask her to start paying rent for the house she occupied? Or, Ronny was afraid that one day she could turn around and say he had not been paying her, something she would never do. She had never lied and had no plans of ever claiming that she had worked without pay.

She fidgeted, questioning in her mind if signing a contract meant that if anything happened to the children, she would be charged in a court of law.

Before she could rethink going to sign the contract, the elevator pinged eighteenth floor and stopped. The two doors parted, and she stepped out and followed the arrow pointing to HR.

After introductions and stating her reason for the visit to the floor receptionist, Angela was directed to the waiting lounge, an expansive space with a panel of windows letting in the morning sunshine to a line of potted flowers.

She sank into one of the eight black leather chairs and gazed at the high ceiling with miniature lights balancing the illumination in the sunlit room.

Before she could focus her eyes on the large wall paintings, she heard the click, click of pumps on the wooden office floor.

A woman who appeared to be in her late thirties or early forties stopped in front of her and extended a hand. "Good morning."

Angela stood up from the soft chair and returned the greeting. "I am Angela. I was sent by Mr. Ronald to come see you for my contract."

"Stella is my name. Welcome."

Angela noticed that they were of similar height, her five feet, eight inches.

Stella looked at Angela from head to her waist. "Come with me, I have your contract." She turned around and walked back in the direction she had come.

Angela followed.

They walked past two glass doors and into a maze of corridors when Stella spoke. "I hear you have done an excellent job, how is the life of working as the housegirl for Henry's grandchildren?"

"Good," Angela said.

Stella seemed to be waiting to hear more from Angela, but nothing was forthcoming. She stopped by an open door into a large office and motioned Angela to walk in.

"Please take a seat." As she pointed Angela to one of the two visitor chairs in her office, right in front of a large desk.

Stella walked to the other side of the desk. "Henry Junior insisted that we include a medical cover in your contract. You look too young to need a doctor. Anyways, read and sign for me," she sneered, handing over papers in a black leather folder.

The first thought in Angela's mind was to throw the contract at Stella's face and march out of the office. Instead, she bit her lower lip, to deter any words she could regret escaping her mouth.

She had wanted to ask Stella if it was only sick people who needed medical cover. Had Stella accepted or rejected a company medical cover herself? What difference would it make to her as head of HR if one more employee received a medical cover?

There and then, Angela resolved that she would not add her son to her medical cover. She would not allow Stella to be the first one to know that she had a child back in the village.

She read the forms. When she reached the section on level of education, she checked the box high school and wrote `going to university soon', beside the box. She signed the forms, placed the folder on Stella's desk and stood up. "Is there anything else you would like from me?"

Stella stared at her before she read all four pages. "I see you are headed to university, which means Ronny will be looking for another housegirl soon. Good, I will keep my ears open."

"Please do," Angela said as she lowered herself back into the leather chair. She did not look at Stella.

"I see you left the section on bank account empty. I don't know how accounts people will pay you."

"I will bring the information soon," Angela said as she vacated the chair. She wanted to leave the office sooner, before she uttered words that she might regret. "Please show me the way out of here."

Stella looked at her with a grin. "I have a feeling you will need a copy of your contract." She stood, and her six-inch pumps clickity-clacked across the wooden floor towards a full-sized copier at one corner.

She inserted all the pages, pressed a button and individual sheets of paper rolled forward. A stapled copy emerged out of the other end of the copier. She gave a copy to Angela. "Keep this for your records, it could become handy when you leave your job."

"For your information, I am not going anywhere soon," Angela said, as she received her copy of the contract and walked out of the office. She retraced her steps back to the reception desk.

She thanked the lady at the desk and walked away, towards the elevators as she heard someone call her name. "Angela, Ronny asked that you see him in his office."

Angela walked back to the desk, though the last person she wanted to see was Ronny. Her wish was to go back to the house and cry out all the tears threatening to fall out of her eyes.

She was led along a corridor and onto an elevator on the other side of the reception desk.

They rode what felt like fifty floors before the elevator stopped on the sixty-fourth floor. The doors parted, and she followed the woman guiding her.

They walked a short distance along a corridor before they stopped at a door bronzed with golden letters, Mr. Ronald Henry Junior, CEO.

The lady opened the door and ushered Angela inside, before she closed the door and walked away.

A smartly dressed elderly woman sat at the only desk in the room. Angela quickly counted four visitor chairs and a door located to the left side from where the woman sat.

The woman rose from her Portuguese leather chair and extended her hand. "Lorna, PA to Ronny. Nice to meet you. He has praised you, your work many times." She smiled. "That fits you well."

"Thank you. It is a pleasure to meet you too." Angela said, hoping to hear more from Lorna on what Ronny had complimented her on.

Lorna apologized many times that Ronny had to suddenly leave for an impromptu meeting.

Angela was relieved that Ronny was not in. She needed more time to reflect on her meeting with Stella, decide on what part to mention to Ronny and which ones to keep to herself.

Lorna left her position behind the desk and guided Angela out. They walked down a long corridor, into a different elevator than the one she arrived in.

Lorna bid her bye. "Sweetheart, have a good day, greet the children for me, tell them it is grandma from Dad's office. That's how they remember me."

Angela's face brightened up with a smile. "I will, thank you and have a lovely day."

"The elevator will take you to the underground parking from where James, not John will drive you home."

"Bye." Angela waved as the elevator doors closed her in. She was glad that the unprovoked loathing from Stella was erased by Lorna's friendliness.

She found James waiting. He drove her home.

The security man at the gate verified who was in the car before he opened the main gate and the car drove into Ronny's compound.

Angela let herself into the house and went to the washroom near the laundry room where she washed hands and splashed water on her face. She sat in the dining room and read the three-year, annually renewable contract one more time.

Annoyance returned. She felt her cheeks and forehead become warm. She was enraged. She would have liked to add her son under the list of beneficiaries. She would have even asked if her grandmother, her brother and father qualified as beneficiaries under her medical cover.

She folded the contract and walked into the kitchen. Opened the drawer where she kept house expenditure receipts and stacked the contract on top of the other papers.

One look at the clock and she realized that she needed to get her usual Friday tasks done quickly, before the children were home from school.

First, a phone call to her brother would be okay. The call went to voicemail before she remembered that he could be in class at that time, teaching.

She called Stephanie her cousin and asked to speak with their grandmother.

Angela shared greetings with Priscah. She asked about her son before more words burst out of her mouth. "*Nyanya*," the Swahili term for grandmother. "I have been trying a job as a housegirl for two months now and I like it."

"Are you telling me you have already changed jobs? You've left your hotel job to babysit?"

The smile on Angela's face faded away. "*Nyanya*, the job is better than at the hotel. It pays well, and I get to save more money." She explained very rapidly.

"A housegirl? Does that mean you work at someone's house, whose house?"

Angela paused for a long moment before she said. "I take care of children of a rich man in the city, while he goes to work. Their mother died."

"God bless her soul, like your mother. How many of you work for the rich man?"

"I do most of the work in the house. I prepare the children for school, and I cook for them. There are machines to wash clothes, floors and dishes. There is a driver who drives the children to school."

"Are you his wife, cleaning and cooking? Listen to me." Priscah called out in a stern voice. "One child is enough for me to take care of now, do not bring more children to me."

Angela thanked God that the person on the other end of the phone was her beloved grandmother. The woman who had taken care of her, loved her, and was now taking care of her child. If the cautionary words had been from someone else, Angela would not have hesitated to ask them what they thought of her and tell the person that her work was not to sleep around with men.

"*Nyanya*, my promise as always. I made a mistake which I have learned from. One child is enough. If I ever change my mind about men, I will bring one for your approval first."

Priscah laughed into the phone. "My child, I guess things have changed. During my time, if a man allowed a girl to clean and cook for him, it meant he loved her. That is why we cooked for our husbands." She chuckled. "Food attracts a man to a woman." She laughed again. "Your *Ta-jiri* must be a good man, you have spoiled me with a lot of money, Babu and I are rich."

"*Nyanya*, I need to go do some work. Please embrace Babu for me. Is he nearby, so I can greet him?"

"That boy never sits still. He is outside playing with other children."

"I will bring you a cell phone when I come home, that way I will be able to talk with Babu. Bye *Nyanya*."

Angela ended the call, tilted her head upwards and smiled. She was happy that, having spent most of her life with her grandmother, she could easily chat with her on any topic about life. And she was glad that her grandmother was an open-minded person, she told her things the way she saw them.

She reflected on what her grandmother meant by `food attracts men to women.' She felt sweat appear on her forehead, pondering on the few times she had caught Ronny looking at her, especially while the family ate dinner. Did that mean he was attracted to her, whenever he ate the food she prepared, which he always seemed to enjoy, and occasionally thanked her, saying she prepared delicious food?

"No, please." She heard the words escape from her mouth. She wished Ronny did not like her. If he ever approached her, she would fight him off, that would be the end of her job as a housegirl taking care of his children.

Fear gripped her with the thought of losing her job. The job she relied on to provide for herself, her son, and to one day pay for her university education. "Time to get back to work on my chores," she uttered the words out loud as she went to the pantry. She removed some chicken from the freezer. Her plan was to prepare a mouth-watering meal for dinner, to celebrate her new three-year contract, working for a family she had come to like.

Chapter 10

Ronny fisted his hand and hit the table. "I have a lot of work to do, go find the answer." He inhaled and exhaled three times, regretted the words as soon as they left his mouth.

Mia looked at her father without blinking.

He stared at her round eyes bulging out of their sockets.

She had asked him to read her school project and explain a few terms she was not clear on.

Mia wiped the tears streaming down her cheeks as she strode to their study station located within the family room.

She logged off the computer. When she lifted her sad eyes, her father was standing next to the TV.

Ronny did not break his stare as he took long strides and cuddled and kissed her on both cheeks. "I am sorry *kiddo.* You caught me in the middle of trying to solve a problem in my head."

"Okay Dad, but next time remember to close your office door if you have problems of your own."

"You got me there." He extended his hand to her with his pinkie stretched out. "Next time I will close the office door when I do not want interruptions." Their fingers sealed the agreement.

He walked away after seeing a smile on her face.

She vacated the study desk, increased her pace, caught up with him and held onto his arm as they stepped inside the kitchen.

Ronny had heard a lively chat from the kitchen and wanted to see what the joy was about. "Hello kids. How's your Friday evening?"

Betty wiped her hands on the white and pink-checked apron flowing down to her ankles. "We are baking a chocolate cake. I am helping Angie with the mixing."

"That is a nice Friday treat," Ronny said as he squatted and touched Nikko on the head.

Nikko looked up from where he was busy pushing a toy-car on the kitchen floor. He returned the smile from his father and back to his toy. *"Pii, pipii, pipiiii* Dad," he uttered as he pushed the toy car closer to his father's feet.

Betty looked at Angela before she turned to her father. "Dad, Mia, go back to your work. We have a surprise when you come to eat dinner."

Mia pulled her father by the arm. "Angela is busy cooking, come assist me with my school project."

Ronny sat with Mia at the study desk. She asked questions and he explained, until she completed her school project.

The other reason that had kept Ronny at the family room was the aroma emanating from the kitchen. The frequent rumble of his stomach reminded him that he was hungry, he needed to eat food.

At seven, Betty walked into the family room. "Mia, Dad. Dinner is on the table.

She held her father by the arm. "Dad close your eyes. If you open them before we reach the table, you will be the last one to eat." She warned while guiding him towards the hand-washing sink.

Ronny did what he knew would excite the children. He inhaled in the food aroma many times. "My nose will hurt if you don't let me see the food," he begged, making the children giggle.

He opened his eyes and blinked several times for their further amusement. He then called them to bow heads in prayer.

The family liked the oven-cooked chicken tikka, masala flavoured roast potatoes and a mixed vegetable salad.

Angela watched from the corner of her eye as Ronny helped himself to a third serving.

After dinner, Ronny smoothed a hand over his stomach. "I will have a glass of wine, after you leave for your bedrooms for the night."

Mia quipped. "Do you have space in your stomach for wine?"

Nikko giggled from across the table. "Dad is big, has a big stomach." He spread out his arms in front of his stomach, to indicate his version of big. There was more laughter at the table.

Mia gathered her used dishes and left for the kitchen. "I need to go bathe."

Angela gathered the food serving bowls into a tray as she addressed Betty. "Carry your used dishes to the kitchen please, as Mia did."

Ronny picked up his used dishes and stood up.

Angela felt sweat on her forehead and armpits, mortified.

She put the tray back on the table and watched as Ronny walked into the kitchen where he left his dishes in the sink.

"Sorry. I was going to carry your dishes." She completed the sentence in a whisper. "I am trying to get the older kids to learn to pick up after themselves. Not you."

"I am the oldest," he chuckled.

With her mouth open, like she wanted to exclaim "Oh," she picked the tray and walked out of the dining room, worried how to undo the shame. She had made her employer, CEO, clear his dishes from the table. Worse still, on a day when he had given her a contract, medical cover and a twenty-five percent salary increment.

Ronny interrupted her thoughts. "I will get Nikko ready for bed."

He spread out both arms and Nikko fell in. He lifted him up high, towards the ceiling, then down to the floor. "Let's walk to your room, that way, the food you ate will dance in your stomach," he said to a beaming Nikko.

Nikko stretched both hands upwards to his father, "Carry me, I want to be tall like you."

Ronny obeyed. They walked away, Betty by their side.

Angela cleared and wiped the dining table. She loaded and started the dishwasher. She then busied herself, wiped the oven and kitchen countertops until Ronny stepped into the kitchen.

"Thank you very much for my new contract." She looked up and met with a stare from Ronny. She lowered her eyes to the floor. "I appreciate the benefits. I will work harder," she said in a trembling voice.

Angela had recalled the words from Stella, when she had asked why Angela needed medical coverage.

"There is no need for you to work harder, you are already working hard enough." Ronny reassured her.

"Thank you. The money will help me, and other people." She debated if she should mention anything about Stella. On further thought, she decided not to. She already had her contract, which meant that she would not be visiting Henry Technologies Inc. soon, at least for the next twelve months when the contract stated she would be due for another review.

Ronny, still watching her, saw as if her facial expression relaxed with a hint of a smile. He decided it was time to voice what had occupied his mind most of the week. He picked the new Smartphone he had placed on the kitchen island. "I will be traveling in and out of town in the coming days, from next weekend."

He watched her for reaction. Not seeing any, he continued. "Will you manage with the children, though a relative will come over, just in case?"

He switched on the phone and handed it to her. "Here is a phone for you to use whenever you want to reach me. It has my private phone numbers. Only for you to reach me when you must."

"I am used to the children's schedule. You may bring a relative." Angela wished she could add that so long as the relative was not Rose. She could not say that though, Rose was his sister, his only sibling.

Fear gripped her on recalling how difficult it had been while training under Rose. Always asking her to perform unnecessary duties and sometimes asking her to do tasks that Rose herself had no knowledge of. Angela recalled how Rose asked her to cook pilau rice, yet she had no idea of the required ingredients, or how long it would take.

On the occasions Rose had visited, or when the family met at church or at their parent's house, Rose always asked her tough questions about the welfare of the children, if Ronny's house was still clean, and reminded her that she was a housegirl for the children.

She felt her eyes close involuntarily on recalling a time when Rose had asked her who cleaned Ronny's bedroom.

Her response had been simple, "I pick any items from the bedroom and bathroom floors when everyone is away from the house. I do that on Tuesdays and Thursdays, when the Rumba is set to clean bedroom carpets and bathroom floors."

Angela had later reflected on the question and got annoyed. Did Rose think she was one of those house girls who would enter their boss's bedroom when he was in the house? She had not done that. "Which relative will come in?"

"One of my in-laws, a younger sister to Bella. You've met Dianna." He stared at her face. "Dianna has been asking to come visit with the children. This will be the right time," he said, smiling now.

His hope was that Angela was not privy to what had been going on within his larger family. Bella's mother had tried several times to bring him an older woman to work in the house with Angela.

Ronny had insisted that they were doing fine with one staff. He was surprised when Bella's mother had resorted to offering Dianna to move in and help him care for the children.

Dianna had visited many times when Bella was alive. Ronny knew well that Dianna was one in need of care herself. In no way would she provide care to his children, or any other child.

Whenever Dianna had visited, her clothes had to be washed and ironed for her.

Ronny did not recall a time when Dianna prepared a meal for anyone, except for an occasional cup of black tea. Worse still, he did not like that she was chauffeured in and out of his compound, by men. A behaviour he would not want displayed in front of his children.

He felt the skin on his face relax on recalling his younger days, before he married at the age of twenty-six. He had found pleasure in picking and dropping girls back to their homes. "But do not expect much help from Dianna. I prefer you continue with the children's routine, as we have it now."

Angela pulled a high stool and sat down at the island. "I too will prefer that."

Ronny was not expecting that response, but it helped him move to his next request. "Since I will be in and out, and after all, you seem to get along well with the children...," He left the side of the kitchen cupboard he had been leaning on, pulled a stool and sat right opposite from Angela. "You will relocate to a bedroom in the house. That will make it easy for you to use the child monitor, in case Nikko needs attention in the night."

"But there is no room for a housegirl in the house."

"There are no labelled rooms or people in this house, we are just family."

"Have you asked the children?"

He made eye contact with her. "Asked is not the right word, maybe informed."

He looked down at the granite countertop. "Some topics I do not like to revisit. The children and I are learning a new life as we move on, looking to find a balance in life."

He crossed his hands on the countertop. "I have informed the children of my upcoming travels. I will let them know that you and Dianna will be with them." He chuckled. "I could ask them to choose a bedroom for you, the fourth bedroom on their side, or the visitor bedroom."

"Tell them I prefer the fourth bedroom. The visitor bedroom will be too far from their rooms."

"Makes sense," Ronny mumbled as he pondered what to do if Dianna decided to overstay in the visitor bedroom. He would not be comfortable sleeping on the same wing of the house with her.

"Don't forget to keep the phone," he said as his eyes turned towards the iPhone on the countertop. "Good night," he leaped off the stool and left for his bedroom.

~~~~~~

Angela opened and closed a few kitchen cupboards, though she had no idea what she was looking for. She paused and stared into one of the hanging cupboards without registering any of the items therein.

She was in deep thought, reflecting on all that had happened to her since she had left the house that Friday morning. She pushed the two side-by-side cupboard doors to close. "It ended well," she muttered to herself. She switched off the kitchen lights and walked away, to the house staff quarters.

Angela worried if her relocation to the main house was Ronny's subtle way to employ another worker. Maybe a male chef to reside in the staff quarters.

Annoyance crept in, though she could not explain why she was getting angry over a thought she generated in her head.

She picked up the brand-new phone and inspected it. She questioned herself if she should call Brenda from the new phone or her old phone. She replaced the phone on the bedside table on remembering what Ronny had said about the phone containing his private phone numbers.

Brenda answered the call on the second ring. "Have you completed your evening chores, or calling me on your boss's time?"

"Did I catch you with your boyfriend?" Angela asked.

"Yes, the boyfriend called school assignments." She laughed. "I wish I lived with a boss like yours, I would stop struggling with these tough term papers."

"Boss, boss." Angela repeated while looking at her bedroom door, like it would open for someone to hear her talking about her employer. "Will you hate my boss if I said our Sunday date is cancelled?"

"Who would hate a boss like yours?"

"Listen, he will be traveling soon. He said I need to be here to watch over the children tomorrow. He has a golf game with his rich friends. Shopping for the month will be on Sunday."

"Aaah. Tell me more." Brenda said.

"I hope you will forgive me for breaking our date. Next week will be ours." She lifted her left hand and slapped her forehead on recalling that Ronny was to travel next Sunday for most of July, which meant the earliest she would meet with Brenda was August.

"Brenda, let us talk and meet once my boss is back from his travel. Wish me luck as I parent the children while he is away."

111

"You would have been his girlfriend or wife by now, were it not for your cowardice. Good night Bestie, I am doing homework," Brenda said before she ended the call.

Angela looked at the clock on her bedside table as she walked into the bathroom to shower.

While in bed she wondered if Stella had talked with Ronny, turned what happened between them against her. Otherwise why would he be thinking of bringing in his sister-in-law to the house?

She worried if Stella had mentioned that Angela would be going to university soon, though that could not be earlier than the three, or four years Ronny was aware of. She needed to save a million shillings to cover her university fees and upkeep for her and her son for at least four years.

Angela reminded herself that one would always find trouble if they focused on problems long enough, as she was doing.

She counted all the positive events of the day. She had a three-year contract, a medical cover, and a salary increase and a new Smartphone. She pulled a bed sheet over her head and said her nightly prayer. She reminded herself of the trust she had earned from her employer, to the extent that he was ready to leave her with his children, soon.

What more could she ask for?

Chapter 11

"You are scaring the kids." Angela said in a raised voice.

Ronny stopped talking midway through a sentence.

Angela wished there was a way to retrieve the words immediately they left her mouth. It was an involuntary response to Ronny's quarrelsome voice. He was giving instructions to the children on how to behave while he was away on travel.

He was flying out to Europe on Sunday morning, so he had gathered the family on Saturday evening. He had repeated several times, how the children should follow their schedule, to make life easier for Angela.

Angela had listened and watched as the children coiled with every instruction from their father. Until she could not take it anymore.

Her fear that she had shouted at her employer vanished when she saw Mia and Betty unfold arms they had crossed tightly on their chest.

She watched as he leaned back on the chair and raised his muscular arms to the headrest.

She braved herself for the worst as she heard him speak. "You could be right. I must be confused, leaving all of you behind."

He stood and paced from the dining room to the entrance to the kitchen and back.

Angela's oval eyes did not turn away as he walked back and sat down. She looked at Nikko seated next to her. He was pushing a toy car on the dining table.

"I know it's not part of my job description to talk, but I can handle the children, and their schedule," she said as she held Nikko's left hand in hers.

She glanced at Mia, then Betty. "Is it okay if you go watch cartoons with Dad while I prepare dinner?" She stood and went to the kitchen.

Ronny watched her until she disappeared into the pantry. He turned back to the children. "Whose day is it to handle the remote?" He asked as he held Betty's hand while beckoning Nikko to follow.

"Toy tracks, toy tracks," Nikko repeated as he walked to the family room where Mia had arrived and had the remote.

Betty freed her hand from Ronny's and ran into the kitchen. "Angie, I hope you are not sad like Dad. I will be a good girl when he goes to other countries for work."

Angela placed the fruits in her hand on a countertop and spread her arms wide. Betty fell in and grabbed Angela's thighs. None of them spoke until Angela saw Ronny walk towards the kitchen. She released Betty. "Everyone is waiting for you, go watch cartoons."

Betty smiled as she sprinted away. "I will arrive before Dad."

Angela went back to the fruits and addressed Ronny without looking up. "I thought you were to be with the children?"

"They seem okay." He pulled a high stool by the island.

She opened a cupboard and retrieved side plates. "Sorry, but you will make my work easier if you mend fences with the children, now."

"Where have you been hiding that confident voice?" He asked.

A smile engulfed Angela's face.

He chuckled. "Anyway, you might find it useful once you meet with Dianna."

Angela pushed the side plates to one corner of the tray and made space for the bowl of fruits. "Is there looming trouble I need to know about?"

Ronny massaged his forehead, like it hurt. He picked a half banana from the bowl. "Not really. Only that Dianna could turn out to be the fourth child around. Best if you ignore her. I will make things clear when I return."

"Anyone in the family I should turn to if I find it hard to babysit the fourth baby?" Angela asked, smiling, without turning her eyes away from Ronny.

She watched him smooth his right hand through his chin, like he was feeling for any new growth, and then he spoke. "Did you say I scared the children? You are now scaring me with that question."

He peeled the banana and took a bite. "You may call my mother, but I pray there won't be any reason for that. She already has enough in her hands, taking care of Dad while worrying about her grandchildren."

Angela wished she could open her arms to comfort Ronny, as she often did with the children.

She cautioned herself that it would not be proper to even think of hugging her employer, even if it was just to give comfort. "I will not let anything go wrong, believe me. You may now go be with the kids."

She lifted the tray and went to the family room. "Here I come with lots of fruits. Please make sure you catch all the juice into your mouths or side plates. Okay?"

She left for the kitchen after receiving a uniform "Yes" from the children.

Ronny joined the children at the sofa. They ate fruits as they talked about his travel and their schoolwork.

Later, Angela prepared dinner, a meal she hoped Ronny would miss until he returned from his travel. A bean-stew, grilled marinated ribs, vegetables, rice and *ugali*.

While cooking, she reflected on each of the thoughts storming through her head.

She wondered why Ronny seemed to be in a bad temper one moment and good mood the next. He had lost his temper while reminding the children of the house rules and their schedule, and then within minutes, he seemed to have sobered up as he chatted with her in the kitchen.

She made many trips to the dining table, forgetting that she could have arranged all the food items and plates in the kitchen trolley. She was reflective. What did Ronny mean by saying Dianna was as good as a fourth child in the house?

On the few times Dianna had visited, she had appeared okay, though always in a hurry. The last time she had come in with her mother, she had left halfway through lunch and did not return until her mother called Dianna to drive her back to their house.

Angela went to the family room and there was no one. She had not noticed when Ronny and the children had left. She walked to the corridor leading into the bedrooms and found the place quiet.

Not wanting the grilled ribs to go cold, she went the direction to Ronny's bedroom. She heard laughter.

She knocked softly on the bedroom door. No answer.

She tried two more times before she heard more laughter and the words, "Come in."

The door opened, and Betty giggled. "We are having a pillow fight with Dad. Come and join."

Angela looked at Betty and wished she could be a child again and play with her father. Growing up, she could not recall a time when her father played with her or her brother, not even after their mother had died. Her father was always serious, waking up and driving to work in the morning and back in the evening.

Later, after the death of her mother, whenever they were home from boarding school, they spent most of their daytime with their cousins or grandmother and only went to their parents' house to sleep. Not play with their father or stepmother. "Betty, tell everyone that dinner is ready, on the table, getting cold." She walked away.

In the kitchen, she busied herself until she saw the foursome flock towards the dining room. Nikko was hanging onto Ronny's chest while Mia was on his back and Betty was trying to hang onto his left arm.

A smile engulfed Angela's face. Glad that the children would stay happy and cooperate with her while their father was away.

If Ronny had left without making peace with his children, Angela was sure they would have transferred whatever anger from their father to her. She was now happy, the only person she had to deal with would be Dianna.

There was near silence at the table except for the click, click, click of spoons and forks hitting plates.

Halfway through the meal, Ronny Spoke, "The food is more than yummy. Is that the reason no one wants to talk?"

His words opened a lengthy conversation about food. The children asked one another to name restaurants and hotels they have visited, which one could compete with Angela's delicious meal.

The children listened keenly as Angela informed them that her cooking was just the beginning of better food to come. She would one day open a big hotel and they were all welcome to visit and taste the food.

Mia supported her cheek on one hand. "Does that mean you will go? Who will cook for us, or stay with us when Dad goes to work?"

Angela forced a smile to shield her misting eyes. She looked at Ronny seated opposite from her before she said, "I will be here for the next three years. After that you would have learned how to cook from me."

She inhaled Ronny's cologne across the table, though she made it appear like she was inhaling the aroma of food. "I will need to leave, go to university before you catch up with me."

Mia counted her fingers. "Three years means I will be eleven, Betty will be nine and Nikko will be only six." She glanced at Ronny who had all along been listening to the conversation between Angela and Mia.

"Why don't you stay with us and go to university when Nikko is fourteen?"

Angela was aware that Ronny was very keen on the discussion. She had finished eating, she stood up. "After ten or eleven years, I will be too old to be a student." She picked Ronny's plates, added Nikko's and stuck them on top of hers.

Betty lifted her glass of water. "How old are you, when is your birthday?" She put the glass on the table. "Did you know that November and December are our birthday months? We eat many birthday cakes."

Angela put the dishes on the tray. "You know what, three years is such a long time, three Christmases. We have enough time to discuss when I will leave for university. After you all learn how to cook and dust the house," she said as she walked towards the kitchen.

Betty and Mia picked up their dishes and followed her.

Mia rinsed her plate and placed it in the dish washer. "Why do you make us pick our plates but not Dad and Nikko, the boys?"

Amused, Angela said, "Nikko's hands are still growing. He will pick his used plates when he turns five years, a year younger than Betty." She stretched her neck out, peeped towards the dining room. "For Dad, maybe because he is very tall. A plate would break if it fell from his hands."

She was surprised that the girls were convinced. They walked away. A moment later she heard them share her response with Ronny.

After loading the dish washer, Angela walked into the dining room. "The girls will come help me carry some of my belongings into the house while Dad and Nikko get ready for bed."

Ronny got the message and walked away with Nikko. Angela, Betty and Mia went to her sleeping quarters.

By the time Ronny helped Nikko to take a shower and pull on his pajamas, most of Angela's belongings were in the fourth bedroom.

She was glad that Mia and Betty were happy with the new arrangement.

On seeing their father, they ran and pulled him, as Mia urged, "Come see Angela's new room."

"Not today. You may take Nikko to see where Angela will be sleeping."

He turned to Nikko. "No need for you to worry that Angela will be far in the other house when I travel tomorrow," he said as he released his fingers from Nikko's grip.

~~~~~

Ronny was reflective as he placed individual suits into protective bags before placing them into his travel suitcase. The suits were delivered to his office on Thursday by the dry-cleaning delivery vehicle.

"Thank you, Lord." He heard words escape from his mouth. He was thoughtful, how bearable Angela had made his life, taking care of his children, and him.

He admonished himself on the thought that Angela arranged his wardrobe better than what his wife used to do. He pushed the guilty feeling aside, comforting himself that Bella was brought up in a family like his, where parents believed in relying on house workers.

Bella's father and mother were in full time employment. Bella, her older brother and sister, and a younger sister were under the care of two workers within the household.

The workers followed a common trend in the city, especially in homes of the rich.

Many house girls and other domestic workers prefer to perform all duties in the house, rather than ask any of the children to take up some tasks.

The house staff feared to have an argument with the children or be reported to the parents as being trouble-makers. They remained quiet and picked up after the children, whatever the age.

The result was that the workers remained on friendly terms with the children and adults of the household.

Ronny was grateful that Angela was different. He had on occasion heard her ask his children to pick up after themselves.

She had taken time to explain to Betty and Mia the benefits of carrying their used dishes from the dining table to the kitchen and keep their bedrooms neat. Put items at designated places.

Of late, he had seen Nikko remove his toys from chairs, place them on a table or toy box.

Ronny liked the idea that his children were learning basics, personal hygiene and food preparation skills.

Looking back at how busy his week had been, he appreciated that Angela had chosen to do his laundry without being asked. He recalled how Angela had relieved him from the task of washing his clothes. He had returned home one Wednesday evening and the first words he heard from her were, "The carpet cleaners were here, the laundry lady finished her work, and I washed clothes from your room, hope that's okay with you."

He had stared, more of wanting to understand the relationship between the weekly commercial cleaners and his clothes.

To ease the strained expression on her face, he had said, "Okay," and only understood what she meant when he walked into his bedroom.

All items in the bathroom - laundry basket, soaps, oils, towels, shaver and combs were at their rightful place.

There was a clean pair of folded bedsheets on his bed. His clean socks, vests, and underwear arranged in the drawers in the wardrobe. He now understood why Angela had appeared confused.

Not wanting to make her feel uneasy discussing his clothes, he had not complained or thanked her. Over time, she continued to wash clothes from his laundry basket every Thursday. He too started to set the Rumba to clean his bedroom floor on Thursday evenings, sure there would be no items in the way of the machine.

He had also noted that Angela never spread his bed. Her only sign that he needed to change beddings was the clean pair of folded bedsheets, pillowcases and a duvet she left on his bed. Subsequently, he had made it a habit to change his bedsheets and place the used ones in the laundry basket. Their silent agreement worked well.

He now had a supply of clean clothing items for his trip.

Ronny was to travel with some staff from his office to Bonn, Germany and then to Sweden to discuss extension of contracts with suppliers of their computer hardware and software.

He would then fly back home and pack another suitcase for the family trip to Thailand. On his return, he would have two nights at home before joining managers of Henry Technologies Inc. at their bi-annual teambuilding gathering in Mombasa.

He was glad that Angela agreed to relocate into the main house, and she chose the bedroom on the same side as the children. His wish was that she would not go back to her sleeping quarters once he returned from his travels, though he did not want to tell her then.

Thus far, most of the tasks that had him worried for most of the week had fallen into place with little effort from his side.

He admired the ease with which Angela had let the children know she was moving into the main house, without use of many words as he had planned to. All she did was ask them to assist her carry her belongings. Their eagerness was their way of saying she was welcome to sleep in the main house.

Ronny wondered what made Angela act different from the workers in his parents' house, or Margaret, the woman who took care of his children before Angela.

Maggie was a competent worker, though she rarely played with the children, or asked them to learn any household tasks, as Angela did. Ronny concluded it was Angela's level of education. Having completed high school and qualified to join university meant she was analytical, good at decision-making. She would qualify, like some of his competent employees in the office who made very feasible decisions.

His thoughts drifted to how harsh he had been on the children earlier in the afternoon. How a simple suggestion from Angela that he join them in their play melted all their fears and the anger they had. In a few hours, they had watched TV, read two short story books and played a pillow fight that made the children happy.

He had also received a list of items they wanted him to buy for them. And Mia had included a handbag and perfume for Angela on her shopping list.

Ronny retired to bed after midnight, content, convinced that Angela would handle Dianna well. So far, Angela had not shown signs of being confrontational, she would let whatever Dianna did or said pass.

He preferred that Angela focused on the children and engaged with Dianna only when necessary.

Knowing Dianna, she would be out of the house early in the morning for work, and back in time for dinner, or after the children had gone to bed. He hoped that he would be the one to talk with Dianna in case she interfered with the children's schedule. Not Angela.

Ronny did not want to return home and find that Angela had left her job in protest. He had a new plan for her.

Chapter 12

Why did she not come as planned? Not now, when I am around." Ronny paced the breadth of his bedroom as he voiced out the question several times.

On arrival from Mombasa, which was the last of his trips, he was glad that Angela and the children had managed on their own. Though on a few occasions, John, his driver had to go grocery shopping. Angela had decided it was hard to shop with three children after they had refused to stay at Rose's house, so she could go buy fresh fruits and vegetables.

Ronny's plan had been that Dianna would come visit her sister's children while he was away. She would have also helped with the shopping or be the adult in the house while Angela went shopping.

Though he had noticed Dianna's absence during the nights he was home before he left for Thailand with his parents, he had not asked. He was now home and confirmed that Dianna never showed up even for a single day. She had called and told Angela that she was held up, would visit once the children closed school for the August holidays, which was now.

Ronny had squeezed his travels into the month of July to free up August, allow him enough time with the children during their school holiday. He now had doubts if he would enjoy the holiday, after Dianna's announcement that she would visit in August.

The next day, Sunday, Ronny was still restless. On arrival at church, he asked the children to follow Angela to where she always sat, near the church choir. He sat with his sister and her family.

Rose must have noticed that her brother was troubled. As soon as the church service was over, she held his hand and guided him away, leaving the children playing outside the church under the watchful eyes of Robert her husband, and Angela.

"Is something wrong?" Rose asked.

"Dianna plans to come spoil my holiday with the children."

"Do not let her step in the bedroom near yours. I will come prepare the extra room on the children's side for her."

Ronny scratched his chin as he nodded. His wish was that Rose could continue to talk, give him enough time to put words together, tell her the only other available bedroom was in the house staff quarters.

"Angela has been using the room near the children while I was on travel. The children like that arrangement."

"You cannot bring a housegirl into your house," she rebuked in a raised voice, attracting attention from nearby churchgoers.

He scowled. "You need to grow up. What did you expect while I was out of town, have the children stay in the house all by themselves?" He shouted back, agitated, at how anyone who heard her statement was going to interpret it. He worried that some people might interpret that to mean he had slept with the housegirl.

He shoved hands into his trouser pockets and stared at Rose.

She thinned her lips and crossed her arms in defiance. But as he expected of her, she recovered from her annoyance very fast, pasted on a smile, made eye contact and said in a lowered voice. "Does that mean we prepare the staff quarters for Dianna? That way you will not see her again if that is your wish."

All the anger melted from Ronny's face. "You are another one, kid sister." He slapped her gently on the shoulder. "Do you want to cut all links with my in-laws?"

Even though Ronny acknowledged the concern of his relatives, that his children were very young and needed a mother figure to guide them, he was not happy with how fast some of them were trying to get him to marry. His in-laws wanted him to take in Dianna, while Rose had her single friends lined up for him to make a choice.

"Time to leave, otherwise we shall be left here with the church mice," Ronny said. Both laughed as they walked to where their families were waiting.

As they approached them, Rose said, "I assume lunch will be at yours, while we wait for Dianna?"

"Not until four. I promised the family some ice cream. Come over for an early dinner," Ronny said as he lowered his body closer to the ground and scooped Nikko. He talked briefly with Robert before they said their byes and left.

On their drive home, Ronny addressed Angela without turning his eyes away from the road. "Can we help you prepare dinner for many people? Rose will come over, and maybe Dianna, as you know."

"That's okay, I will cook." She turned to Betty and Mia on the very back seats of the Toyota Prado. "Maybe the girls will help chop onions and tomatoes. Will that be okay with you?"

Betty agreed while Mia said she had a storybook she wanted to read.

Angela looked at Nikko seated beside her. "And this boy will bake a cake for our dessert." She lifted a hand and pointed at his armpit, sending him into a giggle before he drove an imaginary car to her face. "My cars will chase you from tickling me."

"You are right," Angela said, to give the boy more confidence.

Ronny waited to hear what task Angela would like him to help with. When she did not mention anything in that line, he volunteered himself. "I will set up the barbeque for *nyama choma*. That means a quick stop for fresh ribs, after the ice cream."

~~~~~~

"I had no idea there would be a celebration. Who is my brother welcoming home?" Rose asked as she stepped into Ronny's house through the kitchen door. Her sons entered ahead of her.

She looked from the kids to Angela and to Ronny. "Robert was paged. One of his elderly patients is admitted in hospital. He might join us later." She explained the absence of her husband, but not the presence of Judy, one of her girlfriends.

Rose and Judy had attended the same primary school in the city and continued to meet at the members' clubs and other family events.

Ronny removed the oven mittens and threw them on a countertop. He took a few strides to Judy and kissed her on both cheeks. "It has been some time, welcome to our home."

He turned to Rose. "My family is welcoming me back home from my many travels. My sister is welcome to taste their cooking."

He was glad that he had changed his mind about lighting the barbeque, where he planned to spend time with Robert.

With Angela's help, he had marinated the ribs and placed them in the kitchen grill oven to cook.

Angela was quiet. She mixed flour for a cake before she prepared roasted potatoes, rice, stewed chicken, vegetables and *ugali*. Her target was to set food on the dining table by six o'clock.

The few times Angela spoke was when asking Betty or Mia for the onions or tomatoes she had given them to chop on a manual food processor.

Ronny followed Rose and Judy into the living room where he served them wine. They settled down to a friendly chat, though Ronny made frequent excuses and left for the kitchen to check on the cooking ribs.

At one point, Angela talked without looking at him. "I will make sure the meat cooks well. You may stay with the visitors."

Ronny chuckled and turned his attention to his daughters. "Hi Betty, Mia, would you like to join your brother and cousins David and Donald in the family room?" He asked, aware that the five-year old twins had little in common with their older cousins. He had asked the question to have a feel of their desire to be in the kitchen working.

Betty said she preferred to watch the cake as it baked.

Ronny left for the family room where he chatted with the three boys until Rose arrived by his side, holding her glass of wine. "Running away from us? I see you prefer the kitchen more."

"Jealous that I am entertaining my younger visitors?" He turned to Donald who had the TV remote in his hand. "Young man, please ask your mother what she would like to watch?"

Donald tilted his chin upwards, towards his mother. "No drinks near the TV, as you always tell us." he turned back to Thomas the Train showing on TV.

Ronny leaned over, closer to his sister. "How's your plan. I see you brought an extra hand to assist in the girl fight?"

"Not what you think. We are civilized women, we don't fight." She took a sip from her glass, leaned over and rested her head on Ronny's shoulder. "We are here to help you, in a subtle way." She held Ronny's hand and pulled him away, further from the children's earshot. "Is it okay if you sit closer to Judy when Dianna arrives? Judy prefers it that way."

"Uuuh?" Ronny exclaimed as he held Rose's hand and walked towards the kitchen. "Count me out. The only battles I want are the ones I volunteer to fight in. Not this one." They arrived in the kitchen.

Mia looked up from the recipe book in her hand. "Auntie, I have found a cake I like, and Angie has agreed to help me bake it."

Betty, still wearing the floor length apron protested. "No, Angie said she will teach both of us."

Ronny looked at Angela before he switched on the oven light and checked the ribs. He stood upright when he heard Rose say. "She's transformed from Angela, to Angie?"

Betty jumped on her toes. "Auntie, yes. You can shorten people's names to make them prettier. Like mine from Beatrice to Betty and Miriam to Mia." She ran and held Rose by the arm. "Auntie, what is your full name, Rose for?"

Rose shrugged, "Ask your dad."

Ronny coughed a dry cough. "Ronny for Ronald."

Mia joined in the conversation. "You forgot to add our Nikko for Nicholas." She said as she watched Rose sip from her glass of wine.

Betty untied the apron. "Auntie, what about you, do you have a longer name, to make your short name, Rose, like a rose flower?"

"She is Auntie Roselyn," Ronny moved closer to Rose. "Do you want to learn how to bake cake or shall we leave the girls to enjoy their cooking?"

Rose walked out of the kitchen. "My job of running the school is hard enough. Leave the kitchen to housegirls, though I see my nieces are being trained to be cooks. It is not a real profession."

Ronny caught up with Rose and squeezed her hand. "Why don't we wait and complain after we taste the food? Relax."

They approached and found Judy standing by one window in the living room, talking on her phone. When she finished, she walked back to where she had left her handbag. "I see you have a visitor." Rose and Ronny stood up at the same time.

Ronny saw Rose's strained expression and sensed trouble. He went and opened the door as Dianna parked a Honda Civic on the driveway, right behind Rose's BMW.

"Welcome, welcome my sister," he called out as Dianna stepped out of the car.

"Hi. Do you want to carry my suitcase?" She took a step towards the back of her car.

"No problem. Come in and enjoy yourself. The luggage will be brought in after you eat and are rested."

He was glad when she obliged and followed him into the house. He held her hand and kissed her on both cheeks.

Rose and Judy were in conversation, in lowered tones.

Dianna waved to Judy then walked over and shook Rose's hand. "How have you been? Glad you came over to see the children." Dianna said before she walked away towards the kitchen.

Ronny watched as Dianna took long strides in her six-inch pumps. He then looked at his sister, questioning if the mortified expression on Rose's face was because Dianna had walked on the carpet with shoes or because she had not paused to share a proper greeting with Judy.

"Please go and find out if dinner is ready." Ronny encouraged Rose.

As Rose walked away, Ronny left his position on the sofa and sat on his recliner chair. "How's the world out there? You must be busy, I have not seen you of late," he said to Judy.

He was impressed with the instant smile on Judy's face.

She talked of her last two trips to Europe and how she planned to travel to the US for the New York Fashion Show. He nodded, though his mind was far. He worried if Rose had gone to raise trouble with Dianna in the kitchen.

For a moment, he questioned himself, why he sent Rose to the kitchen. On further reflection, he decided the two were adults. If they exchanged bitter words in his absence, and Dianna protested and left, it would solve his problem without dragging his name in, leave the doors open for his mother-in-law to visit her grandchildren.

"Have you been back to the club since we last ate dinner in that—"

"One day I will make time to attend one of those fashion events," Ronny said absentmindedly, not aware that he had interrupted Judy.

Judy took a sip from her glass and continued to talk about the latest designs and the designers she preferred to buy from.

Ronny watched as Betty ran into the living room. "Angie says dinner is served. And Auntie Dianna says she is not hungry."

Ronny stood and motioned Judy to walk ahead of him.

His quick action was to stop Betty from saying more. To him, there must have been an exchange between his sister and sister-in-law. Why else would Dianna announce that she would not eat?

His hope was that they exchanged their displeasures away from the children, though that would not be possible if Betty and Mia were in the kitchen.

"The aroma from the table is welcoming enough. Where are the boys?" Ronny asked as he walked past the dining room into the family room. On his way, he took a quick glance towards the kitchen where he saw Rose and Dianna on the high stools by the island, in conversation.

He returned with Nikko, David and Donald.

Ronny signaled Judy to the sink. "Please go ahead of the boys, unless you want your designer dress messed up with water."

"That will give me reason to shop for more clothes," Judy said.

Ronny clapped for attention from the boys. "Hi boys, fall into one line to wash hands."

David and Donald shoved one another to be first in line. Donald won, followed by David. Nikko was third.

As the children washed their hands, Ronny pondered what type of life Judy led when the only topic she could engage in well was clothes and fashion shows.

As a professional, always eager to upgrade his skills in modern technologies, Ronny found it hard to understand Judy. How someone with a master's degree in human resources management from a university in the UK could spend her days and years just looking good.

He smiled on remembering that however annoying his sister was on some days, she held a job, managing the private school their parents had invested in for her. Though Rose still found time to meet and chat with her girlfriends, and occasionally travel for the international fashion shows, she worked as the Manager of the school.

Ronny turned his attention to the children. "Boys. Dry your hands and find a chair at the table."

He was relieved when he saw Dianna and Rose walk into the dining room. Rose walked straight to the table and served food into the children's plates.

Ronny looked at Judy and then Dianna. "I am the host, my visitors first," as he motioned the two ladies to-wards the table.

Judy sat next to Rose, and to the left of Mia and Betty.

Dianna sat on the remaining chair at the table as Betty looked at her.

Mia glanced around the table before she asked, "Where will Dad and Angela sit?" Mia stood up from her chair and motioned her father to the seat. "I will eat from the kitchen." She picked her plate of food and walked away.

"My mistake, I forgot to pull out the table to its full capacity." Ronny explained.

Betty stood up. "I will leave my chair for Angela."

Ronny stared. "No, stay on your chair. There are more seats in the kitchen and the store, we can bring over."

Betty sat back. "Okay."

Ronny did not miss the expression on Rose's face as her lips parted. "You encourage the housegirl to eat at the table?"

"We manage as family, no titles in this house," he said as he busied himself serving food into a plate.

Dianna stood and picked her plate of food. "Let me eat from the living room if the housegirl eats from this table." Off she went.

The serving spoon dropped out of Ronny's hand and landed on the table. He replaced it into the serving bowl, sat down and turned to Judy. "More food for you?"

She shook her head and continued to eat.

Rose swallowed the food in her mouth. "As a good Manager, I always give credit where it is due. The food is yummy."

"Thank you. You are most welcome, eat more," Ronny said, relaxed on hearing Rose praise the food. He finished serving and pushed his chair back. "I will be back."

He carried the plate of food and walked into the kitchen where he found Angela and Mia seated at the island.

Mia was eating while Angela had a drink in her hand. He walked to Angela's side and placed the food in front of her, his other hand rested on her shoulder. "Time to eat food." He peered into the glass in her hand. "Juice later."

Ronny sensed as Angela went stiff when his hand touched her shoulder. He pulled his hand away as his eyes drifted to Mia's face. She had seen.

He had been longing to touch Angela. Thank her for her excellent work, especially since he arrived back from his travels and found his children as happy as he had left them.

He worried on what to do if Angela reacted, decided to resign from her job if he looked at her beyond her role as the housegirl.

He went back to the dining room and sat. He glanced around and was glad that Rose and Judy were in conversation, and the children were busy eating and discussing their toy cars, cartoons on TV and their next game. He served food onto his plate. "I will go join our sister in the living room."

His objective was to chat with Dianna, have a chance to know if she was still staying or would leave for her home.

"How is your meal? Hope it is near your high food standards."

"I was enjoying myself until you mentioned that you eat from the same table as the housegirl." Ronny stared at her, he chuckled and sat down on the opposite sofa. "Have you ever considered saying yes to one of your boyfriends? You might have a chance to learn some details, like the vital role of the people you call house girls."

"Do I look like I want children? Never." She chuckled. "Except maybe taking care of Bella's angels." Her face turned into a sad expression. "I can never fall asleep, whenever I think of the suffering they must be going through."

If Ronny's complexion had not been dark enough, one would have seen the hot flashes he felt on his face. "The children are fine. They have a parent and they receive some warmth from Angie."

Dianna laughed aloud. "Angie. Sounds like you always follow that Angie with sweetheart."

He massaged the back of his neck. Even he was surprised that he had referred to Angela as Angie. "I have not called her by that, Angie."

He picked up a grilled piece of meat while staring at Dianna. When she did not say a word, he added. "I hope you will stay with us for long, you need to see for yourself how the children are coping."

"I had wanted to stay, but your sister is too annoying."

"She does not live here with us."

Unlike earlier in the day, he now wanted Dianna to stay, even for one night. She needed to witness how hard Angela worked to make his children comfortable. Dianna would also have a chance to see how close his children had grown towards Angela.

He made a promise to himself that he would do whatever within his means to make Dianna stay, even just for one night. "I see your plate is low on food," he said as he put his plate on the glass coffee table and stretched for Dianna's. He received her plate and walked to the dining table where he served half of her earlier portion.

Rose stopped talking and looked at Ronny as he served. She said, "Tasty food. Isn't your friend interested in more?"

Ronny raised the plate in his hand. "This is for her. I will come with mine later." He walked away, not wanting to see the expression on Rose's face. She was yet to learn how to hide some of her feelings.

He knew Rose was not impressed. Not only that he had come to refill Dianna's plate, she had announced that she would not eat food prepared by a person who was not a trained chef.

The only worry Ronny had was that the children would hear any expletives uttered by Rose, if she chose to make her displeasure known.

Ronny arrived and held the plate of food with two hands in front of Dianna. "For my sister, I'm at your service, in case you need more."

Dianna lifted her empty glass of juice.

He walked to the half wall between the living room and the dining and returned with glasses and two bottles of wine, one red and one white. "Please make your choice."

She pointed to the red wine. He uncorked the bottle and served wine into the two glasses.

Ronny engaged Dianna in general discussions. He did not want to unravel her now jovial mood. He asked about her parents and her siblings. He was surprised when she referred to her nieces as "spoiled brats who will never hand you even a glass of water."

Rose's arrival interrupted their conversation.

She looked at Dianna, then Ronny. "Thanks for the nice meal. We are leaving."

Ronny chewing food in his mouth raised a hand, like he wanted to stop Rose from leaving. Rose added, "We are going to check on Robert. We will come back for the twins."

He swallowed then spoke. "Okay, sounds good." He turned to Judy. "Are you also leaving?"

She nodded and picked her handbag from near the chair where Dianna sat.

He placed his plate of food on the table and wiped his hands with a paper towel. He picked Dianna's car keys from a nearby side stool and followed Judy and Rose outside.

After a brief chat, he bid them bye as he opened Dianna's car and retrieved her suitcase from the boot.

Rose, who was stepping into her car, stood still. Holding onto the open door, she watched Ronny.

He closed the boot of Dianna's car as he said, "Better if I bring Dianna's luggage in now."

Rose sneered. "Looks like you have made your choice." She sat in her car, started the engine and sped off, with Judy in the passenger seat.

A broad smile engulfed Ronny's face as he walked back into the house to the visitor's room where he put down Dianna's suitcase and went back to the sitting room.

He was satisfied with the way events had turned out. With his sister out of the way, he would now focus his energy on managing Dianna.

Chapter 13

At nine o'clock Rose called and asked Ronny to drive her children back home.

It was not possible for Ronny. "I drank some wine, and I don't want to trouble my drivers at this hour of Sunday night." Ronny chuckled. "Better if they stay the night, after all schools are closed for holiday"

She was convinced.

Normally the twins would have shared the double bed in the fourth bedroom, currently occupied by Angela. Ronny ruled the bedroom out. It was the wrong night to ask Angela to move back to the staff quarters, even if it was just for one night.

Having heard the comments made by Dianna and Rose about Angela, they must have uttered more negative words about her while they were in the kitchen. What else could have kept two opponents in the kitchen for the time they sat there?

The big question was how to fit the eight of them in the six bedrooms. He wished he could go sleep at the staff quarters to release his bedroom without raising too many questions from Angela, Dianna and the children.

He called Mia to follow him as he walked to his bedroom. Betty invited herself and went along.

Once they were inside, he closed the door. "Your cousins will spend the night with us—"

Betty jumped up in jubilation as Ronny added. "The problem is that Auntie is staying, so we lack beds. One of you can vacate your room for the boys. Go share a room with your aunt. Use a sleeping bag."

"Not me," Mia said.

From her quick response, Ronny knew he had no luck.

With lips parted, Betty looked at her father, looked at Mia and back to Ronny. "Auntie used mean words about Angie. Dad, we are not supposed to say bad things about other people, especially when they are nearby."

Betty lifted both hands and covered her eyes. "Dad, are we supposed to like mean people?"

Ronny saw Mia's pulled-in eyebrows and knew she was hurting. He said, "I have another suggestion, the two of you, or, all the boys can bring sleeping bags and camp in my room.

Betty uncovered her eyes as Ronny added, "You may even bring your small tent along."

He placed a finger on his mouth. "Do not tell the boys. Too many tents will spoil your fun."

He was relieved when his daughters stood up and gave him a high-five as Mia said, "Best Dad in the world. Can we stay for a week since schools are closed?"

"Let's discuss that after your first night." He did not want to remind them that he was not on holiday from work. "Go shower before you leave your rooms for the night."

They ran out of the bedroom.

Ronny was glad for the moment to himself. He needed time to reflect on how to approach Dianna. Thinking of Dianna, Ronny almost ran out of his bedroom on remembering that Dianna could have gone to the kitchen to torment Angela. He found Angela alone in the kitchen. "How's your evening? Hope we did not overwork you."

Angela looked up and back to the cups she was picking from a tray into a cupboard.

He saw the grief on her face, which he partly understood based on what Betty had revealed and from the earlier comments made by Rose and Dianna. He felt his face warm with anger.

He walked and stood very close to Angela, almost touching. "I wish you could allow me to give you a hug. I know you are hurting, and that hurts me too."

"Please don't." She snapped and turned back to her task of storing dishes in the cupboard.

He obeyed and moved two steps back. "I know you are hurt. I asked Dianna to stay, she needs to witness that you are more than a housegirl." His eyebrows pulled in. "You are a good person. You are special to me."

He started to walk away as he heard Angela exclaim, "Hehe!".

Ronny did not turn back when he heard steps behind him, and a stool scrape the floor. Aware that Angela

145

had sat down, he wondered if she was overwhelmed with his words. Was she still annoyed, or happy to hear that she was of value to him?

Angela had shed enough tears while she loaded the dishwasher. She did not want to replay the words from Dianna who had said over and over that she had come to stay with the children, and she would have no need for the services of a housegirl.

Somehow reassured by the words from Ronny, Angela told herself she would have to wait until the next day to see if she or Dianna would vacate the house.

The thought of leaving her job brought a new stream of tears. She lifted the hem of her skirt and wiped her tears as she slid off the stool. She pulled a broom she had rested against a wall and busied herself sweeping the kitchen floor, oblivious of Ronny standing by the entrance to the kitchen.

He stepped inside the kitchen. "Angie, please give me a chance to wipe those tears off your face. I promise there won't be more than that."

"Go away. I want to go home to my people. My grandmother will welcome me back home." Her voice choked as more tears fell.

"I understand. Please go to bed. I will call you before I sleep." He said in a lowered voice before he walked away. He needed to finalize sleeping arrangements for the children.

Reaching the family room, Ronny waved to the boys who were busy playing games on the family computer.

Though he would have wanted to ask who logged them into Wi-Fi, he did not. Instead he called out, "Time for bed, who wants to follow me?"

"We are waiting for mummy and daddy to take us home," David said.

"Mummy said you could sleep here. She will pick you up tomorrow."

The three boys abandoned the computer and ran towards Ronny, joyous.

Donald raised his hand and held Ronny by his trousers. "Can we stay until school opens?"

"Yes, if your parents agree," Ronny said as he walked towards Nikko's bedroom, the boys in tow.

Once in the bedroom, Ronny squatted, looked at each boy in the eye before he spoke. "You are welcome to stay here, for many days, but Nikko's PJs, shirts and trousers are not large enough for you to wear."

Nikko ran to his wardrobe and pulled out whatever pajamas he could find.

Ronny stood up and stopped him. "David and Donald will come and pick one pair of PJs. Follow me to the bathroom for a bath."

They did.

There was a knock as Ronny read Toy Story to the three boys in pajamas. The doorknob turned, and Mia peeped. "We are ready, may we go sleep?"

"Come, we prepare beds for each boy," Ronny said as he walked out of the bedroom. He knocked on Betty's bedroom door and opened. He came face to face with Betty and Dianna.

He looked at the three boys standing by his side. "Betty has given her room to David or Donald. Who wants to sleep here?"

None of the boys talked. There was a long moment of silence until Nikko said. "We all sleep in my room, not in the girls' room." Sending everyone into laughter, including Dianna.

Betty stood and walked out. "Good night, I have gone to sleep." She ran through the living room and into Ronny's bedroom.

Dianna left the room. Ronny followed her. "I guess you know the visitor room, please make yourself comfortable. Good night."

She paused and looked at him. Her lips parted but no words came out.

He watched as Dianna walked towards the living room side of the house.

Not sure if Angela had left the kitchen, he wanted to be certain that Dianna did not go to the kitchen. Dianna going to the kitchen would result in more misery for Angela.

Assured that Dianna was gone to the visitor bedroom, he walked back to Betty's bedroom to convince the boys to go to bed.

By ten o'clock Ronny had not made much progress with the boys except to get annoyed and then laugh at their jokes. He gave up when the three curled up on Betty's bed.

Ronny brought the child monitor from Nikko's room and positioned it on the nightstand. He switched on the bathroom light and left the bathroom door ajar, switched off the bedroom lights and left the room.

The kitchen lights were off, he knew Angela had gone to bed. He proceeded to his bedroom.

He knocked on his door before walking in. Mia and Betty were already asleep, each in their pink sleeping bags.

Ronny tiptoed to his walk-in wardrobe, picked PJs and proceeded to the bathroom. He reached the door and turned back to the nightstand and picked his phone.

After securing his bathroom door he dialed the number of the phone he had given Angela. The phone rang several times without a response. Assuming she was already asleep, he walked to the door of the bathroom, stopped and walked back.

He had wanted to go get the child monitor receiver he had forgotten in Nikko's room. He typed a message. "Hi. The child monitor is in Nikko's room. Please take it to your room. Thanks. R."

Ronny busied himself brushing teeth while debating if he should go for the monitor. There was no way he would leave the monitor unattended, with three young boys curled up together on one bed.

He heard an SMS drop into his phone and read, "Okay. I will go for the monitor. Good night."

Ronny pressed the redial button on his phone and waited for Angela to answer her phone. She did not.

He was glad she had responded to his SMS. He finished brushing and walked into the shower section of his bathroom, though on weekends he preferred to soak in the Jacuzzi located on the far end of the bathroom.

Halfway through his shower, he heard his phone ring. He walked out of the shower to the sink countertop where he had left the phone. He saw the missed call was from Angela. He wrapped a towel around his waist and redialed. He was glad when she answered the call.

"Are the children okay?" He asked.

"Why are they all on one bed, Betty's bed? Nikko's and Mia's rooms are empty."

Ronny chuckled. "Are they asleep?"

"Yes."

"They refused to stay apart, they insisted on sharing one bed. The reason I want you to have the monitor."

"Okay."

"If I am not asking for too much, please check on them again before morning."

"I will. Good night."

"Angela!" Ronny called, but he heard the phone disconnect from her end.

He retreated into the shower while he reflected on how to approach Angela the next day. He would ask her to reconsider her words about abandoning her job.

Next, he pondered how to talk with Dianna and ask her to let Angela continue with her role of housegirl, which Angela had extended to include advisor for his children.

~~~~~~

Angela checked on the boys four times that night. The fourth time was at six o'clock before she went to the kitchen to start her workday.

She was busy with her morning duties in the kitchen when she heard pump, pump sounds. She looked up to see Dianna hurrying into the kitchen.

"Do you have coffee ready? I need something to wake me up."

"I have tea on the table. We can buy some coffee today." Angela watched as Dianna walked to the dining table. She reverted to her tasks when she saw Ronny walk to the dining room. He stopped and exchanged morning greetings with Dianna before he proceeded to the kitchen. He greeted Angela as she walked out with a jug of fresh juice.

Ronny stayed in the kitchen until Angela returned. "How did the babies on your side sleep?" He asked, inspecting her from head to waist. "Mine will require a drum beat to wake up."

"The boys slept well. I checked on them several times. They are fine."

Ronny taped a hand on his thigh. "I will work from home until Rose comes for her boys." He opted to wait for Rose. He did not want to take chances, leave her a chance to torment Angela.

151

Angela walked into the pantry as she murmured. "Any coffee in this house for the visitor?" She asked, though she knew the answer. No one in the house used coffee.

He went to the dining room and joined Dianna. "How's your breakfast?"

"Good. I will grab a cup of coffee on my drive to work." She made eye contact with Ronny. "Please carry my luggage to the car." She stretched her head out, like she could see inside the kitchen from her position in the dining room. "Or can your housegirl do that?"

"Are you leaving?" He asked as he uncovered his bowl of porridge before he served juice.

Dianna stared at him. "I see the housegirl knows her work," as she waved a hand to indicate the breakfast items on the table. "Who knew a housegirl could prepare porridge for the boss? I wonder what else she can do."

"She's mainly here for the children, I only get the side benefits."

He stared at Dianna, glad to see his response had the intended effect.

Dianna's eyes opened wide. "Benefits?"

He lifted the glass of juice closer to his mouth. "On school days all I do is walk to the table, eat breakfast and leave. She feeds the young ones and accompanies them to school."

He reflected on how comfortable his life at home had become because Angela implemented most of the required tasks for him and the children. He took a sip of juice, swallowed then chuckled. "Before she gets back home and continues with her daily chores."

"You must be mean," Dianna said, smiling.

Ronny put his glass on the table. He watched as she spoke.

"Why not employ a cook or cleaner to assist the housegirl?"

He bellowed. "Her name is Angela, Angie." He paused and turned toward Mia and Betty walking towards the dining table.

Betty looked at Dianna and then her Dad. "Good morning Auntie. Dad, can we use your toilet?"

Ronny threw his arms wide open. "I need a morning hug, if you are not pressed," he said as Betty ran and fell into his open arms.

Mia ran past the family room and into the corridor leading to the children's bedrooms.

Betty hugged Dianna before she walked into the kitchen where she hugged Angela. "Good morning Angie," as she tried to encircle her arms around Angela's waist.

Betty positioned a stool and hoisted herself up. "Angie. Are we supposed to follow our schedule when school is closed? Please say no."

Angela laughed out loud, paused and said, "Can we ask Dad after breakfast?"

Betty slipped down from the stool. "I will go ask him." She walked away.

While Mia and Betty were away from the dining room, Dianna asked Ronny where the girls had slept. "If I was a visitor, I would assume there was a third bedroom on our side, where my nieces emerged from."

"The boys were supposed to take over the children's wing. They overturned my sleeping arrangements, they shared one room, they are fine, Angela checked on them many times in the night."

"You are totally lost." Dianna said as she stood up and threw her cloth napkin on the chair. Her lips parted like she was going to say more but did not. She watched as Betty walked to the dining table.

Dianna sat back, looked at her unfinished breakfast before she addressed Betty. "Betty, please ask the housegirl to bring my luggage to the car."

Betty stopped and looked at her father before she went back to the kitchen.

Ronny stood and walked the direction of his bedroom. On his way back, he met with Angela and Betty. He waved them back as he wheeled Dianna's suitcase and placed it near the kitchen door and went back to the dining room. "Let me check on my boys," he said as he walked away.

After about five minutes, Ronny was back to the dining room. He listened as Mia and Betty explained their usual morning routine to Dianna before Mia said, "Dad, are we going to write a different schedule for our school holiday? Like watch more TV?"

Ronny checked his Rolex. "I will go to my office and work for two hours. After breakfast, bring a paper, sit with Angela and write down your holiday activities." He turned to Dianna as he continued to address the children. "Indicate what you will do in the house, within the compound, at church, at the clubs, and travel out of the city."

I need to get to work," Dianna said. "How's traffic from here in the morning?" She glanced at Mia and Betty. "Bye, girls, hug all the boys for me." She lifted two fingers to her lips and flashed them a kiss.

Instead of walking to the kitchen door to go outside, Dianna walked towards the children's bedrooms while explaining. "The boys might cry when they find their aunty gone. Let me say bye."

Dianna opened Nikko's bedroom door and found no one. She took a few steps and opened the door to Betty's bedroom. She peered, took one step back and slowly pulled the door closed and walked away.

Betty called out as Dianna neared the dining room, "Auntie, you forgot to take your breakfast dishes to the kitchen, as we do."

Dianna grinned. "Bye girls. The housegirl will clear the table."

She walked to the kitchen where she encountered Ronny and Angela in conversation. "Am I interrupting?"

"I will be back," Ronny said to Angela before he took the few steps to the kitchen door, disarmed the house alarm, lifted Dianna's suitcase and walked out of the house.

Angela stared at Dianna as she followed Ronny. She admired how Dianna balanced comfortably on her six-inch pumps. She called out, "Bye Dianna, have a lovely day."

Dianna did not respond. She walked outside, clicked her car key to open the doors.

Ronny loaded the suitcase into the car boot before he waved bye to Dianna. He retained a broad smile as he watched her drive down the driveway to the gate and out of the compound.

He went inside the house, glad that Dianna was out of his way. He could now embark on the next challenge, to mend fences with Angela. Whatever fences that had been broken by his sister and sister-in-law.

It was hard for him to picture his house and his children without Angela. He was ready to protect her from any sadness.

Chapter 14

However hard he tried, there was no way Ronny could hide his happiness.

It was December, schools had closed in November for the long holiday and his parents would be traveling back to town in three days' time.

Ronny had missed his mother and father. Though he held a Skype call with them at least twice a week, he still felt the seven-thousand two hundred kilometers distance between them, Bangkok and Nairobi.

He worried of their comfort even after he had settled them in a serviced apartment type of hospital accommodation, comparable to a five-star hotel.

During the Skype conversations and from information shared by the doctor, Ronny was certain that his father's health had improved very much.

His happiness had increased when Rose finally agreed to fly to Thailand to travel back with their parents.

The only challenge he had now was to convince Angela to shorten her December leave from one month to a few days. He tried to talk her into rescheduling her travel to the New Year. When all that failed, he said he would pay her for the leave days at a rate of one and a half of her normal pay, if she cancelled her travel altogether.

Though Angela had informed him in August that she planned to go on leave in December, he still wondered why she could not stay and earn more money that she had said she needed.

"This important person that you will be going to see, is it a husband? Can you visit them from next week and be back for Christmas?" Ronny asked before he realized he had almost shouted the question to Angela. He was jealous. He had developed feelings for Angela.

He saw one side of her cheeks push upwards into a sneer. He could tell that she was not pleased with his question.

There was a moment of quietness. He assumed she was considering his request.

"I will tell you tomorrow," she said without looking up from the vegetables she was sorting to cook for the evening meal.

Angela asking for time to decide had nothing to do with cancelling her travel. She needed time to call Joshua, her brother, and inquire when he planned to travel home from Nakuru where he worked. She had not seen his wife and son for more than a year.

After dinner, Angela called Joshua. When she finished talking with him, she opened the book where she recorded her bank transactions. Though she received quarterly account statements, she preferred to keep her own records which she could refer to any time.

Satisfied that she had saved seventy thousand shillings in seven months, she decided to send some money to her brother as a Christmas gift. He had told her his family would not travel home for Christmas as his wife was expecting their second child.

The next day, Angela caught Ronny off guard as he walked into the house after work. "If you let me travel home next week, I will come back before Christmas."

Ronny paused and scratched the back of his neck. "Two weeks? Can you make it one week, that way I take the children to be with their grandparents once they arrive? Please."

He was guilting her by mentioning the children. Over time, Ronny had noted that Angela had developed an emotional, almost motherly attachment to his children. He knew that by mentioning care for the children she might reconsider her being away for two weeks.

"Next year I will travel half my leave days over Easter and the remaining half in December for Christmas."

"Deal sealed," Ronny said as he picked up the computer bag, he had placed on the kitchen island. He was content, for now. He would handle next year when the time came.

He walked a few paces then paused. "On Friday I will come home early so that you can go do your travel shopping. Are there many people you want to purchase items for?"

"Thanks. They might prefer money."

"Use the card I gave you for house shopping. Purchase some gifts since you will miss being with them on Christmas."

"Thank you, but I will be okay." She stole a glance at him and looked away quickly. "I will travel home first, on my way back I will stop in Nakuru and visit my brother before I come back to Nairobi."

"If you do not mind, I...we can come pick you up from Nakuru. The children will be excited to go on a road trip," Ronny offered.

Angela turned down the offer, saying "I will find my way back to the city."

~~~~~~

It was just after six o'clock when Angela arrived at Nyametende, her home village.

She stretched a hand through the small opening on the main gate to unbolt the gate to the compound of her parents. She walked down the long driveway, admiring the well-trimmed internal fence.

Instead of turning left into the house of her parents, she turned right and walked on, to Priscah's compound.

She unhooked the metal rod bolting the small gate and entered.

Priscah, who was walking back to her house after locking the chicken house, saw Angela.

Angela followed the footpath. She made frequent glances at the short life fence surrounding Priscah's house.

She walked on, watched her grandmother and her son. They did not talk, call her name. And she did not call them either.

Angela reached where her grandmother stood. The bag in her hand dropped to the ground. She did not attempt to pick it up.

Priscah stood still, stooped by her seventy-six years, hands clasped to her back. She looked at her granddaughter without touching or greeting her.

After a long moment, Priscah said, "You have become a woman. Who knew that my thin worried girl would one day look this beautiful?" She smoothed her wiry hands on Angela's rounded cheeks.

Angela spread out both arms and cuddled her grandmother. "*Nyanya*, I have missed you." She directed her eyes to her son nearby. "How are you and Babu?"

She watched as Babu, standing behind his great grandmother, like he wanted to hide, lifted a hand and greeted Angela, the same way he did to visitors to their home.

Since the age of two, Babu had seen Angela come for short periods of time, a week at most, then leave. As he grew older, now four, he was more accustomed to Priscah and his younger cousins who were constantly in the village with him. They were his family.

Babu had come to learn that he was related to Angela, and she wanted him to call her Mama. He could not.

161

The people children called mama were always at home with the children, like Priscah whom he called mama.

His cold reaction forced Angela not to embrace him, afraid that he would scream and run away from her. That would break her heart.

She took a long stare at her son and realized that ten months were such a long time for a child. She had last seen him when she traveled home in February. He had now grown taller, but thinner. She had missed him more in September. She could not be with him on his fourth birthday.

Angela only realized she was in tears when she saw raindrops wet the well-swept ground below her. She wiped more tears as she held Babu's hand and they walked into the house.

Angela was glad to be home, though she was sad that Babu struggled to call her mum or mama, a term he effortlessly used whenever he needed Priscah's attention.

It was getting dark, Priscah switched on the lights and checked on the potatoes boiling on a charcoal stove for their supper. She had leftover vegetables from their lunch.

They sat at a table on one corner of the large room that served as the living and dining room. They ate as Angela listened to stories from Priscah until she could no longer keep her eyes open. They prayed together, said their good nights and went to bed.

Angela was more troubled when Babu refused to sleep in the same room with her. He vacated his bed for her and went to sleep in Priscah's room.

The next morning Babu refused to eat breakfast, which Angela realized was to do with his new clothes. The boy was afraid that the breakfast food might drop or spill and make his new clothes dirty. Babu's reaction was not strange. Wearing new clothes was a rare event for many children in the village. A new outfit, most often acquired over Easter or Christmas, could make one's stomach full, from joy.

Angela was aware that in the coming days village kids were likely to come – some from afar, to admire Babu's new clothes. Some of them would attempt to touch his clothes yet fear that their action may leave dirt on his new clothes.

Babu rarely had new clothes, except when he was a newborn baby, too young then to recall.

Before Angela left for the city when Babu was only two years old, she had raised him without an income. She did not receive any financial support from Luka her father, except for the food he bought for Priscah, which Angela benefitted from since she lived with her grandmother.

Luka, a manager at a hotel in their local town, had made it clear that he would not provide support to Angela. In his words, she had let him down when she became pregnant and could not proceed to university.

Having grown up in the village and worked in his local town, Luka had little information on the many rich and educated people in other towns and cities. He considered himself a village hero. Unlike many in his village, he worked in town and his son had qualified as a secondary school teacher from the national university. When Angela qualified to study at the national university too, Luka had looked forward to more pride, maybe elevation into an eldership position in his clan.

Angela had shouldered through the pregnancy, with some encouragement from Priscah, who had been like a mother to her for many years.

When Babu turned two, Priscah had encouraged Angela to go find a job to provide for her son. Priscah had volunteered to care for the child, feed him the same food her sons and other grandchildren gave her.

Angela had milked her social networks dry, telling everyone who cared to listen that she needed a job.

Brenda, her best friend from high school had introduced Angela to Cynthia, her aunty who worked as a housegirl in the city.

Cynthia was touched by Angela's story and had asked that Angela travel to the city and try a restaurant job where one of Cynthia's cousins worked.

Luckily for Babu that morning, Angela had bought some large bibs for him, like the ones Ronny's children used during breakfast, to protect their school uniforms.

Priscah watched as Angela went into her bedroom and returned carrying items. Priscah stared as Angela pushed the stretchy bib down Babu's head. "It will not hurt, it is made a little bit tight to fit well, protect your shirt," Angela explained.

The bib rested around his neck, covering the collar and top part of his shirt before it flowed down to his waist. Babu sat upright, like he had been dressed in a second new shirt, with his chin lifted high up so that the bib, which he must have thought was another new shirt, could be seen well.

Angela stepped back and admired Babu. "Grandma will be helping you to wear your bib only when you have your church clothes on. She will help you until you learn to do if for yourself," Angela said as she squeezed the two press-on buttons on the left side. She took one step to his right and pressed similar buttons.

All the while, Priscah was looking and wondering what Angela was up to, dressing Babu with a nice fitting new shirt and then spoiling the look with a smaller tight vest which should have sat in the inside of the shirt. She questioned if the city had confused Angela instead of enlightening her.

When Angela sat back on her chair, Priscah's eyes sank further into their sockets, making them appear smaller and inquisitive, as she said, "You have learned so much in the city, except that they wear vests inside, before shirts," as she pointed to the bib.

Angela smiled, sniffing back the tears dampening her eyes as she looked at the tiny structure of her son. Babu had a pronounced collar bone, a sign of lack of enough food for a child his age. The playful stage when children need to eat many times a day.

"The children I take care of use similar ones, they are called bibs," Angela said as she watched Babu leave his chair and walk outside. She called him, "Babu, where are you going? You need to eat your food."

"*Aiiya*, it is not a vest?" Priscah retorted.

Priscah waved Babu away. "He never goes far, only to your uncle's house to play with the children there." Priscah was referring to her younger son whose house was nearby. "I think he wants to show them his new clothes."

Babu walked back and sat down.

Priscah lifted her cup of millet porridge, which she preferred in place of tea. She replaced the cup on the table without taking a sip. "He is excited, let him go show his new clothes to your cousins, he will come back."

"He needs to eat." Angela turned to Babu. "Finish your bread and eggs, then go outside to play." She held back more words. Angela was afraid to say how thin Babu was but feared she would make her grandmother feel she was not doing a good job, feeding Babu using the money Angela sent to her.

Babu sat and picked the half-eaten bread from his plate. He had not eaten much, maybe from too much excitement.

Priscah watched Babu as he lifted the bread with both hands and took a large bite. She stretched her hand and touched one side of the bib. "This thing, what did you call it, *ebibu* looks new." Her wrinkled face furrowed more. "You have not become like some girls I hear of, who travel home with clothes of children they take care of."

Angela's eyes opened wider, wrinkling the skin on her forehead. She relaxed on remembering that Priscah was renowned in the village as the granny who always said what was in her mind. "The children I take care of are good children, and their father is good, I cannot take any of their belongings." She smiled. "He has money. If I ask, he would give me whatever item, no need for me to steal."

Priscah smoothed a hand down her new cotton skirt. "Sounds like a nice man. Has he found another woman?"

"I don't know. I have not seen him bring any woman home." Angela said, not wanting to imagine Ronny being with another woman.

She was jealous. She lifted the handbags she had brought from the bedroom when she went for the bib. "What do you think of this for cousin Stephanie, and this for Sarah? I will give some money to their mother to buy a gift of her choice for herself."

"The girls will look smart in their new sweaters and bags. But tell them not to run away from school." Priscah laughed. "They might assume that going to the city will get them same luck as you have."

Priscah stretched her slender neck towards the door, like she was making sure no one could hear her. She looked at Babu, then Angela. "I have a feeling that you found a good employer."

Angela nodded as she smoothed her hand through her son's head. "Grandma never leaves any hair to grow on your head. One day I will take both of you to visit the city." She watched the smile on Babu's face broaden.

He turned his head upwards, to get a better view of his mother. "And you will buy for me and Mama more clothes?"

"I bought these clothes from the city," she touched the sleeve of his light blue shirt, then his khaki trousers. "If I take you to the city, you will stay for two days then come back home."

Priscah touched Babu on the shoulder "Ask your mother where we will sleep. She herself stays in the house of her employer."

"I have a two-bedroom house, as big as your house." She spread out both arms. "Though I moved to the main house when my employer started traveling for work."

Babu stood up and looked at Priscah. "Mama," he lifted his empty plate closer to Priscah. "I am a good boy, may I go out now?"

Angela wanted to interject, ask Babu one more time to call her Mama. Maybe he would accept now that she had brought him new clothes and toys. Before she could pick the right words to use, she saw Priscah wave him away. "Remember to come back to finish your milk. I will give you more bread."

Angela and Priscah watched Babu as he walked to one corner of the house, picked one of the toy cars Angela brought for him and walked out of the house, his head held up. He went to Stephanie and Sarah's home.

Priscah turned back to Angela with a wry smile in her eyes. "Maybe my granddaughter has been married by her rich man, but she is afraid to tell me."

Angela laughed aloud. "*Nyanya*, my employer is a good man. But remember what I told you about me and men?" She turned to the doorway, like she had seen someone.

There was no one at the door. Angela had turned, afraid there would be someone nearby to hear their conversation. "I am done with men. All I want is to save money and go to university. Then one day you and Babu will come and we live together in the big city. *Nyanya*, I will soon take you to see the city."

"Have you told your *Tajiri* that you have a boy at home, or are you afraid he will lose interest in you?"

"As I told you, I am not looking for a man, and not my employer. *Nyanya*, I am there to work and earn money." She laughed.

"The man has fed you well. You have transformed into a woman. You could let him marry you."

Angela smiled as she watched Priscah lift her cup of millet porridge. She sipped and placed the cup on the table and said, "Girls eventually get married, and if you are already taking care of his children, what else is remaining?"

Angela picked up her cup and sipped tea, more out of her need to have more time to reflect on the words from her grandmother. She had caught Ronny many times staring at her and on a few occasions, he had told her that she was a nice person, he liked her. Her biggest fear was what had happened the last time she had been too close to a man. Babu was born – nine months later.

"When I go back next week, I will tell him about...," Angela pointed to the chair Babu had vacated without mentioning his name. "That way, he will lose any interest he has in me."

"That is not very clever. Waiting for him to like you before you tell him about your baby."

"*Nyanya*, stop building so many castles in the air. My plan is to save money, go to university and then get a decent job."

Priscah chuckled. "Why struggle, when all you need is money. You can marry a man with the money," she said, her eyes focused outside the house through the glass window.

Priscah watched as Clemencia, her daughter-in-law by her younger son's wife, walked into the house.

Angela stood up, greeted her aunty, walked to a nearby cupboard and returned carrying a cup and plate. "Auntie, I was going to come to your house after breakfast, but *Nyanya* here has endless stories."

"No need to worry," Clemencia said. "Babu is busy showing his friends how you pulled the bib down over his head. Come over for lunch, your older cousins will be home at that time."

Angela opened the paper with bread and put four slices on the plate. "How is uncle?"

"He is fine, busy as always."

Angela lifted the kettle and poured tea into the cup as she said, "*Nyanya*, tea for you or are you stuck with your porridge?"

Priscah lifted the cup to her mouth and sipped the last drops of porridge. She replaced the cup on the table. "Tea is for people in towns and cities."

"How much millet did you harvest in July?" Angela asked, diverting Priscah from talking about cities. She was afraid Priscah might talk about her employer and marriage.

Chapter 15

On the third day since her arrival, Angela left home, leaving Babu's cries behind her. The cries broke her heart, but her consolation was that she was coming back in the evening.

She had tried without success, to explain to him that she was going to town to meet with a friend. She would be back home in the evening.

Babu would not hear why Angela could not go with him if she was not leaving for the city. "You like to leave me here with Mama. You said you would take me and Mama to the city, now you leave us here," he cried.

"Babu, I promise I will be back in the evening. I will bring you cake to eat when you drink your milk," Angela said, wiping his tears as she sniffed back her own.

Angela wished she could cancel her appointment with Brenda who had traveled home from university for the Christmas holiday. She could not, she needed to talk with her friend, get her opinion on Ronny.

She boarded a *matatu* and traveled to town where she met with Brenda. They only broke their long hug after someone bumped into them in front of Mwalimu Hotel, their meeting venue.

They disentangled except for their hands, still tightly entwined.

Brenda watched the young man who came between them walk away as he flashed thumbs up. She chuckled. "We need to call that young man back, tell him how happy we are to see one another."

Angela waved her to no. "The only problem is that he might take our good gesture as an invitation to join us. Do you need anyone to come between our happiness?"

"No way," Brenda said as they stepped inside the hotel. Being only eleven in the morning on a working day, the place had many empty seats.

They chose a table by a window facing the street and sat on chairs facing each other.

Brenda touched Angela's hand. "Nice to meet after a long time. How have you been, and how is the man you have refused to love back?"

"I wonder why my best friend wishes me to marry a much older man, while she has a young one."

Brenda laughed, then stopped when she noticed two men at the far end of the restaurant turn in their direction.

With both hands resting on the table, she leaned towards Angela. "Whoever told to you that a man is old at thirty-six?"

She placed a finger across her mouth, like she was going to tell a secret that she did not want repeated. "Never mention this near my Mr. Mathew. There is a rumour that men are better when a little older than the woman."

"Whatever," Angela said before she waved a waiter to their table.

They ordered drinks. Angela asked for tea and *mandazi* while Brenda opted for fresh mango juice.

Brenda waited for the waiter to walk away before she said, "You need to visit me more often at university. Almost everyone has a man in their life. A fellow student, an employed boyfriend or husband, or an ATM to cater for their financial needs."

"Are you telling me there are girls already married? Are there any with children?"

"Some in comparable situations to yours, young mothers."

"Eeeh?" Angela wondered.

"Do you think you would have gone to work as a housegirl if your mother was alive? God rest her soul in peace. She would have screamed at you to proceed to university, then screamed at your father to pay the fees. He too would have screamed at her to take care of her grandchild."

Both ladies laughed.

A tear from Angela's eye landed on the table.

Brenda extended a hand to Angela's shoulder. "I am sorry for bringing sad memories into your cute face. All I was saying is that there are many students at university who have babies. You would not be alone."

Angela took a bite of her *mandazi* while staring at Brenda. "Are they married to men with three children?"

"You would be better off, sister. Imagine yourself married to Ronny, the heir to Henry Technologies. All you will do is give instructions to your many workers in the house, attend classes at university while he goes to his CEO office."

"I am employed as his housegirl. Who would do the work?"

"It goes without saying. Once you move to his bedroom, he will employ someone to work in the house while you are away at school."

Brenda scanned the restaurant, like she was making sure no one could hear them before she said, "Auntie Cynthia has been sharing some ideas with me since I took my Mathew to visit her. She told me that many good men would not mind who cleans their house, if you serve them breakfast, dinner and keep them warm in the night."

Angela chuckled as her face brightened with a smile. Her secret acknowledgement of what she had already noticed with Ronny. He had relaxed over the months, become more lenient with his children. He had changed from the man who used to shout even at his three-year-old son, to a friendlier father. She wondered if the cause was the delicious food that she served the family each breakfast and dinner, on time.

Angela bit a large piece of *mandazi*. She wanted to appear occupied, a chance to reflect. She questioned if Ronny's frequent mention of how good a job she was doing was another way to tell her that he liked her, had feelings for her. "What will people say if he made advances and I accepted?"

"Which people? The ones who are helping you take care of Babu or paying your university fees?" Brenda mocked.

"His relatives. His sister, her friends, his in-laws, my brother, my father, and you?" Angela finished the list and lifted her cup of tea to her mouth. She did not sip, she just held the cup in front of her nose, like she was hiding from Brenda.

"I would be happy for you. What would your sweet grandmother say?"

Angela giggled and placed the cup on the table. "My grandma is more nuts than you." She lowered her voice into a whisper. "You should have heard her tell me that the man has taken good care of me, so I should take care of him."

Brenda extended a hand to Angela, like she wanted to shake her hand, congratulate her. "Tell your grandmother she's my best friend." She chuckled. "Did you not see me stare as you approached? I avoided telling you that the man has brought happiness into your heart." She glanced over her shoulder and back to Angela. "You cannot hide it from showing on your smooth face, body curves and relaxed muscles."

Angela pitched Brenda's cheek softly. "Who looks curvier? Look at your figure eight."

Brenda laughed. "It will be hard to convince anyone that you are not already sleeping with your boss, your housemate."

Angela touched her lips before lifting her pointer finger upwards. "Take my word, I have never slept with the man. I just found happiness in taking care of some motherless kids. And I am paid well for the job."

She touched the remaining piece of her *mandazi* but did not pick it from the plate. "I perform my tasks, and no one shouts at me, calls me names like when I lived in the village. They treat me well, greet me, smile at me and say thank you. The kids give me hugs, they say sorry to me and to each other, they ask me questions, I assist them with their school homework. Their father seems happy with my work, and he defends me whenever his relatives or friends are mean to me."

"Really?" Brenda's eyes widened.

Angela glanced around before she said, "For your ears only. In August, two ladies brought themselves into the house. No," Angela grinned. "This is how it was. One lady was brought in by his sister and the other is his sister-in-law. Instead of competing amongst themselves, they wanted to fight with me for cooking the best meal for the family."

Brenda leaned in closer, like she did not want to miss a single word. "Who won?"

"None. His sister walked out with her friend, in protest. He called some of his children to spend the night in his bedroom." She chuckled. "I guess to show me that the sister-in-law in the guest bedroom, two doors away from his did not sleep in his bedroom."

"And then?" Brenda asked.

"We should leave. You are becoming too excited," Angela chuckled as she reached for her handbag on a nearby chair.

Brenda reached the bag first and pressed it to the chair. "You can't leave without narrating that nice story. Please," she begged.

"Why do you want to know so much?" Angela grinned. "The man offered to give me a hug, pleaded. I was not ready for that."

"Why do you say that the man has not made his feelings known to you?"

"He was worried that I would pack up and leave after his sister and sister-in-law kept referring to me as the housegirl." Her eyebrows pulled in. "Each time we meet, they want me to stay ten meters away from the family. Yet the man treats me like family."

"So why are you worried of what his relatives will say if the man is already on your side? Whatever they say will be his to handle. Your task will be to learn not to become a stepmother to his children."

"I can never be mean to any child, step or not. I am not that type."

All the previous glitter left Angela's face. "I believe in Karma. Blessings trickle down, my grandmother took care of me, she's taking care of my son while I take care of someone else's children. That could be the reason I am paid like I work in an office."

Angela placed a finger on her. "Don't tell anyone I am paid well."

Brenda looked at her wrist for time. "Sounds like you have a story for me. Let us order a meal before offices close for lunch and workers swarm this place." She touched Angela's arm. "You'll pay for our food. Looks like I should start saving money for my dress as a bride's girl. I volunteer myself as your best maid."

"I will pay for the food, because I will be your best maid when you say yes to Mathew. Make it happen soon."

"Mathew and I will have to first complete our study program and find jobs and save money. That will be long after your wedding."

"I like your optimism," Angela said as she picked up the plastic-covered menu, scanned the page and put it down. "Do you think Ronny would be interested in marrying me once he gets to know I have a child in the village?"

Angela was surprised by the instant sneer on Brenda's face before she spoke. "Which planet do you live on? Let's put it this way, would you be interested in marrying a man who has three children when you have only one?"

Angela did not respond. She could tell that Brenda was serious with her words. On reflection, she saw the sense in the question. Before she could think further, Brenda interrupted. "I cannot wait for January, to invite you to another session with Aunty Cynthia. That woman has too much wisdom to share."

People streamed in and out of the restaurant. It was past three o'clock when Angela and Brenda decided to leave.

Angela pulled a paper bag out of her handbag and handed it to Brenda. "My Christmas gift to you. Please pass my best regards to your parents, Auntie C and your Mathew, in no particular order."

She saw Brenda's eyes mist up on seeing the Michael Kors handbag.

Not wanting to give Brenda a chance to complain on the prohibitive cost of the bag, Angela took one step forward and cuddled her. "Nice bag for my best friend."

"Thank you, I am very touched." Brenda placed a hand on her chest and leaned closer to Angela's ear. "I don't want to ask why you spent so much money on me, good you had said you are paid well."

Angela placed a hand on Brenda's shoulder. "When you get back to Nairobi in January, please come with me we go buy a nice gift for Auntie C. Her job reference has transformed my life for the best."

They walked out of the restaurant and stopped at a nearby shop and bought bread and queen cakes.

In almost total silence, the two friends walked to the *matatu* terminus. They exchanged hugs again before each walked away, to find a *matatu* and travel to their different homes.

Angela was in deep thought for most of the journey. She reflected on some of Brenda's comments. That, together with those from her grandmother made Angela to ponder on what was riskier for her?

Should she welcome future good gestures from Ronny? Or remain focused on her job as a housegirl and one day realize he has married Dianna, or Judy or some other lady. Then to find that they would never stop referring to her as housegirl. Worse, the new wife could terminate her work contract and employ an older woman, a preference of many young wives in the city.

Chapter 16

"What is keeping you in the city for so long, what happened to university?" Luka asked.

Angela did not make eye contact with her father. She had not done it since she discovered she was pregnant. Today was her second visit since her arrival in the village four days ago.

She thought of telling him she needed to work, earn money to pay for her university education. But from his words, she sensed that he now was willing to pay her fees. But she needed his confirmation. "I need to save for my fees."

"Did you say you resigned your job at the restaurant? I have not heard of anyone making a saving from the salary of a housegirl."

Her employer paid her well. She was currently earning more than double her last salary at the restaurant.

Angela stared at an old family photo on the wall in front of her. Was her mother staring back at her, asking her not to reveal the much money she was paid.

Afraid of what Zippy, her stepmother, seated on a nearby chair might say, Angela decided not to tell her father what she earned, or that she had saved a good amount of money. "I will try. If my position of a housegirl does not work, I will find a different one."

Zippy's round face brightened up, her legs swinging from side to side. At a height of five-foot, her feet rarely reached the floor while seated on the dining chair. She had learned to elevate her height, always wore a thick head-scarf, tied high, to the top of her head.

Though she rarely wore high heeled shoes, Zippy was known to take quick short steps, chest forward and head held high, like she was always inspecting taller peo-ple. She said, "Before you know it, you will be a mother to many children. Girls who start off like you, getting chil-dren with unknown men never end well. They get more babies."

Instead of showing how agitated she was, Angela lifted her left hand to her forehead, feeling her warm face. "Mother, God has plans for all of us. If that is His for me, let it be."

She turned to her father, hoping that he would say something to protect her from the uncalled-for words from Zippy. She saw his mouth open, he said, "The other option is to get married to the father of your child. We can compel him to pay for you through university."

Angela looked at her hand, like she was looking for something on her fingers.

Luka raised his voice, "If you were interested in bet-tering yourself, by now you would have reported him to the authorities. You need to go to university."

Angela turned her eyes to the floor, reflective. Babu's father was still at university and did not have a source of income to support her. She would consult with her friends to establish if he had a girlfriend. She wouldn't be interested in him if he did. If he did not, maybe she could learn to love him, and he in turn learn to love her, and it wouldn't be a forced marriage after all.

She spoke without looking up. "I will find out where he is."

Zippy chuckled. "What are you saying, that you are not with him in the city? Does that mean you're already sleeping with different men?"

"Mother, you are embarrassing me in front of Dad."

Zippy laughed, mocking. "I assume embarrassment ended when your growing tummy revealed what you had been doing with men at an immature age."

Luka cleared his throat, stood and walked out of the house. "Did you say you will visit your brother on your way to the city? Come, call one of the workers to go harvest some bananas for you."

On her way out, Angela stared at Zippy. She could tell Zippy was not happy that the discussion had ended abruptly.

~~~~~~

Angela let her tears flow freely as she cuddled her son one more time. She could not believe that her one-week visit was over, and she was leaving Babu and Priscah behind, to return to the city.

As she wiped her tears, she questioned why she had turned down her brother's suggestion that she take her son to Nakuru. Joshua had said he would take Babu back to the village in the New Year. She had not given the idea much thought until now, when she found it hard to bid Babu goodbye.

At one point, she considered calling Ronny to extend her holiday. She changed her mind on recalling how he had tried to get her to forfeit her leave days in exchange for money. He needed her to be with the children while he attended the many company parties and other year-end events.

She gave up trying to stay, the reason to leave were more compelling, her job.

She showed her grandmother one more time how to use her old cell phone that she had brought for her.

From the corner of her eye, Angela noticed her cousins watch her with envy. She had a new Smartphone, and she was traveling back to the city.

More surprises came when Luka drove Angela to town from where she boarded a vehicle to Nakuru. Joshua picked her up from the bus station.

Angela was ecstatic to see that her brother had a personal car. Though not new, and nothing close to the many cars owned by her employer, it was a good car.

They loaded the bananas and vegetables that she brought along from the village.

Brother and sister shared many stories on their drive to Joshua's house near the high school where he was a Physics and Chemistry teacher.

"Dad does not appear happy," Angela said.

"How can you tell? He never shows his emotions." Joshua chuckled. "How is the wife, our new mother?"

"She turned down the money I gave her as a Christmas gift." Angela expressed her concern that their stepmother had remained the same bitter woman she was when their father married her, almost ten years ago.

"Based on what happened while you were in the village, it will be best if you removed Babu out of home. Think about it, we can bring him to Nakuru to be with his cousins."

"What about Grandma? Whom will she stay with? She is used to the boy."

Joshua tapped on the steering wheel. "At seventy-six, that woman is very old. She will be with her other grandchildren in the village."

He glanced at Angela and back to the road. "Or did you forget we are not her only grandchildren, though she brought us up."

"What I noticed is that she is used to being with Babu. It will be hard to take the boy away."

"She is old. Let Grandma be cared for now. Not to take care of great grandchildren."

Angela sensed that Joshua was giving a directive, not a suggestion. "I will think about it."

On arrival, Angela went inside the house and held a lively conversation with Florence, Joshua's wife.

~~~~~~

"Angie is back. Angie is here, Angie."

Mia, Betty and Nikko shouted from behind the short fence shielding the playground from the driveway.

They ran off, to the back entrance to the house and emerged at the living room windows facing the driveway.

Joseph parked the car on the driveway. He turned to the back seat where Angela was gathering her sweater and handbag. "You must be special. What makes the children chant your name that much?"

"They are naturally friendly kids, and I bake chocolate cake. I should bake one for your wife before Christmas."

Joseph stepped out of the car. "I will be waiting for the cake. Do you have your key, or do I call Ronny?"

"I left my key in the house. Who is in with the children?" Angela asked as the door opened, and Ronny walked out.

Ronny touched Angela's shoulder before he shook the hand she had extended to him.

She lowered herself to receive hugs from the children, while she answered Ronny's question on how everyone at home was doing.

Ronny moved away to talk with Joseph as Angela walked into the house with Mia, Betty and Nikko by her side. "You have all grown taller in the few days I have been away, what have you been eating?"

"We stayed with Grandma, Grandpa and went and stayed with Auntie Rose," Mia explained.

"Good. You must have had fun." Angela stopped and looked at each child before she spoke again. "I have been traveling all afternoon in a bus. I will go shower and then come and tell you about my grandmother."

The children waved her off at the family room as she proceeded to her bedroom.

Ronny was standing by the cooker preparing tea when Angela came into the kitchen after a shower and change of clothes.

He winked at her. "Nice to have you back. I ordered take away, you may rest tonight. How are the people you went to see at home, and your brother in Nakuru?"

"I was afraid my grandmother would get a heart attack from too much happiness, but sad that my son is forgetting me."

Angela stood still on realizing what she had just revealed. She wished she could retract her words or rewind the clock back to yesterday when she was still in Nakuru, discussing her son with her brother without any reservations. She wished she was dreaming and could wake up and continue with her normal life, of a housegirl.

Ronny frowned. "A husband I should know of?"

Angela blinked her misty eyes. "I am not married, never been married."

He smiled, then stopped immediately he saw the horror on Angela's eyes. "What happened to the father of your child?"

She sniffed back the tears in her eyes. "He walked away. He has never seen his son."

Ronny wondered what to tell his kids if they came to the kitchen and saw Angela in such a sorry state. He lowered his voice. "Please go to the laundry room and dry the tears. The kids might blame me." He said in a pleading voice.

Angela walked away as Ronny's phone rang. He answered the call from the security man informing him the food delivery had arrived.

Minutes later, Angela walked into the dining room without a trace of her earlier tears. She took her position at the table and served food. "Hi young man, did you miss me the way I missed you?" She touched Nikko's arm while asking.

He showed most of his milk teeth. "We went to Grandma. Grandpa gave me a red and white plane. I will show you." Nikko said as he turned back to his pizza.

The family ate dinner while discussing the children's visits with their grandparents, while Angela was away.

Angela was brief about her trip, promising the children more details the next day, after she was rested. She was glad that Ronny did not give any hint of what she had uttered. From the way he stared at her, she guessed he had a million questions for her.

After reading bedtime stories to the children, Ronny walked into the kitchen where Angela was rearranging dishes. She had found them stored on different shelves, not where she preferred them to be.

When Angela started work as the housegirl, she had rearranged items in the kitchen cupboards. She knew where dishes were, to the extent that she could open a cupboard and pick out a cup or a plate without looking. On her return to the kitchen that evening, a quick inspection of the cupboards revealed that some items had been moved around. She wanted to arrange the items before she resumed her normal duties the next day.

Ronny pulled a high stool and sat at the island. "Did you pass my greetings to your grandmother?"

"I did, to everyone. My grandmother was glad that I work for a good family. She was happy with the presents I took to them. Thank you."

He glanced towards the dining room, like he expected someone to walk in. He turned back to Angela. "I am not digging into your private life, but what happened to the father of your child?"

She continued to arrange the dishes. "It was my most stupid mistake, immediately after high school. I don't want to talk about my pain," she said as she stood on her toes to reach a top shelf. She stored a vegetable chopper.

"You can tell me more tomorrow. You must be tired after your travel, please go to bed." He slid off the stool and left the kitchen.

Part of the reason he walked away was he did not want Angela to see the happiness on his face. He had been worried since her travel home, assuming she had gone to visit a boyfriend. What else could have made her forgo extra pay to travel?

He had also worried that she might not return to her job. Afraid that some man in the village might convince her to marry him, as happened to many during the December festive season.

It was a relief to him when she confessed that she had traveled to see her child, and that she was not in touch with the father of her child.

Angela watched Ronny walk away, leaving his familiar scent behind. A smile engulfed her face, she liked how assured his step had grown over the months. It was that type of gait confident people have, like they are humming a song to guide them along. He turned to the living room, leaving her staring into emptiness.

She switched off the kitchen lights and went to her bedroom. She bit her lower lip, punishment to her mouth for failing her, mentioning her child without much thought. A new worry came to mind, that Ronny walked away from the kitchen because he was no longer interested in her on hearing that she had a child.

As she closed the bedroom door behind her, she heard a message drop into the phone which she had left in the room. She had one missed call and messages from her brother and Ronny. She had forgotten to call her brother upon arrival.

She checked the time and decided that it was too late to call back. She typed an SMS instead. "I traveled well. Sorry I missed your call. My phone was in the bedroom.

Everyone is fine. I will call you tomorrow, my regards to your family."

Next, she read the message from Ronny. "No need to get disturbed about your child. I am glad the father is not with you. Let us talk more later."

She read the message again and wondered what Ronny was trying to communicate. Was he happy that a man had used her then walked away? Was he happy that she was struggling alone, to raise a child? She felt the tears in her eyes and reminded herself that it was time to retire for the night.

She set a six o'clock alarm and switched off the lights. She was glad to be back to her bed, the soft mattress, so comfortable compared to the worn-out mattress at her grandmother's house.

Instead of her eyes closing for the night, she felt a stream of tears run down her cheeks.

Chapter 17

Christmas was exactly what Ronny had planned for until Rose showed up with her friend Christine, and worse, asked why Angela had returned from the village so soon.

To celebrate the return home of his father from medical treatment overseas, Ronny was hosting Christmas dinner at his house for close family members. He was overjoyed to see his father perform several tasks on his own.

Compared to five months ago, Henry could now walk short distances without support. His left hand which had been almost immobile from the stroke could now lift light objects such as a cup of tea or a piece of fruit.

His mother Pauline was assisting in food preparation as all her house workers were away, to celebrate Christmas with their families.

Ronny greeted Rose, "Good to see you kid sis. All food goes there." He kissed her on both cheeks, ushering her to place the fruit platter she had on the kitchen island where other food items were.

Christine walking right behind Rose received a similar greeting from Ronny. "Hi Christine, so good you could join us. How's your family?" he asked as he kissed her on each cheek.

The glitter on Christine's eyelashes revealed her sparkly eyes. "They are fine, enjoying the tiring parties of the season," she said as she placed a basket of assorted chocolates on the island.

Ronny wondered how Rose managed to pull Christine away from her family. What excuse Christine must have used to miss her family Christmas dinner, a lavish celebration they were known for in the city.

Christine was a daughter of a renowned politician in the country, and a church leader where the Henry family attended. Though Christine rarely turned up for service, always preferring to meet with her parents at the local members' club for Sunday lunch.

After greeting and welcoming Christine and Rose, Pauline said to Rose. "I am glad you are here. I need you to measure rice and start the rice cooker."

Rose looked at her Sandy Liang patterned shirt dress, all the colors somehow matched with her Suzanne Rae Mary Janes. "What if I watch over the children? Measurements can be done by Angela."

Pauline looked at Angela and back to Rose. "She is busy with the *ugali*, which will not cook well if she stops halfway."

Pauline was aware that Angela needed help with some tasks. Angela had prepared and cooked many dishes within two hours of their arrival from church. She had placed the goat meat she marinated the night before into the grill to roast. She whisked cake flour and covered it to rise then moved on and mixed flour for chapatti and rolled while frying them in a nearby cooking pan. She was now cooking *ugali* while Pauline fried green vegetables and chicken stew.

At one point, Pauline had asked Angela to take a break, otherwise she would collapse out of exhaustion. Angela had turned the offer down, saying she would take a break after dinner.

At four o'clock, Pauline stood at one end of the dining table and inspected the Christmas meal one more time. She was happy that within five hours of sorting, cutting, cooking and flipping food, there was enough for everyone to savour.

Angela walked into the family room and clapped to get the children's attention. "Kids, in case you have forgotten, today is Christmas, and food is ready. Come, time to eat."

Pauline went to the living room where Ronny, Robert, Henry, Christine, Rose, and Charles, Henry's cousin, were all engrossed in discussions on how various families celebrated Christmas in the city and village.

Pauline looked at Rose for a long moment before she asked her, "How are the children?" She then welcomed the rest of the group. "Come, Christmas meal is served at the table, unless you prefer to eat from here?" She said while looking at her husband.

Henry nodded as Ronny said, "Better if we all sit at the dining table, bring Christmas back to our house."

Ronny stood and watched his father struggle out of his chair, until he stood up without any assistance. Ronny followed behind as they walked to the dining room.

As the adults arrived in the dining room, the children washed hands and sat at one side of the table.

The day before, Ronny had extended the table to its full length of a twelve-seater and added four seats from the store.

Pauline said a prayer and welcomed all to enjoy the meal.

Betty picked a plate and called out, "Angie! I can't reach all the food, come."

Angela walked into the dining room.

Pauline who was serving food into Henry's plate paused and addressed Angela, "I will serve the children. You may go back."

"Mum, it is okay if Angela serves the children, she knows what they will eat," Ronny explained.

Angela walked back and served Betty.

Rose cleared her throat to attract Ronny's attention. "Are you trying to say Mum does not know how to serve children?"

Ronny stared at his sister with a smile on his face. He knew there would be chaos at the Christmas table if he asked Rose why she had served herself instead of serving the children first.

Pauline finished serving Henry and sat down. She watched as Angela served each child. Angela finished and left for the kitchen.

Ronny's eyes remained on Angela's back until she turned into the kitchen. He turned back to his food, aware that his mother and sister had noticed his gaze.

He had noticed the reaction of his sister as she watched Angela serve the children. He knew better not to call Angela back to the table to serve her food. He was also aware that she might refuse if he asked her to come.

Rose, seated between Christine and Robert, chatted with Christine who sat on her left-hand side. She occasionally asked the children if they were enjoying the food or wanted more.

The other people at the table engaged in a conversation on the booming retail business in December, the cause of the January slump in the economy.

Halfway through their meal, Ronny asked Christine to pass him a plate from a side table closer to where she sat. He served food, pushed his chair back and walked away into the kitchen. He placed the food in front of Angela who had sat at the far end of the kitchen. "Merry Christmas to our dear Angela. We miss you at the table," he said before he walked away.

Rose and Pauline watched Ronny until he was back on his chair. He sat down saying, "Good if we all eat at the same time. It's Christmas after all." He briefly joined in the discussion before asking Christine, "More food for you?"

She shook her head to no.

Ronny smiled, more from the relaxation he noticed on the face of his sister. He had asked to serve Christine out of courtesy, as the host.

After two hours of eating and chatting, the family went into the living room from where Pauline served dessert.

The people in the living room congregated into smaller groups. Pauline, Rose and Christine sat on one sofa. Robert conversed with Henry, while Ronny conversed with his uncle. The children watched the lights on the tree flicker in rhythm to the Christmas melodies.

Christine kept checking the gold hands of her watch until she received a message that her family driver had arrived. She stood up and waved to everyone in the room, "Merry Christmas to you all." She turned to Pauline. "My driver is here. I need to join my family in the remaining part of the celebration, the night party must be starting now."

All faces turned to Christine. Rose appeared to be surprised that Christine was leaving.

Christine had typed a message to her mother asking for a driver to pick her up. No one knew of her plan until she made the announcement.

Rose glanced at Ronny before her eyes darted back to Christine. "I hope you had some fun. Tomorrow, you and Ronny can meet at my house for the drinks you'll miss tonight."

Ronny was too astounded to comment on the plan made by Rose without consulting him. He smiled, after all Christine was leaving.

~~~~~~

It was past two in the morning when the last guests left.

Angela was pleased that she would now have some deserved rest. That was until she checked her phone which she had left in the bedroom all day.

She had three missed calls from her brother and one from Stephanie her cousin. She checked time on the phone and wondered if she should return the missed calls at that time of night.

While thinking on whom to call, between her brother and cousin, she heard her phone ping with a new message. More anxiety as she clicked the inbox and noticed that she had more SMS messages that she had failed to take note of.

The message at the top was from Ronny. "Good night my dear. I am pleased you served our visitors well. Mum was impressed."

She clicked the next message, from Joshua. "Hope your phone works. Call me before I travel home tomorrow."

The phone dropped out of her hand. Her first thought was there was an emergency at home. What else could make Joshua want to travel on short notice. He had made it clear that his family would stay in Nakuru over Christmas. She felt cold sweat on her warm forehead. She was worried.

"God have mercy," she said as she stretched and picked up the phone from where it had landed on the carpet next to her feet.

She could hear her heart pounding in her chest as she read an SMS from Stephanie. "Hi. Hope you had a good Christmas day. *Nyanya* has been crying all day, someone tried to take Babu from her at church, Christmas mass."

"Uuuuuuiii," Angela screamed before she could stop it. She lifted a hand to her mouth to muffle the sound, to stop herself from waking up the children in nearby bedrooms.

She dialed Stephanie's number and listened through the rings, as tears streamed down her cheeks.

She disconnected the call and dialed again, not wanting to give up, in case her son had been taken away by whoever.

Stephanie answered the call on Angela's fourth trial. "Is Babu at home, is he okay?" Angela did not waste time on greetings.

"Mmhhh," Stephanie grumbled. "Waking me up, you will wake the boy up. *Nyanya* was very scared, Mum brought Babu to our house. Go to sleep."

Angela heard Stephanie end the phone call.

She exhaled, was relieved, the was better than what she was expecting to hear. She took another look at her phone in case she had more messages.

She thought of calling her brother but quickly decided not to. Three o'clock was too early in the morning to wake his family up.

Angela cried herself to sleep, wondering who could have tried to take her son. She tried to find a reason. Maybe it was the smart clothes she bought for him from the city. Or was it someone who had seen her looking well-groomed and thought she had a lot of money? Was it someone who needed money for Christmas, imagined that the boy's parents were rich? By taking the boy, the parents would give money to get him back.

More fear gripped her as she thought of how she had no money to give, especially if the person asked for millions, far more money than she had in her savings account.

Angela lifted her heavy head from the pillow with the first ring of her alarm at six in the morning. She threw her blankets back and walked to the bathroom and brushed her teeth. She was thoughtful of what to do next.

Back in the bedroom, she lifted her reluctant fingers and pressed her brother's name on her contact list.

Joshua answered on the second ring. "I thought you had lost your phone, and I do not have the phone number of your boss."

"What happened to my boy?" Angela asked, ignoring what Joshua had said.

"The boy is fine. After talking with *Nyanya*, Dad, and a few people, your secret is out."

Angela did not ask what Joshua meant by *your secret is out*. She preferred to wait and hear whatever explanation he had about her son.

Joshua broke the silence that was ensuring. "The father of your boy and his mother wanted to have Babu with them for Christmas."

The phone dropped onto the pillow on the bed. Angela's vision blurred by numerous shiny stars, but she could still hear the voice of her brother.

Minutes later, she touched her face, to be sure that she was awake and not dreaming.

The phone dropped to the floor. She picked it up, hoping that it did not break. She needed it, to call and ask more about her son.

She saw a missed call from Joshua. She dialed, and he answered on the first ring and said, "Good, you are still there. Please give me the phone number of your employer. I'm finding it hard to hold a conversation with you."

The words caught Angela's full attention. No way would she give Ronny's telephone number before asking him, and not today.

She still needed to come up with a strategy on how to face Ronny that morning. She was yet to comprehend why he gave her presents when the family exchanged Christmas gifts. She had unwrapped her gift after the visitors left because Ronny's children refused to go to bed before seeing her gift.

Angela had sat and taken her time to unwrap the gift, afraid to see what was inside, more afraid that the children sat and waited, their eyes focused on the gift. Ronny had given her a bottle of Arizona perfume by Proenza and a box of Swiss chocolates.

She needed time to think on what to do with the gifts and what to say to Ronny. She could thank him, or, not mention the gifts at all.

"The number is saved in my phone. I can check it for you after we talk," Angela said.

She listened as Joshua spoke. "Next time you visit home, avoid all those fancy clothes, toy cars and other presents for everyone. Your future mother-in-law believes you have too much money and wants some via the boy."

Angela blinked fast, many times, like she was trying to hear with her eyes instead of her ears.

"Mmhhh!" was her only response, which encouraged Joshua to say more.

"I assume you have her phone number, your mother-in-law. Call her or send her money." He chuckled, "You, rich girl."

Angela wanted to throw her phone at the wall, the easier way to make her brother know the pain he had brought to her heart. Instead, she summoned all the energy left in her weak body. "Maybe I have not told you before. That woman never came once to see me as I suffered through the pregnancy. She never came to see the baby. I am surprised that all along she knew her son was a father."

Joshua chuckled. "Now you have money."

"I am just a housegirl, trying to get myself to university."

"Send me the phone number of your boss. I am headed out and will talk with you after I return with Babu from the village."

"Thanks," she whispered into the phone.

"Do not call me until I am back. Do me another favour."

"Yes?"

She was more scared when Joshua said in a raised voice. "Do not call or talk with anyone at home. If you do, the boy could be taken away before I arrive." He ended the call.

Angela stared at her phone. She wondered what to do next, how to spend the time until Joshua called back.

She folded her fingers, one by one, counting. It would take a minimum of six hours for Joshua to travel to the village and back if he found public transport. Or was he going to drive his car the two hundred and ten kilometers to the village? Four hundred and twenty for the return journey.

Angela picked up her phone. She wanted to call and ask if she could send him money for transport or fuel. She changed her mind on recalling how stern he had sounded when asking her not to call him. He was the one to call her.

She went to the bathroom to shower. While there, she resolved that the only way to forget about the many hours she had to wait, was to make herself busy.

Angela felt dizzy as she walked into the kitchen. A feeling she attributed to lack of enough sleep and the thoughts tormenting her mind.

Staying busy was the answer. She whisked millet porridge, left it to simmer while she arranged breakfast on a tray - potatoes, milk, cereal and bowls for the children. She decided that it would not hurt if the children missed eggs, fresh juice and other breakfast necessities just once.

Angela went back to her bedroom at seven-forty in the morning. She needed to call more relatives while she waited for Ronny to wake up.

The night before Ronny had suggested that everyone sleep late the next morning and wake up after ten. She edged towards her bed. She needed to lay down, for she felt the skin on her forehead pulling tight. She had a headache and her legs felt wobbly.

Chapter 18

Ronny hit his alarm clock to stop at eight. He had set an earlier alarm. His plan was to be in the kitchen before Angela and prepare breakfast for the family. His way of showing gratitude for all the work she had done in the last eight months, taking care of him and his children.

He stayed in bed long after his alarm had gone off, reflecting on the twenty months gone since the burial of his wife.

Sorry that they had celebrated their second Christmas without her, he rested his right hand on his chest, closer to his heart, he thought of the friends and family members who had helped him wade through the tough times.

He appreciated how resilient his children had been, learning to live without a mother. They had talked less and less of their mother. He was unnerved by the thought. He questioned why it took so few months, less than two years for children to forget their lost parent. He then excused them, on remembering some people mentioning that the children, being young, could recover faster than him, especially if they received loving and consistent care in their daily life.

On several occasions, some of his relatives and friends had urged him to marry sooner, find a new wife to take care of the children. Their reasoning was that once they got older, the children would outgrow the need for a mother's care. Then he would have a challenge of convincing them otherwise if he ever decided to marry later.

In the last few months, he had felt the need for a woman in his life. He attributed part of the feelings to his life getting back to some normality–his children were happy, so he was able to spend time reflecting on his life, his wellbeing, his needs.

Reflecting on the way his mother provided care to his father, before and after he suffered the stroke, Ronny worried. Who would provide such loving care to him if he was incapacitated by a stroke or any other illness?

He needed to find himself a wife, before his sister delivered one to his bedroom. He was convinced she would do that. She had tried many times in the past, the latest being less than twenty-four hours ago when she turned up with Christine at the family Christmas party.

He looked at his bedside clock and heaved himself out of bed.

While shaving, he checked himself in the mirror and smiled, acknowledging that he still looked youthful enough to find a young wife. He stopped smoothing the shaver on his face. What qualities would he be looking for in his next wife?

For his first wife, he had focused on what many of his friends and age mates did. He had spent time analyzing the many girls in his social circles, wanting to compete and win the girl coveted by his friends. Ronny had added two criteria to his list: the girl had to show in public that she loved him, and mention children as part of her future dreams. Bella had come to the top of his list.

His love for Bella had grown with time. He had loved her more when she accepted to get pregnant for a third time. He knew she would do it for child number four and even five. He was a happy man and had successfully discouraged Bella from going back to her job after Mia was born.

Having grown up in a small family, Ronny wanted many children in his life. He had never stopped imagining how interesting life would have been if he had brothers and more sisters. Knowing there was no way he could influence the decision of his parents about children, he had looked forward to having many children of his own.

There was enough money in the Henry family to provide for the needs of many children in terms of house workers, best food, education, medical care and holidays.

Acknowledging that he now had three beautiful and well-behaved children, he wondered what else to look for if he married again. "Someone who would love and care for the children," he said aloud, then tilted his head towards the bathroom door, wondering what he would give her in return. He thought of how short life could be, he needed to love more, let people in his life know he loved them.

Back to the mirror, he contemplated on which of the single women he knew would fit into what he would be looking for. He crossed out Judy and Christine from his mental list. They were too busy loving themselves, flying out to international fashion shows. They would never have time to focus on what was going on in the house or be with the children.

In November, a month ago, Mia and Betty turned a year older, nine and seven respectively. In December, Nikko turned four. Ronny and Bella had planned the birth of their children well, to turn a year older before the school year in January. Many competitive schools admitted students based on year and month of birth, - neither too old nor too young for a class.

In less than five years, Mia would be a teenager, then Betty. Teenage age hood is; an unstable period in life when they will need a parent figure to help comfort and anchor them. Would he be there for them while he worked hard as CEO of Henry Technologies Inc.?

Ronny had noticed that part of his father's healing depended on the success of the company. Henry had put in a lot of energy and time, to grow the company from the ground up. He would not want to see it become less successful because of his medical condition.

As Ronny inspected his now clean-shaven face, the name Dianna flashed through his mind. He told himself that she would be a burden, not only to him, but to any worker in the house. Fear gripped him with the thought that if Dianna was to come to his house with some sort of authority, as his wife or even just to live with his children, he was sure that she would show Angela to the door within the hour of her arrival.

Thinking of Angela, Ronny asked himself why he had not added her to his list. She was already taking care of his children, and him. She went out with a driver and bought groceries and prepared food for the family. She was home every Wednesday when the commercial workers came in to clean the house and do laundry. She made sure the children completed their homework, showered, ate and went to bed on time. She joined in their play time whenever time allowed. And she now did his laundry. What if he convinced her to cross over, be his wife?

He brushed and rinsed his mouth. Reminded himself that he needed to plan well before approaching her. There were chances she would turn his request down, then scamper out of his house. She had made it clear to him that her focus was to save money for her university education, though now he knew that her need for money included to provide for her son.

He pulled on a faded pair of blue men's Levis and a fitted Hugo black Polo. Satisfied with his physical appearance, he hoped that preparing that day's breakfast could also help convince Angela that he cared.

He stopped halfway as he approached the dining room. It was only a few minutes past nine and Angela had prepared breakfast and set the table.

He increased his stride towards the kitchen, ready to hug her for a morning greeting. If she objected, he would explain that the hug was out of gratitude for her devotion to her work for the family.

More surprises awaited him. There was quietness in the kitchen and the rest of the house.

Back in the dining room, he noticed that there was no tea, juice or eggs or sausage. He gave Angela credit for not overworking herself that morning, to cook the usual full breakfast.

He would go to the kitchen and prepare tea after he ate breakfast. He had noticed that she never missed drinking a cup of tea each morning.

~~~~~~

After setting tea and boiled eggs on the table, Ronny saw his children stream to the dining table, one by one. All in their PJs.

The children looked around and asked where Angela was.

Ronny had a quick excuse for her. "Let her sleep, she must be tired from all the work she did yesterday. We can wake her up at lunch time."

By mid-day, Ronny was getting worried if Angela was fine, or even, if she was still in the house. He sent an SMS, "Good afternoon Angie, sorry for overworking you yesterday. If you're hungry we can bring you some food in bed."

He waited, taking frequent glances at his phone. There was no response and there was no Angela.

At one o'clock he walked into the kitchen to reheat leftover food for their lunch. While in the kitchen, he called Mia. "Please go check on Angela in her bedroom, but do not wake her up."

Mia ran back to the kitchen in less than three minutes. "She is fast asleep, on top of her duvet. Is it okay if I go cover her without waking her up?"

"Let her sleep. Maybe she felt the December warmth and decided not to cover herself," he said.

Mia went to the kitchen drawer where tablemats were stored. "I will set the table while you heat up the food."

Ronny did not say yes or no. He was happy that his children, under Angela's guidance, were learning to do some chores within the house. That simple thought warmed his heart for Angela. There and then, he wanted Angela to stay on, be part of his family, be his wife.

During lunch, Nikko once again noticed Angela's absence. "Today I have all this space to myself," as he pointed at the empty dining seats on his left and right side. "Where is Angie to sit here?" pointing to the chair on his right.

Ronny reassured the children, told them Angela was enjoying her off day in her room. "I will go check on her after lunch, to find out if she wants to eat," he said.

The family finished eating, cleared the table and loaded the dishwasher before Ronny told his children,

"Choose one, go bathe and change from your PJs or watch TV while I go do some work in my office."

"TV," was the uniform choice.

Though he did not tell them, TV was the response he wanted to hear. All the children being at one location would give him the reassurance and courage he needed to walk into Angela's room. He had never been to her bedroom since she moved in.

It was approaching two o'clock and she had not appeared, even out of hunger, unless she had eaten enough food when she prepared breakfast.

He knocked on Angela's door softly, like the door hurt. He knocked twice. When he did not receive a response, he pressed the knob slowly and walked inside. There she lay, asleep.

He was startled by the vibration from her phone on the bedside table. He watched the name Brother Joshua dance on the screen until it stopped. When he saw the phone vibrate a third time, he assumed that Joshua could have tried all morning to reach Angela. He might worry that she had not answered his calls.

Ronny answered the phone while he touched her shoulder, to wake her up.

"Ronny speaking. I walked in to check on Angela and found her asleep and saw you struggling to reach her. Is everything okay?"

Ronny asked the last part of the question as the person on the other side asked the same.

"Yes, she could be tired, she worked all day yesterday serving visitors." Ronny said as he saw Angela open her eyes. He continued to explain. "She has been in her bedroom the entire day, the reason I just walked in to check if she was fine. She is now awake," he said while looking at Angela. "Your brother," he said as he pointed to her phone on his ear.

"Tell her not to worry. The boy is okay. We are back in Nakuru," Joshua said.

Ronny's round eyes widened as he handed the phone to Angela who had stood up. He asked her, "Was there a problem? I wish you had told me."

She took the phone and put it to her ear while looking at him.

He could tell that she wanted him to leave the room. He decided to stay. If he left, he would have no excuse to come back, and that would mean not knowing what the problem was with her son.

He walked to her dresser table near the window and sat on a stool, aware of Angela's eyes following him.

His eyes remained focused on her as she uttered many "okays" into the phone.

Ronny relaxed as he saw the expression on her face change, more relaxed before she said, "Thanks. I will call you later to talk." She ended the call and turned to Ronny. "Where are the children?"

"They are okay, watching TV. They were worried about you, so I came to check if you were well. It was becoming tough for us to continue with the day without knowing if you were fine, maybe we overworked you yesterday."

He looked out the window. "Sorry that I answered your phone. It worried me when I saw three successive calls with your brother's name on the screen. I thought he could be in some sort of distress, an emergency." He turned her direction, "Is everything, everyone okay at home?"

Angela took one step back and sat at the edge of her bed. "I have no idea why God is trying to punish me, when I have been so good."

"I can attest to that."

She continued, like he had not interrupted. "When I thought my life was getting better, God sends people who claim to be family, to take my son."

Ronny jerked out of the seat and went closer to Angela. "Did someone try to kidnap your son? Is he fine in Nakuru?"

Angela nodded as she wiped tears. She stood up.

Ronny extended his phone to her, "I do not want to stress you more, please dial your brother, so I can speak with him."

She took the phone and punched in ten-digits and handed the phone back to Ronny.

He did not accept the phone. "Tell him you dialed for me."

She looked at him as she talked into the phone. "Joshua. Talk with my boss while I go eat something. Supper was my last meal." She handed the phone to Ronny and walked away, into her bathroom and closed the door behind her.

Ronny walked out of the bedroom while talking with Joshua. He introduced himself, praised Angela for the excellent job she had done thus far. On reaching the family room, he sat down on the sofa while he talked.

When the children glared at him, like he was interrupting their enjoyment of the TV program, he stood up. He had wanted the children to take note that he had left Angela's bedroom. He waved at them and walked away to his office.

Twenty-five minutes later, Ronny shook his head as he uttered bye, ended the call and placed his phone on the desk.

He paced the room, he needed to think. What would he say to Angela if she asked to travel to Nakuru or to her village? What if she said she would resign from being a housegirl, to take care of her son?

Though Joshua had reassured Ronny that Babu was safe and would now live with his family in Nakuru, he was not sure if Angela would be comfortable with that. He hoped she would.

Pausing by the window, he looked outside without registering whatever was out in the trees.

He walked to the living room, disarmed the house and walked outside. He ended up at the main gate into the compound where he chatted with the security man. Noting that the guard was different from the one of yesterday, he asked him about Christmas and how his family celebrated.

Back in the house, he found the children had showered and changed into different pajamas, and Angela was in the kitchen cooking. "I was going to call the food delivery people, we could leave the kitchen to rest till tomorrow, or the day after." He said, aware that he was struggling to start a conversation with her. It was hard to guess her mood from the neutral expression on her face.

She stirred whatever she was cooking. "Cooking is my next best thing, unless you don't like the food."

He raised both hands. "Say the opposite of that." He pulled a stool and sat down. "Thanks for letting me speak with your brother. That must have been a scare, your son. Good that everything is okay now."

She paused from stirring the pasta. "Nothing is okay if someone wants to abduct my child."

Ronny noticed her agitation before he said, "Joshua said the boy's father is already married. His mother has no right to take your son without his or your consent."

Her eyebrows pulled in. "Whose consent? A person who has no idea what his son looks like? I even wonder if he knows my son's name."

A smile appeared on Ronny's face, which he could again tell got her agitated. He wished there was a way to tell her what was making him happy.

The moment Angela revealed that there was no relationship between her and the father of her son, and that the man had never expressed any interest in the boy, made him optimistic that she would accept to marry him. He would take them in, mother and son. "What if you tell him the boy is not his?"

Ronny regretted the words as he saw her stand still and address him. "I am not what you think of me. I have never slept with another man, if that is what you thought." She stared, made eye contact. "Why would I tell a lie, when I am not a liar?"

She turned back to the cooker, picked a tin and emptied pasta sauce into the cooking pasta. She threw the empty tin on a countertop. The tin landed, then fell and rolled over. Angela did not appear to take note as the tin rolled on the granite countertop and stopped near the sink.

Ronny watched her. He tasted his words, trying hard to get them right this time. "I am sorry. I should have not said that. What I wanted to communicate was that there's a difference between being a father and being a dad."

He looked at her to gauge the expression on her face before he uttered his next words. "Do not worry, you already have all legal rights to your son. Whose name was he registered in, on the birth certificate?"

"My father's, I made him like my little brother."

His face brightened up again. "Means I can have both of you, if you allow me," he said as he stepped down from the stool and walked her direction.

Angela watched him.

He stopped and leaned against a cupboard near her and crossed arms against his chest.

She turned her attention back to the food. She was still infuriated by what had happened to her son. She wished there was a way she could shout at Sabrina, the woman who had tried to take him.

Angela wished Ronny could allow her to travel home, go tell Sabrina the many words in her head. She would then travel back to the city and continue with her job, which she needed now more than ever.

Her future salary would be sub-divided into three; some money to her grandmother, money to her brother for the care of her son, and some money to her savings account for her university education.

Soon she would need more money to pay school fees for her son. Schools in towns and cities required children to attend nursery school for admission into class one. Babu would attend the same private school his cousin Dave, Joshua's son, attended.

Angela set dinner on the table. She was convinced that her son would be safe under the care of her brother. What she needed was to work hard, earn the money she needed now, more than ever before.

Chapter 19

The family was having breakfast when Ronny exhaled loudly. He could tell that Angela was no longer herself, one day after Anne, his mother-in-law arrived in his house.

Ronny worried what Dianna might have said to Angela when she visited, to bring her mother to his house.

Angela glanced at Ronny before she put the cup she had lifted back on the table, without taking a sip of tea.

Ronny was thoughtful, juggling ideas in his head on how best to tell Angela he loved her and ask her to marry him.

A good strategy was what he needed. One wrong word and he might scare her into packing her bag and leaving. He was aware that she was competent enough to find another a position in the city, but he might never find someone to replace her as his efficient housegirl, and the wife he wanted to make her.

And now his mother-in-law had come to visit until the New Year, four days away.

He felt okay when he thought of the opportunity the presence of Anne afforded him. He could leave the children with Anne in the house and take Angela out for dinner. But that would drive Anne crazy. She was still hopeful that Ronny would welcome Dianna, to live with him, be his wife and take care of her sister's children.

After breakfast, Ronny was the first one to leave his chair. He walked around the table to reach the side of Nikko who sat between Angela and Anne.

Ronny stood between Angela and Nikko's chairs. He intentionally brushed his thigh against Angela's shoulder as he softly poked Nikko's shoulder.

Nikko raised his head upwards for a better view of his father. "Dad wants to fight now," he sniggered as Ronny shifted his hand to Nikko's armpit.

Nikko slipped off his chair. Ronny was quick to grab him, and in the process, his hips pushed on Angela's arm.

Ronny supported Nikko on his feet and handed him his breakfast bowl and cup. "Today you will carry your dishes to the kitchen. I will show you where to place them," he said as he stretched to the opposite side of the table and picked his used dishes.

Father and son walked to the kitchen.

Angela, Mia and Betty watched them before Betty said. "Nice, Dad. Not only the girls should be carrying dishes to the kitchen."

She stood, picked up her dishes and turned to Anne. "Grandma, I will carry your dishes." She arranged the smaller ones on top of the larger ones and placed them on a tray. "Grandma, did you say we can go outside and enjoy the morning sun?"

Anne nodded. She had a constant smile on her wrinkled face as she watched Mia and Angela gather the remaining dishes from the dining table. She stared as they walked to the kitchen. Anne shook her head and mumbled, "She overworks my grandchildren."

Mia and Betty ran back to the dining room. Mia went and held Anne by the arm. "Grandma come we go sit by the guava trees. I like to watch birds as they get food for their chicks."

Betty walked ahead and opened the kitchen door, she let Mia and Anne walk ahead.

Nikko, who had been busy helping his father arrange dishes in the dishwasher, looked over his shoulder to see the kitchen door close behind Betty.

"I want to go outside, to ride my bike." He screamed as he let the spoons in his hands drop to the floor. He ran to the door, held the doorknob and looked back into the kitchen. "Dad, the door has refused to open for me."

Ronny opened the door and Nikko went outside. Ronny watched until Nikko caught up with his sisters and grandmother.

He closed the door and walked back to the kitchen. An opportunity had availed itself, he would be foolish not to maximize it.

Ronny hastened his stride towards the dishwasher where Angela was loading the remaining dishes. He stood very close to her and crossed arms on his chest. "I am not happy."

His words prompted Angela to tilt her neck upwards for a better glimpse of him. He completed the sentence, "Loading the dishes was my task today. You need a good rest before the new year, next week," he said as the smile on his face widened.

He noticed that Angela had received his words well. She grinned. "Thanks. You've already done too much of my work, carrying plates from the table."

She added a cube of dish washer detergent, touched the appropriate buttons and the machine started the wash cycle. From the corner of her eye, she saw that Ronny was gawking.

"I wish I could help you more. Please give me a chance," he said.

Noticing the change of expression on Angela's face, he took steps backwards, reached the island, pulled a stool and popped himself up. He leaned with his hands on the countertop. "I mean it, you need to have a good rest before schools open."

"You could be right." As soon as she uttered the words, she lifted a hand to her mouth, baffled, for admitting to her employer that she needed a break from her regular job. Though she felt the need for a break, even travel to Nakuru to attest that her son was fine, not injured physically or psychologically, she was still scared to admit it.

Ronny stretched his neck to one side of the kitchen windows, like he was ascertaining that there was no one nearby. He turned back to Angela who was busy wiping kitchen countertops, "I am thinking of a two-day get away with the children, down the Rift Valley. Would you like to join us?"

"Not really. I will stay here with Anne while you are away," she said without looking up.

"What if I need help, someone to mind the children, now and then?"

She stopped wiping and looked at him, "Would their grandmother do?"

He shook his head. "She came to visit the children, not drive around with me. Anyway, she will leave soon, once she realizes I am not in favour of her plan."

"Plan?" Angela sneered.

"How has it been, between you and her?"

"Nothing to report about. She mentioned that Dianna will come in tomorrow."

Ronny remained quiet for a short while. His mind was running at top speed as he tried to think of how to handle the arrival of Dianna. "Let's all drive to Nakuru tomorrow. You may come with us to our hotel, or we drop you at your brother's if that's what you prefer?"

He felt Angela's arms around his broad shoulders while she uttered, "thank you," many times.

Ronny sought her face and kissed her on the cheek.

She pulled away saying, "Sorry. What did I just do? Forgive me. I will never do that again." She walked out of the kitchen to the family room.

Ronny slipped down from the stool and followed her. "Why are you sorry? I am not," he said.

She halted her step and turned his direction. "I understand if you are not sorry. Please forgive me and let me continue to work for pay, for the children," she said before she walked on.

She stopped at the children's study area and rearranged some books to new positions.

Ronny scrutinized her. He saw that she was frightened, not focused at all on what she was doing, just fumbling.

"Angie, listen to me."

She paused, stood still, her arms hanging to her front side.

Ronny felt pity at how scared she appeared. He knew she worried that he could dismiss her for hugging him. He wished she realized how he loved the hug, the feeling it brought to his body.

He walked the remaining steps between them and reached her. Held her by the waist and pulled her closer to his body. "Let me do likewise, that way both of us will be guilty, forgiving and loving." His mouth covered hers with a kiss, quelled whatever she had tried to say.

He released her, and he took one step back. "I have nothing to complain about, I hope it is the same with you." He shoved both hands into his trouser pockets. "Please stop looking so scared, I will not do anything without your interest and consent."

Angela lifted a hand and wiped her tears as she smiled. "Thanks for letting me have my job. You confused me. It was too good to be true when you offered me the chance to visit my son."

She turned back to the study table and touched the computer keyboard, though the computer was off. "You don't know what that means to me. I can go visit him, even for one hour," her smile broadened. "I promise to come back whenever you want me to, please."

Ronny closed the little space between them and spread his arms out. "Please accept this, nothing but to lessen the pain you have."

Angela fell into his open arms and rested her head on his shoulder as tears flowed down her cheeks. He leaned back from her, placed two fingers below her chin and lifted her head to have a better view of her face. "I wish you could let me wipe all those tears away." He kissed her.

He felt her body relax before she opened her lips and returned his kiss. He tightened his hold on her back and pressed his body more to hers.

She must have panicked, maybe afraid that Anne and the children could walk into the house any time. She placed a hand on his chest and pushed him away as she took one step backwards. "I will be okay. Go check on the children while I gather clothes, to put in the laundry machine."

Angela was happy and frightened at the same time, she needed something to distract them away from another embrace.

On regular days, she did not clean the house or do laundry, except her clothes and Ronny's. There was a commercial company contracted to do the job, but they won't be coming until after the New Year.

The cleaners came in every Wednesday to clean carpets, windows and polish the woodwork. A laundry lady spent hours in the laundry room, washing and ironing the children's clothes.

All that Angela did was take laundry baskets filled with used clothes from each of the bedrooms into the laundry room.

A woman in her fifties drove in with other workers. She was dressed like she was going to work in a big office in town. She changed into cream overalls and flat shoes before loading clothes into the machine. She spent time loading the washing machine, shifting clothes into the dryer. From the dyer she ironed the clothes and arranged them on hangers in the clothes trolley or folded and arranged them on the folding table.

When the team of workers left the house, Angela took the clean clothes back into individual bedrooms and arranged them in wardrobes. She stored the smaller clothing items such as panties, underwear, vests and socks in drawers.

Each Thursday Angela arranged items in Ronny's bathroom before the evening cleaning by the set Rumba. She hauled his laundry basket to the laundry room and let the machines run. By lunch time she would have ironed and arranged the bedsheets, vests, underwear, socks and t-shirts in his wardrobe. She still had no idea who cleaned his shirts and suites.

On Friday, she carried her clothes to the laundry room, washed and ironed them.

Ronny coughed to get her attention. When he did, he lowered his eyes to his groin, adjusted himself before he walked away, the direction of his bedroom.

Angela stared until he turned the corner.

She released a breath, went to the kitchen and sat at one far end. She needed some minutes to catch her breath, let her pounding heartbeat settle. She worried why her heart raced, yet she had a nice feeling in her lower stomach.

Was it the kiss, or the fear that someone would have walked into the house to find her in Ronny's arms?

She mumbled to herself. "He's not a bad man, he will let me see my son. I will be a better housegirl." She chuckled. "Whatever the outside world brings, I will find a way around any forces."

Chapter 20

Angela had a new wave of energy as she lifted the tray filled with lunch dishes and walked into the dining room. She wasn't sure if her happy feeling was because she would be traveling to see her son, or from the kiss.

Within two and half hours, she had carried four laundry baskets to the laundry room and loaded the washer, one basket at a time. The cleaners were away until the New Year.

While the machines washed, she stayed in the kitchen preparing lunch. She responded to each *ndeeee, ndeee* of the bell from the laundry room.

After placing the final food item on the dining table, she went to the laundry room and put in the third load of clothes into the washer.

She walked to the kitchen door, opened and scanned the front side of the compound.

Spotting Nikko on his bicycle, she called out, "Nikko."

He turned and looked back as the front wheel made an abrupt turn and he fell with the bicycle.

Mia arrived by his side ahead of Angela. She helped him get up. "Big boys don't fall off bikes, and you are a big boy."

Angela reached their side. "My fault for calling your name, I should have walked here." She turned to Mia, "Please call the others, lunch is ready." Angela turned her attention back to Nikko. "I will carry your bike to the shed before we go to the house and eat lunch."

Nikko soothed his scratched elbow.

Angela squatted. She held his elbow and blew air to sooth him. "There is no blood. Come to the house, I will wipe off the dirt." She extended her hand and Nikko held on. She lifted his bicycle with her other hand.

They arrived in the house and found Ronny, Anne, Mia and Betty at the table, waiting for them to arrive.

Angela sensed some tension as the family ate lunch. It did not take long before her fear was confirmed.

Anne put her fork on the plate and said, "Angela, Ronny tells me you will travel to Nakuru to see your family."

The spoon in Angela's hand dropped to the table before she could tighten her grip. She feared what she would hear next. She worried if Ronny had mentioned that she would be going to see her son.

Anne added, "He has invited me to travel with him and the children." She looked the direction of Ronny. "I am too old for leisure travels. I will go visit Pauline instead."

Angela and Ronny exhaled at the same time. Ronny covered up the uniform reaction by saying. "It is sad you are not able to join us, to spend more time with your grandkids."

Ronny's plan was that if Anne traveled with them, he would leave her with the children and accompany Angela to see her son. He wished to meet with Joshua, talk with him, mention to him he would like to propose to his sister. He had decided it was too important a matter to discuss with Joshua on phone. They had talked on phone often, since Boxing Day.

"Dianna would be a better companion, though I fail to understand why you turned her offer down," Anne said.

Ronny forced a cough. "No need. The kids and I will be fine."

Angela toyed with the food on her plate as she listened to the conversation between Ronny and Anne, with Mia and Betty chipping in. She cleared the food from her plate into her mouth before she turned to Nikko. "More food for our growing boy?" she asked as she added more bananas and beef stew into his plate.

Angela glanced at Mia and Betty before she stood up. "Sorry I have to go, I need to fold the clothes in the drier before they cool down." She picked her dishes and went to the kitchen.

Five minutes later, Angela looked up in surprise as the door to the laundry room opened and Anne stepped in. "You work so hard," she smiled.

Angela returned the smile.

231

"The problem is that you could spoil this man. He needs a wife, not a maid."

Angela put the shorts she had folded into Nikko's laundry basket. She picked up a shirt and folded as she reflected on what to say next. She knew she had two options: to tell Anne that she had no business in the wife-matters of his son-in-law or say something to please her and make her leave the laundry room. "I will leave for university when he brings the wife."

"Good plan," Anne said as she picked up a vest and started to assist Angela with the folding.

From the corner of her eye, Angela saw Anne's eyebrows pull in. She could tell that Anne was struggling with something in her mind. The words did not take long to come out. "Would you continue to stay in Nakuru with your family, if Dianna comes in tomorrow?"

Angela made an abrupt turn of head. "Better if you make that decision with Ronny. Not you and me," she said as she emptied the next load of clothes from the washer into the drier.

She sensed that what Anne was driving towards was to get her out of her job. Get Ronny into a desperate situation of having no worker in the house, then have reason to bring Dianna in as a helper.

A vision crossed her mind to a few hours back, when Ronny had held her close to his body and the nice warm feeling she felt. He had promised he would not force her into doing anything she did not want. He had kissed her gently and only increased the pace after she relaxed and returned his kiss. Though she had been too scared when he pulled her tightly to his body, it felt nice. His embrace had brought a floating sensation into her stomach.

Angela worried that if she left her job that week, Ronny would not know what to do with the children. The New Year was a few days away and schools would be opening in less than nine days.

She panicked on the realization that losing her job would mean no more money to pay nursery school fees for her son. "On second thought, I need my job." She made eye contact with Anne. "I want to work for the children, all children. If Dianna comes, I can still continue as the housegirl."

Anne chuckled. "I saw you've trained the children to do tasks for themselves. They will manage without you."

Angela added detergent and softener to the washer. "Is it okay if we check with Ronny on who will prepare food for the family?"

"What am I doing here arguing with a housegirl?" Anne's raised voice startled Angela.

Angela remembered how secure she had felt when Ronny held his arms open for her. He had embraced her, like he would never let her go. She had felt protected when he held her tightly.

She pressed the washer buttons and started a new cycle. She picked up Nikko's laundry basket and opened the door. "Not your type of housegirl," Angela said before she walked away without looking back at Anne.

Angela strode past the family room, struggling to hold back the tears brimming in her eyes.

The children were watching TV, they did not turn her direction as she walked past. But Angela noticed the concerned expression on Ronny's face.

Satisfied with how she had arranged Nikko's wardrobe, she left his bedroom, walked along the corridor, and instead of turning right to exit into the family room, she continued forward, to her bedroom.

She picked her phone from the bedside table, checked the time and was satisfied that her grandmother would be home. She dialed her number.

Angela thought of giving up on her third trial. Before she could do that, she heard Priscah on the other side of the phone. "Allo, arro, Arroh?"

Angela burst out into laughter. "*Nyanya,* you are supposed to say one hallo and listen to hear who is calling and what they have to say."

After exchanging niceties, Angela could tell that her grandmother had a lot to talk about. She interrupted. "Stephanie told me she gave you the money I sent via M-Pesa. What will you buy to celebrate New Year?"

"Your brother took away my boy. How do you expect me to celebrate?" Priscah sounded irritated.

"Okay, that means no more money from me, if you do not want to celebrate the end of one year and welcome a new one."

"Hahaaha," Priscah laughed loudly, prompting Angela to move the phone away from her ear. She heard

Priscah add, "Is that city making you lose your sense of humour? I was letting you know how I miss the boy."

Angela chuckled. "Babu is fine. I will go visit him tomorrow. My *Tajiri* will be traveling to Nakuru and will give me a ride."

Priscah laughed again. "Drive you to Nakuru? Does that mean your *Tajiri* is not afraid to be seen with you? Make him marry you."

"*Nyanya*, I will end this phone call if you continue to say such things. I told you I want to go to university."

"Where is this *ounibasiti* you keep talking about? Is it a place you cannot go to if you are married?"

"Bye *Nyanya* I will talk with you from Nakuru. That way you will greet Babu and Dave." She ended the call and threw the phone on the bed.

Angela stood on one heel and made a 360-degree spin. She lifted her head upwards, to the ceiling and crossed her hands to her shoulders. "Thank you, Lord, I am happy."

Talking with her grandmother always brought her joy. Joy she could not explain, she only felt it.

She sat on her dresser stool and looked outside to the ever-green lawn. Though it was December, a dry month of the year, Ronny's grass was well-watered through the underground sprinkler system. Water came from a borehole whose location she had never been shown.

Angela remembered that she had work to do.

She walked out of the room, wondering if she would ever be married. Would Ronny or any other man she married let her attend university? She walked to the family room where she paused and asked the children what program had kept them so engrossed. She left for the kitchen, ignoring a wink from Ronny.

In the kitchen she looked out of the window, turned and walked towards the living room where she had spotted Anne. She sat on the opposite sofa from Anne. "I am going to the kitchen to prepare an afternoon snack, would you like millet porridge or tea?"

Anne tried to shield the smile engulfing her face by not looking up. "I see you want to spoil me as you have done to everyone in this house." She made eye contact with Angela. "I will eat whatever you prepare for Ronny. I need to taste whatever you give him that has given you a big head."

Angela went and prepared fruits for the children and cooked porridge for Ronny and Anne.

After setting the table, she called Betty. "Please go and call your Grandma and everyone else to the table."

"Okay," Betty said as she ran off.

Satisfied that the children were settled at the table, Angela went to the kitchen. She drank tea while she busied herself perusing through a cookbook.

She had decided that she would cook grilled ribs, *ugali* and vegetables for dinner, and a chocolate cake for dessert. She was aware that Ronny liked to eat that dish. She would serve it to show Anne the sort of food that she had spoiled Ronny with and given herself 'a big head.'

The family streamed into the kitchen, except for Anne.

"I was going to come clear the dishes from the table," Angela said while smiling at Ronny. "I see you have a plan to work me out of my job?"

He nodded with sparkly eyes and proceeded to the double sink. He took a cup from Nikko and placed the dishes inside the sink.

On his way back, he talked without stopping. "We have saved you by leaving dishes in the sink. Why did you not come to the table?"

Angela ignored his question. She turned to Mia and Betty who were studying the recipe book beside her. "Would you like to help me bake a cake for dessert? Choose one." She stepped down from the stool and went to the dining room to wipe the table.

Ronny and Anne sat at the dining room. They stopped talking while Angela gathered the remaining dishes and wiped the table. As she walked away, she heard them talk, though she could not comprehend the words.

Later, Anne walked to the kitchen. She paused at the entrance and glanced from one child to another. Nikko balanced on a high stool, riding his toy cars on the island top. Betty and Mia were busy decorating the ready cake from a kitchen countertop. "I was wondering where the children were, I see you are being overworked," Anne said, addressing no one in particular.

Angela focused on the *ugali* she was stirring as she heard Betty laugh aloud. "Grandma, this is not work, we're decorating a cake. You cannot taste it now."

Betty turned to Angela. "Angie, tell Grandma how we begged you to allow us to decorate the cake."

Angela had baked a chocolate cake for dessert, and the girls had implored her to let them practice adding coloured icing sugar to match the cake in the recipe book.

She focused on the *ugali* while listening to the chat between Anne and her grandchildren. She stirred the *ugali* less and listened as Mia said, "Grandma, if you stay with us a few more days, we can show you how to bake a nice cake, like this one."

"As I told you, I will leave tomorrow. Dianna will pick me up and drive me to Pauline's house. I cannot stand to see my grandchildren being trained to be house girls."

Mia sneered.

Betty laughed until she rested her head on the countertop.

"Grandma," Mia called out. "Learning how to bake cake does not mean we will become housegirls. I want to be a doctor and save people's lives." She turned to Betty who had stopped laughing. "Betty wants to be an astronaut." She turned the direction of Nikko. "Our brother must be driving himself into being some car engineer."

Betty said, "And Angie told us she will go to university to study food service, then she will open a huge hotel." Betty spread out her arms to demonstrate the big size of the hotel. "Then we can all go and help her bake a huge cake, to serve many people, like at weddings."

Anne retorted, addressing Angela. "You can bake a cake for their father's wedding. He said one day he will marry again."

"What? Whom will Dad marry?" Mia asked.

Betty jumped on her toes while she clapped. "Will the new Mum teach us how to cook, bake cake, just like Angie?"

The smile on Anne's face broadened. "Mums don't need to know how to cook. Your Dad will employ a chef to prepare food for everyone in the house."

Betty went and stood beside Angela. "Angie, can you become a chef, then you can come prepare food and cake for us?"

Angela served steaming *ugali* into a plate. From the corner of her eye, she had noticed that Anne was staring at her, so she said. "I will consider your request."

Betty did a happy dance as Angela completed the sentence. "If Dad and Mia, and Nikko and Betty need me, and ask me to stay, I will consider."

Anne walked out of the kitchen, muttering, "Never, that's a bad dream."

The rest of her words were drowned as Betty called out, "Grandma. Come you see how we decorate the center of the cake."

Anne walked away and turned the corner to the corridor leading to the staff quarters where she slept.

The family ate dinner in record time. Betty and Mia urged everyone to eat quickly so that they could carry the cake to the table for dessert.

Fearing that the children might eat too much cake, Angela reminded them of the usual practice. "Remember we will eat a small piece of cake after dinner. We will eat some tomorrow after lunch and the remaining after dinner."

"Dad said we are going away for two days. May we eat all the cake tonight?" Mia asked.

Angela looked at Ronny sitting directly opposite from her at the dining table.

Ronny swallowed before he said, "We will drive out tomorrow morning to Nakuru, then come back on 30th to get ready for the New Year."

As the family retired to bed, Angela planned to wake up early the next morning, prepare breakfast and help everyone get ready for the trip.

The earlier she got to see her son, the better for her. She would need time to chat with Babu, to find out if he was still scared from the Christmas day incident.

Chapter 21

Ronny heard his alarm go off and was glad. It was six o'clock and by eight, Dianna would have picked up her mother. If not, they would drive her to his parents' house on their way to Nakuru.

He had been restless most of the night. His mother-in-law's words replayed themselves in his head most of the night. Anne had insisted he terminates Angela's contract, employ a chef and a cleaner to help Dianna while she stayed with the children.

Not wanting to get into a verbal conflict with his mother-in-law, Ronny had sat and mumbled, "Okay, I will see," as Anne gave all sorts of advice on childcare.

What Ronny would have liked to tell Anne was that Dianna would be nothing close to Bella as a wife.

He was infuriated when Anne said she had discussed with Angela, and Angela had agreed to resign her job and proceed to university. He prayed there was no truth to that.

The family left for Nakuru, stopping by the house of Ronny's parents where they left Anne.

Angela was excited when Joshua came to pick her up from the WeFlamingos Country Club. But she had to wait for Joshua and Ronny to finish whatever discussion had kept them standing near the entrance like they were in a hurry, but never opened the door to leave.

She wanted to go see her son.

Tired of waiting, she joined the children who were playing a board game, until she heard Joshua reassure Ronny that he would bring her back.

Angela was delayed more when Nikko held onto her skirt. He wanted to go with her.

Joshua watched as Angela tried to convince Nikko that she would be back before he went to bed, which made him cry more.

Ronny intervened. He spread his arms out for Nikko. "Who wants to show Dad how tight they can cuddle?" Nikko ran into his father's arms, giving Angela a chance to leave.

Ronny lifted Nikko and walked towards the gym within their hotel quarters. "We need to build our muscles." He fisted a hand and stretched it in front of Nikko. "When Angie returns, we will ask her to choose who has the biggest muscles." He held Nikko up, in front of him. "And I know my boy will win." He lowered Nikko to the floor.

Nikko ran towards a treadmill. Ronny followed closely.

Joshua and Angela left the Club premises for his house forty minutes away. On their drive they discussed a variety of issues including his plan to apply for a promotion. He had been teaching at the school for five years.

They discussed a home-based business that his wife planned to start. They talked about crops grown in the village and in Nakuru. The only topic they did not bring up was Babu, until Joshua parked the car outside the single-family house at the edge of the school compound.

Angela saw Babu and Dave peek from the door of the living room. Her son did not sprint to her as she walked towards the house, which worried her.

Dave walked outside. Babu followed him and asked Angela, "You have come again to visit us. Uncle drove me from Mama's house."

Angela bent and cuddled Babu and then Dave, hearing Florence, her sister-in-law, welcome her into the house.

Still holding onto Babu's hand, Angela squatted and made eye contact with him. "I too am Mama."

She stood up and embraced Florence while avoiding squeezing her stomach, eight months pregnant. "I see the name mama being transferred to you and not me, time to take this boy away with me."

"Did you find a house or the house of your *Tajiri*?" Joshua asked as he entered the house right behind Angela.

"I have seen some workers who reside with families in the staff quarters. I will find out how they do that." Immediately, she remembered what that would mean, she had to move back to the staff quarters. What would she do whenever Ronny needed to travel and asked her to move into the main house? Would she move there with Babu?

Angela also recalled that there was no school nearby for Babu to attend, though that would wait as he had one

243

more year before he turned six to start class one. Then it occurred to her that unlike the practice in their village, towns and cities were different. Children went to school as young as three years, starting in baby class, nursery and kindergarten from where they graduate into class one. This was the schooling system that Nikko was going through.

Florence awakened Angela from her thoughts. "Come to the table, time to eat."

Angela, still holding onto Babu' hand, looked at him. "Son, would you like to come with me to the city?"

Joshua stopped washing hands and looked at Angela over his shoulder. "No need to promise what is not possible, we do not want trouble with the boy after you leave." He lifted his wrist and checked time. "Which is in less than two hours, as your boss asked."

"Really? I do not recall him mentioning time."

"He requested that we drive back with Babu and Dave to drink evening tea together, before I drive them back."

Angela supported her forehead on one hand. "I had no idea you agreed to a plan before consulting me."

Joshua chuckled. "I thought my sister works as a housegirl, interesting to hear that the boss needs to consult with her."

Not wanting to get into a conversation about her boss, a conversation that could get her excited and by mistake mention that he kissed her, she decided to divert their talk. "Do you have any additional information from grandma?" Angela asked.

Joshua shook his head no.

Angela pulled a chair and sat down. "I talked with her yesterday." She scanned the people at the table. "That woman has aged, all she talks to me about is getting married. She cannot understand when I tell her there is university for me, marriage is the last item on my bucket list."

"Why?" Florence asked. "I had no idea marriage was that bad. Find someone loving, and you will never regret a day in your life."

"I will consult you once I am done with my university studies."

"Good. When did you start?" Florence asked.

"I have not started. My plan is to save enough money first and start university in the next two to three years. For now, I need to work and save. My boss is not bad, and he needs my services." Angela stopped talking. She was getting excited whenever she mentioned her boss.

The drive back to the Country Club took a little longer compared to the morning one. There were many people on the road at four o'clock. Some were traveling from places of work, and being the end of the year, there were also people traveling to and from shopping in town.

Angela spent the travel time chatting with Babu and Dave. She asked about their holidays and what they planned to do when schools opened. Babu told her he would be starting school in January, which Joshua confirmed.

Angela knew that Joshua, being a trained teacher, must know the best way to prepare children to succeed in their journey of education.

They arrived at the Country Club as the sun set, casting a yellow glow on the west side of the lake.

Within minutes, Babu and Dave made friends with Nikko, Mia and Betty.

Angela watched, wishing she could have a free heart and will like a child. Unlike adults who took time to earn one another's trust, children trusted one another sooner, until they found reason not to.

Ronny announced that he and Joshua were going outside for a drink. The announcement worried Angela. What would the two men discuss?

~~~~~~

Joshua and Ronny walked to a gazebo, a stone's throw from the club house.

While they ordered their drinks, Joshua could tell that Ronny was uneasy. He fumbled in his trousers and jacket pockets in search of his phone. When he finally found it, he touched the screen before replacing the phone back to the jacket pocket.

"How is your sister finding the work she does? Are we overworking her?" Ronny asked without making eye contact with Joshua.

"Hard to tell, partly because I have not asked for details. Any complaints on your side?" Joshua asked.

Ronny wiped his forehead with the back of his hand. "Nothing but praises. I wish she could allow me to be with her."

"Is she leaving?" Joshua asked. "She had said she would work until she's ready to go to university."

"I meant live with me. Us." He fumbled in his breast pocket. "Live together with her."

Joshua stared as the waiter arranged a tea kettle, two cups and a plate of *samosas* on the table that separated his chair from that of Ronny.

The waiter poured tea into each cup, stood at attention and said, "Enjoy your tea, Sir," and walked away.

Ronny sipped from his cup and looked at Joshua. Not getting any response, he said, "I like your sister. She is a nice lady. I would like to propose to her."

Joshua replaced the teacup he had lifted closer to his mouth back on the table. He looked at Ronny. "Mmhhh."

"She's willing, though she is worried of something I am not able to determine."

"What about her studies? The university she plans to proceed to?"

"I have no objection. We can organize whenever she wants to start, even on Monday," Ronny said before he picked a *samosa* into a side plate and took a large bite nearly filling his mouth.

Joshua just watched as Ronny took a second bite.

"Has she told you how old she is? Is she ready for marriage?" Joshua asked.

"Twenty-three, four in February. I have tried to talk with her. Let her know that she has done an excellent job with my children. How I fell in love with her. She is all that I could ever ask for. Pleasant, loving to the children, kind to my family and friends, and ready to serve."

"Mmhhh." Joshua made the sound again as he took a bite of his *samosa*.

"Has she always been that fearful, even to talk?" Ronny asked.

Joshua took a sip from his cup. "As you have said, she is a young girl, scarred at a very young age. I am glad to hear she is being careful with her life."

Ronny shook his head. "I fully understand." One side of his mouth twitched upwards, into a smile. "Between you and me, I have not touched your sister and will not without her consent."

Joshua smiled, partly to help Ronny loosen up. He could tell that Ronny was almost pleading for his intervention, though he had not made his request clear.

"I hate to say this, but my sister could be worried, maybe you have a girlfriend, Are—"

"No, no," Ronny interrupted.

Are you trying to approach her because she is always in the house?" He chuckled. "As your employee, she would not know how to handle that."

Ronny tilted his head upwards, like he was in search of heavenly intervention.

"I have had many people bring ladies to me without my asking. I am sorry that some of them have been mean to her." He forced a dry cough. "The truth is, they are not my girlfriends, but daughters of family friends."

"That makes it worse for Angela, ladies that are already known to your family."

Ronny chuckled. "You are a married man. I do not need to tell you the difference between getting a wife and a woman. What I want is a wife, a friend to compliment me. For the time Angela has been with my family, I know she is the one."

Joshua checked his watch, picked up his cup and finished the tea.

Ronny lifted the kettle to refill Joshua's cup, but Joshua held his hand up, to stop him as he said. "Why not tell her what you have said to me, about not touching her without her consent. Then start your conversation from there." He shot up from his chair and extended a hand to Ronny. "As you know, no man should ever be told how to hunt for what he cannot live without."

Both men laughed and tightened their handshake as Joshua said, "Good luck. You have my support and blessings." He chuckled. "On one condition, promise never to hurt my kid sister. She's had enough in her life this far. What we want is a better, happier life for her onwards."

Ronny placed his left hand on Joshua's shoulder. "Take my word, I promise to love and take care of Angela and Babu. I will find a way to remove all her fears and doubts."

The two men walked towards the house. On their way, Joshua inquired if Ronny had received clearance from his children.

"You need to pay us a visit in the city, witness how trusting the children are of Angela. If you did not know yet, you have a wonderful sister. She knows how to talk the kids out of situations where I would have had to fight. She has a way of teaching them basics of life with minimal protests."

Ronny paused, and Joshua did the same. Ronny said, "Unlike homes where some of us grew up, my children now clear the dining table after a meal and organize their bedrooms."

"Good you have mentioned that," Joshua interjected. "I know Angela is a very focused girl, she will eventually make something big out of herself, after university. We were raised by an employed father and a mother who stayed at home, raised us without the support of house workers. How do you plan to fit into her world, and her into yours, business families?"

"She will be okay. Angela has a lot of wisdom and knowledge. She is not afraid to separate me from my office, the money. She has on occasion called me out when I was stressed and being hard on the children. I loved her more since that day."

"She has a subtle and confident way of getting around those who try to step on her way. And she is neat, dresses smartly each day for her job. What else does one need to fit in? We go to church together, we have taken the children to various clubs and restaurants, and I have not seen her behave different from the other people there."

The two men reached the veranda of the house and stopped. Ronny offered his hand to Joshua. "Thank you very much. I will take care of your sister. I promise to give her the respect she deserves."

He removed the door card from his wallet. "We can revisit this next month." He inserted the card and pushed the door open. He was hopeful, happy with the results of their short meeting, the beginning of a family conversation.

Joshua declined an invitation to sit, explaining that it was getting dark. He needed to take Babu and Dave home.

Angela was upset when Babu waved bye to her, held his uncle's hand and they walked away towards his car.

During the three days Babu had been in Nakuru, he seemed to have developed a strong attachment to his uncle.

Angela wondered what Joshua did to attain that relationship, or, was Babu now at an age he needed a father-figure in his life?

251

Chapter 22

Angela had one worry that hindered her enjoyment of dinner. Soon the family would retire to bed for the night and there were only three bedrooms, where would she sleep?

When everyone could not eat any more dessert, the family left the dining room for their house. On arrival Ronny informed Angela, "I have a meeting with a friend, please see that the children shower and get to bed on time."

Mia looked at her father, then Angela. "We are on holiday. Can we stay awake longer?"

"Schools will open in few days' time. It will be better if you start to practice school sleeping hours." He cuddled each child, including Angela, wished them a good night and walked out of the house.

Angela was tongue-tied by Ronny's embrace. By the time she collected herself, she remembered she had not asked him about the sleeping arrangements.

She questioned why whoever designed the Club house did not have four or five bedrooms instead of the three large ones. Making the rooms smaller would have allowed for an extra room for her.

She looked around the large living room and decided that the three-seater sofa would do.

The children showered, she read them a story book from the living room before she escorted each child to their beds, starting with Nikko.

When all was quiet, Angela went to the living room and read a clothing fashion magazine until she heard the door to the house open.

Ronny walked inside, closed the door slowly and asked in a whisper, "How are the children?"

She sat upright. "Fine, they showered, we read a story book, said prayers and they are now in bed."

He looked at his Rolex. "I see it is getting late, did I keep you waiting?"

"Is my room on the outside? I could not leave the children alone."

He chuckled, picked the remote and switched on the TV. "You could sleep in the room." He pointed towards the master bedroom. "There's more than enough space in there."

He stopped talking on seeing the horrified expression on Angela's face, eyes wide as she asked. "Is that not the master bedroom? Your room?"

"There are no rooms with names here," he said as he removed his black leather jacket and sat down on a two-seater sofa, opposite from Angela. "Do you mind sitting here so we can talk?" He patted the left side of his seat.

Angela stood up. "No. I want my job as a housegirl."

"Who said you would not have your job? You would, but not with the title of housegirl."

He watched her walk away towards the kitchen. He stood up, switched off the TV, then switched it on again. He followed her to the kitchen. "Whatever you decide, please don't think of leaving your job, the kids need you, and I do too," he said before he walked away to the master bedroom.

Angela comforted herself that she would finally lay down on the sofa for the night. She would get the extra duvet and bedsheets from Nikko's room. The sofa would be fine for the night. They would be leaving for the city the next day.

Questions flooded her mind. Did she react too fast to the invitation to sit next to Ronny. There would be no problem sharing a chair with him, even a kiss. She recalled how nice she had felt when he kissed her the day before. Why had she objected to be near him, to get the warm feeling again.

Her thought process was interrupted by the opening of a door. Ronny walked out. He had changed into grey and black striped pajamas.

He had his travel bag in one hand. "Enjoy your night in the bedroom, I will take up residence with Nikko."

Angela's lips parted, ready to say something, but no words came out.

Ronny closed the few strides between them. The bag in his hand dropped to the floor as he cuddled her, supported the back of her head and kissed her. "I did not communicate well. I just wanted us to sit together, hold and talk about our future. Good night, I will miss you."

Angela's eyes opened wider followed by a smile and lowering of her eyelids.

He picked up the bag and went into Nikko's room.

Angela sat on the nearest sofa. She bent her head to her knees. She could hear her heart throbbing in her chest, she felt a sweat on her neck. The same nice feeling she had felt when Ronny kissed her in Nairobi returned to her stomach. She wondered if that was what women call love.

She worried why Ronny wanted her to sleep in the large king-size bed, while he slept on a smaller one, a double-sized bed. She had never slept on such a large bed.

She would not enjoy sleeping on a bed reserved for the master. That would be like sleeping on his bed back in the city. "No way," she uttered.

She leaned on the armrest and supported her head on her hand. Her mind drifted back to the events of that day. She had visited her brother's family, taken care of Ronny's children, and now had no place to sleep.

A tear escaped from her eye as she thought of how wonderful it would be for her to continue working as the housegirl. With that thought, she was glad about what Ronny had said that whatever her decision, she would keep her job.

Then the words from her grandmother and Brenda about getting married sprang in her head. Before she could dismiss them, the words from Florence, "Find someone loving, and you will never regret a day in your life," echoed in her ears, like she had just heard them.

She had a feeling that Florence was right about loving someone. From the few interactions she had had with her brother and his family, she had concluded that they were a happy family, even with the one salary they relied on.

She wondered how some women manage to find men who love them. The last time she thought a man loved her, based on the love letters she had exchanged with Japheth while in school, he had walked away and left her pregnant. How would she ever trust another man, however much he said he loved her?

Angela was reflective as her tired head fell to the armrest of the sofa.

The living room became cold as the night progressed. Fearing to fall sick, she picked her travel bag from the corner where she had left it when they arrived. She tiptoed into the master bedroom, promising herself that all she would do was find some warmth. She would run out if Ronny had tricked her and came back in the middle of the night.

She went and showered, all the while afraid that the door would open, and Ronny walked inside.

All was quiet when she stepped out of the shower, dressed and went into the bedroom. She set her alarm for six o'clock, pulled an extra duvet from a nearby wardrobe and coiled herself on one end of the bed, on top of the bed coverings.

Did the wrong alarm go off? That was the first thought in Angela's mind as she silenced her wake-up alarm.

Where was she? Not in her bedroom in the city.

She stepped on the soft carpet and looked back at the bed, to confirm that Ronny had not sneaked in while she slept.

In a hurry, she tiptoed to the bathroom, washed her face and brushed her teeth. She changed into a clean purple cotton dress, pairing it with a floral jacket. She tied her braids to the top of her head and left two hanging to the side of her head.

She picked up her travel bag and walked out, placing it at the exact place in the dining room as the night before.

~~~~~~

Angela noted Ronny's gaze as they ate breakfast.

Not wanting to talk much in case the children asked to see her bedroom, Angela focused her attention on her food and on Nikko. She was glad when she heard Ronny ask the children to be nice as he would be going away to play golf with friends. That was when she learned that he had extended their stay by a day.

The family strolled along nearby fields where the children pointed to birds and a monkey here, a monkey there.

They reached one fence of the Club where Ronny called the children to come see some giraffes a distance away.

Angela excused herself to make a phone call. She walked away and called Florence. She thanked her again for accepting to host Babu in her house. She was surprised by the response from Florence.

"No way I can host Babu in my house." The words froze Angela on the spot before Florence completed the sentence. "Babu is like my child, he will live with us as one of my children, not a visitor."

"I hope you are not planning to take my son away from me, he is the only one I have."

Florence laughed. "He is not the only one. Go open your heart to the man and make many more cute babies."

"Which man? did you find one for me?"

Florence chuckled. "You and I know about the man who loves you. Open your eyes, sister," she said. She wished Angela a good day and ended the call.

Angela walked further away from Ronny and the children. She called her grandmother and informed her that she was in Nakuru and had been with Babu the day before.

"I was told you are there with your man and children. Are they good children you can call your own?"

Not wanting to ask her grandmother what she meant by 'your man', Angela responded to the second part of the question. "The children I take care of are well-behaved, otherwise I would have looked for another job by now."

"Good. Promise me you will take care of them well, even after that man marries you."

Angela laughed. "*Nyanya*, all you think about is marriage. I am too young for—"

"Young?" Priscah interrupted. "You are a woman with a son. Any man would know you can produce more. Accept that one so that you can take care of all the children."

Angela looked back over her shoulder, to be sure no one would hear their conversation.

Priscah added, "The children your father's wife has refused to have."

"Bye, bye *Nyanya*," Angela said, ending the call. She did not want to talk about her stepmother. People had said she did not want to have children. Angela had decided she would not engage in such a conversation, for she was not very sure if Zippy did not want to have children or she was not able to have them.

Angela rejoined the group. She lifted Nikko up and put him down. "My grandmother sends greetings to all of you," she said as she extended a hand and tickled Mia on the arm, sending Betty into laughter without being touched.

"What about your mummy?" Betty asked.

Angela remembered she had never told Betty or Nikko that her mother had died. "My mother died when I was a little bit older than Mia. My grandmother is now like my mother."

"Do all mothers have to die?" Betty asked.

Ronny held Betty by the shoulders. "They all have to die at some stage in life. Some die when young, others live for a long time. That is why my mother, your Grandma is still alive, and the mothers of many of your friends and children at school."

He tickled Nikko. "You will one day have another mother, she will live with us until we are all very old."

Angela looked at Ronny. She turned away when he winked at her.

~~~~~~

Ronny suppressed a smile as he recalled what Joshua had said to him - it was his job to woo Angela. He had also learned from Joshua that Angela and Priscah were very close confidants, and Priscah was encouraging her to get married.

Ronny felt fortunate that Joshua had not reacted the way he had feared. He had assumed Joshua would accuse him of trying to take advantage of Angela because she was desperate for her job.

He remembered the passing time. "Kids, I see its time for me to go play daddy's sports. Angie will guide you back to the room. Watch some TV, go to the swimming pool, eat lunch and then play at the children's playgrounds."

He then addressed Angela. "I will be back in time for dinner."

They walked back to the Club house.

Angela and the children followed Ronny at a slower pace. By the time they arrived inside, Ronny had changed into crispy white Zegna trousers, a matching golf-shirt and a pair of Air Zoom 90 IT golf shoes. "Remember to enjoy every minute, we are on holiday," he told them before walking out.

Nikko waved with the TV remote in his hand, "Bye Dad."

As he strode towards the golf-club house to be allocated a cabby, he reflected on how involved Angela had become with his children. He would soon allow her to take up further responsibilities. She could accompany the children to their local members' club in his absence. Take Betty and Mia to the Mall to shop or window shop, and to the cinema house to watch movies.

He thought of inviting Angela to the children's parent-teacher meetings. He would start by visiting with her, assess her interest before asking her to join other parents whenever the children had a sporting activity. She could also frequent Nikko's kindergarten to read a book to the class or narrate a story as many parents, mostly mothers, did.

~~~~~~

The house was quiet when Ronny returned at six-fifteen.

"Where are the children?" He asked Angela who sat on the sofa reading a novel.

"They played themselves silly. They are fine and asleep."

"Really?" He questioned as he walked away, first to Nikko's room and then to Betty and Mia's.

Angela, with the book still in her hand, watched Ronny until he walked back.

"You must have done an excellent job entertaining them," he said as he walked away to the master bedroom. Halfway, he paused, went to Nikko's room and walked out with his travel bag.

At seven Ronny walked out of his room having shaved, showered and dressed in his Levi's jeans along with a button-down white cotton shirt. He was barefoot.

Angela gawked, wondering how a man could disappear for forty minutes and re-emerge utterly changed. He appeared younger than his thirty-six years.

Still lost on his beauty, impressed by how refreshed and alive he looked, she did not budge when he sat next to her on the sofa. He held her by the shoulder and kissed her cheeks. "Do you think hunger will wake them up?" He lifted his chin to the side of the children's bedrooms.

"I will go wake them up." She stood from the sofa.

"No, no. That is not what I meant." He stood, walked to the door and slipped feet into his open pair of leather shoes. "I will be back with dinner for everyone. Any preferences?"

She inhaled his cologne, and she could not stop admiring how radiant he looked. She regretted leaving the sofa so fast. "Surprise us," she said as she walked back to the sofa and picked her book from the coffee table.

He held onto the door handle. "I will include some red wine for us, after dinner." He opened the door and walked out.

262

Chapter 23

The door swung open and Ronny walked in without a single item in hand.

Before Angela could ask if he changed his mind, two waiters struggled in pushing a food cart.

They nodded at Angela as they directed the cart towards the dining side of the room, pressed down two brake handles, wished them a nice evening and walked out.

The grin on Angela's face rescinded on realizing that Ronny's eyes were on her. She walked to the cart and darted her eyes from one foil covered tray to another. "I had no idea you were such a fast chef. So much food within minutes." She patted his arm and walked away to the children's bedrooms.

Ronny shook his head, walked to the sink and washed hands. He pulled on a chef's apron and cap hanging on one side of the cart. He picked plates from the cart and set them on the six-place dining table.

"Wash your hands. Time to taste your Dad's cooking," he told Betty and Mia as they walked into the living room, rubbing sleep from their eyes.

Ronny lifted a serving spoon and swung it in his hand, to Nikko's amusement.

"Be seated. Do we start with a prayer or my guests food choices?" Ronny asked.

Everyone burst out with laughter before Mia said, "You forgot the small booklet for taking our food orders."

Ronny held his fore finger to one side of his jaw, thoughtful. "One does not need to write when they serve at our five-star hotel. I qualified for the job after reciting all the dishes on the menu."

Angela asked everyone to bow for prayer. The amen was followed by Ronny uncovering the first food tray and looking at Nikko. "Good manners demand that we start with the most important dinner guest, the youngest. Would you like some rice?"

"Start with soup, a starter before the main meal," Angela advised.

"Good reminder," Ronny said before he ladled soup into five bowls and handed them out.

Ronny stole glances at the children as they enjoyed their soup. He could tell they were hungry, they must have played a lot during the day.

Nikko picked a plate in front of him and lifted it towards Ronny. Betty and Mia followed, and Angela did the same.

Each time Ronny served a food item, he added the same to a plate near his side of the table.

He unwrapped the aluminium foil covering green vegetables, fried chicken, roast potatoes, grilled goat meat, marinated lamb, steamed cauliflower, kidney beans, rice, *ugali* and chapattis.

Once all the plates were filled with food, he removed the chef's cap and placed it on a nearby stool. "The chef will only serve dessert after everyone has had a second serving." He sat down and joined his family in eating.

Forks, spoons and knives clicked on plates, competing with stories from each child on the fun they had that day.

Quietness followed when Nikko hit his spoon on a plate for attention. "Did you cook all the food when you left us in the morning?"

Angela and Ronny's eyes met before Ronny said, "You now know how good a cook your dad is."

Betty laughed as Mia said, "I remember, a long, long time ago, when Dad burnt all the breakfast eggs, after saying Mum had served half-cooked eggs."

Ronny stood up and put on the chef's cap. It had been long since any of the children mentioned their Mum at the dining table. The children only referenced her occasionally, whenever their father said no to a request.

Ronny had a strong urge to continue the conversation in a positive way. "Mum is in heaven with the angels, guarding us every day." He glanced at each child, to ascertain their reaction. Not seeing much astonishment like it used to be one year ago, he asked, "Would you mind if Angela stayed with us, to continue providing loving care to us like Mum used to?"

His hope was that the children would decipher the hidden message in his question. But he worried what to say if they asked what he meant. He held his breath when he saw Nikko's lips part. "Will Angela go away when Mum returns? I want her to stay."

A strained smile crept onto Ronny's face. "Mum will not return from heaven. We will only see her one day, when the angels take us away." He looked at Mia, Nikko and then Betty. "But that should only happen after many, many years, when we are old, older than Grandpa."

"Dead people don't come back to life," Betty said while looking at Mia.

Ronny saw the agony on Mia's face. He lowered his body and reached the dessert on the lowest level of the food cart.

He stayed longer than necessary because he was thinking of what to say next, weighing how welcoming the children would be if Angela accepted his proposal.

He stood upright. "Chef Dad presents the best dessert." He stared at Nikko who had a broad smile on his face. Ronny wondered if his son, at the tender age of four, remembered his mother or missed her after twenty months of her absence from his life.

"Taste and tell us which one you prefer, Dad's dessert or the one served by Angela at home."

Mia looked at Angela while she spoke. "Angela prepares the best desserts, even Aunty Rose likes them."

"Does that mean Dad should not take over Angela's work at home?"

Among all his children, Ronny knew that Betty always said things as she saw them. Mia being older, now nine years, she always paused and reflected before she spoke.

He listened carefully when he heard Betty speak. "Dad will shout at us if he comes from his office and goes to the kitchen to cook for us."

"Does that mean you do not want me in the kitchen?" he asked.

Mia held her hand up. "Dad can go to the kitchen to grill *nyama choma*, Angela to cook all the other food."

Ronny turned to Nikko. "Hi young man, why are you so quiet?"

Nikko lifted a side plate towards his father. "I am waiting for that," he pointed at the dessert.

They all laughed.

Nikko looked at his father, confused by the laughter.

Ronny picked a dessert plate, uncovered the chocolate mousse cake and served a piece. "You asked for it boy," he said as he handed the plate to Nikko.

Nikko dug a spoon into the cake. "Thank you, Dad."

"Anyone else wants Dad's cake or are you waiting for Angela's when she opens her big hotel?"

Mia extended her right hand towards Ronny, like she was receiving something from him.

Betty stood up and stretched her neck for a better view of the dessert. "I know you did not bake the cake. The hotel did." She sat back.

"Why did you say that?" Angela asked.

"Because Dad is not a good cook. Don't go away and leave him to cook for us."

Ronny rewarded Betty with a piece of the cake and then turned to Mia. "What do you prefer sweetie?"

"I too will eat hotel cake, served by my sweet Dad."

"What about you my dear?" Ronny asked Angela.

~~~~~~

Two hours later, the family vacated the dining table.

The children brushed their teeth and went to bed with little prompting. They were still tired from their participation in many physical activities during the day.

Angela's worry returned as she cleared the table. Where would she sleep?

She arranged all the dishes and leftover food back to the cart. "What do we do with the leftover food? Store it in that small fridge?" She asked Ronny as he returned from reading a bedtime story to the children.

"That will make the hotel manager a sad man. I will call them to come for the cart."

Minutes later, there was a knock at the door. Ronny opened, and two waiters walked in. They acknowledged Angela with a slight bow and went to the dining room.

One of the waiters said, "Madam, next time please leave the table for us to clear."

Angela wondered how to tell the waiter that she was the housegirl. She turned her attention to the main door on hearing Ronny converse with a third man whom he directed into the living room.

The waiter placed a silver pail containing a bottle of wine on the coffee table. He lifted the bottle and wiped off the icy droplets with a small towel. He turned the bottle in front of Angela and then Ronny.

Ronny nodded.

Assured that it was the right red wine, the waiter popped out the cork. He served a splash of wine into the two glasses, handing one to Angela and the other to Ronny.

He watched as Angela sniffed hers but did not taste.

Ronny sniffed the wine then took a sip. When he nodded, the waiter filled the two glasses and replaced the bottle back into the cooler.

The waiter turned to Angela with a slight curtsy, then to Ronny. "Enjoy your evening Madam and Sir." He walked out of the house, behind the two men who had wheeled out the food cart.

Ronny bolted the door, walked back and sat on the sofa, beside Angela. He picked one wine glass and lifted it to her. "To Angie, for making each one of us happy."

Angela accepted the glass. She held it and toasted Ronny. "To all of you, for taking me in as your housegirl."

She saw the smile fade off his face. She placed the glass on the table. "Thanks. I am yet to learn how to drink wine, or any alcohol," she said with a grin.

He put his glass on the table before he asked, "Never had alcohol? How is that?"

She laughed aloud. "Sorry, I am waking the children up. That is how we grew up. No alcohol in the family, though Dad has started to drink beer nowadays."

"He never drank. Not even wine?"

She shook her head.

"But you can learn." He lifted the glass of wine and gave it to her.

Angela received the glass and placed it on the table. "I am ready to learn and taste new food recipes, but not beer. And not while in Nakuru."

He took another sip from his glass. "Is it okay if I order tea while you make up your mind?"

She lifted her hand towards Ronny, like wanting to stop him from leaving his seat. "Thanks, no tea for me at night. What I need most is a place to sleep."

"What if you try some wine, then go back to your room of yesterday?"

"No!" She realized she had shouted. She lowered her voice. "I wish you had reserved a room, a bed for me."

He took another sip of wine. "I had assumed that we could discuss our future together, agree and share a room. Get to bond, nothing else—"

"I don't sleep with men," she interrupted him.

He put his glass on the table and shifted on the sofa, more to her direction. "Sorry. I am not 'men', I like you. Let's talk and see what we can agree on."

Her oval eyes opened wider. "You want to chase me away from my job. Not now, I need the job, the money."

Ronny stood up and stretched his neck towards the side of the children's bedrooms. "I will repeat myself until you get this one right." He sat down. "Whatever your decision between me and you, I want you to continue providing the same loving care to the children. They have no one."

"Stop making me feel guilty." She looked at the entrance into the house, prompting Ronny to do the same.

"That is not my idea. I prefer that you continue to be with the children. You have done an excellent job this far."

He rested his hand on her knee. The move was more out of fear that she planned to scamper out of the house, when she had taken a glance at the entrance.

He would not let that happen. He knew the consequences would be more than losing a hardworking housegirl. There would be a story from the night watchmen, to the Club's kitchen staff, to the hotel management and to his friends.

People in each of those groups would formulate their version of a story. What could have made Angela to dash out of the house late in the night. "Angela, dear, you know I do not have a wife. Thanks for helping my children out."

She raised her eyes in his direction.

He continued, "What if you extended that to me? I know we will complement one another well."

Tears welled in her eyes. She tilted her head towards the door again.

Ronny pressed his hand more on her thigh. He loosened the hold by massaging her, praying that she would not shovel his hand away.

He emptied the few drops of wine in his glass into his mouth. "I am not asking you to accept me tonight, or even tomorrow. Think about it in the new year."

Her face brightened with a smile.

"Tell me, what scares you so much about men?" he asked.

A tear escaped onto the sofa before she wiped more tears from her cheek. "The only experience I had pains my heart," she said in a choking voice.

He wiped tears from her cheeks with his thumb. "I am sorry to hear of your unpleasant experience. Your future experiences will be fine. I promise you."

"You don't know what I am talking about."

"I don't. Would you like to talk about it?"

"No." She stood up.

He did the same.

"Is it okay if I give you a hug, to lessen the pain?" He asked as he encircled his hands to her back.

He took the risk, hoping that she would let him hug her, at least in the name of easing her pain.

Ronny was surprised when she did not push him away. He continued to cuddle her until he sensed she had relaxed. He lowered his head and kissed the tears on her cheeks. Too tensed up himself, scared of what her next reaction would be.

When she tilted her head upwards, he was expecting the worst. Without much thought, he planted a kiss on her mouth. He felt her lips part and her hands leave her side and wander to his waist.

He relaxed, pulled her closer to his body. Her hands left his side and encircled his neck. She took over the kissing and only stopped as he groaned her name.

Angela pulled away.

He stepped back and waited.

She took two steps backwards. "I am too tired to think. I wish I had a place to sleep."

Ronny held out a hand for her. She obliged. He guided her to the corner of the room where her travel bag lay. He picked it up, "Come this way, to your room."

Angela followed, mainly because he was walking away from the direction of his bedroom, to the side of the kitchen.

He opened a door that she had all along assumed led outside, to the back of the house.

He stood by the door and placed her bag on the carpeted floor. "Will this room do? Though I prefer if you chose to spend the night with me, in the other room."

He noticed a genuine smile on her face as she said, "Next time I will be more adventurous. I would have found this room—"

Ronny quietened her words with a kiss on her mouth. "Good night my dear, hope you will spend part of your night to reflect on my plea."

He ushered her into the room, stepped inside and pushed the door to close behind them.

She stared at him, questioningly.

He chuckled. "I do not have plans other than to see you into your room, and chat if you are comfortable with that."

"I am too tired to discuss difficult topics."

He went and sat on a chair next to a study table. "What if you ask me all the difficult questions? I will do the talking."

Angela sat on the edge of the double bed. "Why did you follow me into this room?"

"To share my feelings for you and assure you that I will not do whatever you are scared of."

She smiled. "What about feelings?"

"Your good behaviour, hard work and love for the children has guided my heart towards you. I want to know if you will accept me."

"I am too tired to discuss such heavy matters. Is it okay if you leave so that I can go to bed? I have sleep of two days."

He stood up and offered his hand to her. "I fully understand."

Angela used his hand as support, pulled herself up and walked with him towards the door.

Instead of opening the door, Ronny turned and spread both arms. He cuddled her, but she struggled to pull away. He held her tightly and stood still until he felt her relax in his arms.

He loosened his hold and held her hands at arm's length. "I see a lot of sleep in your eyes." He bent his head to reach her face. She lifted her head upwards.

After a long kiss, Angela pulled away and pushed him by the chest. "Good night. I hope I will not regret this tomorrow."

"You won't. Please think about my request." He opened the door. "Good night my dear, sleep well." He walked out and pulled the door closed behind him.

Chapter 24

Angela felt dizzy as she walked back from the door.

She sat on a nearby chair and held her face in her hands. "God, what did I do? I kissed my boss again." She heard the words escape from her mouth. She scanned the room and noticed the door was not bolted.

Fearing that her weak knees would not provide the support she needed, she walked along the wall of the room to reach the door. She bolted the chain hanging on the door frame.

Assured that no one would enter her room without her hearing, she slid along the wall back to the chair. Her heart was pumping on her chest, hard.

A smile appeared on her face as she recalled the confident pause of Ronny as he pretended to be their chef that evening. She felt shy, acknowledging that he looked handsome, more of beautiful. If she had been a stranger and walked into the room, no one would have convinced her that he was old enough to be the father of his three children.

With the thought on age, she wondered if that was the reason the waiter had addressed them as madam and sir.

The sound of a message on her phone distracted her thoughts. She read, "I miss you already, but I will respect the time you need, good night my love."

She read the message again, placed the phone on the nightstand and walked into the bathroom. She brushed while she admired her face in the mirror. She wondered what it was that attracted Ronny to her when he had all the women struggling to get him to marry them.

Angela questioned if Ronny was just one of the many stories in town. Like other men who told their housegirls how they loved when they wanted to sleep with them. Once the woman became pregnant, the men denied they had ever slept with her.

She slapped her cheek. "Grandma said not all men are bad." She pulled off the hair band holding her braids together, shook her head twice and liked her heart-shaped face. She held the braids together at the top of her head and took a few steps to reach the shower nearby.

While in the shower, Angela recalled the warmth she felt when Ronny cuddled and kissed her. At the beginning she had resisted the feeling, until she could deny it no more. She recalled how her heart rate increased with each kiss.

She wrapped a towel around her body, pondering if that was the feeling men and women summed up as love. She had liked it more as Ronny held her tight to his body, as she felt his muscles harden around her. A giggle

277

escaped from her mouth followed by the words, "I wish for more."

She stopped by the mirror and gave herself a broad smile before she switched off the lights and walked into the bedroom.

As she set her morning alarm, she saw a missed call from Ronny. She set her alarm and put the phone on the bedside table and heaved herself onto the soft cotton bedsheets.

As she lay her head on the soft down feathers pillow, a question popped up in her mind. "What if there was a problem with one of the children and Ronny needed her help?"

She threw the sheets and duvet back and stepped out of bed to go check on the children. She reached the door, looked at her see-through nightie and walked back. She typed a message on her phone. "I was taking a shower, just seen your missed call. Hope the children are fine."

She heard a new message drop in and read, "Thanks for thinking of the children. You forgot to ask about me, the one who's unwell."

"What do you advise, I call the hotel reception for a doctor?" She wrote back.

Another message dropped in, a laughing *emoji* with the words, "Not that type of doctor. You are the doctor I need. Next time allow me to assist as you take a shower."

She chuckled, out of relief from the contents of the message. She would not know what to do if Ronny fell ill while with only her and the children.

In the city she had a list of the doctors to call for the children, for herself, for an adult within their compound, or if Ronny's parents were unwell. She made a mental note, to ask Ronny for information on what to do in case one of them fell ill while they were out of the city.

She typed a message. "Stop promising yourself things that are not possible. Good night. I need to catch up on the sleep I lost last night."

She switched off the lights and involuntarily looked at her phone, wishing to read another message from Ronny. She saw the blue light flash on the screen.

Supporting her head on one elbow, she read, "Please give me a chance to prove that all things are possible. Good night my love."

Angela pulled a bed sheet over her head. In the quietness of the December night, she wondered what it would be like if she became intimate with Ronny.

How would he transition from respecting her as his housegirl, to his partner, lover? She almost shouted out that she liked her job and would prefer their current relationship of housegirl and boss. She would not like to try something else that could jeopardize her job, her only source of income.

She rested her right hand on her chest as she uttered her nightly prayer.

In a moment, it was morning. Angela stretched a hand to her phone without opening her eyes. She knew that a random touch would silence the annoying wake up call.

She was surprised the next time she woke up, it was eight in the morning. She panicked, worrying that everyone else could be awake except her. She walked to her door and put her head to the door frame. There was quietness in the house.

After a quick shower, she dressed in a Valentino dress she had bought at a second-hand shop. She dotted it with drops of the perfume Ronny gave her as a Christmas gift.

A little sunshine would brighten her day. She drew open the curtains on the only window in the room and faced a huge tree nearby. There were monkeys jumping from one branch to the next.

Angela walked out of her room and found Betty and Mia in the living room watching TV.

"Where did you appear from, the kitchen?" Mia asked.

Angela beckoned the two girls. "Is Nikko awake? Come, I want to show you something." They followed her into the bedroom.

Mia verbalized her surprise. "I did not know there was a room here."

"Where did you think I was sleeping?"

Mia turned to Betty who had excitement written all over her face from seeing the jumpy monkeys. "Maybe on the extra bed in Nikko's room, or on the large bed with Dad," Mia said.

"Wooi! Can you imagine me sleeping with Dad?" Angela asked as the nice warm feeling crept back to her stomach. "How would that be?"

"I don't know," Mia shrugged her shoulders. "Auntie Rose asked if you sleep in Dad's room at home."

The smile disappeared from Angela's face. "What did you tell her?"

"I was with Betty," Mia said as she took the few steps to reach the window where Betty was, jumping up and down as she watched the monkeys hop from one branch of the tree to the next.

"Betty, remember when we were with Grandma and Auntie asked about Angie?" Mia smiled at Angela. "I told her you sleep in your room, the one next to our bedrooms."

"What would you do if I slept in the same room with your father?"

Betty turned away from the window. "I don't know. Will you wake up early, before it is time for us to go to school?"

Angela did not answer. Instead she looked at Mia.

"Okay," Mia said. "My friends at school say that every daddy should have one woman he sleeps with, otherwise he will sleep with many different women from the streets." Her eyebrows pulled in. "I don't want that to happen to Dad."

Angela spread out her arms and embraced Mia, as Betty asked, "Angie, will you sleep with Dad in his bedroom? We do not know the women from the streets. We know you."

A monkey screamed when another one scratched it. Surprisingly, the sound did not distract Betty as she continued. "You like us. You cook the best food for us, you arrange my wardrobe, and you give us hugs."

Angela's eyes welled up. She pulled Betty into an embrace. "Thank you."

The three watched the monkeys in silence.

Betty ran out of the room saying, "Nikko will miss this."

"I will be back." Angela said as she followed Betty to keep her from waking Nikko.

Angela saw Ronny in the living room. Betty was pulling him by his hand. "Dad, you must come and see the monkeys."

Angela looked at the two. "I thought you were going to wake Nikko up."

Betty lifted her chin towards Angela. "I was, but I stopped here when I saw Dad. I want Dad to go see the monkeys from your room."

Angela walked to Nikko's room as she heard Ronny ask, "No morning greetings for me?"

"Sorry. Good morning, Sir," She winked at him as she walked away and met with Nikko walking out of his room.

Angela squatted. "Good morning Nikko. Did you have a nice sleep? I was coming for you. We need to go climb a tree and play with monkeys."

"Dad said not good to go near animals or touch them," he said as Angela held his hand and they walked to her room. Nikko struggled out of her hold.

Ronny stood up and extended a hand to Betty. "Come, I'll show you something different."

They walked to one of the two windows in his bedroom. "What animals do you see out there?" He pointed outside.

Betty pressed her face to the glass window. "Zebras!"

She ran out of the room, to Angela's room and pulled Mia by the arm. "Come, there are more animals to see from Dad's room."

They finished eating breakfast at ten and sat outside, basking in the sun until the driver arrived at midday to drive them back to the city.

The children objected, they wanted to stay another day, watch wild animals in the night from the windows of the house.

The children agreed to board the car after Ronny called out for their attention. "Today is the thirty-first. The end of 2014. We need to travel to the city, shower and change into nice clothes. We will go visit Grandpa and Grandma."

They obeyed as he added, "And John needs enough time to travel and be with his family before the clocks strike New Year."

Chapter 25

Schools opened for the new school year and the children effortlessly got into their school schedule.

Ronny was on international travel for most of February.

March came and dragged on as the children counted the days to their Easter school holiday.

Angela felt less tired with each day, week and month. She had fully adapted to her work routine with the children. She liked her job more and Ronny had become more loving towards her, and he respected her no.

Assured that the children were happy at home and school, Ronny spent more time at the office, which worried Angela.

She questioned herself, if she had pushed him away with her many rejections whenever he approached her. She had not given him an answer to his question, if she would be interested to stay on, marry him.

Though he kissed her each time he left for work and when he arrived back home, she had refused to move to his bedroom. Yet, she missed him most of the day when he was away at work.

Angela never forgot to say her daily prayers, show gratitude for her job and salary. She welcomed more tasks. She now had an added task, attending sporting events and other extra-curricular activities of the children at school and at various clubs in the city.

Over time she had overcome her fear and started to join the children in the swimming pool.

It had taken her many weeks of deliberation before she gathered courage and joined in the competitive parent activities at the children's schools.

The first time Ronny asked her to join other parents, she had said, "But I am not one of the parents."

To which Ronny had asked, "Are you telling me that you are not a parent to Babu? Go join the other parents."

She had looked around to confirm that no one heard that she had a child whom she was trying to deny. She could not imagine doing that to her son.

To compensate for the guilt she felt, she joined parents at the children's school.

The other change was that Angela had increased her phone calls to her brother and sister-in-law until Joshua asked her to limit the calls to once a week. He explained that Babu needed time to adjust to his new home and school life.

Feeling dejected but not wanting to argue with her brother, Angela turned her many phone calls to her grandmother. The more she called, the more Priscah asked about Ronny's children and if she was already married to him.

Angela's response remained the same, "*Nyanya*, you will be the first to know the day I sleep in the same bed with the man. Don't forget that you are the one to marry me off."

"Your father is still alive. Has life in those cities made you forget you still have a father?"

"*Nyanya*, I still love my father, I call him often."

Priscah chuckled. "Has he told you that your stepmother wants you to bring Babu for her to take care of?"

Angela had stayed quiet until Priscah assumed the phone had disconnected and got into a monologue. "These phones talk, talk, then stop. Hope she will call to hear more."

On hearing her grandmother's monologue, Angela asked, "*Nyanya*, what does that mean, about my son?"

"I do not know. For now, my advice is that continue to love your father but do not bring your son to Zippy. She's been your stepmother when you needed her most, now she wants Babu, your money," Priscah said followed by laughter.

"*Nyanya*, I need to go back to work. I will call you tomorrow to talk more."

Angela ended the call, tapped on Joshua's number and typed a message. "Hi. How is everyone? Let me know when we can talk, I hear Babu is needed at home."

Her phone rang. She was attentive, she could tell from the poor phone reception that Joshua was in motion.

"The boy is fine. What do you mean by Babu to go home? Back to Grandma?"

"Are you at school? It's a long story, we can talk later."

"I walked out of the staffroom, no need to wait."

"I just talked with Grandma, and she asked if Zippy has told me that she wants Babu to go home, for her to take care of him."

"And you agreed?" Joshua shouted into the phone.

"I have not spoken with Zippy. And Dad never mentioned such information the last time I spoke with him."

"Today?"

"No, yesterday. I call him every Sunday and Wednesday."

"Good. Babu is fine. Promise me—"

"Yes," Angela said without waiting for Joshua to complete the sentence.

"Avoid any calls from Dad. I will talk with him tonight and get back to you."

"Okay," she whispered back.

Joshua chuckled. "Ronny wants Babu in the city with you, seems to me like the right time for you to bring them together."

"But...,"

The phone disconnected before Angela could respond to what Joshua said about Babu and Ronny. She lifted the phone from her ear and looked at the screen, the disconnection sound she heard was real.

The day dragged on. Angela did Ronny's laundry before she left to accompany Nikko to his karate classes while Joseph went to pick up Mia and Betty from school.

Nikko had asked to go for the classes after his friends told him that only babies stayed at school after lunch, so they could sleep. He had convinced his father by crying that he was four, a big boy. He went for the classes twice a week, Tuesdays and Thursdays.

Mia and Betty had Table Tennis lessons on Fridays, after school. Angela and Nikko would sit in the gym and cheer for the girls until the game was over. They traveled home together.

While waiting for Nikko to complete his karate lesson, Angela spent most of the ninety minutes looking at her phone, waiting for Joshua to call.

She consoled herself that in April, less than a month away, she would travel to Nakuru to visit Babu. She would also go to her village to visit her grandmother.

Chapter 26

Angela arrived at her grandmother's house before lunch time. The journey from Nakuru to Nyametende took three hours.

She had not informed her grandmother or her parents of her travel, so it was a pleasant surprise when Priscah saw her.

Angela was unbolting the small gate to Priscah's compound when she heard Priscah say, "That looks like my son's daughter, though she should be in the city."

Angela entered the compound where she preferred to visit first whenever she arrived home. "*Nyanya*, the city has moved closer to our village."

Priscah struggled to stand up from her wooden recliner chair.

Angela quickened her step and reached Priscah's side before she stood up. She let her travel bag drop to the ground, spread her arms out and embraced Priscah. "I missed you *Nyanya*, how have you been?"

Priscah pushed Angela out of the embrace and held her by the hands. "Who knew my baby would grow into such a beautiful woman." She tilted her neck up, faced the midday blue sky. "Your mother must be smiling from the ancestral lands."

Angela embraced her grandmother again. "I had assumed that my life was the worst without a mother, until I met the children I work for." She squeezed Priscah's shoulders. "Three of them. One is younger than Babu, and without a mother." Angela picked up her bag and walked into the house, with Priscah tagging along.

"Come, I have greetings for you from Babu, Joshua and his family. I have been in Nakuru."

"I was wondering if your *Tajiri* brought you in one of those fast-moving cars from the city," Priscah said while serving her drinking water.

Angela chuckled but did not say what was in her mind. She had wanted to tell Priscah that Ronny would be more than ready to drive or fly her to the village if she allowed him.

She gave Priscah gifts she had bought for her. Two Kitenge dresses designed by Recho Omondi, which were once chic. A cotton dress, a wool sweater, rubber shoes, cotton bedsheets and socks.

Priscah received and kissed each item with mumbles, "Thank you, may you be blessed many times, God has heard your prayers, our ancestors never sleep."

She held the last gift, a floral headscarf in front of her and said, "Babu might forget his other mama. Why did you not come with him?"

Angela scanned the entrance to the house before she responded. "I would have brought him, but I thought better if I come alone and hear why our mother now wants to have my child with her."

Priscah extended her wrinkled hand and softly drummed Angela's thigh. In a lowered voice, she asked, "Did you see your stepmother out there?"

Angela shook her head.

"Trouble," Priscah said. "She is now friends with Sabrina, Babu's other grandmother."

"What?" Angela raised her voice. "I had no idea they knew one another."

Priscah walked to the side of the kitchen within the house. She opened a paper box and retrieved a paper bag.

Angela watched as the aroma of ripe bananas revealed why Priscah had walked away. "*Nyanya*, does your farm ever run out of bananas?"

"The soil was made to serve us, if we give it good care." She brought seven bananas in a tray. "I have potatoes to eat with the bananas."

Angela went to the sink and washed her hands, "Thank goodness it is April, there is water." She returned to her chair as Priscah placed one large potato on the table. "I ate not long ago," she picked a banana and held it without peeling it. "Don't you know that birds of a feather flock together? They want money, not the boy."

Angela waved her grandmother aside. "What money, from who?"

Priscah stared at Angela for a long moment before her lips parted. "Have you married your *Tajiri* and his children, or are you waiting for him to bring another woman for you to serve?"

Angela made a face, stretched her tongue out to Priscah. *"Ng'oo."* She stared at her grandmother. She needed a moment to decide if to share the details or not.

She was reflective, asking herself who else she had in her life to share such information with other than her grandmother. She trusted her brother, but details of her life with Ronny were not the type of information she would share with him.

She had friends from high school, but she knew where she stood with them. Some had drawn away from her once they got word that she was pregnant. Others had been urging her to introduce them to Ronny after she told them she worked as a housegirl for a widower, the heir of Henry Technologies, Inc.

A smile engulfed her face. "My *Tajiri* said he wants to marry me, but—"

"Children of today," Priscah interrupted with a chuckle. "That must be a very good man, go and marry him." She waved Angela away.

"How do you know he is a good man?"

Priscah poked Angela on the cheek tenderly. "You live with him, cook for him and he has not made you pregnant." She laughed.

Angela smiled back. *"Nyanya,* nowadays if a man sleeps with you by force, you can report him to the police, and they will take him to court."

"Eeeh," Priscah mumbled, made eye contact with Angela and asked. "The man who was to be taken to the police is the father of Babu, not a man who asks you to marry him. How long have you lived with that man, your *Tajiri?"*

Angela swallowed the food in her mouth, took a sip of water before she said, "A year next week." She then reflected on what Priscah had said. She looked up and found Priscah staring at her.

Angela considered if her grandmother could be right that Ronny was a good man. She had heard stories of some men who force their housegirls, or other workers, or even office employees to sleep with them. Whenever the women reported them to the authorities, the court cases took long before such a woman received any hearing. By that time the woman would have moved out of the city or was busy struggling to feed her baby if she had become pregnant. Like she was now, struggling to earn money and take care of Babu. "Do you think he will marry me when I have Babu?"

"What do you call the ones he has, the ones you are taking care of? Will you marry him when he has children?"

"They are good children, I like them, and they like me."

Priscah pointed a finger at Angela, something she had not done for long.

Reflecting, Angela recalled that the last time her grandmother had appeared that serious was when she had touched her stomach and declared that Angela was pregnant.

Priscah interrupted her thoughts. "Better if you marry a man with his own children, it makes it easier for you to bring yours along."

Priscah must have noticed the scared look on Angela's face, so she smiled. "Do you have another man wanting to marry you? I am told Babu's father found another girl and made her his wife."

Angela scratched her head. "I will think about it," she said though she knew that she did not have much time. In recent times, Ronny had crossed some of the boundaries she had set, including not to cuddle or kiss her in front of the children.

Whenever she asked him, his reply was that he loved her. He wanted her for him and for the children. At other times Ronny asked Angela why she freely cuddled the children but not him.

He bought her gifts whenever he traveled: perfume, a handbag, or a book. He also encouraged her to have her hair and nails done when she accompanied Mia and Betty to the beauty salon.

In the beginning, Angela had turned down the offer until she found the waiting time at the salon too long. When she finally decided to have her hair washed, blow-dried and set, the lady at the salon declined her money, told her that all the bills from any member of Ronny's family were invoiced to him, under his account.

The warm nice feeling engulfed her stomach as she recalled the kisses she and Ronny had shared.

The muscles on her face tightened as she questioned how she would feel if Ronny brought a woman to the house, as a wife or girlfriend. "What will Dad say if I told him I want to get married, and to a man with...," she mumbled.

"Go back to the city and tell your *Tajiri* you will marry him, then come home and inform your father." Priscah stared at Angela as she continued, "Have you told your brother, does he know?"

"No and yes. I did not tell him, but he is good friends with my *Tajiri*." Angela looked out the door as her cousins, Stephanie and Sarah knocked on the door and walked in.

Chapter 27

On Saturday morning Angela went to her parents' house.

Zippy welcomed her warmly, unlike before. "Come in, come in for breakfast." Zippy invited her into the house and brought a cup for her to join in the breakfast they were eating while she asked, "How is the city? It has done you a lot of good."

Angela was baffled by the enthusiasm. She greeted her father Luka and pulled a dining chair for herself. Though she was aware that her stepmother wanted to take care of Babu, she was not expecting such instant change.

"Good," Angela said. "I have a lot of tasks to do, but I am fine with that."

She did not want to say something that would make her parents ask more questions. If she told them that she lived with an understanding family, they might ask what relationship she had with them to say that they were good.

Luka nodded.

Zippy said. "We assumed you would come with Babu, before he breaks your brother's marriage."

Angela put the teacup on the dining table. "How?"

"Bring Babu back home so we can take care of him. If your sister-in-law is overworked from taking care of children, she might divorce your brother," Zippy explained.

Angela cast her eyes to the outside through the panel of glass windows. She wished Zippy could realize that Joshua's wife had no ill feelings about Babu residing with them. "Divorce? I pay his school fees. I contribute some money for Babu's upkeep, a sisterly gift though Joshua discourages me from paying."

Zippy chuckled. "Maybe he wants you to remove the child from his house. Accepting your money would be saying yes to have the child stay."

Angela held the cup close to her mouth. She worried if it was true that misunderstandings could develop between Joshua and Florence over Babu being in their house. But then Angela recalled that during the three days she spent in Nakuru, the family appeared fine and Babu had already become great friends with his cousins, Dave and Angelica, the baby.

"I will make a stop-over in Nakuru, on my way to Nairobi." Angela said as she looked from her father to Zippy. She saw Zippy's eyes soften with a smile.

Angela added, "I was in Nakuru for three days and all I saw was love and happiness in Joshua's family. He sends his greetings," she said while looking her father's direction.

Zippy went to the nearby kitchen. "Remember, we still have two extra bedrooms in this house. Babu can spoil himself with choices."

"He's already in school. It will be hard to transfer him here," Angela said, trying her best not to reveal the anger she felt. She wondered how her stepmother who never liked her or Babu in her father's house, was now offering her and Joshua's childhood bedrooms freely.

Angela bit her lower lip, questioning what good had entered Zippy's heart to now ask to take care of her child. How was it that she now cared about Joshua's marriage, when Zippy had never hidden her dislike for him as well.

"It's better if that boy is cared for by us," Zippy said. "That way, his other grandmother will not take him away from you."

The cup dropped from Angela's hand and landed on the table, splashing the little tea that was inside.

"Sorry. The cup dropped," Angela said as she stood up, grabbed a paper towel and placed it on the table, stopping the tea from dripping down to the cement floor. "Sorry, my hands must be shocked, that now my child has grandparents," She mumbled.

"Was there a time he did not have grandparents?" Luka asked.

"Not really," Angela said as tears welled up in her eyes.

The question from her father had reminded her of all the suffering she had gone through while pregnant and after her baby was born. She recalled like it was yesterday. It was her grandmother who had escorted her to the government hospital in town when it was time to deliver the baby. It was her grandmother and her two older cousins who asked if she had had something to eat, and it was her cousins who paid for the taxi that drove them back home with the newborn baby. "Babu will be better off staying with his uncle and aunty," Angela said, more out of anger.

She turned to Zippy. "Does this other grandmother know what Babu looked like when he was born?" She chuckled. "Not until she was ready to steal him on Christmas."

Her hope was that Zippy would apply the question to herself as well. All she had done was ridicule Angela when she could no longer hide her pregnancy. Angela had not forgotten how her stepmother had made fun of her pregnancy, asking where she was getting all the food that was making her stomach bulge out that way.

Zippy broke the silence. "It will be better for you to bring the boy here. That way, some man can marry you without knowing you have a baby."

Angela pushed her chair back, away from the table and turned toward her father. "The man who wants to marry me wants me and my baby." She stood up and extended a hand to her father. "I am leaving right now, I want to get to Nakuru before darkness sets in."

Angela walked towards the door as her father called out, "Do you have some minutes to wait we harvest a banana for Joshua?"

"Yes, about thirty minutes," she said while walking out, aware that the stare from Zippy was still pinned onto her back.

It was past two o'clock when Angela boarded a vehicle to Nakuru. She chose a window seat and was in deep thought for most of the journey. She was oblivious of the high speed the Nissan traveled, above the legal one hundred kilometers per hour.

The ringing of a phone startled Angela. It was her phone. She listened as Joshua asked, "Hi, how is everyone? Did they stop you from traveling?"

"She whispered into the phone. "Thanks for calling, I forgot to send a message. We are near Njoro, thirty minutes away from Nakuru considering the speed at which we are moving."

"See you then. I will pick you up," he said.

She kept her phone in the handbag that she held securely on her lap and reflected on her future. If she was to be married by Ronny, or any other man, she would state her preconditions upfront. She would want a wedding. It had been part of her dreams as a young girl. She still treasured the image of her in a tight-fitting wedding dress with a long veil, five meters flowing behind her. She would not move in with a man until after her wedding. Would Ronny support her condition if she agreed to marry him?

Angela then thought of Rose, Dianna and the other people who could object to her marriage to Ronny.

She worried that she might arrive in the city the next day and find that Ronny had taken in one of the many women that Rose had in waiting. Did the matatu come to a complete stop, or her life?

~~~~~~

Ronny and his family returned to the city two days before Angela was to be back. The family had traveled to their home village of Kongunga, for Bella's second memorial.

On arrival in the city, Ronny decided it would be easier if his children visited with their cousins. He took them to his sister's house.

Ronny was by his car, ready to leave when he heard Rose calling, "Junior, wait for me."

He checked time before he turned to Rose standing by the front veranda to her house. "Did I hear my name?"

She gave thumbs up. "No, you heard my voice," she said as she descended the steps to reach the driveway.

Rose waved at John on the driver's seat, then back to Ronny. "Is there someone home with you or should I tag along?"

"Come." Ronny motioned her into the car. He was astonished when Rose jumped in and sat back left, his usual position. He walked around the car and sat back right.

John started the engine before he asked, "Home or club?"

"Home," Rose said and then asked Ronny, "Or are you hungry for the club?"

Ronny shook his head.

As Joseph drove out, Ronny questioned what could make his sister choose to accompany him after he had brought his children to her house. On further reflection, he determined it was good she came, an opportunity for him to tell her about his love for Angela.

Ronny spent their travel time chatting with John, asking about his home. Ronny had encouraged John to go spend time at his rural home after he had dropped them at Kongunga.

Fifteen minutes later, they were at Ronny's house.

John parked the Toyota Prado and drove off in a Subaru Impreza, the car he normally drove to his house in the city.

Rose marched into the house behind Ronny. She embraced him. "Such an emotional speech you gave at the memorial. Why did you say future memorials will be five years apart?"

Ronny exhaled. "Time to move on sister, we will continue to pray for Bella." He motioned her, and they walked into the living room where he occupied his recliner chair.

Hands held akimbo, Rose said, "Two years have passed, and you have refused to move on. Eeeh?"

He pointed her to a chair. "Let it be on my time, not other peoples' time." He tapped the armrest. "My time, my children's time, those are the people who matter the most. My time has come."

"I am happy to hear you've decided to move on. Who's the lucky lady?"

He chuckled. "Reverse your sentence, I am the lucky one. I will introduce her to you after I convince her. Unless you want to convince her for me." Ronny said though he knew there was no way he would draw his sister into his love affair, let alone to convince Angela for him.

Ronny tapped his fingers to a silent song before he asked. "Will you talk her into accepting me, if it happens to be none of your friends?"

"In no way can it be a different person." Her eyebrows pulled in. "I hope you have not bought into the idea of our crazy sister-in-law, Dianna."

Ronny cast his eyes to the ceiling. He lifted both hands and intertwined the fingers behind his head. "Their culture, not mine. I cannot marry the aunty of my children."

He liked the smile that appeared on Rose's face as she said, "Let me know who to bring. Judy, Christine, Mercy or Daphne?"

Ronny stood up and picked his cell phone from a nearby stool. "Would you like me to call for evening tea or can you come fix something in the kitchen?" He chuckled. "Now I miss our Angela."

Rose walked towards the kitchen and Ronny followed as she admonished him. "Angela, Angela, Angie. How many times will you utter that name before you scare away your new wife?"

He massaged the back of his neck before shifting the hand to his chin as they arrived in the kitchen. "What if I convince her to be the same person?"

Rose sneered. "The next day's headlines, a city gentleman marries his housegirl."

Ronny laughed out loud, pulled a stool and sat by the kitchen island. "Do you know where the cooking pots are, or should I call for dinner from your house?"

Rose picked the phone she had placed on the countertop and dialed a number as she walked out of the kitchen. She returned while giving instructions on the food her driver was to deliver.

She opened two floor-level cupboards and banged them closed. She walked into the pantry.

Ronny could tell that she was angry, so he gave her time to cool down. He picked up his phone and scrolled through until he heard her speak.

"Can you ask your Angela to label some items? What would you do if she fails to turn up tomorrow? I cannot find simple things in your kitchen."

Rose's words alarmed Ronny. What would he do if Angela did not return as agreed?

He slid down from the stool, walked to a cupboard on the right side of the cooker, opened and removed tea leaves, sugar and tea masala. He went to the cupboards across from the island, opened one and pulled out an aluminum cooking pot with a cover. He stared back at Rose, aware that she had been looking at him.

He crossed hands on his chest to match hers, as he said, "Are those enough? It is not possible to cook masala tea in the kettle."

She unclasped her hands, picked up the cooking pot, went to the kitchen sink and added water.

Ronny chuckled as he walked back to the island. He picked his phone and typed a message. "Hi, my dear. How was home? Are you already in Nakuru?" He clicked send and placed the phone on the countertop.

Since December when Ronny first kissed Angela and she returned his kiss, he knew there were high chances he would convince her to marry him. It was now April and Angela had accepted his kisses as normal. He had also learned that she felt shy if he kissed her in public, he had tried to limit showing his affection by only holding her waist or shoulder in public.

He had another reason. He had wanted to keep some distance between him and Angela as he waited to celebrate Bella's second memorial. His plan was that after the anniversary, he would do whatever it took to get Angela to agree to marry him.

The sound of a message coming into his phone interrupted his thoughts. He read, "Thanks. We are fine. I will travel back as planned. I miss the kids, my regards to them."

A smile engulfed his face as he typed, "Thank you."

Aware that Rose was staring, he clicked send and raised his chin her direction. There she was, holding a one hand akimbo with thinned lips, like she was ready for a fight.

He beckoned her. "Come fight your brother. Easy prey since you cannot fight your husband, or your crazy in-laws."

Ronny had always been surprised that Rose was meek to her in-laws. Here she was, tough on him like nails, trying to dictate whom he could or should not marry.

Rose walked to his side and poked his shoulder. "You look lonely, you need a wife to keep you on your toes."

He pulled out a stool for her. "My CEO work and my lovely kids keep me busy enough." He chuckled. "I need a wife to love me, love the kids, and me to love them all." He spread his hands out wide and brought them together in a mock embrace.

"On a serious note, which among the girls I named did you choose?" Rose asked.

"None," Ronny said as he slid off the stool and took long strides towards the boiling tea, almost overflowing the pot. He switched off the gas and lifted the pot to a different side of the cooker. "Come serve me. That way I will have an idea on how your friends will serve me," he said, smoothing a hand down his chest.

"Are you looking for a wife or a worker? You already have a housegirl, though you should replace her with a chef and a cleaner."

Ronny looked at her as she sieved the tea into a flask. "You are my sister, my only sibling. I will be happier if you let me choose a partner. House workers? Maybe I will get someone to load dishes and sweep the kitchen."

"What about cooking?"

"Angela will continue with what she loves, cooking and minding the kids, until she starts her study program."

He could see that his words had had the intended effect. He grinned as he listened to her speak.

"My ears must be muffled with wax." She placed a tray filled with tea items - a tea flask, cups, sugar and tea biscuits, on the island countertop. "Am I hearing that your housegirl has bewitched you into desiring her?"

"Yes, if that is what you call my love for her." He poured tea into two cups, added one spoonful of sugar to one cup and stirred. "What do you have against Angela?"

"I will tell Mum."

He pulled Rose's left hand to his mouth and kissed her fingers. "Please do that, tell Mum she will have another ready-made grandson."

He made an imaginary checkmark in the air with his finger. "One important item off my to do list."

He took a sip from his cup. "The one you call housegirl has provided the conducive environment I need to perform my office duties." He placed the cup back on the counter as Rose spoke.

"Does that mean you have relegated the care of your children to a housegirl? And did you say she has children?"

"Just like my sister and most of the rich families in the city have done, left the care of their children to workers in their houses."

He waited until she finished laughing then added, "I will be better off with my so-called housegirl as my friend, lover, and the person I entrust the care of my children to."

"What will you tell Mum, Dad, our relatives and friends?" she asked.

"That I have found a nice girl to marry, and we both have and love children?"

"No." How will you walk around with her?"

He pulled Rose's right hand and hooked it to his bent elbow. "Like this."

She pulled her arm away and elbowed him softly on the arm.

Ronny tickled her. "I will show you once I convince her." He pointed to her cup. "Your tea is getting cold."

She waved him off, lifted her cup and sipped. She put the cup down. "No sugar for me?"

"I hear there are ladies who don't see eye to eye with sugar because of their waistline." He scooped a spoonful of sugar.

She moved her cup away. "That is too much sugar. Less than a quarter of that will do."

They drank tea in silence before Ronny spoke. "Do me one favour."

She replaced her cup on the table as he continued to speak. "Please do not scare her away, even if it means you not visiting for now."

"That's how confused you've become, chasing away your family?"

"Not really. Just trying to find some happiness for myself," Ronny said as his eyes stayed focused on a wave of lights filtering through the kitchen window. He put his cup on the table. "Is that the food I have been waiting for?"

He asked as he vacated his seat and walked towards the kitchen door.

He was not able to see the outside well through the nearby window at that time of day because of the light inside the house. He walked to the house phone and pressed one key and asked. "Whom did you let into the compound?"

The rule was that the security people at the gate were to call and speak with someone in the house before letting people in, especially at night. Unless it was one of his family members or the office drivers driving in a family member.

"Robert for Rose," was the response he received from the night watchman.

"Okay, thanks." Ronny replaced the receiver. He went and swung the kitchen door open to let Robert in. "Hey, man, good to see you. Come in, come in," Ronny said while ushering Robert into the house.

Robert walked to the kitchen island. "Today I have followed my wife, to feed her," he said as he placed a food warmer on the countertop.

Ronny closed the door and joined Rose and Robert. "I will get your wife here more often," he said as he removed the multi-level hotpot from the carrier bag.

Ronny went for plates from the hanging cupboard at one end of the kitchen. After placing them on the countertop, he went back for silverware. "Angela is not here to see me bring cutlery in my hands. She prefers a tray."

"Have you become her prisoner, in your own house?" Rose asked.

"Who's become a prisoner?" Robert asked, on his way back from washing hands.

Ronny chuckled. "Me, to my Angela."

Robert patted Ronny on the shoulder. "Well done man, for finding someone. "

"I had no idea you would marry a housegirl," Rose said while she served food.

The two men turned toward each other, but neither one spoke. Each must have been wondering if Rose's message was directed at them.

It was ten o'clock when Rose and Robert drove out.

Ronny was happy with the way the evening had gone. He had managed to tell Rose of his love for Angela. His hope was that Rose would stop parading her friends to him.

He stopped by the door to his bedroom and typed a message. "Hi. I wish you were here. I am all alone. I left the kids at Rose's house. Just had dinner with Rose and Robert." He clicked send and walked inside. He scanned his bedroom, like it had suddenly become too vast for his liking.

A message dropped in, he read, "Good to hear the kids are taken care of, and you've eaten. I was worried. Good night." Angela did not explain what her worry was. She had been worried that she might return and find Ronny had brought a girlfriend to the house.
He read the message twice before he put his phone down on a bedside table and went to the bathroom.

Chapter 28

The two-hour journey from Nakuru to Nairobi seemed longer than usual for both Angela and Ronny, though for different reasons.

Angela was apprehensive that Ronny had changed his mind while she was away. She planned to be more friendly, responsive to his love, lest he assumed she was not interested.

Ronny on the other hand was waiting for Angela to arrive so he could serve her tea and tell her that he loved her. Ronny had taken time to reflect, questioned why Angela seemed to want him whenever they kissed, then pushed him away. Maybe she was afraid he was out to take advantage of her. His plan was to spend the evening with her, reassure her that he loved her and wanted to marry her.

John parked the car on the driveway near the kitchen from where Angela used her key to get into the house. There was quietness as she punched her code to quieten the alarm that was quickly counting down to zero.

Then the drop of a cooking pot on the kitchen floor startled her, threw her into panic mood. Had she not completed punching in the code, the fear that gripped her would have erased the code from her mind.

Ronny did not pick the pot that had accidentally dropped. He walked to Angela before she screamed and dashed for the door to go outside.

"I have never been this scared in my life. A very quiet house and when I thought I was the only one in, a pot hit—"

She lost the remaining words as Ronny embraced her. He kissed her on both cheeks and the mouth before he released her. "Welcome back home."

He held both her hands and examined her from head to waist. "I missed you each day you were away. Do you prefer to start with tea, or do you need to reach your room first?" He asked as he pointed towards the kitchen island where he had set the tea.

She picked her luggage, her other hand on her chest as she said in a shaky voice, "I will be back for the tea." She walked away.

Ronny stared until she turned a corner.

Angela paused by the family room where she had expected to find the children watching TV or playing a game. They were nowhere. She walked on.

As she pushed the door to her room open, it occurred to her how different sleeping quarters could be. From her worn out mattress at her grandmother's house, to the futon bed she slept on at her brother's house in Nakuru, and to what she now considered a magnificent room in the city.

After showering she dressed in a floral pink and cream full-length nightie and added a complimenting cream gown. Her plan was to eat whatever Ronny had prepared and go to bed early. She was tired.

She held the door handle to leave the bedroom when she realized she would be sending the wrong message to Ronny by appearing in her night clothes. She changed into grey sweatpants and a matching T-shirt.

Ronny stood from a high stool. "What took you so long?" He asked while pulling a stool for her to sit beside him.

Angela walked to the opposite side of the island and pulled out a stool for herself. "How are my friends, the children?" She asked, climbing onto the stool, making herself comfortable and crossing her arms on the countertop.

"Interesting evening. I pull a stool for you, you walk away." He chuckled. "Then you answer my question with a question."

He served tea into the two cups. "You have no reason to wake up early tomorrow." He added sugar, one teaspoon into each cup. "The children are being spoilt by their aunty, Rose."

"Thank you for the tea. Tomorrow is Monday, unless you are not going to work."

"I will work from home," he said as he lifted his cup. "How is everyone at home, and Joshua and family, and Babu our boy?"

"Fine. Grandma, as interesting as always. She makes me miss the village."

"You must be very close to her?"

"She brought me up, after our mother died."

He extended his long arm across and trapped her hand to the granite top. "Sorry for your loss. And Joshua?"

"He was in secondary school and later proceeded to university."

"Hope your life was not very hard?"

She placed her cup back on the table without taking a sip. "Pray you do not marry someone like our stepmother. She never wanted us in our house, she now wants my son."

Ronny intertwined his fingers with hers, pondering how best to respond to her comment about her stepmother. "What do you mean by 'wants your son?' Is he not with Joshua?"

"He is. Out of the blues she told me she is ready to take care of Babu. A child she never carried, even when he cried all day out of hunger."

Ronny set her hand free and stepped down from the stool. "Are you saying that your second mother did not take care of you, or your baby?"

"That is a detail I would rather forget." She watched as he reached her side and placed his arm on her shoulder.

She felt shivers down her spine as he mumbled. "I am here to make the rest of your life, the best."

She tilted her neck upwards to look at him. She lost her breath. Ronny clasped her lips into his mouth and licked on them until she gave in, returned his kiss.

He held her shoulder and helped her descend from the stool without disentangling their mouths. Once her feet were on the floor, he encircled one hand around her slender waist and pulled her closer to his body. "I missed you so much, hope you missed me too." He guessed her answer was yes from the way she licked his lips.

Still holding onto her, Ronny guided her away from the kitchen.

She pulled back. "What are we doing?"

"Whatever you agree to," he said.

She freed herself from his hold and walked back to her stool. She felt warm and could hear the pounding of her heart. She sat down, hoping her heartbeat would slow down and help the warm feeling in her body recede.

Ronny followed her. "Did I do something wrong?"

"No," she said, still panting. She exhaled.

He was glad, she was not mad with him for kissing her. He knew she had enjoyed the kiss as much as he did, until something he could not figure out made her push him away. He had noticed on several occasions that she would return his kiss and suddenly push him away.

The trend worried him. He needed to know what caused that fear in her. "Are you hungry for food or we go relax from the living room?"

"I could do with some food." She stepped down from the stool and went to the fridge.

He followed her and stopped near the oven, switched it on and set a timer. "We can have more tea or a glass of wine while the food heats up."

"Did you cook for me?" She stood on her toes and kissed him on the cheek.

He attempted to pull her closer, but she was too fast for him. She took the few steps to reach her stool. "You make me feel very special. I will sit here and wait to be served." She sprang onto the stool.

Ronny followed and sat opposite from her. "You've always been special. Give me a chance to show you more," he extended a hand across to her side of the island. His plan was to take a good look at her fingers, get an idea on the size of her engagement finger. He planned to buy her a ring as he was now convinced she would accept his marriage proposal.

Without warning, Ronny stepped down from the stool, went and stood beside her. He held her wrists, bent and lined his forehead with hers.

"What?" she asked without pulling away.

"Did you remember to tell your parents, your brother and dear Grandma about us?" He lowered his mouth to her lips.

She struggled and freed her mouth. "How do you expect me to answer without a mouth?"

Ronny laughed out loud. "Right on spot," he said before he sat on a nearby stool and entwined their fingers. "Did you?"

"Not really, though Grandma has not stopped thinking that I am growing old."

Angela did not elaborate on what Priscah had said about being at her prime age for marriage, or not to let the good man be taken by another woman.

He leaned closer to her. "That is her way of saying you are very beautiful, in and out. You need to agree to my request." He tightened his grip on her hand. "Please."

"What do you need a wife for? To me you look happy, complete by yourself and the children."

He held her earlobe between his lips. "Thanks for taking care of the kids. Please give me a chance to show you how much peace you have brought into my mind, our house."

She groaned. "Any housegirl could have done that."

"I know what I am talking about. Come, join me we raise all the children together. We can make more if you agree."

Ronny saw her thin her mouth while she tapped on the table. He knew it was something to do with his mention of children. "Did I scare you with my talk of children. It is not a must to have more since we already have four."

"Children are cute, but not the struggle of bringing them into the world." She cast her eyes to the panel of windows facing the driveway.

Ronny could tell that she was in agony, blinking many times, like she was fighting back tears or some pain.

Angela was reflective as the pain she had felt that night poured back into her mind.

The pain heightened when she remembered her twelve hours at the labour and maternity wards. Then she recalled the pain on her breasts whenever Babu struggled to suck out more milk. Milk she did not have all the time, partly due to lack of a proper diet. "No more children for me."

317

He shifted his hand to her waist. "I am here to help lessen your pain, and, medicine has advanced to keep childbirth pain away."

"You don't understand." She pulled out of his grip and walked into the kitchen. She arranged dinner dishes on a tray and took them to the dining table.

She spent more time than needed to set the table. She was reflective, how to tell Ronny that what scared her most was the sting as Babu's father forced himself into her, and then the awful labour she endured to bring Babu into the world. The experience had ingrained pain in her mind as synonymous with having one's own children.

Ronny's eyes followed her from the dining room to the kitchen. He followed her near the oven on hearing the timer call out.

He placed a hand on her shoulder. "Was it the childbirth process or something else?"

She leaned on his chest. "It took less than five minutes to conceive my baby, a very agonizing moment. I never want to experience that again."

Ronny felt her tears on his shirt. He knew she was in great agony. He did not move.

After about three minutes of silence, he decided that better take advantage of her willingness to talk and help her banish the anguish from her mind and heart. "Thanks for telling me of your tormenting experience." He tightened his hold on her waist. "Did the guy take you against your will?"

"I don't know. We were both young and stupid, at a party. We walked out of the room, to the back of the house. Before I knew what was happening, he had entered me, he pulled out when I screamed."

"You might not agree with me now, but I promise, I will never hurt you. The boy hurried you, there is a better way. I will help you like it."

He waited for a long moment before he added. "The reason you see married people get more and more babies." He kissed her. "Please allow me, I will show you how pleasurable love-making is supposed to be."

Angela spaced into a gaze at her tea on the table. She thought about how sweeter the tea tasted since she'd kissed Ronny. She said nothing, and when he spoke, his words were distant. She didn't hear him say, "Not today, or tomorrow. Only when you are ready. I promise."

With two fingers, he lifted her chin and held her mouth in his.

She did not pull away. She reluctantly joined in the kissing. When he released her, she turned her eyes to the oven.

Ronny chuckled. "Time for us to eat. Mum will not appreciate if the food she prepared is not eaten today."

He slid on oven mittens and pulled out a large glassware covered with aluminum foil. He walked to the dining room, Angela in tow, carrying a thick table mat.

"Don't burn the table, I have the mat."

"You are what I need in a partner." He waited for the mat before placing the food container on the table.

319

They ate in silence for the first few minutes before Ronny put his fork down and hit the table with both hands, softly. "We need to discuss a few things before the children come in tomorrow, or the day after."

Angela held a piece of meat to her mouth. "Mmhhh!" she responded, her eyes focused on the painting hanging on the wall behind Ronny.

He picked up the fork. "It has been a long time since I was with a woman. I have a feeling Bella is asking me to move on, live life."

She stopped chewing.

He spoke again. "You are the one I want to spend the rest of my life with."

"Why me? What about the children?"

"Why you? Because you are you, a good person."

She bit on her fork though it had no food.

Ronny continued, "I have talked with the children. They were excited that you could continue to stay with us."

"You are not serious. You talked with the kids?"

"I did. It was a difficult talk, but I had to. They surprised me with their responses."

"What did they say?"

"I still have this image of them as babies, but they have grown. As you know from their last birthday celebrations, Mia turned nine and Betty seven. You will have to start talking with them about teenage hood and girl things, soon."

He stopped talking, expecting her to say something. When she did not, he continued. "You should have seen me break into a sweat right in front of my mother."

"Ooh. Did you talk with the children while with your mother?"

"I had no idea how they would react on hearing that I plan to bring them another mother. I had my mother nearby, to wipe away the tears I expected."

"You expected? What did you get?"

"Difficult statements." One side of his mouth pushed upwards into a smile. "Mia said her friends had told her something about fathers without wives getting women from the streets in the night. Ooh my God!" Ronny exclaimed. "I have never done that. I assured her of the same."

He massaged his jaw. "Before long, Betty asked if I could ask you to be my wife since you are good, you cook for them, show them how to arrange their rooms, teach them how to cook and go to the mall with them." He choked on the last words.

Angela noticed that his eyes were misty. She extended a hand across the table and touched his, scratched his palm softly.

Not wanting to see the tears he was fighting back, she distracted him. "The food was yummy, tell Mum I said so." She patted his hand. "Is there chocolate cake for our dessert?"

He grinned. "Chocolate cake is your specialty, no one can compete." He stood and gathered the plates onto the tray. "Or did you want to take a photo of the almost empty bowl for Mum to see?"

"You served me a lot of delicious food. I should clear the table."

He did not respond. Instead, he picked up the tray and walked to the kitchen, glad that he had thought of getting their supper. From the way both ate the meal, they would never have enjoyed a take-away dish in the same way. And, it would have been unfair for him to expect Angela to cook after her travel from Nakuru.

He made a mental note, to add private transport for her future travels to the village or to Nakuru. He had enough cars within the compound, five to be exact, before counting the many company vehicles. Angela could use any of the vehicles since her work contract was with the company.

With the thought on the company cars, he remembered that her contract would be up for review soon. He would increase her salary and ask her to add Babu to her medical cover.

Angela finished wiping the table and joined him in the kitchen. "Thanks for feeding me. I will wash the dishes tomorrow." She smoothed her stomach. "I will retire to bed, if you do not mind."

"I do mind," Ronny said as he shut off the tap. "The food I ate will digest better with a glass of wine."

He retrieved two wine glasses from a cupboard. "I could also teach you how to drink some wine."

"Are you planning to get me drunk?"

"No need to worry about that. Remember my promise, not tonight or tomorrow?"

He returned one glass to the cupboard. "Today, I prefer you remain sober, that way we can discuss how to forge our future forward, together."

Chapter 29

Angela was surprised at how fast Ronny agreed to her travel request, until she remembered what his plea had been in the last three months. He had been urging her to inform her father that she planned to get married.

Her answer had remained the same. "Such information can only be shared at a face-to-face meeting."

Joshua had informed Angela of his plan to travel home with the family in August. He asked if she could join them in the village.

Angela was excited. She looked forward to seeing her son and grandmother.

However, her enthusiasm waned as the travel date approached. Though she knew that her grandmother would be excited by the news of her considering marriage, Angela worried how to explain to her father that she was thinking about marrying her employer.

Angela boarded the Land Rover Cruiser that Ronny insisted she use. She sat in the back and read a book until they arrived at her local town from where she focused on directing James to her home village, Nyametende.

They arrived at four o'clock. James declined an invitation to visit with her parents, insisting he needed at least two hours to drive to Kisumu, his next destination.

Angela did not argue much as her son and his cousins were pulling her arms, waiting to tell her about their holiday in the village.

As was her tradition, she visited her grandmother before returning to the compound of her father.

Being a Saturday, Luka was home, in his dining room having a chat with Joshua who had arrived three days ahead of Angela.

"Good, you have arrived," were the first words from Joshua as he stood and hugged his sister.

Angela's hand was shaky as she greeted her father, while she pondered what Joshua's words meant.

Joshua pointed her to a chair. "Sorry, I had no intention to scare my sister."

"I don't know," Angela said as she wiped her forehead, she felt warm, sweaty. She sat opposite Joshua at the dining table.

Needing something to distract her from the thoughts rushing through her head, she served tea into an empty cup at the table. "Thank you for the tea," she said.

Angela was worried that Joshua had told her father about her relationship with Ronny. What would she say if Luka asked about her wanting to get married before acquiring university education?

Luka chuckled. "Even if there was something to concern you that is not how we welcome visitors." He pointed her to *mandazi* on a plate.

Angela shook her head. She picked a *mandazi*, took a bite and looked at her father and then her brother.

Joshua laughed. "I am learning now that I have a coward for a sister."

Zippy arrived home from the shopping center and greeted them. After, Joshua excused himself and left for his house.

A few minutes later Angela followed Joshua to his house. She joined Florence to prepare supper now that she was busy taking care of three children, Babu, Dave and Angelica.

While they ate supper, Joshua held Angela's left hand. "That Ronny guy is slow, no ring yet?"

Florence paused from eating. "I need to reduce the amount of food I eat, I must look good at my sister's wedding. When is the day?"

Dave and Babu giggled, prompting Angela to ask them. "Do you know about weddings? Why did you laugh?"

Babu pointed back to Angela. "People eat cake and nice food at a wedding. Uncle and Auntie took us to a wedding."

"Would you like your Mama to have a wedding?" Angela asked while pointing to herself, annoyed that Babu still referred to Priscah as Mama.

"Yes," Babu grinned. "We can eat food and play in the large field and come back to eat cake."

Angela turned to Dave. "What about you Dave, do you want your aunt to have a wedding?"

Dave nodded as he had just scooped a spoonful of rice into his mouth.

Florence interrupted. "When is the big day, and who is the lucky guy you have hidden from me?"

Joshua had been updating Florence each time he spoke with Ronny or his grandmother who always had the latest information from Angela.

"Any story from Grandma?" Joshua asked Angela.

"I did not have story time with her yet." Angela checked time. "I need to go before she locks me out of the house."

After supper Angela cleared the table and washed dishes. She wished everyone a good night, picked a spotlight and walked to the house of her grandmother.

"*Nyanya*, what was your supper like?" Angela asked though Priscah had told her she would cook millet *ugali* to eat with *Sagaa*, an indigenous vegetable, and sour milk.

"I have been waiting for you," Priscah said as she stood and walked to the kitchen.

Angela followed and embraced her. "I have eaten supper with Joshua and his family."

"I too have eaten, Stephanie came over and we ate, but we can eat again."

Angela touched her stomach. "My stomach is too full, I will eat that food tomorrow, at breakfast."

"What is Joshua saying, has your stepmother stopped asking to take Babu to town?"

"Town? For what?" Angela asked as she opened one of the foldable chairs and sat.

Priscah left the kitchen and walked back to her chair. "I hear you were brought home by your man, did you not want him to greet me?"

"Ooh *Nyanya*, that was his driver. I will inform you many weeks in advance, that way you can slaughter a goat for him when he comes. He will come before Christmas."

Priscah held on to the arms of her chair and stood up. She held Angela's hands and fondled them. "Did he marry you already?"

"No, he just asked me. He is waiting for my answer and your answer."

She kissed Angela's fingers. "I see my other daughter, Joshua's is doing an excellent job, another baby. I want to see more great grandchildren before my time to join our ancestors comes."

Angela sniggered. "Children, children, children are all *Nyanya* thinks about. I already have four. Do you want more *Nyanya*?"

Priscah looked at her hand, like she was counting her fingers. "Is the man marrying you to look at you? More children are good," she said while laughing. She stopped suddenly and asked, "Have you talked with your father?"

"About what? I greeted him, and we drank tea together."

Priscah pointed a finger at Angela. "Tomorrow, don't do that. Stay home with the boy. They are planning to marry you off to that man, the father of your child."

"*Nyanya*, no need to worry, he has a wife, unless they have chased her away."

"Tell me tomorrow, but you have heard my words." Priscah walked towards her bedroom and stood by the door.

Angela knew not to ask for more. She would count the hours to morning and go ask Joshua if he had any information on what her grandmother said.

She watched as her grandmother stretched a hand and fumbled for the switch on the bedroom wall. The light came on, a sign that she had found the light switch.

She followed and hugged Priscah goodnight.

Angela went to the indoor bathroom and took a shower. The cold water reminded her of the hot showers she enjoyed back in the city. Thinking of the city, she remembered that she needed to call Ronny.

After the shower she wrapped a towel below her shoulders and walked out of the bathroom, for her room. She typed a message to Ronny. "Hello. How is the work of babysitting? We traveled well, arrived home in great comfort. Thank you and have a good night. Love you."

Barely a minute after she clicked send, she heard a message drop into her phone while she pulled a nightie over her head. She was glad Ronny had responded so fast, he must be missing her already. She read, "Tomorrow come to my house before you go to Dad's. We need to talk."

She typed, "Okay" and clicked send back to Joshua. She could now connect her grandmother's words and the message from Joshua.

Angela wished it was already morning, for her to know what was going on. The worst part was if it was true that Babu's father now wanted to marry her, a man she did not know well. She worried if he planned to stop her wedding. Even though she was not his wife, he might use the case of Babu to disrupt her day.

The ringing of her phone distracted her thoughts. Ronny's name on her screen announced who was on the other end of the line.

"Hello. How is your evening with the children?"

"The children are fine, in bed, I miss you a lot."

She chuckled. "Same here."

"I wish you could come back earlier than next weekend. May I ask James to pick you up tomorrow now that you have seen your folks?"

Angela was glad that they were talking on phone and not face-to-face. In no way would she want anyone, including her grandmother to see how worried she looked. How was she going to tell Ronny that there were new developments at home that she must attend to, but she did not have the full details? "There are some issues that require my presence here."

"Is everyone okay?" Ronny asked in a hurried voice.

"People are fine. I will update you tomorrow after lunch, good night." Angela ended the call and switched off her phone.

Chapter 30

Angela said she had no appetite for breakfast which was ready on the dining table. She sat on a sofa at one corner of Joshua's living room, waiting for him.

She had tossed throughout the night, juggling thoughts in her mind on what Joshua wanted to tell or ask her. She wondered what her parents had to say about the new development, worse still, the reason her parents were planning to marry her off without consulting her.

The phone became her companion. She scrolled through messages. She had three missed calls from Ronny last night and one at six in the morning. His last message asked if she still had the phone.

She lifted her head towards the dining table and locked eyes with Joshua. She turned back to her phone and typed a message to Ronny. "Good morning. We are fine. I will get back to you soon. Regards and miss you and the children."

Angela addressed Florence at the dining table. "Flo, I guess the baby is too young for church today, means we can all stay home?"

Florence who had been breastfeeding while eating breakfast lifted her eyes to Angela. "The church service will be over by the time I get everyone ready."

"Babu," Angela called. "Greetings from Grandma. She asked when you will go sleep in her house, as you used to."

Babu and Dave looked at one another with smiles on their faces, not saying a word, their mouths full of food.

She asked Joshua, "Ready? I am developing a worry ulcer, right here in your house."

"After all these years, you should be tough enough not to be scared by the panic of other people," Joshua told her.

"If only you knew what I am going through. I haven't slept."

She was relieved when Joshua stood up and walked to the door. "Come," he beckoned her before turning to his wife. "Please make sure the children stay in sight." He walked outside, and Angela followed him to their parents' house.

Zippy welcomed them to the table for breakfast.

Joshua declined, explaining that he just stood from eating breakfast.

Angela said she was okay.

Joshua and Angela sat in facing sofas in the living room.

Luka sat on the one-seater always reserved for him.

Zippy carried a chair from the dining room to the living room, her cup of tea in one hand.

Angela sat upright with her hands crossed on her chest.

Joshua looked at her for a long moment. "Angela, yesterday I sat here, and our parents mentioned something I thought best if you hear it from them."

Luka looked at Zippy while he said, "Your mother has details. In short, the parents of Japheth want you and the child."

"For what?" Angela asked, not caring if her father had finished talking or not.

"Your mother-in-law told me its time she had her grandson and daughter-in-law come to live with her," Zippy said.

"Father, we need to be clear on what we are talking about," Joshua said. "Is Sabrina asking on behalf of her son Japheth or for herself?"

Zippy interjected, "Once Sabrina has them in her compound, it means they belong to Japheth."

Joshua raised his voice. "Is that how they want Angela's life to be, full of interruptions?"

Zippy lifted the cup closer to her mouth without taking a sip. "We could ask Sabrina to come and explain—"

Luka interrupted her, "That's an important matter. We do not call strangers to my home just like that."

"I mean we could organize to have a delegation come over to get Angela and Babu," Zippy explained.

Angela stood up from the sofa. "Which Angela are you talking about? This 24-year-old single mother? I am no longer the naive girl you threw out of this home."

She sat after Joshua motioned her to sit.

Joshua addressed Luka, "I can say something here. I married Florence not too many years ago." He chuckled. "It was an agreement between her and me before I informed you and she informed her parents. It was never between the parents."

"But Angela has their baby," Zippy said.

Angela bit her lower lip before she spoke. "Whose baby? If you have forgotten, Babu is my baby, especially when I suffered to take care of him without an income. Where were you?" She stared at Zippy. "Where was Sabrina? All she did was ship her son to the city to hide. He now has his degree before I even start mine. She wiped a tear from her cheek. I see the plan, bring me and Babu to stay with Sabrina and be her farm workers, while her son puts on a necktie and drives to work. Eeeh?"

Luka waved her to stop talking.

She addressed Luka, "Dad, I have my own plans, big plans." She chuckled. "I am getting married and going to university."

A smile appeared on Zippy's face. "The more reason you should let Sabrina take their baby, before your man learns you have a son and runs away from you."

Angela's eyebrows pulled in. "I would have answered you if you were not the wife of my father."

Luka stood up. "It seems like things are getting out of hand, can we talk later about this?"

Angela lowered her voice. "I prefer you give me few minutes to tell you what I think and know."

She smiled when her father reclaimed his chair. She explained, "Babu is my baby and I will take him along when I get married. If Japheth or Sabrina have claims, let them follow the proper channels. I will be waiting to hear from them."

Angela turned to Zippy and grinned. "Please, I will need Japheth's phone number. You never know."

Zippy went to the dining room. She picked her cell phone from a side stool, pressed keys and walked away into the kitchen while speaking on the phone. She returned and handed a small piece of paper to Angela. "Tell him we would like to see the two of you together."

Angela smiled her appreciation. She went to the dining table and saved Japheth's number on her phone. She looked at the screen of her phone again before she tucked the piece of paper in her dress pocket and went back to her seat.

Joshua and Luka were in conversation, as Angela thanked Zippy again.

"Will it be okay if plans for any future meetings are done via father here?" Joshua said as he pointed to Luka. "That way, we do not confuse one another."

"I will let Dad know when Ronny can visit," Angela said as she turned to her father. "Unless you want to come to the city?"

Luka chuckled. "Things are not done that way. His people must come and consult with me in my home, not your house in the city."

Angela's lips parted but Joshua spoke ahead of her. "Better if they visit our home, though Nakuru would have been the better venue, mid-way between Nairobi and here."

When a quiet moment arose, Zippy asked, "And if Sabrina and her people want to visit? Are they to come here or to the city?"

Angela's eyes opened wide. "What are they coming to do? Please tell Sabrina to follow established procedures to claim me and my son." She walked to the door and stopped. "I have not had a life for many years, no one is going to interfere with my future."

~~~~~~

Angela walked to Joshua's house and entered without knocking.

Florence smiled and pointed her to the breakfast waiting for her on the dining table. She continued to sing a lullaby to put the baby to sleep.

Angela pulled a chair and sat down but did not move closer to the table. "Where are the boys?" she asked in a whisper.

Florence pointed to one of the three bedrooms in the house.

Angela typed a message on her phone, "I should not be telling you this. I am ready to travel. Babu will come with me for one week." She clicked send to Ronny and placed the phone on the table.

She served tea and sipped after which she talked without looking up. "I am not annoyed with you, just me." She rested her forehead on her hand. "Each time I imagine my life is getting back to normal, someone comes in and takes away the light. I am in darkness again."

Joshua walked into the house as Florence said, "I hope no one is giving you a tough time. I saw you use your phone. Is everything okay in Nairobi?"

"Nairobi is fine. Most of my problems are here, at my father's house."

Joshua reached Angela's side and placed a hand on her shoulder. "You did well, told them you are not pleased with Zippy's plans. She is talking on phone, I think with Sabrina." He walked into the living room and sat next to his wife.

A message dropped into Angela's phone. She read, "I am more than happy. May I ask James to come for you today or tomorrow?"

She typed a response, "I am surprised you are not asking why I am cutting my holiday short." She clicked send and immediately her phone rang. She rejected the call and typed another message. "Will call when @ Grandmas. Can't talk now."

Angela walked to the bedroom where the children were playing with their toys. "Are you ready we go play with my Grandma?"

Babu picked his toy car and Dave followed with a similar one.

Angela walked out with the two boys on either side. They stopped at the living room, Angela informed

Florence of her plan. "I will go prepare some food while the boys play with Grandma before we leave for the city."

"What?" Florence and Joshua asked in unison.

Angela chuckled. "Today or tomorrow. I will go with Babu and bring him to Nakuru over the weekend when you guys are back." She walked out, holding the boys' hands.

Angela was glad that her grandmother was back from church. "*Nyanya*. I have brought your great grand-kids. They need to laugh at one of your funny stories before we go back to the city."

"Are you going back to the city so soon? To your husband?" she chuckled.

Babu stopped pushing his car on the cement floor and tilted his head upwards, to Angela. "Do you have a husband?"

"Not yet, but soon. I will take you to the city to meet him."

Babu ran towards Angela and held onto the skirt of her dress. "Is he good like my uncle, Joshua?"

"Yes. You will play together with his other children and become friends. All of you will be my children."

Dave stood up from the sofa where he was pushing his toy car. "Auntie, will I come to Nairobi with you, with Babu my friend?"

Angela massaged Dave's clean-shaven head. "I will ask your parents and hear what they say. Okay?"

He nodded and went back to his toy.

Angela went to the kitchen and opened a cupboard, like she was in search of something. She called to Priscah, "*Nyanya*, I want to prepare some food for you."

She turned on the two-burner electric cooker and prepared *ugali*. Priscah sat nearby, they conversed in hushed tones. She updated her on the meeting with her parents and what her position was.

By the time Angela served lunch – *ugali*, vegetables and beef stew, she had shared her plan and received Priscah's approval.

The foursome sat at the small round table to eat lunch. Immediately they said Amen to the prayer before food, Angela heard the ringtone of her phone go off. She accepted the call and walked to her bedroom while motioning the rest to proceed with lunch.

"You timed me well, I just set lunch on the table."

"Should I call later?" Ronny asked.

"No. Grandma is eating with the kids. I will join after we talk."

"I guess it will be late for you to travel now, unless you want us to meet in Nakuru, then travel to Nairobi in the morning?"

"Are you in Nakuru?"

"In the city, but if you leave today, I can travel to Nakuru. We'll meet there."

"Joshua and family are still here, there is no one in Nakuru," Angela told Ronny.

"I meant we meet and spend the night at a hotel, then proceed to Nairobi tomorrow."

Angela tilted her head upwards, like the answer was written on the corrugated metal roof of the house. "That sounds complicated. I can leave tomorrow morning and come to the city. I will bring Babu along."

"Yes, yes. I cannot wait to welcome the two of you."

Angela wondered if she should mention the reason she was traveling back so soon. After a moment's reflection, she decided to wait and tell him after she arrived in the city.

Her plan was to be with Babu in the city until she contacted Japheth. After that she would return with Babu to Nakuru the coming Saturday, before schools opened the following Tuesday.

"Thanks," Angela said, hoping Ronny had not said something while she was in deep thought. "Let me go and eat, then help Florence with some cooking before tomorrow."

"Sounds yummy. What will you cook?" He asked.

"I will turn lots of chapattis and some pilau and maybe a cake. Food to last them until they leave for Nakuru. Bye and thanks for calling." She ended the call, threw the phone on her bed and walked out to join the rest at the lunch table.

~~~~~~

Luka was surprised when Angela knocked on the door early on Monday morning. He had just finished eating breakfast and was getting ready to leave for work.

She had timed him well. Aware that he liked to leave the house by six-forty-five to drive to town before the morning traffic. "I came to say bye. I am going back to Nairobi today."

"Did you come for only the weekend?"

Angela took a moment before she responded, "I need to take Babu to the city, see the people I work for. I will take him to Nakuru on Saturday.

Luka picked his leather office bag, prompting Angela to stand up while she said, "I will call you to discuss when my visitors can come."

She gave an envelope to Babu. "Give that to your Grandpa, fuel for his car."

Babu took the envelope, lifted the flap and looked at Luka. "Grandpa, you have a lot of money." He handed the envelope to Luka who received the envelope before he massaged Babu's head, "Thank you, young man."

They walked out to where Luka parked his car.

Angela was glad that Zippy did not show up while she talked with her father. She had a feeling the conversation would have turned sour.

She bid good day to Luka and went to Joshua's house. She helped prepare and serve breakfast for the family - tea, millet porridge and *mandazi* she had cooked the night before.

They discussed farming activities in the village and progress made by their cousins while eating breakfast.

341

Angela could tell that Joshua wanted to ask her a million questions, but he did not.

They heard a car park outside.

Angela embraced Florence, thanking her many times for the welcome. They all walked out and greeted James. Angela introduced him to Joshua and his family.

She loaded her bags and excused herself to go say bye to her grandmother and cousins.

Ten minutes later, Angela and Babu returned. Babu sat in the car and pressed his face to the window, with a broad grin.

As James got into the driver's seat, Joshua pulled Angela aside. "I hope you are not taking the boy away from me."

She chuckled. "We will be back at your house in Nakuru on Saturday for lunch." She moved closer and hugged her brother.

Instead of walking to the car, she went to Joshua's house where she hugged Florence, Dave and the baby bye and left as tears welled up in her eyes.

When Angela reached Joshua's side, she said, "Please support my idea that Dad meets with Ronny's parents in Nakuru. I have a feeling Zippy will cause trouble here."

He patted her on the shoulder. "As you say, kid sister. No worries. Your life from now on will be a happy one."

Chapter 31

Nikko, Betty and Mia rushed out of the house as James parked the car on the driveway.

After an exchange of hugs and many words of welcome with Ronny's children, Angela looked at each of the three kids. "I have brought you a friend to play with, my son. His name is—"

"Babu." The children said in unison before Angela could utter the name.

"How did you know his name?" she asked.

"Did you forget we met in Nakuru, shared snacks and played together? Where is Dave, the other boy?" Mia said.

Betty clapped her hands. "Dad told us you would bring us a brother to live with us." She touched Mia. "One," then touched her chest. "Two girls." She pointed to Nikko, then Babu, "One, two boys. Nice, two girls, two boys."

They went to the house through the living room and walked to the family room where Angela placed the luggage. She walked into the kitchen and waved a greeting to Rebecca, the senior house worker at Pauline's house. "Thanks for coming to help while I was away."

Rebecca was busy preparing a snack for the children and waved back. "Welcome, welcome back home. We missed you."

"I will be back after I settle in," Angela said as she left for the family room, picked up the bags and walked to her bedroom.

She was surprised to see a large blue envelope with four full blown balloons attached to the bedroom door. There were huge letters spelling, "Babu, welcome home."

Angela heard many footsteps behind her. She dropped the two bags on the floor and waited until the four children arrived.

Mia explained without being asked. "Dad helped us decorate the door to Babu's room. We assisted the people who brought the bed to move your clothes to the visitor's room, near Dad's room."

Mia's eyes darted from Betty to Nikko before she continued. "Dad said you will sleep there until you have a wedding and then you will move to his bedroom."

Angela felt like her legs could not hold her any further. Fearing that she would fall, she opened the door and dragged the bags inside. The children followed her.

There were more surprises inside. The room had been redone to match Nikko's. A double bed in the shape of a Jeep car, blue beddings, a side table and a chair, which she sat on, dazed.

She watched as the children followed one another, showing Babu his empty wardrobe, which they said would soon be full of clothes. They walked to the bathroom from where she heard as they pointed to his basket for dirty clothes and the stepping stool to reach the sink.

When her wooziness subsided, she opened her handbag and pulled out her phone. She typed a message to Florence to inform her that they traveled well. She called her father and grandmother and informed them of the same.

She then sent a message to Ronny. "Hi. Thanks for the ride. We traveled well. I am in the house and have no words."

Her phone rang as soon as she put it in the bag. She answered, and Ronny asked, "Is everything okay?"

"No. What is all the arrangement of a room for Babu? He is going back to Nakuru on Saturday."

There was a long pause before Ronny said, "Sorry, I assumed Joshua had briefed you, the reason you traveled with Babu."

"Joshua? Bringing the boy?" she said.

"I will be home soon. Is it okay if we talk when I arrive?"

"Okay," Angela said.

"Bye, I love you. See you soon," Ronny said before he ended the call.

Angela scrolled to her contact list and dialed Joshua's number.

He answered on the third ring. "Hi Sister. Thanks for your message that you traveled well."

"I was well until I arrived here."

"Is everyone okay? What happened?"

"I had no idea you did not want my son to stay at your house."

"What? Are you in your right mind?" Joshua asked.

"Ronny prepared a room for Babu. A new bed, beddings and everything else. He said you knew about it, he talked with you, but you did not tell me."

"Okay, okay." Joshua said. "I was going to tell you his request, to travel to the city with the boy. But when you announced that you were going back to the city with Babu, I assumed you had discussed it with Ronny, that was the reason you changed your travel dates. Otherwise, I would have not let you leave with Babu."

She exhaled into the phone.

Joshua chuckled. "No need to faint. Did you not say you would only allow Ronny to marry you if he accepted your son as well? Your own words."

"December is not now," Angela said.

"What's the difference? It is better if the boy stays there, gets used to his new father before the wedding. I guess you do not want Babu to appear at the wedding and divert attention from the bride. Let people get used to him now."

"You could be right. I do not like surprises. Now I have to relocate to a room near his."

"Not *in* his room? You must have found the last well-behaved man in that city. Do not look back. Bye, kid sister."

Angela smiled as she said, "Bye."

She walked into the bathroom to check on what the running water and giggles were all about. She was glad that the four children had not blocked the sink in whatever water experiment they were doing. The open taps drained well.

Angela heard a new message notification from her phone as she guided the children out, towards the family room. "Some TV will do you good," she said to them before she read the message, "My Dear. I have ideas on how to lessen the confusion I caused. Get ready to go out for dinner. Rebecca will stay with the children tonight."

"I have no bathroom to shower from."

A reply came in a moment later. "That's even better. I am on my way, we can shower from my room."

Angela picked her bag and almost ran to the guest room where she found more surprises. The bag in her hand dropped. She crossed both hands on her chest, wondering how Ronny had transformed the two rooms within the two and a half days she had been gone. Her bed from the other room had replaced the visitor bed.

The curtains had changed from the usual purple floras to a light lime and brown, her favourite colours. The beddings had changed into a pricey duvet and several pillows of assorted sizes. There was a new two-seater sofa instead of the one-seater previously in the room. The soft brown chair blended in well with the window curtains and the duvet on her bed.

Not knowing what to say or do, she lowered herself onto the chair, and held her head between her hands.

The ringing of her phone startled her, Ronny. She let the call go to voice mail. The ringing stopped, and she heard a message drop in. She read, "I am almost home for our bath."

She jerked out of the chair, walked to the wardrobe to pick a gown to wear after bathing. There were more clothing items. On one side of the double wardrobe were the clothes she was familiar with. On the remaining half were many new clothing items. She saw a Vera Wang jacket, some Phlemuns separates, TylynnNyugen slip, and two denim jeans. She questioned why Ronny had to go to such an extent. In no way would she accept that. With a smile on her face, she acknowledged that he got her size ten right.

She picked a night gown and went to the bathroom. Her plan was to bathe, then walk back to the wardrobe to select a dress to wear, but not any of the new clothes.

Looking for a way to reflect on events of the last three days, she filled the bathtub. She sprinkled lavender oils and bathing salts lined up nearby and immersed herself inside.

After about thirty minutes of quietness, she left the bathtub. With only a towel wrapped below her shoulders, she admired her smooth skin in front of the full-length mirror.

She turned around for a better view of herself as she applied lotion. She smiled at her rounded hips and questioned if that was what made her grandmother insist that she was now in her prime age. With the thought, she wondered how she would look in some of the new designer dresses in the wardrobe.

She went to the bedroom and returned with three dresses still in their hangers. She let the towel drop, pulled on panties and a bra before she tried on the blue jeans. The fit was out of this world, and the cuffed hem hit her legs at a flattering length. She pulled from the pile randomly, ending up with a TylynnNyugen slip. She removed the jeans and pulled on the deep purple dress. It felt as slippery as buttered hands. She turned to admire her backside when she heard a knock and the bedroom door opened.

Angela straightened the dress down her hips and walked to the bathroom door. She opened a small space and there was Ronny in the room.

"Hi," was all she mumbled before closing the bathroom door.

Time was not on her side. She needed to decide fast on how to walk out of the bathroom, in her night gown or in the dress. After a moment she opened the door and walked out of the bathroom.

Ronny took long strides and reached her. She was in his arms before she knew it. After they kissed, he held her wrists and took one step back. "You look stunning, elegant, beautiful." He moved closer and cuddled her again.

Angela was tongue-tied. She asked herself how she made the mistake of not carrying any of her regular clothes to the bathroom. To her, Ronny was going to assume that she was getting ready for the dinner outing.

"Did you go to work dressed casual today?" She asked, for he always dressed in a suit when going to the office.

He lowered his eyes to his casual black trousers and a crisp white cotton shirt. "I arrived home as promised. I took a shower and changed. I came to check on you after several messages and no reply."

She turned to her phone, but he held her by the waist. "I played catch with Babu. A pleasant kid he is. I like that he is talkative."

When her lips parted, ready for her to say something, he captured her mouth with his and guided her to the loveseat, they sat down. "Did you tell your parents about our dream wedding in December or earlier if you allow me?"

Needing time to reflect on how to answer his question. She held his hand and tickled his palms. He was enjoying the massage until she said. "Ask your friend Joshua. You two seem to share a lot of information about me."

"I will. Promise me you will agree to whatever month Joshua and I choose." He stood and extended a hand to her. "I am hungry. Let's go to a club for tea and dinner."

Ronny had not been very convinced of dining out until he arrived home and found the four children bonding well. He felt comfortable leaving them with Rebecca. He needed to be alone with Angela to hear details of her visit home. If she informed her parents about him and a future visit by his parents.

Ronny picked Angela's phone and guided her out of the room. He could tell that she wanted to retrieve her handbag, an aged black leather bag that she had carried on her travel home. He did not let her go. Tonight, she would walk without a handbag.

He guided her to the family room where the children were watching TV while playing Scrabble. He paused for a moment, told the children that he and Angela were leaving the house and would be back after dinner.

Angela kissed each child bye. She held onto Ronny's arm as they walked to the kitchen. They conversed with Rebecca before they walked out to the car garage.

Ronny helped Angela into the passenger seat of his Jaguar.

She waited until his seat-belt was in place then said, "What a bad start. What type of future parents drive out and leave toddlers in the house?"

"Not bad for one day." He started the engine, pressed the garage door opener and reversed the car out. "For every seven days, at least two evenings should be ours, the two of us. That will leave us five dinners with the kids."

Angela was quiet. She found his suggestion fair enough. She did not want to talk more, lest she introduce a topic she did not want to discuss, like how she decided to bring Babu along, yet she had not heard any news from Joshua.

She also needed a clear mind on how to walk into the club with Ronny by her side. Though they had been to the club many times before, they had taken the children.

She pondered if she should ask him not to hold her by the waist while at the club. She changed her mind, maybe Ronny had not planned to hold her, but mentioning it would prompt him to hold her.

He parked the car and walked around to hold the door as she stepped out.

As she had feared, he snaked his hand around her waist, gave her a light kiss on her full lips covered in lavender lipstick. "Remember to enjoy the evening. My friends will be glad to see me with you." He chuckled. "Do not be surprised if some girls and women are not happy with us."

She paused. "Do you have other girlfriends?"

He tightened his grip on her waist. "No. You already know the ones who were being pushed to me."

She held onto his waist. "Do not chase them away yet." She lowered her eyelashes. "My parents have plans on who to marry me to."

"Are your parents that ancient? You are mine, and I am yours," he said as they stepped into the club.

Ronny swiped his membership card at the front desk machine, returned a greeting from the lady behind the desk and they walked on. Inside the club they sat at a table with two other couples.

At seven o'clock the group of six left the bar for the dining room where they ate dinner. The other couples were Michael with his wife Beauta, and Richie with his wife Sophia.

During their chat, Angela learned that Richie was the younger brother to Michael.

Angela was glad that though the men were louder in their talk than she would have liked, she was able to join in the conversation. Her initial fear had been that Beauta and Sophia might talk about diamonds and international fashion shows. They did not. She was glad that all she had received were congratulatory messages when Ronny introduced her as his girlfriend.

Angela planned to start reading fashion magazines, just in case next time she shared a table with women who wanted to talk nothing but fashion. She would start by reading about the designer clothes in her wardrobe - the designers, awards they have received, and where they preferred to show their fashions. She would also read books and watch movies about the old houses, and social media for contemporary brands.

After dinner Angela held Ronny's wrist and checked his watch, though she had her own. Her intent was to remind him that it was time for them to go home.

He got the message and announced that Tuesday being a workday, he was ready to leave.
Michael, Richie and their wives agreed. They all stood and walked out to the car park.

Chapter 32

On their drive home, Ronny took several quick glances to Angela's side before he said, "So, whom is my future father-in-law planning to marry you off to?"

She pressed both hands onto her seat. "I have my doubts if my father is part of the scheme. He is letting himself be dragged into schemes of two women." She ended in a high tone, indicating her displeasure.

She felt Ronny's hand on her knee. "That sounds like your mother and—"

"For now, she is called Zippy, together with her new friend co-conspirator, Sabrina, Babu's grandmother," Angela said.

There was a long moment of silence. Ronny turned the car off the main road onto the private lane leading to his house. The night watchman let them into the compound.

He parked in the garage, switched off the engine and turned to Angela. "Give me a chance tonight, to chase away all your fears. I will be gentle with you." He unbuckled the seat belt and leaned towards her side.

Ronny had panicked on hearing that there was someone else who wanted Angela. She might be taken away from him if he did not act fast, convince her to move into his bedroom.

Angela talked without turning her eyes away from the windscreen. "I need space and time to reorganize the thoughts in my mind, from talking with my father, to taking Babu to Nakuru on Saturday."

Ronny could tell that Angela was tense, afraid of something. He wished there was a way to get her to share the information without getting agitated. "You mentioned the mothers. Does that mean Babu's father is not part of their plan?"

"He is busy somewhere in this city with his life."

He squeezed her hand, relieved to hear that Babu's father was not the one after her hand in marriage. He said, "Sounds like someone wants to break our family. We should not let them." He held her by the shoulder. "What would you say if I stayed home with you tomorrow, take the day off?"

"Two unemployed people in one house is not good."

"Thanks for reminding me. We need to discuss your resignation from the company."

The distant smile on her face disappeared. "Am I losing my job?"

"No. Just removing you from the office payroll. You will still receive your salary."

The smile returned to her face. "If Babu does not go back to my brother, I will need the money to put him in a school, maybe a boarding school."

He chuckled as he got out of the car, walked around and opened her door. "I have already reserved a place for Babu in nursery school. They need a copy of his birth certificate. Do you have one?"

She placed a hand on his chest. "You are moving too fast for me, Babu will be back in Nakuru over the weekend."

"Tomorrow we can discuss how you would like us to go through the adoption process, add my name to his."

She pulled away from his grasp. "Adoption. For what, why?"

"That way we become one large family upon marriage." He walked few steps and opened the door into the kitchen. Angela asked Rebecca, "How was your evening with the group?"

"Nice kids," Rebecca said, perched on a high stool at the kitchen island. "They said they will not go to sleep. They are waiting for their evening prayer and story. Babu cried at one point."

"Thanks Rebecca," Angela said as she held Ronny's hand and they went into the family room.

The four children sat on one sofa watching TV.

Angela greeted them before she said, "If we all pray together, there will be enough time to read you bedtime stories from your bedrooms."

There was no objection to her suggestion.

After the prayer, Mia stood up from the sofa. "I will read myself a bedtime story. I have a book I like."

Betty raised a hand to attract attention. "Can I read my cartoon book to myself? I have two pages left."

Angela glanced at Ronny and their eyes locked. It was the first time Mia and Betty ever turned down listening to bedtime stories.

Ronny read a bedtime story to Nikko and tucked him into bed. Angela did the same for Babu. She took advantage of being alone with him to ask how his evening was and if he missed her.

"I want my uncle, aunty and Dave," Babu choked on the words. "When are we going to Nakuru?"

Angela was not prepared for the question. She had assumed that Babu would be okay being with her in Nairobi. "We will visit them one weekend. Would you like to stay here, with me and Ronny, and Nikko, Mia, Betty and Rebecca?"

He shook his head no.

"What about you stay here so that we are one large family?" She threw her arms open. "You can go to school with Nikko. Over the weekend we will travel to Nakuru and come back to Nairobi."

She switched on his bedside lamp. "Another time, Uncle Joshua will drive his family to come visit us here." She returned his smile. "One day we can even ask Uncle and his family to come stay in the city."

Angela was glad when she saw Babu close his eyes. She kissed him on the forehead, stood from her kneeling position and tiptoed to the door. She switched off the lights and walked out, to the family room.

Ronny looked up from the magazine he was reading. "How did it go, is he asleep?"

"Yes. I had a lot of convincing to do. The boy is missing my brother and his family."

Ronny stood up, held her hand and they walked towards the dining room.

The lights in the kitchen were off as Rebecca had left for the staff quarters.

He set Angela's hand free. "Time to bond with my lovely lady now." He picked a bottle of wine from the mini fridge in the dining room and asked her to bring two glasses. He walked into the living room, placed the bottle on the coffee table and watched as she approached, carrying one wine glass.

"Good choice. That means you are with me tonight, in your clear mind."

She walked back to the kitchen and returned with a second glass. "I would rather force myself to drink than what you are proposing."

He laughed. "I had no idea you detest good things in life."

He beckoned her to come sit by his side on the sofa. He served wine into one glass and lifted it to his mouth. "Think about it."

She made eye contact.

He read the confused expression on her face and provided a clarification. "Think about Babu adding the

Henry name. It will be better if all the children use one family name. Even the ones we will have one day," he said as he smoothed her stomach.

She held his hand away from her stomach. "Give me time to think."

"Is one week enough, before schools open next Tuesday?"

She nodded.

Chapter 33

Rose sat back and cupped her cheeks between her hands while looking at Ronny who sat on the opposite chair.

He did not show anger or happiness. He had been thoughtful most of the evening.

Ronny and Rose had traveled to their parents' house for dinner on Thursday evening which was unusual. They normally visited their parents on weekends, unless one of the parents was unwell, which was not the case this time.

Afraid that Angela would travel to Nakuru on Saturday, in two days' time, to return Babu to her brother's house, Ronny had decided to hasten preparations for their marriage. By doing that, he hoped that Angela would let Babu live with them in the city.

Ronny had made a weekday appointment with his sister and parents for dinner but had not informed them of his wish to marry Angela.

After discussing the company business with his father who had made remarkable progress in his recovery, Ronny felt energized enough to introduce his objective for the visit.

He waited until everyone had filled their plates with food before he said, "As you might have heard during our last memorial service for Bella, I wish to do what she would have wanted, provide proper care to our children."

"Mmhhh," Henry encouraged.

Rose and Pauline paused from eating but remained silent.

Ronny continued, "I have weighed the pros and cons of mourning Bella forever, at the expense of the family."

He forked a piece of broccoli into his mouth, chewed, swallowed and said, "And you my family and friends have voiced concerns for my wellbeing for long." He made eye contact with Rose. "That includes my dear sister. I have now given in, to people, and most importantly to myself."

Rose smiled. "My brother is finally seeing sense. Otherwise the family name was being tarnished with stories formulated in people's heads."

"Tarnished?" Ronny queried.

"No one would say that to your face. They tell me." She looked upwards, to the chandelier hanging from the ceiling on top of the dining table. "Why do you think was I burdening myself to find you a good girl?"

"Thank you for trying," Ronny said.

Pauline looked from Ronny to Rose. "Who's the girl? The one you chose?"

Rose crossed both hands on the table. "He refused all the good girls."

Henry interjected. "Give Junior a chance to explain." He looked from Rose to Pauline.

Pauline placed her fork on her plate. "No one is stopping him from explaining himself."

Henry shook his head. "What if we give him a chance to complete his story, his choice." He looked at Ronny seated on the far end of the table, opposite from Rose. Pauline sat on the left side of Henry.

Ronny took a sip from his glass of wine. "There are people out there talking, though I cannot call that tarnishing." He smiled. "Let's call the stories interesting for now. I have heard some in the office, at clubs and other places, including from my children's school."

"School?" Rose asked.

"Some parents and students ask my daughters how they manage without a mother." The expression on his face softened. "Luckily for me, the questions gave my children a chance to share about the incredible job done by Angela."

Rose sneered. "Angie."

Ronny continued. "For more than fourteen months she has cared for those children like her own. Getting everyone ready for school, feeding us home cooked food, checking their homework and holding them close whenever they are hurting."

"We have heard and seen," Pauline said.

"Mum," Rose mumbled.

Ronny cleared his throat and regained their attention before he continued. "The efforts of Angela have

362

afforded me energy and time to focus on my office work —
"

Rose interrupted, "We all perform our office work because of the workers in our houses, though you seem to imagine that the housegirl in your house is different, special."

Ronny's eyebrows pulled in as Pauline waved Rose to stop talking.

He looked at his father. "Yes, we have had workers in the house before. Angela is very special. I have asked her to marry me."

Rose placed her knife and fork on the right side of her plate, an indication that she had finished eating. "That is if you did not marry her a long time ago."

Both Henry and Pauline turned to Rose's direction without saying a word.

Ronny added, "I wish that was the case. I would not be seated here if she'd accepted." He waved a hand around. "I am asking you to help me convince her."

"Count me out," Rose stated.

"What I would prefer to hear from you is a promise, that you will not interfere with my choice."

"I am not concerned about your choice, but with the welfare of my nephew and nieces."

"To your nieces and nephew, add another nephew. We now have Babu with us."

"Is that the visitor I heard about?" Pauline asked.

Ronny answered with a question, "From Rebecca? Yes. New addition to our family. He turns five next month."

Henry looked away as the door to his study opened and his personal health assistant stepped out. He excused himself, "Time to take my medicine and physio exercise. Your mother will brief me on your decision." He held onto the table and pulled himself up, to his feet.

The rest of the family remained quiet, watched as Henry pushed the chair back and walked out of the dining room.

Ronny had a smiley face as his father walked away. He was happy with the rate at which his father was recovering. In the ten months since his medical travel to Thailand, he had progressed from using a walker, to a walking stick, and now walking within the house without any support.

More than ever, Ronny resolved that he needed Angela in his life. If she continued with childcare as she had done so far, he would have more time to focus on the family business. The better the company was managed, the faster it would take his father to recover and return to work someday. Ronny was aware that Henry had built the company from scratch, the last thing he would want to see was his many years of effort go into waste.

"What I need is your support. Not advice on my choice," Ronny said, getting the attention of his sister and mother.

Rose thinned her lips. "My support? While I watch you marry a housegirl?"

"A very good girl, the love of my heart." He returned her glare.

"Good girls do not have five-year-old sons at such an early age," Rose said.

"She had a misfortune at a youthful age. Someone took advantage of her innocence, the reason she did not proceed to university on completion of high school. I can attest that she is a good girl—"

"All bad girls call having children before marriage a misfortune." Rose tightened her lips.

Pauline glanced from Ronny to Rose, "I am getting worried by this exchange. Other than the baby, is there something else we should know about Angela?"

Rose pursed her lips. "He lives with her, let him tell us."

"Exactly. What I have been trying to get you to understand. I live with Angela and I know she has all that I need in a wife." He fisted the table. "I bring three children and she brings one child. I bring my busy office work routine, she brings her willingness to take care of the children. And we love one another."

"Whose child is she bringing?" Pauline asked.

"She said it was a one-time contact. The man, her age-mate walked away and has no idea what the baby looks like," Ronny said in a calmer voice.

Pauline stared at the window coverings in front of her. "What if you encourage her to clear with the man, before you proceed? You know those stories of the other parent turning up to stop a wedding?"

"Mum! Are you letting him marry that girl?"

"Your brother is a grown man. He can make good decisions as a CEO, the company, his life, children, and his wellbeing."

Rose stood up and threw her napkin on the table. "Count me out, especially when she brings you problems."

"Thank you for that promise sister. Though I do not see or anticipate any problems from Angela."

He turned to his mother. "If you ever hear of a misunderstanding between Angela and I, blame me, not her."

Rose remained quiet.

Ronny broke the ensuing silence. "I am chasing time, Angela plans to take the boy back to Nakuru on Saturday, I will need someone to talk her out of that."

"What is her reason?" Pauline asked.

"My wish is for the child to stay with us." He took a glance at Rose and back to his mother. "We will have a wedding in December, so we need to visit her family soon."

Pauline took a sip from her cup of tea and put it back on the table. "Have you talked with your father to ask his brothers to travel since he is unwell?"

"I wanted to hear from you first. Will it be okay if Angela's parents are asked to come meet here, in the city, or Nakuru?" Ronny asked.

Rose stared. "Why go through all the marriage processes, like you are young people without children?"

Ronny flexed his muscular arms upwards, like he was about to lift a heavy load. "We are very young, in age and mind. Angela needs to have her first wedding."

He lowered his arms. "Angela has always wanted to pursue her degree program in food service and hotel management, the reason she took up the job, to earn money for her university education."

"Did I not hear you say you want her to take care of the kids? Now she will go to university?" Rose questioned.

He waved her away. "Leave that to me and her. We will find a way for her to pursue her career while being a wife and mother."

Ronny chuckled. "Tell me, dear sister," pointing to Rose "how you balance your life, managing the school and all those tasks in your house."

Everyone broke into laughter before Rose said. "It never works, there's no balance. Encourage her to take those distance studies, online classes." She chuckled. "That way she can add graduate to her Mrs. Junior, Ronald Henry."

One side of Ronny's mouth pulled up into a grin. He questioned if Rose was being sarcastic about Angela becoming his wife and gaining a degree. But he liked her suggestion. Online university courses would save her on travel time. To him, if Angela chose to pursue online courses, it would be easier to convince her to have one or two more children.

The smile on his face widened as he thought of how pursuing online courses would make more sense. Angela would be home with the children whenever he was busy in the office or on travel.

"What if you share your joke with us?" Pauline asked Ronny on seeing the smile on his face.

"It is not a joke. I am happy with my sister's suggestion, for Angela to pursue an online program for her university studies, so she'll have time to mind the children."

"What is stopping her? Am I not your mother, though I stayed home with both of you, instead of being in employment?"

Ronny reflected on how to persuade Angela to be a stay-at-home mom. His worry was what to do if people at the members' clubs or children's school referred to her as the housegirl or a high school dropout. He knew such words would hurt her, more so that she had qualified for university. "Mum, we live in a new world, full of expectations and pressures."

"What if you learn to live your life as you want, not the way other people want it for you?" Pauline asked.

Ronny stood up, then sat down. "I wish it was that easy." He stood up again. "I need to get back home before everyone retires to bed. I need to talk with Angela before she plans her weekend travel."

He stretched both arms upwards and yawned. "Mum, I will bring my family for tea and supper on Saturday." He turned to Rose, "You are invited, come meet with my large family." He extended both hands to Rose, but she did not leave her seat.

Pauline stood up to see him off.

Rose picked her Valentino Crossbody and followed them. "Let me hike a ride with my brother, that way he might convince me, or better, I convince him to change some of his plans."

Ronny hugged her. "You're out of luck kid sister. Come, we discuss my wedding and the role you prefer to take up."

Rose nuzzled to his chest. "I prefer to be the one to stop the wedding."

He kissed her on both cheeks before they walked out, bidding their mother to a good night.

Ronny held Rose by the waist and whispered into her ear. "You are my beautiful sister, too young to invite a heart attack to your heart. I will marry Angela."

She pulled his arm down, as she always did when they were young. "You have turned down all my choices. I have no option but to wish you the best in life." She lifted his hand to her lips. "You have my blessings.

Chapter 34

Angela was glad that Ronny was away that Thursday evening.

She assisted Rebecca in the kitchen. After dinner, she entertained the children with stories of her early childhood in the village.

The children found the stories to be more of fiction than her real life, very different from their experience.

Angela tucked the last kid, Nikko into bed.

On her way to the family room, she saw Ronny walk towards his bedroom. Angela paused and only proceeded after he had turned a corner.

She had looked forward to the children going to bed, for her to have some quiet time. She needed to plan how to solve the many questions in her head before Saturday, when she was to travel to Nakuru with Babu. He had not stopped asking her when he would visit his uncle.

Being Thursday, Angela had only Friday left to contact Japheth. She needed to talk with him, know his position. That way she would give feedback to Ronny who was still waiting for her response to his request to marry her.

She went into her bedroom, picked a nightie and on her way to the bathroom she saw Ronny's photo dance on the screen of her phone. She let it go to voicemail. She closed the bathroom door behind her as she heard a knock on her bedroom door.

She filled the bathtub and added lavender bathing salts and oil that she had become accustomed to. She stripped and lowered herself into the bathtub, hopping that Ronny would leave her room on finding out that she was in the bathroom.

The bathroom door opened, forcing her to fully submerge her body except the head. "How was your evening? I am having my private time," she told Ronny.

He looked at her for a long moment. "I can see that." He raised one hand and blocked his eyes, pretending to give her the privacy she asked for. "Does this work? I came to brief you about my evening. I will wait for you." He left, closing the bathroom door behind him.

Angela turned her eyes to the soapy form covering her body, grateful that her naked body was not exposed. She wondered what it could be that had taken Ronny to his parent's house on a weekday. She prayed that his father was not unwell, one thing that she knew would stress Ronny.

She pondered on what to tell him if he asked about her insistence to travel to Nakuru with Babu on Saturday.

Angela knew she would not have an answer for Ronny, she had not talked with Japheth.

The last time she sent a message to his phone, he had replied with two words, "Which Angela?"

371

She had waited for an entire day, giving him time to remember which Angela, just in case he knew of many other girls by that name.

By Wednesday she had not heard from Japheth, she had sent another message, "The Angela you knocked out that December night and walked away from. I am told that your dear mother wants me by her side."

Japheth had responded immediately. "I had assumed you never wanted me when you kept quiet for many years?"

"Yes, that is your part of the story. Can we meet? I need to hear when you plan to marry me, take me home to your mother."

"Please. Can you elaborate on what you mean? I thought you left me and moved on?" Japheth pleaded.

Angela had then written and told him that what news she had for him could not be discussed on phone. It was better if they held a meeting somewhere in town.

He had agreed to meet on Friday, over lunch.

Friday was less than twelve hours away. Angela needed time to reflect on how she would approach Japheth, and more importantly, if she should let Ronny know of her plan and when. She wondered if Ronny would discourage her if she informed him that night, or if he would complain if she informed him after, on Friday evening.

There was the issue of how she would travel to and from town as well. Though she had access to a car and a driver whenever she needed one, she did not want

Ronny's employees brought into the issue, more so if her meeting with Japheth did not go well. She preferred to handle everything on her own. There was also the issue of what she would tell Rebecca and the children before she left for the meeting.

She felt cold under the warm water when a small voice at the back of her head asked how she would leave the house if Ronny chose to work from his home office. She uncorked the bathtub drain and let the water out. She rinsed the soap off her body and stepped out of the bathtub.

Angela hurried through drying her body. She put on the nightie she had carried to the bathroom, a sheer white dress dotted with pink roses.

She flung the door open and stepped out, with high hopes that Ronny could have not waited that long.

He had left. She picked her phone and scrolled through new messages, all from Ronny.

The last message to her was five minutes ago. He had written to inform her he would take her out for dinner on Friday evening, then brief her on his meeting with his sister and parents.

He also let her know he had meetings most of Friday, he would leave the house early.

Her prayer was answered. She typed a message to Ronny. "Hi. I needed to soak my body and think. Good night, I will join you for dinner tomorrow." She clicked send and climbed into bed as she heard a new message drop in. She read. "Thanks. I will come home at six, we leave at seven for dinner. Good night."

"Sounds like you will have a long day. What time will you leave the house?" She wrote back.

"Around six-thirty. Good night my love."

"I miss you. Good night." Angela changed her wake-up alarm from six-thirty to five-thirty. She switched off the bedside light and pulled a bed sheet over her head.

Her plan was to prepare breakfast for Ronny before he left for work. She knew he loved his porridge with sweet potatoes, especially when he had long workdays. She would eat breakfast with him and mention her planned travel to the city center for a lunch meeting with a friend.

~~~~~~

The next morning Angela stood by the door and kissed Ronny, wishing him a good day.

She went to the kitchen, prepared and set breakfast on the table for the children before Rebecca walked in, they exchanged morning greetings before Angela said, "Rebecca, I need to catch up on sleep, I will not join the children for breakfast, and I will be away over lunch time."

Angela had been in such a hurry to leave, she failed to see the smile on Rebecca's face.

Angela hit the clock to quiet her nine o'clock wake-up call.

She showered, dressed and went to the family room. "Good morning kids. Put on sports shoes and follow me outside, it is playtime."

While outside, she called and booked a car to leave at noon for a one o'clock meeting in town.

She sat under the shade of a tree and watched the children as they rode their bicycles. Later, she moved with them to the playing area behind the house where they played on the swings and sandpit.

Angela was glad the children did not object when she asked them to go back to the house. She informed them that she needed to travel to the city center for a meeting.

Angela dressed in her favourite pair of black Zara trousers, a cream silk blouse and a black button-down sweater with a waist belt. She wore her comfortable black leather heels and carried a matching black leather bag.

She hugged each child before she walked out. "Goodbye kids, goodbye Rebecca, see you after lunch."

There was traffic on the stretch from Thika Road to the Museum Hill exchange before they drove along University Way and off to City Hall Way.

On arrival at Our Meridian Restaurant building, Angela asked James to pick her up after one hour. She bid him goodbye and walked inside. She found where Japheth sat at a corner table, waiting for her.

They exchanged greetings as she took a nervous scan of the place. She was worried that someone who knew her and Ronny and might start a rumour that she was on a lunch date with Japheth.

Her choice to meet at that restaurant was to lessen the chances of meeting Ronny's colleagues, family or friends. The place was mostly frequented by workers who could afford a simple one course meal for lunch.

Japheth and Angela sat on opposite sides of the table without talking for about five minutes. Each focused on their drink until a waiter brought their food.

Angela was anxious, noticing Japheth was too. She watched him and noticed as he darted his eyes in the room, encircled his glass of juice with both hands and immediately removed them.

At one-point Japheth removed an iPhone from his trouser pocket, placed it on the table, then returned it to the pocket.

His actions gave Angela more confidence, she considered he was more worried than she was. "I guess we need to talk and leave this place in time for work." She noted that her words had startled him.

"Yes. I have been waiting," he said.

"I was home last week, in Nyametende." She watched as he placed the glass of juice, he had lifted back to the table without taking a sip. He placed both hands flat on the table, like he wanted to push himself out of his chair.

Angela continued, "People greeted you. I was told that your mother wants us to go live with her."

She stopped talking, hoping that the couple on the nearby table was too busy with their own chat to hear her words.

"I am a bit lost. Who is us?"

Angela smiled, tapped her fingers on the table as she drew in slow, steady breaths to hold her anger back. "Exactly. I too want to know if by *us*, your mother means you, I and our baby." She watched as his facial muscles tightened.

He spoke in a muffled voice. "What did you tell her?"

"Nothing. I need the answer from you, what to tell her."

Japheth looked around, at the people waiting to be seated, and back to his food. "I don't know. My mother knows I am married. And I thought you had proceeded on with life."

"I have not moved on. I have been very busy, struggling to raise your child, waiting for you to provide some support."

"I wish you had told me," he whispered.

She was silent except for the sound of her chewing that echoed in her ears. She liked the sound, it gave her something to listen to internally while she juggled ideas in her head on what to say next. She made eye contact. "It is not like the child is now a fully-grown adult. So, I am reminding you that you have a son."

He pressed the fish on his plate with one finger. "Is it okay if we agree on a plan?"

"I am listening." She noticed that he had not eaten any of the fried fish and *ugali* he had ordered.

"I did not ask my mother to come talk with you."

"What I am hearing is that I am the one trying to get myself to your home, to live with your mother?"

He took the first bite from his plate, a small piece of fish. "Not me." He touched the ring on his finger. "I can contribute whenever I have money, but I do not live in the village where mother wants you."

"I know you reside in the city with your wife."

His eyes opened wide. He sat up straight. "Yes, I do."

"The days when I needed your money, your support, are now behind me."

She stopped talking when she noticed a twinkle in his eyes. She retrieved her phone from her bag, checked the time and put it back. She then checked time again on her watch.

"I am sorry, I had assumed you were fine," Japheth said.

"I am tired of hearing what you assumed." She lowered her voice when she noticed some patrons turn their direction. She added, "Assumptions are not good. Please, ask your mother to stop making assumptions about my life—"

"I will," he interrupted.

"What I prefer you do is totally different. I see you are already someone's husband. It is not my plan to interrupt your life. That's if you do not interrupt mine."

"Exactly."

"I am here to give you a task for tomorrow. Please travel home and agree with your mother to forget that she ever heard of me or my baby. Have you ever longed to know the name, or what the baby looks like?"

Japheth said nothing. He squeezed the bridge of his nose, like the place hurt.

Angela stared at his forehead. "There's no need to worry yourself." She stopped talking when he removed the hand and blinked, like her words had surprised him.

She chuckled. "The baby has my name and will soon add the name of my fiancé." She stood up. "I will do you one favour though. I will one day tell him who his father is, if he asks."

She looked at her watch and saw it was a few minutes to one. James would arrive soon. She tapped the table for Japheth's attention. "Please call me from home. It will be best if I hear the promise from your mother, that she will never try to interfere with my life."

Angela opened her handbag like she was in search of something before she turned her eyes to Japheth. "Guess I will not burden you if you pay for my lunch. It will be your small sacrifice."

She saw him nod yes. She left the restaurant, reached outside where James was waiting. She exhaled once she entered the car.

Angela focused her eyes outside, towards the restaurant. She hoped Japheth had recollected himself enough to plan for his impromptu travel home.

Based on the expression on his face, she knew his wife was not aware that he had a son with her. She would wait for his call the next day from the village.

Chapter 35

However hard Ronny tried to show his love to Angela that Friday evening, she did not tell him if she would travel to Nakuru the next day, or not.

She had raised his hopes when she said she had changed her travel plans from Saturday to Sunday. She would provide a confirmation on Saturday evening.

Ronny tried to get her to say more, all in vain. Her only response was that she was waiting for someone to call before she could reach a decision.

He wondered who the important call was to come from but did not ask.

During breakfast on Saturday morning, Ronny announced of the family visit to his parents' house for afternoon tea and dinner. He also informed the children that Rebecca would be going back to her job at his parents' house.

The children were excited, while Angela's worry increased. How to introduce Babu to Ronny's parents. She was not aware that Rebecca and Ronny had already done that for her.

Angela dressed in a peach patterned Diane von Furstenberg wrap and pulled on some black mules. She was unusually quiet. She watched Pauline call out and embrace her grandchildren, one by one.

She waited for Babu's turn and was surprised when her son ran with open arms as the other children had done. Angela heard Pauline call out his name before they embraced.

Pauline hugged Babu. "Look at me well young man. You too are my grandchild. Okay?"

Babu's face brightened with a smile. "Are you now my new Grandma?"

Pauline hugged him again before she loosened the embrace and pointed towards Ronny. "And that son of mine is now your daddy."

Pauline called the four children together and asked them to give her a huge hug. She asked them, "Is there space left for more grandchildren?"

"Yes," the four children said in unison.

Ronny locked eyes with Angela. He had turned to see her reaction to the question from his mother to her grandchildren.

He held Angela's hand and kissed her palm. They watched as Pauline walked away towards her bedroom side of the house, the children in tow. He guessed she was going to wake Henry from his siesta and introduce Babu.

Ronny walked outside when he saw Robert drive in with his family. Angela did not follow him.

On most days when they visited Ronny's parents, Angela would be in the kitchen where she helped Rebecca to prepare and serve food. Ronny had discouraged her when they arrived, asking her to stay with him.

Angela exchanged pleasantries with Robert, Rose and their sons.

Ronny asked David and Donald to go find their grandmother in her bedroom. The twins ran off.

Angela stayed in the living room, watched as Ronny, Robert and Rose engaged in conversation until her phone rang. She excused herself and walked out of the room and house, aware that Ronny was watching her.

She listened as Japheth talked from his rural home. "Angela, my mother had made a big mistake. I have asked her to cut her interactions with Zippy and she has agreed." He released a breath. "My mother said that the idea of you and Babu going to reside at her home was from Zippy. Please talk with her."

Japheth did not give Angela a chance to talk or ask him a question. He handed the phone to Sabrina.

Sabrina did not even answer to the greeting from Angela. She was busy explaining, she called upon her ancestors to confirm that the idea came from Zippy.

The only chance Angela had was to say, "Okay" before she heard Japheth's voice. "My mother has made her promise. Is it okay if I leave for the city now?"

Angela felt pity when she heard Japheth beg. She said, "I will only have problems with you if your mother collaborates with my stepmother to make my life difficult. All the best and enjoy your life," Angela said before she ended the call. She walked back into the house where she joined the rest of the family to drink tea.

Ronny spent most of his time looking at Angela and noticed that she relaxed as time passed.

After tea, Angela asked the children what cake they would like for dessert. She left for the kitchen where she joined Pauline, Rebecca and Rebecca's daughter in the kitchen.

Rebecca had worked for Ronny's parents for many years. She had become a trusted member of their family. Rebecca's contract was with the company, which enabled her and her children to benefit from the medical and educational fund. She had paid for three of her five children's schooling and into university. The youngest was the one in the kitchen, she lived with her mother and attended university.

Ronny walked into the kitchen as Angela set the timer for the cake in the oven. He held her by the shoulder. "I hope it is chocolate cake. What did the kids ask for?"

Angela washed hands, removed the apron and walked with him to the dining room. "Today's cake is for the children, not you," she said with a grin.

He held her by the small of her back, "Are you enjoying your evening, or I take you away to a more interesting place?"

"I am fine. I will stay and help watch the children."

"You have been so tense, there's no need to keep you here if you are uncomfortable."

She smiled. "Better if I stay now and know how uncomfortable it can get, before I say, 'I do'." She went to the living room and joined Robert, Rose and the children who were watching TV.

Ronny walked back to the kitchen where he spoke with his mother in lowered tones. He then left for the living room as Pauline walked away towards her bedroom.

Ten minutes later, Ronny watched as Henry took calculated steps to the living room, without any support. Ronny stood up and greeted his father and assisted him to his recliner massage chair.

Henry made himself comfortable before he waved to his family in the living room. He contributed to the ongoing conversation on general topics including hospitals, politics, business and schools.

Angela was glad that she had of late been reading newspapers, magazines and listening to radio broadcasts. It was easy for her to join in the conversation.

When the one hour of TV the children had been allowed was over, they walked as a group and sat on the floor on both sides of Henry.

Henry took time, asked each child for a story, after which he would tell them a story about Mr. Hare and the Elephant.

Halfway through the children's story telling session, Angela excused herself to go check on the cake, though she knew that the oven was on a timer, would switch itself off.

She returned the smile from Pauline as she arrived in the kitchen and asked, "Do you have any icing sugar? The girls like to do simple decorations."

Pauline went into the pantry nearby and then to the fridge. She came back carrying a tray with icing sugar, food colouring and the decorating tubes.

Angela excused herself, "I will be back." Minutes later, she returned with Betty and Mia.

By the time Angela, Rebecca and Pauline finished setting food on the dining table, Mia and Betty had decorated the cake with their version of a wedding cake, two people standing on a blue cake.

The family took their choice of seats at the sixteen-seater dining table. Henry sat at his usual armchair at one end of the table, Pauline on his left-hand side. The six grandchildren rushed to seats nearest to their grandpa or grandma, forcing Pauline to shift three seats away to accommodate three children to her right. Three other children sat on the right side of Henry.

When it was time for dessert, Pauline left for the kitchen and Ronny followed her. They conversed in lowered voices before they walked back, Pauline carrying bowls on a tray and Ronny had a mega-container of ice cream. Rebecca carried the cake.

Ronny went to where Angela sat, to the left of his chair and tapped her on the shoulder. "It's our time now."

Confused by his words, she pushed her chair back and stood up. From the corner of her eyes, she saw Rose staring.

Ronny looked at his father before he removed a small box from his shirt pocket and went down on one knee. He tilted his head up, eyes to Angela. "Angela my love, will you marry me with all our children?"

He opened the box, retrieved a ring and extended it to her left engagement finger.

Angela looked at Rose. She saw the broad smile on her face and a thumbs up from Robert. She turned to Pauline and received a nod. She glanced at Henry and the children and back to Ronny. "Yes, I will marry you." She answered in an unsteady voice.

There was loud clapping from the adults and giggles from the children before they joined in the clapping.

"Thank you, my love," Ronny said as he pushed the five-carat diamond ring into her engagement finger. "Thank you, we will be happy the rest of our lives," he said, choking on his words.

"Thank you." Angela lifted her left hand in front of her face and looked at the ring again. "I don't know what to say. I am happy, we will make it work."

Ronny cuddled and kissed her on both cheeks and then her lips. He held her hand and they sat down to more clapping.

When the cheering subsided, Ronny turned to the children. "Cut the cake, we will make a toast to one another before I leave with my fiancée."

Betty stood up. "Is this your wedding cake?"

Laughter filled the dining room.

"No," Rose said. "I will bring the biggest wedding cake in December. This one is for dessert, to celebrate Angela's engagement to Ronny."

Ronny lifted his glass of wine high and toasted Angela to a long life together. Next, he toasted Rose. "Thank you for your offer, it means more than just a wedding cake."

Angela, still nervous, walked around the table carrying a glass of wine. She toasted to Pauline, Rose, Robert and Henry. She picked up a glass of juice and toasted with each child.

After chatting and sharing the cake, Ronny stood up and extended a hand to Angela. "May we leave?"

Angela held his hand and stood up. He held her by the waist and looked at his father. "I hope you had enough rest during the day, to entertain your friends," as he waved a hand from left to right of the children. "Kids. Rebecca will go to our house and get you a change of clothes. Good night." He kissed his fingers and threw a flying kiss to all.

Nikko started to cry.

Mia comforted him. "We are here with you. Grandpa and Grandma are here, and we can eat more cake after this ice cream. Say bye." As she lifted his left hand to wave.

Angela waved at Babu. She noticed that he looked sad. She knew he would be okay with Rebecca, the other children, and his new grandparents.

Chapter 36

As soon as they stepped outside the house, Angela turned to Ronny. "You never cease to surprise me."

Ronny lowered his head and brushed his lips on hers. "I love you and I want us to talk tonight. Just you and—"

He was interrupted by the opening of the front door.

Rose ran after them, her hands spread out. She reached Angela and hugged her. "My brother loves you."

Ronny edged closer to them as Rose added, "He loves you because you are lovable. Thanks for helping him transform from the irritable man he was becoming, back to the brother he used to be."

"Thank you," Angela said.

Ronny embraced the two, massaged their backs, each with one of his hands. He then shifted his hand from Angela's back to her face, wiped tears from her cheek with his thumb.

Rose raised her eyes heavenwards, "In wanting to help my brother as he mourned Bella, I forgot to see that he needed more than sisterly comfort, he needed someone to touch his heart." She directed her eyes to Angela, "He found you, he loves you. Please do not hesitate to love him back."

She pushed Angela and Ronny from her hold. "Go home, Mum and Dad are happy with both of you. I will come visit as your loving sister."

"Amen." Angela heard the words escape from her mouth.

Rose's action and words had been more of a prayer come true for Angela. She had never imagined that such a time would come. A time when Rose would not only hug her but embrace her as part of the family. More than ever, now Angela looked forward to a life with Ronny.

Rose waved them bye and retreated into the house.

Ronny shook his head vigorously, opened the car door for Angela before walking to his side.

Angela buckled up and waited for him to do the same before she asked, "Can we go back to the party if I cancel my trip to Nakuru?"

He unbuckled his seatbelt and held her face between his palms. "That is music to my ears." He kissed her like he was being chased by a lion, angrily.

After a long moment she freed her mouth from his. "People are watching us from the house. And I asked a question, I did not say I cancelled."

He secured himself to his seat and the engine of the Mercedes Benz roared into live. "You are my best friend, which means we shall agree on something once we arrive home."

"Where will the children sleep, who will take care of them?"

Ronny provided an anecdote of when they were growing up and all his cousins would visit. Up to ten of them would find a place to sleep in that five-bedroom house.

They drove, quiet, each one lost in their own thoughts. Ronny turned off the main road and drove along the long stretch to reach the entrance to his compound. The security guard opened and stood on salute as Ronny drove in. He parked the car in the attached garage. They walked into the kitchen.

Ronny filled the kettle. He crossed arms on his chest and leaned against a kitchen cupboard. He stared at Angela while waiting for the kettle to boil.

Angela finished drinking water and looked at him. "You, standing near that boiling kettle reminds me of the day Rose interviewed me." She chuckled and turned the engagement ring on her finger. "What was on your mind then?"

He thundered with laughter, walked to her side and held her waist. "I was afraid she would make you run away. I don't want to think any further, if you had turned the job down." He laughed again. "How hard was your heart pumping?"

"Your sister. How was she as a young girl? Will she ever learn to like me?"

"She already does. Did you not see it in her smile? Her offer of our wedding cake was her way to welcome you into her former family. She now belongs to her husband's family. Welcome to mine." He kissed her before he walked away and switched off the boiling kettle.

Angela placed cups, tea bags and drinking chocolate on a tray and followed Ronny into the living room.

He mixed one cup of tea and another of drinking chocolate before he pulled her closer to his chest. "Please tell me you are not taking Babu back to Nakuru. You will break my heart. You will break his heart."

Angela lifted the cup of drinking chocolate to her mouth and blew air to cool it before she sipped. "I need to talk with my boy. He still wants to visit his uncle."

Ronny noticed that she was getting emotional and cuddled her more. He did not move, giving her time to cry. He wished she would voice out what had been disturbing her since Thursday. He stroked her curled hair backwards.

"I will stay here with my boy," she said. "I hope your people will not complain."

He sat upright on the sofa, held her face and nibbled on her lips. "Which people? Did you not see my mother, my father, my family welcome Babu into their arms and house?"

She nodded.

"Do me one favour?"

She wiped a tear from her cheek as she nodded.

"Please learn not to imagine what other people think of you. I am not being arrogant, but all they will do is admire you, envy how you won my heart, accepted me. The rest is their problem, not yours. Okay my love?"

She nodded and rested her head on his chest. "You may go ahead and add the Henry name to his."

He stood and pulled her along. "You deserve more than a party tonight. You are the greatest, giving me an instant son."

The rest of his words were lost as his lips captured hers. They stood there for long moments, kissing, taking a break to catch air and tangling their mouths repeatedly.

Ronny broke the silence. "I wish you could agree we get married even next week or we share a bed tonight."

"What type of wedding will that be? I told you I wanted a proper wedding."

"Just name a date and watch me perform the miracle for you." He cuddled her tightly until she voiced her discomfort. "You are squeezing all the food out of my stomach."

He loosened his grip on her. "Come, we should sit down." He motioned her back to the chair. "You have no idea how much I need you. Too many cold showers are killing me." He pulled her hand to touch the crotch of his overstretched trousers.

By the time they finished their drink, Angela had responded to questions from Ronny. They had shared stories from their childhood, what food they liked, their best friends, relatives they were constantly in touch with, and things they disliked or that could easily irritate them.

Ronny was pleased to hear that Angela had not followed up to get the birth certificate after Babu was born. The practice was that at birth, the hospital gave a birth notification to all new mothers. It was their responsibility to go to a government registrar in their town and apply for a birth certification. Angela had been too busy learning to adapt to motherhood to follow-up with the registration.

She went to her bedroom and returned with a large envelop. "I feel like I am giving away my child," she said as she pulled out a government stamped paper and handed it to Ronny.

Instead of receiving the paper from her, he pulled her and sat her on his lap and whispered into her ear, "To a good man. Remember I too have given you my three children, plus myself." He smoothed her hair backwards, in the process messing her beehive hairstyle. "Why do you keep forgetting that?"

She leaned over and kissed him.

Ronny studied the paper. "This should be okay. I will seek legal guidance on Monday, then start the process."

Angela slid from his lap and sat beside him. She stared until he said, "I assume you are clear on the position of his father. Will he come saying I stole his baby?"

"I had a meeting with him yesterday. The lunch meeting." She pulled Ronny's hand between her two palms. "He pleaded, wished me peace in my new life, that way he too can continue with his marriage."

"Is he married?"

"He traveled home today, called to tell me his mother had agreed she would stop tagging along with my stepmother, the hatcher of those plans."

"Are you serious?"

"About what?" Angela asked without batting an eyelid.

"That the scheme was Zippy and not Sabrina?"

"No idea. Japheth appeared surprised, so he traveled home today to consult with his mother. He called me. Remember when I walked out to answer my phone?"

Ronny looked at the framed photo of his family with Bella on the wall. "I had no idea that you guys have been in touch." He said in a raised voice, in disappointment.

"Never. I got his phone number when I was home in August. Zippy called Sabrina and wrote the number on a piece of paper for me. That was after I told her I wanted to contact him about our staying with his mother."

Angela shook the large envelope and a white small piece of paper fell out. "There. The paper she wrote the number on."

Ronny picked the paper that had landed on the coffee table. "I see you kept it well."

"I saved the number in my phone, I will delete it, and block it. I kept the paper, in case Zippy denies that she ever gave me the number, though Joshua and Dad were in the room, both saw her give it to me."

He held her hand in his. "Don't worry, I trust you."

She eased herself upwards and kissed him on the side of his neck. "I too trust you. Many people don't understand that you never tried to force me into doing anything I did not want, including sleeping with you. You are a noble man, I love you."

Ronny snuggled. "Is it okay if we celebrate our wedding in December by trying for our next child?"

"Why so fast?"

He pulled her closer and rested his chin on the top of her head. He did not want to tell her his reasoning. He was concerned that Angela might take too long to transition from her current housegirl-employer relation with him, into his wife. Having a child with him would be one way to seal their marriage, blend their family, help her transition into a partner on equal terms.

Ronny too was afraid he might sometimes instinctively relate with her as the housegirl she had been. That needed to change immediately. "All the children need to grow up together. We can discuss that tonight, or tomorrow, we will not fail to agree," he said.

"You are right, we need time to discuss that, adding more children, yet all the bedrooms are occupied."

He held her by the waist and sat upright. "For now, we can discuss what will be better for us and the children. To wait and have more sisters or brothers after you complete your degree, or we have them immediately, so they all grow up together." He smiled. "That way, you can pursue your degree program as the children grow."

Angela's lips parted like she wanted to say something, but Ronny held his hand up. "Not tonight. Take your time and reflect on the two ideas. I will support your choice."

"I might choose going to school first, to have a career, a job, a source of income."

"I do not know about you, but in my father's house, his money was family money, for our mother as well. It will be the same in our house, the money in my personal accounts is our money, family money."

Noticing that she had lost the grin on her face, he tickled her into laughter and said, "Taking care of children is a full-time job. You don't have to be employed if you choose to stay home and take care of the children, as you have been doing."

"Will there be enough money for all our needs, plus more children?" She lamented.

"There is enough money for the four children, or even ten children," Ronny said. He pondered how to tell Angela that there was enough money in the Henry family to provide for the needs of two more generations. And even more generations if the company continued to generate income at the current rate. "You do not need to be employed, unless you will be looking for a way to spend any extra time on your hands."

He cuddled her. "But I will oblige you to pursue your degree program. Let me know what you prefer, an online program or traveling to university every day. If online, choose one based in Europe, to give us an excuse to travel there. If local, you will have a dedicated driver to chauffer you there and back."

"I will tell you after I check tuition costs and starting dates."

"I will pay university tuition and other costs for my fiancée, soon to be wife." He lifted her hand to his mouth and kissed her ring. "No need to worry about that. My money is our money, we will pay your fees from the money. I will soon introduce you to my bankers, add you as a signatory to my personal account."

There was silence. Angela pondered on what Ronny had said about having more children and pursuing her degree. "Thank you for asking me to marry you."

"You have no idea what your yes means to me, to our family." Ronny said. "Thank you again for accepting to be my wife, accepting to continue to take care of all the children."

"There are things we need to talk about." She inched away from him.

Ronny stood up. "Does that mean I can boil more water for tea or bring wine?"

"None for me please."

He sat back. "Today is our evening, ask all the questions you have."

"What will happen with Dianna and the other ladies who used to come over with Rose?"

He laughed, then stopped on realizing that she was serious. "Leave that to me. Dianna is out, she's already busy with another man. We cannot stop her from coming to visit her nieces and nephews, and to important family functions. Likewise, with the rest of her family. It will be proper for the children to know them, part of their family."

He intertwined his fingers with hers. "Who were the others?" He asked and proceeded to answer his own question. "I have already discussed with Rose not to bring any of those friends of hers here. Though some are like family, so you will continue to encounter them at the clubs and other family functions, including our wedding."

"Okay," she whispered.

"You will see how friendly many of them will turn out to be. They might be from rich families, but they too have normal human fears, like you, me and every other human being." He paused before he continued. "No one is immune to that emotion."

"Thank you for the reassurance. I will always turn to you whenever my side of fear glares at me."

"I will share with you as my best friend, my fiancée." He said while playing with her ring, turning it around her finger.

She softly scratched his palm. "Thank you for the ring. I like it." She giggled. "And I love you, have loved you for a long time, especially for respecting my no. I used to fear you would—"

He cuddled her to his chest, to keep her from seeing the tears in his eyes. "Thanks." He stared to the wall in front of him, the family photos. He questioned what he should do with Bella's photos. Would the children complain if he removed the larger photos? Would the photos interfere with his love for Angela if he retained them? What if he just added Angela's photos to the wall? "Please continue to be strong, be yourself, voice your needs. I like it that way," He said.

He sniffed back the tears and tickled her, distract her from hearing how emotional he had become on hearing her words, appreciating how he had respected her as his housegirl.

After a moment of silence, Ronny said, "I remember it all, from your first day of arrival, the interview, your dedication to your job. Your love for my children. Your focus on serving them helped clear the angry outbursts in my heart. They were not a part of me, never were. The anger was out of my many questions to God. The sad part was that my heart transferred the anger to my children, to my friends and to my employees at Henry Technologies."

He sniffed again, surprised how quiet Angela was. He concluded she was listening, so he continued, "Now everyone gives me compliments, that in the last year I have become my old self again. I lack the words to tell them about the new angel in my house. Your devotion to my family brought back the peace we used to know. There's no way to let you leave, you need to stay and enjoy the peace with me, with us. Is that not what we call life?" He tickled her more.

Angela freed herself from his hold and held his head between her hands and kissed him. "I will try, we will succeed in our new life."

Ronny stood and strode to his home office.

While he was gone, Angela became reflective. She questioned herself, why it had taken her that long to realize that it was okay to get married to any man who loved her, however rich or poor they were.

She thought of how hard she had worked, loved the children she took care of. In return Ronny had loved her back.

She silently told herself that she would continue to love and take care of all their children, her children now. She would let Ronny provide for all the family's financial needs. Was it not her need for money that had brought her to his house as a housegirl? It was okay to embrace her new position in his house, his fiancée, his wife. She would take up the role and responsibility, give it her attention, embrace it as her new passion – a lover, a mother and a wife. A daughter, a sister, a granddaughter, a daughter-in-law, a sister-in-law.

Ronny's return interrupted her thought process. He handed her a sketch book. "Please write down your dream wedding colours and other ideas to get us going. Also, the people you would like to invite."

"Mmhhh. A wedding before the mandatory meetings with my parents?"

He sat down next to her. "Joshua has done an excellent job so far. The entourage from your home will meet with mine in Nakuru in October. I have a feeling our parents will agree with our plan." He gave her the pencil he was holding. "We can start organizing the wedding while we await their blessings."

She launched into a monologue. "My grandmother, my brother, my sister-in-law, my nieces and nephews and my cousins. My aunties and uncles."

"What about your parents?" Ronny asked.

"I have no choice there. Those are a given."

"What colour for men, that way the ladies can choose colours to blend?" She asked.

"Men? Black or grey suit, white shirt, a floral necktie, and a colourful half-coat. Nothing complicated, I've never been complicated" he said.

She scribbled notes on the paper.

They discussed the venue and foods to serve. They listed special roles for their children who would also be part of their wedding line-up.

It was approaching two in the morning when Angela yawned for the tenth time. "I am very tired. I wish there was a machine to bathe me."

Chapter 37

Ronny lifted her off the sofa and carried her away. He stopped by the door to his bedroom, kicked it open with one leg and rushed inside.

The next morning Angela knew where she was. She did not regret her experience and what Ronny had taught her. Within the short hours of their night, he had aroused her. She felt fulfilled as a woman.

She gently lifted Ronny's hand off her waist. Stepped out of bed, picked his PJ shirt from the floor and slipped it on before she walked into the bathroom.

Five minutes later, Angela returned to the bedroom, ready to sleep. It was seven in the morning. She felt alert enough to start her day, but she had slept less than two hours, she needed more rest.

She climbed into bed as the door to the bedroom opened and Ronny entered, carrying two glasses of juice. She stared at his chest before her eyes lowered to his PJ trousers, hanging low on his hips. She bit her lower lip.

He sat on the bed. "How was your night my love? Thank you for allowing me to show you how a man should love his woman, my fiancée." He handed one glass to her before he gulped all the cold juice from the second glass.

He took her empty glass and placed both on the bedside table. He leaned over, cuddled her as he pulled his PJ off her body. "We have the day to ourselves, let me know what else you prefer we learn together."

She grinned, encircled both hands around his neck and snuggled. "Why did I not agree to this earlier than today?"

The End

One last request

If you enjoyed reading this novel, please post a brief review on Amazon. I read all reviews, as they help me gain a better understanding of you my reader and make improvements on my books for your enjoyment. Thank you again for your support

About the Author

K is for Kwamboka

Eileen K. Omosa, Ph.D., writes on change and adaptation. She is the author of the book series: *The African Woman's Journey, Trending Tomorrow, Grandma Food Stories,* and, *An Immigrant's Journey.*

Eileen grew up in Kenya until the day she packed that grey suitcase and left for the city – and she's never stopped traveling the world except for her long stopover in Canada.

During the day she works as a research consultant on household food security, the reason she cultivates vegetables in a city. Visit her online at EileenOmosa.com

Books by the Author

The African Woman's Journey Series

1. Ignited by Education
2. Slowed by a Baby
3. Trapped Inside the Family Box

Trending Tomorrow Series

1. The Housegirl Becoming Angela
2. A Husband for Her Daughter (2019)
3. We don't talk with them (2020)

Book 1: Ignited by Education

Does romance distract women from their career goals?

Sophia Marko is focused on building her career, uplift her family out of poverty, when Richie Broaders crosses her path. He floods her work desk with roses and wants to marry her, but she vows not to let it happen.

Desperation kicks in when she learns that Richie is the son of her employer, the billionaire owner of the Broaders Group of Companies. She's aware of her employer's rule on romance between employees, one of them must resign.

Leaving from her job is tantamount to falling back into the poverty she has worked so hard to overcome.

Evading Richie is not Sophia's only challenge. Marko, her father summons her to the village to marry a local schoolteacher. Can she object without straining existing family relations or jeopardize her job?

Ignited by Education is a contemporary women's fiction with a romantic twist. The book focuses on change and adaptation after the African girl-child acquires education. What's her journey to becoming a career woman?

Buy this first book in *The African Woman's Journey* trilogy for a story where education, culture, ambition and love intertwine.

Book 2: Slowed by a Baby

Can she lead a lifestyle different from her husband?

Sophia can't give up all when she's confronted with a new reality - being a millionaire's wife, and, pregnant is an automatic ticket out of the world employment.

Richie and Sophia are back from a ten-day honeymoon when he asks her to resign from her job and stay home to manage their household. His wife continuing in employment will reflect negatively on his capability to provide.

Sophia agrees they continue to reside with Richie's parents until she delivers her baby. In the process, her mother-in-law provides the comfort she needs to continue going to work.

How will Richie convince Sophia to become a stay-at-home-mom, provide the comfort he needs to put more effort into his managerial, and soon to be directorship tasks – be the financial provider for his family.

This Book 2 in *The African Woman's Journey* series is a tale of change and adaptation, where ambition, social expectations, and love intertwine.

Book 3: Trapped Inside the Family Box

Wait, did happiness for the larger family come at her cost?

In this third book, in *The African Woman's Journey* trilogy, Sophia and Richie tackle a task that the other Broaders family members have failed in for nine years.

Richie convinces Sophia that a holiday will help her rejuvenate after she's overwhelmed from months of taking care of their newborn baby. She travels with him to the USA where he reconnects with James, his brother.

While in the USA, Sophia realizes that Richie is not as confident in dealing with family issues as he is with his office tasks. She steps in, but little does she know of the significant favour she's done the Broaders family.

Will Sophia ever accept that being a full-time mother is as fulfilling a job as any other career choice?

Read this book and get entertained on the intricacies within families, as you discern how Sophia, an educated African girl from a humble rural upbringing transitions into a Broaders, a billionaire family.

Grandma Food Stories

1. Grandma Harvests a Banana: and the children learn the African Cinderella Story
2. Grandma Arrives in the City: and our baby is clean-shaven
3. Cooked pumpkins for a village

The Immigrant's Journey

1. My Journey Overseas
2. An Immigrant's Food Choices (2020)